The Good Father

DIANE CHAMBERLAIN

The Good Father

Recycling programs
for this product may
not exist in your area.

ISBN-13: 978-0-7783-1346-5

THE GOOD FATHER

Copyright © 2012 by Diane Chamberlain

For questions and comments about the quality of this book please contact us at Customer_eCare@Harlequin.ca.

www.Harlequin.com

Printed in U.S.A.

First Printing: May 2012
10 9 8 7 6 5 4 3 2 1

For Nolan and Garrett, Claire and Olivia,
who are so lucky to have very good fathers!

1

Travis

Raleigh, North Carolina
October 2011

IT WAS NINE-FORTY WHEN I WOKE UP IN THE back of the van. Nine-forty! What if Erin had already left the coffee shop by the time we got there? *What if she's not there?* That sentence kept running through my head as I got Bella up and moving. She'd had a dream about her stuffed lamb and wanted to tell me the whole thing, but all I could think about while I changed her into the cleanest clothes I had for her was, *What if she's not there?*

On the phone yesterday, Roy had told me I was making the smart choice. "You can get rich doing this, bro," he'd said.

I thought of the gold watch he wore. The red Mustang he drove. "I don't care about getting rich," I'd answered. "I just want enough money to keep me and Bella fed till I get a real job." I felt smarmy just talking to him on the phone. The dude was a total cretin.

"You feel that way right now," he said, "but wait till you get a taste of easy money."

"Look," I said, "just tell me where to meet you and when."

"We'll come to you about eleven tomorrow night," he said. "You still hanging in the same place? The lot by the Target?"

"Yeah."

"Just make sure you've got enough gas to get us to the Virginia border and back," he said, and then he was gone from the line.

So, now I'd have all day to freak out about my decision and, if things went according to my plan, I wouldn't have Bella with me. My chest tightened at the thought. I wasn't sure I could do this. Erin was a good woman, though. I could tell. Plus, Bella knew her and liked her. The only thing was, she might be *too* good. The kind of person who'd call the cops on me. I just had to trust her not to.

My hands shook as I scratched a note on the back of a gas receipt and stuck it in Bella's pants pocket, sneaking it in there so Bella wouldn't ask me about it or try to pull it out. I remembered the tremor in my mother's hands. "A fine tremor," the doctor had called it and he'd said it was harmless and barely noticeable. Mine wasn't so fine. I could hardly help Bella get her socks straight on her feet.

"I'm hungry, Daddy," she said as she pulled on her shoes.

I opened some Tic Tacs and shook a couple into her hand. "We'll get breakfast in a minute," I said, as she popped the Tic Tacs into her mouth.

I pictured Erin finding the note. She *would* find it, wouldn't she? If she didn't, then what? I thought of all the things that could go wrong and my head hurt like a bitch.

First things first, I told myself. First I had to get to JumpStart
before Erin left or else the whole plan was going to cave in.

"I got to go potty," Bella said.

"Yeah, baby, me too." I ran a comb through her dark hair,
which I really should have tried to wash in the Target restroom last night like I did once already this week. Last night,
though, washing her hair had been the furthest thing from
my mind. She needed a haircut, too, but it wasn't like I'd
thought of bringing scissors with me when we left Carolina
Beach. Her bangs were almost long enough to put behind
her ears now, and I tried that, but as soon as she hopped out
of the van, her hair fell into her face again. Poor kid. She
looked like an orphan nobody cared about. I prayed to God
she didn't become one tonight.

I held her hand as we walked toward the coffee shop.

"You're hurting my hand, Daddy," she said, and I realized
I was holding on to her way too tight. How could I do this
to my baby girl? I couldn't even prepare her for what was
going to happen. *Bella, I'm sorry.* I hoped she was so young
that she'd never remember this. Never think of it as the day
her daddy abandoned her.

Wildflowers filled the grassy strip of land next to the
coffee shop and I had a sudden idea. They were nothing but
weeds, but they'd do. "Look, Bella." I pointed toward them.
"Let's pick some of these for Miss Erin." We stepped onto
the lawn and began picking the flowers and I hoped Bella's
bladder could hold out one more minute. The flowers were
the only way I could think of to thank Erin for what I was
going to ask her to do.

She was sitting in the brown leather chair where she always sat, reading something on her iPad, as usual, and brushing a strand of light brown hair out of her eyes. I felt a crazy
rush of relief and a crazy rush of disappointment. If she

hadn't been there, I would have no way to do what I was going to do tonight, and that would have been a good thing. But she *was* there and she smiled like she'd been waiting for us.

"There she is!" Bella shouted loudly enough for the two girls at the corner table to look over at us. They were close to my age. Twenty-two. Twenty-three. One of them smiled at me, then went red in the face and looked away. I hardly glanced at her. I only saw the thirtysomething woman sitting in the leather chair. I felt like hugging her.

"Hey," I said, like it was any other morning. "How's it going?"

"Good." She reached out to run a hand down Bella's arm. "Good morning, honey," she said. "How are you today?"

"We had Tic Tacs for breakfast," Bella said.

"Well, we'll get something a little better here," I said, embarrassed.

"Did you?" Erin asked. "Were they yummy?"

Bella nodded, her bangs falling over her eyes.

"We need to use the bathroom, don't we, Bell?" I said, then I looked at Erin. "You'll be here a minute?"

"Oh, I'm not going anywhere," she said.

"These are for you." I held the flowers toward her and wished I'd thought to tie them together with something, but with what? "Bella picked them for you this morning."

"How pretty!" She took the flowers from my hand, sniffed them and then put them on the table. "Thank you, Bella."

I spotted a kids' book on the table next to the flowers. "Looks like Miss Erin has a new book to read you," I said, hoping that was true. A book would keep Bella busy while I... I couldn't think about it.

"I got to go potty, Daddy," Bella reminded me.

"Right." I reached for her hand. "We'll be back in a sec," I said to Erin.

In the restroom, I rushed through the teeth-brushing, the going potty and the face-washing. My hands were like a guy with DTs and I mostly let Bella brush her own teeth. It was all I could do to brush mine. I didn't bother to shave.

Erin had moved the book to the arm of the chair by the time we got back.

"I think you're going to love this one, Bella," she said. She held her arms out to my four-year-old daughter, who climbed into her lap like she'd known Erin all her life. *Thank you, God,* I thought. What I was going to do tonight was as wrong as wrong could be, but the fact that Erin had been put in my path this week made me think maybe it was supposed to happen.

"I'm going to grab my coffee and our muffin," I said. "Can I get you anything, Erin?" I asked, like I could actually afford to buy her something.

"I'm fine," she said. "I picked up an OJ for Bella."

I knew—and had known from day one—that it was Bella she was into and not me. That was fine. Perfect, actually. "Okay," I said. "Thanks."

I ordered my coffee and a muffin and a cup of water for Bella. When I went to pick up the water from the counter, I knocked the damn thing over with my not-so-fine tremor. "Sorry!" I grabbed a handful of napkins from the holder on the counter and started to mop up.

"No problem," said Nando, the barista who waited on me every morning. He called to a girl in the back who came out and cleaned up my mess while he got me another cup of water. He put the cup and the coffee and muffin in one of those cardboard carriers, and I lifted it carefully and took it back to my seat.

Erin and Bella were deep in their story. Bella asked her questions, pointing to things in the book. She rested her head against Erin's shoulder, looking kind of sleepy. That dream had gone on and on last night, she'd said, and we woke up so late. She looked as totaled as I felt. I'd use some of the money I'd make tonight to find a clinic and get her checked out. She wasn't exactly eating a great diet these days, either. I was about to break the muffin in half to split with her, but decided to give her the whole thing instead. I didn't think I could eat this morning, anyway.

I sat down on the couch, wondering how to time things. I couldn't wait too long. I had no idea when Erin would leave the coffee shop. I sipped my coffee and it felt like acid going down. *You suck as a father,* I thought to myself.

Erin came to the end of a chapter and said they'd take a little break while Bella ate her muffin.

"Come over here to eat so you don't get it all over Miss Erin," I said to Bella.

"Oh, she's fine here," Erin said. "Just set the water on the table."

I did, although I wanted Bella back right then. Yeah, I was glad she was so happy on Erin's lap and all that, but I wanted to hold her right now. I'd scare her, though—holding her too tight the way I'd squashed her hand when we walked across the parking lot. It was better this way. Now, how to make my graceful exit. I hadn't quite thought through that part. Maybe I'd say I needed to use the restroom again, but they'd be able to see me if I left the restroom and went out the door.

"So, just a couple more days till you go back to work?" I asked Erin. I needed to make sure she didn't need to go back to the pharmacy any sooner than that. I hoped I'd figured this out right.

"Don't remind me." She rubbed Bella's back. Bella had blueberry stuck in her teeth and I was glad I'd remembered to put her toothbrush in her little pink purse.

"Do you ever feel, you know, *tempted* being around all those drugs all the time?" I asked. Why the hell did I ask her that? I had no idea. Nerves. I was a frickin' mass of nerves.

She gave me a look like I was a total lowlife. "Not even a little bit," she said. "And please don't tell me you *would* be tempted."

I tried to smile. "No way," I said, "It's not my thing." Why'd I even go there? I worried she could see how I was shaking today and think I was using something. Suddenly, I knew how to handle the next few minutes. "I've got another interview today," I said.

"Great! You found something on Craigslist?"

"No, my friend came through." I tapped my sweaty fingers on my thighs. "I hope this one works out."

"Oh, me too, Travis. I guess it's in construction? Is it for a business? Or residential? Or—"

"I've got the info in my van," I said, getting to my feet. "Can you watch Bella a sec and I'll go get it? I can tell you the address and maybe you can tell me how to get there."

"Sure," she said. I couldn't move all of a sudden. I wanted to take Bella back into the restroom and hug her so hard, but I had to get this over with. Just do it. I bent over and kissed Bella's head, then walked away fast. Out the door, across the parking lot, into my van. Fast, fast, fast, before I could change my mind. I turned the key in the ignition. I couldn't leave the van here where Erin and Bella would be able to see it when they came out of JumpStart. I drove all the way to the other end of the lot, nearly crashing into parked cars, my foot jerking all over the gas pedal, the whole wide world a blur in front of me and one word on my mind.

Bella Bella Bella.

2

Travis

Six Weeks Earlier
Carolina Beach, North Carolina

YOU KNOW HOW EVERY ONCE IN A WHILE happiness kind of comes over you like a bolt of lightning, surprising you so much it makes you laugh out loud? That's how I felt as I worked on the molding for the kitchen cabinets of the oceanfront house. I'd been doing construction four years and always thought of it as a job I hated, just something I had to do to put food on the table for me and Bella and my mom. But construction jobs were hard to find at the beach these days, especially in Carolina Beach, which wasn't exactly overflowing with high-end properties even though the ocean was just as blue and the sand just as white as the rest of the coast. Plus, it would always be my home. The foreman on my last job watched me work on a deck addition for a few days and he must have seen something in me because he asked me to do some custom work inside the house. He was teaching me stuff, like the detailing on this molding. He was grooming me. I didn't know I was learning skills that, on this late August day, would make me laugh out loud when I realized I was actually enjoying the work. I was glad I was alone in the kitchen so I didn't have to explain my reaction to any of the guys.

I was on the ladder working on the molding when I heard sirens in the distance. A lot of them, but far away and echoey, hardly loud enough to cut through the sound of the ocean, and I didn't pay all that much attention. After a while, they became part of the white noise of the sea as I kept working. I was climbing down from the ladder when I heard someone rushing up the stairs to the living room.

"Travis!" Jeb, one of my coworkers, shouted as he ran into the kitchen. He was red-faced and winded, bending over in the middle of the room to catch his breath. "It's your house, man!" he said. "It's on fire!"

I dropped my hammer and ran for the stairs. "Are they safe?" I called over my shoulder.

"Don't know, man. I just heard and ran here to tell—"

I didn't hear the rest of what he said as I nearly slid down the stairs, stopping a fall with my hand on the banister. My brain was going crazy. Was it the screwed-up electrical in the living room? Or one of those scented candles my mother liked to burn to get the musty smell out of the air of the old cottage? Or maybe it was her damn cigarettes, though she was careful. She wasn't the type to fall asleep smoking, especially not with Bella in the house.

Bella. Oh, shit. *Let them be okay.*

I ran out to my van and as I turned it around to head toward my house, I saw smoke in the sky. It was the pale gray of a fire that had burned itself out, not the black you'd see if the fire was still raging, and that gave me hope. The gray billowed into the sky and then hung in an air current drifting toward the mainland. I made the four miles to my house in three minutes flat.

There were two fire trucks, a couple of cop cars and one ambulance in front of the charred shell of the small cottage that had been my home for the past eight years and would never be my home again. Right then, I didn't care. I jumped out of my van and headed straight for the ambulance. Ridley Strub, a cop I'd known since we were in middle school together, showed up out of nowhere and grabbed my arm.

"They took your mother to the hospital," he said. "Bella's in the ambulance. She's going to be fine."

"Let me go!" I pulled away from him and ran to the open rear of the ambulance, jumping inside without waiting for an invitation.

"Daddy!" Bella's cry was muffled by an oxygen mask, but it was strong enough that I knew she was okay. I sat on the edge of the stretcher and pulled her into my arms.

"You're all right, baby." My throat was so tight that *baby* came out like a whisper. I looked up at the EMT, a girl of about twenty. "She's okay, right?"

"She's fine," the girl said. "Just needed a little O2 as a precaution, but—"

"Can we take the mask off?" I asked. I wanted to see her face. To check her all over for damage. I wanted to make sure the only thing she'd suffered was a scare. I noticed she had her stuffed lamb clutched tight in one arm, and on the floor of the ambulance I spotted her little pink purse. The two things she was never without.

"I want it off, Daddy!" Bella picked at the edge of the plastic mask where it pressed against her cheek. She hiccupped like she always did when she cried.

The paramedic leaned over and slipped the mask from

Bella's face. "We'll leave the O2 monitor on her finger and see how she does," she said.

I smoothed my hands over my daughter's brown hair. I could smell the smoke on her. "You're okay," I said. "You're perfect."

She hiccupped again. "Nana fell down in the living room," she said. "Smoke comed out of the windows."

"Came," I said. "That must've been scary." My mother fell? I remembered Ridley saying she was in the hospital. I looked at the EMT again. She was checking some monitor on the wall above the stretcher. "My mother," I said. "Is she okay?"

The EMT glanced toward the open doors and I didn't miss the relief in her face when she saw Ridley climbing into the ambulance. He put a hand on my shoulder. "Need to see you a sec, Trav," he said.

"What?" I didn't look up from Bella, who was clutching my hand like she'd never let it go.

"Come outside with me," he said.

Mom. I didn't want to go with him. I didn't want to hear whatever he was going to tell me.

"Go ahead," the EMT said. "I'll be here with Bella."

"Daddy!" Bella clung harder to my hand as I stood up, knocking the monitor off her finger. "Don't go away!" She tried to scramble off the stretcher, but I held her by the shoulders and looked into her gray eyes.

"You have to stay here and I'll be right back," I said. I knew she'd stay. She always did what I told her. Nearly always, anyway.

"How many minutes?" she asked.

"Five at the most," I promised, glancing at my watch. I'd never once broken a promise to her. My father'd never broken a promise to me, and I remembered how that felt, knowing I could always trust him no matter what.

I leaned down to hug her, kissing the top of her head. The smell of smoke just about seared my lungs.

Outside the ambulance, Ridley led me to the corner of the lot next door, away from the fire trucks and all the tourists who'd gathered to watch somebody else's disaster.

"It's about your mom," he said. "Neighbor said she was outside hanging laundry when the fire started and it went up like a…just real fast. Your mom ran in for Bella and she was either overcome by smoke or maybe had a heart attack. Either way, she fell and—"

"Is she okay?" I wanted him to get to the point.

He shook his head. "I'm sorry, Trav. She didn't make it."

"Didn't make it?" I asked. The words weren't getting through to me.

"She died on the way to the hospital." Ridley reached a hand toward my arm but didn't touch me. Like he was just holding his hand there in case I started to keel over.

"I don't get it," I said. "Bella's fine. How can Bella be fine and my mother's dead?" My voice was getting loud and people turned to look at me.

"Your mom saved her. They think she fell and Bella knew enough to get out of the house, but your mom was—"

"Shit!" I pulled away from him. Looked at my watch. Four minutes. I headed back to the ambulance and climbed inside.

"Daddy!" Bella said. "I want to go home!"

I bit the inside of my cheek to keep from crying. "One thing at a time, Bell," I said. "First we make sure your lungs are okay." And then what? Then *what?* Where would we go? One look at the house and you knew everything we owned was gone. I closed my eyes, picturing my mother running into the house through smoke and flames to find Bella. Thank God she had, but God had done a half-assed job this time. I hoped my mother had been unconscious when she fell. I hoped she never had a clue she was dying. *Please, God, no clue.*

"I want to go home!" Bella wailed again, her voice loud in the tiny space of the ambulance.

I held her by the shoulders and looked her straight in the eye. "Our house burned down, Bella," I said. "We can't go back. But we'll go to another house. We have plenty of friends, right? Our friends will help us."

"Tyler?" she asked. Tyler was the five-year-old boy who lived a few houses down from us. Her innocence slayed me.

"*All* our friends," I said, hoping I wasn't lying. We were going to need everyone.

I saw something in her face I'd never seen before. How had it happened? She was two weeks shy of her fourth birthday, and overnight she seemed to have grown from my baby daughter to a miniature adult. In her face, I saw the girl she'd become. I saw Robin. There'd always been hints of her mother in her face—the way her eyes crinkled up when she laughed. The upturn at the edges of her lips so that she always looked happy. The rosy circles on her cheeks. But now, suddenly, there was more than a hint and it shook me up. I pulled her against my chest, full of love for the mother I'd lost that afternoon and for the little girl I would hold on to forever—and maybe, buried deep inside me where my anger couldn't reach, for the teenage girl who'd long ago shut me out of her life.

3
Robin

Beaufort, North Carolina

JAMES AND I STOOD UP WHEN DALE WALKED into the waiting room. Dale always seemed to have a gravitational field around him and sure enough, the seven other people sitting in the room turned to look at him as he walked toward us. They would sail right through the air toward him if they hadn't clutched the arms of their chairs. That was the sort of pull he had on people. He'd had it on me from the first moment I met him.

Now, he smiled at me and gave me a quick kiss on the cheek, then shook his father's hand as if he hadn't seen him at home only a few short hours ago. "How's she doing?" he asked quietly, looking from me to his father and back again.

"Eight centimeters," I said. "Your mom's with her. Alissa's miserable, but the nurse said she's doing really well."

"Poor kid," Dale said. He took my hand and the three of us sat down again in the row of chairs. Across from us, an older woman and man whispered to one another and pointed in our direction, and I knew they'd recognized us. I had only a second to wonder if they'd approach us before the woman got to her feet, ran her hand over her flawlessly styled silver hair and headed toward us.

Her eyes were on James. "Mayor Hendricks." She smiled, and James immediately stood up and took her hand in his.

"Yes," he said, "and you are…?"

"Mary Wiley, just one of your constituents. We—" she looked over her shoulder at the man, most likely her husband "—we have such mixed feelings about your retirement," she said. "The only good thing about it is that your son will take over."

Dale was already on his feet, already smiling that smile that made you feel special. I once thought that smile was only for me but soon came to realize it was for every single person he met. "Well, I hope that's the case," he said modestly. "Sounds like I can count on your vote."

"And the vote of everyone I know," she said. "Really, it's a given, isn't it? I mean, Dina Pingry? She's completely wrong." She gave a little eye roll at the thought of Dale's opposition, a woman who was a powerhouse Realtor in Beaufort. Of course, the people we hung out with were all Hendricks supporters, so it was sometimes easy to forget that Dina Pingry had her own fans and they were fanatical in their support. But James had been mayor of this small waterfront town for twenty years, and passing the torch to his thirty-three-year-old attorney son seemed like a done deal. To us, anyway.

"It's never a given, Mrs. Wiley," Dale said. He was so good at remembering names! "I need every vote, so promise me you'll get out there on election day."

"Oh, we work the polls," she said, nodding toward her husband. "We never miss an election." Her eyes finally fell on me, still in my seat between the two men. "You, dear, are going to have the wedding of the decade, aren't you?"

I didn't stand, but I shook the hand she offered and gave her my own smile—the one I had quickly learned to put and keep on my face in public. It came pretty naturally to me. That was the thing Dale said first attracted him to me: I was always smiling. For me, it had been his gray eyes. When I saw those eyes, I suddenly understood the phrase *Love at first sight*. "I'm very lucky," I said now, and Dale rested his hand on my shoulder.

"I'm the lucky one," he said.

"Well, we're waiting for our daughter to have her third." The woman gestured toward the double doors that led to the labor rooms. "And I guess you're waiting for Alissa…?" She didn't finish her sentence, but raised her eyebrows to see if she was right. Of course she was. Alissa was the Hendricks' barely seventeen-year-old daughter, my future sister-in-law and the poster child for Taking Responsibility for your Actions. The Hendricks had turned what might have been a scandalous event into an asset by publicly supporting their unwed pregnant daughter. This was a family that didn't hide much, I'd discovered. Rather, they capitalized on the negative. To the outside world, their actions might have looked like complete support, but I was privy to their inside world, where all was not so rosy.

"Mrs. Hendricks is with her," James said to the woman. "Latest report is she's doing very well." He always called Mollie, his wife, Mrs. Hendricks in public. I'd asked Dale not to do the same to me after we were married. I'd actually wished I could keep my maiden name, Saville, but that wasn't done in the world of the Hendricks family.

"Well, now," the woman said, "I'll leave you three in

peace. It's the last peace you'll have for a while with a baby around, I can tell you that."

"We're looking forward to the chaos," Dale said. "So nice meeting you, Mrs. Wiley." He gave a little bow of his head and he and his father sat down again as the woman returned to her seat.

I was tired and wished I could rest my head against Dale's shoulder, but I didn't think he'd appreciate it here in public. *In public* were words I heard all the time from one Hendricks or another. I was being trained to become one of them. I think they'd started grooming me from the moment I met them all two years earlier, when I'd applied for the job to assist with running their Taylor's Creek Bed and Breakfast at the end of Front Street. It was a job I'd handled so well that I was now the manager. I'd met with all three of them in the living room of Hendricks House, their big, white, two-story home, which was right next door to the B and B and almost identical in its Queen Anne–style architecture. They told me later that they knew I was right for the job the moment I walked in, despite the fact that I was barely twenty and had zero experience at anything other than surviving. "You were much younger than we'd expected," Mollie told me later, "but you were a people person, oozing self-confidence and full of enthusiasm. After the interview, you left the room and we all looked at each other and knew. I picked up the phone and canceled the other applicants we'd scheduled for interviews."

I'd wondered later if they knew then I would become one of them. If they'd wanted that. I thought so. It had been funny getting that glowing feedback. I was only beginning to know the real me. I was only starting to live. I was one year out from my heart transplant and still learning that I could trust my body, that I could climb a flight of stairs and walk a block and think about a future. If I wore a perpetual smile, that was why. I was alive and grateful for every second I'd been given. Now I was living that future. There were days, though, when it felt as though my life was no more in my control than it had been when I was sick. "Everyone feels that way," my best friend, Joy, told me. "Totally normal." I'd had so little experience with "normal" that I could only hope she was right.

Mollie walked through the double doors into the waiting room. She wasn't smiling and I suddenly felt afraid for Alissa. This time, I was the one to get to my feet. "Is everything okay?" I asked. I loved Alissa. She was so real. So down to earth. She was five years younger than me, but I felt as though we were kindred spirits—in ways only I truly understood.

"She's very close," Mollie said, "but she wants *you* with her." She looked at me. "You want to go in?"

"Me?" From the start, the plan had been for Mollie to be in the delivery room with her daughter. "She wants you, honey." Mollie sounded tired.

Dale stood up and put his hand on the small of my back. "You okay with that?" he asked quietly. He was always protective of me. Sometimes I appreciated it. Other times it reminded me of my father, cutting me off from the world.

"Sure," I said. I was no stranger to hospitals, though a delivery room was unfamiliar territory. I hoped someday to have a career in medicine, though Dale said I'd never have to work if I didn't want to. My only hesitation in being with Alissa was stepping into a role that had so clearly belonged to Mollie.

"I'll show you where," Mollie said, and she led me through the waiting room and the double doors and into a hallway. She pointed toward a doorway. "Just hold her hand.

Be there for her. She's tired of me." She gave me a smile that let me know she was a little bit hurt that Alissa wanted me with her rather than her mother.

I heard Alissa the second I opened the door. She was halfway sitting up, panting hard, a look of intense concentration on her face, and I guessed she was in the middle of a contraction. "Robin!" she managed to say when she could catch her breath. Her face was red and sweaty, her forehead lined with pain.

"I'm here, Ali," I said. One of the nurses motioned toward a stool at the side of the bed and I sat down and took Alissa's hand in both of mine. I wasn't sure what to say. *How are you feeling?* seemed like a ridiculous question to ask. It was pretty clear how she was feeling, so I just repeated myself. "I'm here," I said again. Someone handed me a damp, cool washcloth and I pressed it to her forehead. Tendrils of her auburn hair were plastered to her face and her brown eyes were bloodshot.

"I couldn't take one more minute of my mother." She spoke through clenched teeth, then let out a long, loud groan. I watched the monitors on the other side of the bed. The baby's heartbeat was so fast. Was it supposed to be that fast?

"I think she's okay with it," I lied.

"I hate her right now. I hate them. All of my stupid family. Except you."

"Shh," I said, pulling the stool closer to her. I wondered if delivery room nurses had to keep things they heard confidential. I bet they heard all kinds of gossip in here. The last thing Dale needed was for the world to know all was not well with Beaufort's first family.

"*Will* should be with me," Alissa whispered. "That's how it's supposed to be. Not like this."

I was surprised. Will Stevenson was completely out of the picture and I'd thought she was finally okay with that. He'd created a mess the Hendricks family had needed to clean up, but now wasn't the time to get into a big discussion with her about it. I'd never even met Will. Alissa had kept that relationship even from me, and I had to admit I was hurt when I found out about it. I'd thought we were closer than that. But she'd done me a favor. I didn't want to feel as though I was keeping secrets from Dale—at least, no more than the secrets I was already keeping.

She had another contraction and nearly broke my fingers as she squeezed them. The baby's heartbeat slowed way down on the monitor and I glanced nervously at the nurses, trying to gauge if something was wrong, but no one except me seemed concerned.

"This baby's going to wreck my life!" Alissa nearly shouted when the contraction had ended.

"Shh," I said. It wasn't the first time I'd heard her say that and it worried me. If Alissa had had her way, she'd be putting this baby up for adoption, but that would never have been acceptable to her parents. "You're going to love her," I said, as if I knew about these things. "Everything's going to work out fine. You'll see."

An hour later, baby Hannah was born and I watched my future sister-in-law change from a screaming, fighting, panting warrior to a docile and beaten-down seventeen-year-old. The doctor rested the tiny infant on her belly, but Alissa didn't touch her or look at her. Instead, she turned her head away, and I saw two of the nurses exchange a glance. I wanted to touch that baby myself. How could Alissa not want to?

One of the nurses took Hannah to the side of the room to

clean her up and I leaned my lips close to Alissa's ear. "She's beautiful, Ali," I said. "Wait till you get a good look at her." But Alissa wouldn't even look at me, and as I wiped her face with the washcloth, I wasn't sure if it was perspiration or tears I was cleaning away.

The nurse brought the baby back to the side of the bed. "Are you ready to hold her?" she asked Alissa, who gave the slightest shake of her head. I bit my lip.

"How about you, auntie?" the nurse asked me. "Would you like to hold her?"

I looked up at the nurse. "Yes," I said, draping the washcloth on the metal bar of the bed. I reached out my arms, and the nurse settled Hannah, light as feathers, into them. I looked down at the tiny perfect face and felt the strangest emotion come over me. It slipped into my body and locked my throat up tight. I'd rarely related Alissa's pregnancy to my own. That denial had been easy, since I'd blocked so much of my own experience from my mind. The baby I'd had didn't exist for me. But suddenly, holding this beautiful little angel in my arms, I thought, *This is the part I missed.* This was the part I'd never realized I was missing and that no one must ever know that I missed. And as I pressed my lips to the baby's warm temple, I cried the first tears ever for the empty place in my heart.

4

Erin

Raleigh

MICHAEL SET ONE OF THE BOXES ON THE granite counter of my new, small kitchen. Through the window over the sink, I could see the sun disappear behind dust-colored clouds. The sky would be opening up soon with a late-summer storm. I was glad we'd gotten all the boxes in before the rain started.

"This is the last one," Michael said, brushing his hands together as if the box had been dirty. He walked into the attached dining area and looked out the window with a sigh. "You're way out in the boonies here," he said.

I knew what he was seeing through that window: the sprawling Brier Creek Shopping Center. Acres and acres of every big box store and chain restaurant you could imagine. Hardly the boonies.

"It's not that far," I said, although it was a good fifteen miles from our house in Raleigh's Five Points neighborhood.

"You don't know anyone out here," he said. "I don't get it."

"I know you don't," I said. "That's okay. It's what I want, Michael. What I need right now. Thanks for just…for tolerating it."

He looked out the window again. The gray light played on his ashy brown hair, the same color mine would be if I didn't lighten it. The color my roots were. I was really late for a touch-up, but I didn't care.

"Let me be the one to live here," he said suddenly.

"You?" I frowned. "Why?"

"I just…" He turned his head toward me. "I don't like to think of you in a place like this. You've worked so hard on the house. You belong there."

"It's perfectly nice," I said. "It's new, for heaven's sake." I was deeply touched; he still loved me so much that he'd be willing to live in this bland little furnished apartment so I didn't have to. But he didn't understand. I couldn't be in our house any longer. I felt Carolyn's absence everywhere in that house. Her room, which I hadn't walked into once in the four months since she died, taunted me from behind the closed door. Michael had actually suggested we turn her room into an exercise room! It was like he wanted to erase Carolyn from our lives. He found this apartment depressing. I found it safe, away from my old life. My Carolyn life. The friends and their children I could no longer bear to be around. The acquaintances I didn't want to bump into. The husband I no longer felt I knew. I didn't think my friends wanted to be with me any more than I wanted to be with them. They'd been wonderful in the beginning, but now they didn't know what to say to me. I was a horror to them, a reminder of how quickly their lives could change.

"What do I tell people?" Michael asked. "Are we separated? Getting a divorce? How do I explain to people that you've moved out of the house?"

"Tell them whatever makes you comfortable." I didn't care what people thought. I used to, but everything was different now. *Michael* still cared, though, and that was the difference between us. He was still living in our old lives, where what people thought mattered and where he wanted to find a way back to normal. I'd given up on normal. I didn't care about normal. My therapist Judith's reaction when I told her that? "That's normal," she said, and the old me would have laughed, but I didn't laugh anymore.

Michael gestured to one of the boxes on the stool by the breakfast bar. "This one says *bedroom*. I'll carry it in for you."

"Great. Thanks." I watched him lift it into his arms. I used to love his arms, probably more than any other part of his body. He worked out every day and his arms were undeniably ripped. Michael was that rare combination of brains and brawn. "A geek with a great body," one of my friends had once told me, when we were watching our husbands playing with our kids in someone's backyard pool. Watching him now, though, I felt nothing.

I walked the few short steps to the living room windows and looked at the reassuringly unfamiliar landscape. Absolutely nothing to remind me of my bubbly and beautiful daughter. *You want to run away,* Judith had said when I told her my plan to rent this apartment. There was no accusation in the way she said it, although I knew she didn't think it was a good idea. But she didn't do the lecture bit like Michael did. "You might be able to run away from home," he'd said, "but you can't run away from what's inside your head." I'd wanted to slug him for saying that. I was sick of his advice and his finding fault in my own personal style of grieving. Never mind that I found plenty of fault in his. I had deep questions he simply couldn't relate to. Mystical questions. Would I ever see Carolyn again? Was her soul someplace?

I felt her around me. I heard her voice sometimes. When I asked him if he did, he said, "Sure" in a way that told me that he didn't.

Michael came into the living room and stood next to me at the window. He put his arm around my shoulders and I felt the tentative nature of the touch. He no longer knew what I would welcome and what I would shrug off. Judith tried to get me to have some sympathy for him, but I was too busy having sympathy for myself. I had no energy to pay attention to what Michael needed these days. He'd turned into someone I'd once loved but could no longer understand. I knew he could say the same about me.

"I'm worried about you," he said now. His arm felt too heavy across my shoulders.

"Don't be."

"I think it's wrong for me to let you do this."

"'Let me'?" I walked away from his arm and sat down on the sofa. It was uncomfortably firm, nothing like the big, cushy sofa we had at home. "What are you? My father?"

"When are you going back to work?"

"If you ask me that question one more time..." I shook my head in frustration. I'd tried going back to work. I'd lasted half a day. I made a mistake with a medication that could have cost a person his life and I took off my white coat, turned the order over to the other pharmacist, and walked out of the building without looking back.

"You're going to sit here in this—" he waved an arm through the air to take in the combined living room/dining room/kitchen "—this *place* and ruminate. And that scares me, Erin." He looked at me head-on then and I saw the worry in his eyes. I had to look away. I stared down at my hands where they rested flat on my thighs.

"I'll be fine," I said.

"You need to stop going over every detail of it the way you do," he said, as though he was telling me something he hadn't already said twenty times. "You have to stop asking yourself all the what-ifs. It *happened*. You need to start accepting it."

I stood up. "Time for you to go," I said, walking to the door. I'd moved into this apartment, in part, to get away from exactly this. "Thank you so much for helping. I know it was hard for you."

He gave me one last frustrated look before walking to the door. I followed him, opening the door for him, and he leaned over to hug me.

"Do you hate me?" he whispered into my hair.

"Of course not," I whispered back, even though there were moments when I did. I could honestly say he was the only man I'd ever loved and if anyone had told me we would one day fall apart the way we had, I would have said they just didn't know us very well. But here we were, as fallen apart as we could be.

I opened the door and he walked into the hallway.

"Bye," I said. I started to close the door behind him, but felt a sudden rush of panic and pulled it open again. "Don't touch her room!" I called after him.

He didn't turn around. Just waved a hand through the air to let me know he'd heard me. I knew he was in pain—maybe tremendous pain. But I also knew how he would deal with it. He'd invent some new video game or work on a repair project. He'd lose himself in activity. He certainly wouldn't *ruminate*. He didn't even know how. I had it down to an art. It wasn't deliberate. It just happened. My mind would start one place—making a grocery list, for example—and before I knew it, I'd be going over every detail of what happened as if I were describing it to someone. Who was I telling it to inside my head? I needed to relive the details of that night the way an obsessive-compulsive person had to wash her hands over and over again. Sometimes I felt crazy and I'd make myself think of something else, but the minute I let my guard down, I'd be at it again. This was why I loved the Harley's Dad and Friends group I'd found on the internet. It had been started by the father of eight-year-old Harley, a little girl who was killed in a bicycling accident. The group was full of bereaved parents I'd never met face-to-face but felt as though I knew better than I knew anyone. Better than I knew Michael. They understood my need to go over and over what had happened. They understood *me*. I spent hours with them every day, reading about their struggles and sharing my own. I actually felt love for some of those people I'd never met. I didn't even know what most of them looked like, but I was coming to think of them as my best friends.

So, now I was safe. I was creating my own world, in a new neighborhood, with new friends in the Harley's Dad group and a new apartment. I turned around to take in the living room, thinking *my escape*. But instead of the bland furniture and the small room, I saw a sky the color of black velvet and the long, illuminated ribbon of the Stardust Pier, and I knew that no matter how far from home I ran, that horrible night would always, always be with me.

5

Travis

BELLA RAN AHEAD OF ME ON THE BEACH AND I watched the sandy soles of her feet flashing in the sunshine. Labor Day had passed and we nearly had the beach to ourselves. Bella's brown hair flew behind her like a flag and her pink purse slapped against her side as she ran. She looked so free. I wished she could always feel the way she felt right this second. Free and happy. That's why I brought her out on the beach today, so she could run and just act like a kid. My wrecked house was only a couple of blocks from the beach, and I usually brought her out here nearly every day, but we hadn't been once in the week since the fire and she'd become this totally serious and confused little girl. Sort of like her totally serious and confused dad. Our lives had turned to shit overnight. I didn't want her to know that. I didn't want her to feel scared, ever. But she was no dummy. She knew everything had changed.

We were staying with one of my mom's church friends, Franny, but it wasn't good. She had a slew of grandkids running in and out of the house and a bunch of cats I thought Bella might be allergic to, and you could tell she was letting us stay there because it was the Christian thing to do but that we were in the way. Bella and I shared the sagging mattress of a pull-out sofa and I thought we were getting flea bites in the middle of the night, but it wasn't like I could say anything about it. We didn't have a lot of other offers and about three times a day, Franny asked me if I'd found a place we could move into yet. I had—a shithole of a trailer that sat in a row of other trailers along the main road. It was nothing but a one-room tin can, and a good nor'easter would probably send it flying down the street, but it was going to have to do. There was a double bed I'd let Bella sleep in and a futon that would work for me. I thought it was okay for little kids to sleep with their parents, but the books I'd read said it wasn't cool once they were three or so. Bella was really good at sleeping in her own room at home. At Franny's, though, we didn't have much choice and anyway, Bella needed me close. I needed her close to me just as much.

If she asked me one more time when Nana was coming back, I didn't know what I'd do. I told her Nana was in heaven and had to stay there and then she worried someone was keeping her in a locked room or something. So I explained about God and how heaven was a good place, but I got scared maybe I was giving her the message that dying was a good thing and I didn't want her to start thinking she should die. Then she started asking me if I'd go to heaven and leave her. Franny told me I was overthinking the whole situation and making it too complicated. She said to Bella, "Your nana's gone to sleep in heaven with Jesus and when you're a very old lady, you'll get to see her there again," which seemed to satisfy Bella, or so I thought, until about an hour later when she asked me, "Can we go see Nana in heaven today?"

Man, I wished we could.

Mom hadn't been perfect. She'd smoked and had diabetes and was overweight and didn't take care of herself at all, but she'd loved Bella and she'd been happy to watch her while I worked. It turned out the fire was caused by some malfunction in the wiring behind the stove, so it wasn't anything I could blame on my mother and I was relieved by that. I didn't want to be angry with her now. I didn't want that to be the last feeling I had toward her. Instead, I felt grateful. She gave her life for Bella. I couldn't wrap my head around that—my fat, wheezy mom running into the burning house to save her. "God was working through her," the minister said at her funeral, and even though God and I had never been on the best terms, I liked that thought. I was holding on to it.

I never realized just how much I'd come to depend on my mother. Now I was it for Bella and it scared the shit out of me. I had no job now. Couldn't work with a kid to take care of, and no job meant no money. My boss found somebody else to finish up the work on those cabinets in the oceanfront house. There'd been about a hundred guys waiting to step into my shoes.

The thing that really sucked was that I'd been getting paid under the table for my work. That meant cash, and my most recent pay envelope had been in the house. Four hundred bucks, up in smoke. I'd had about a hundred dollars in my wallet when the house burned down. That was what stood between Bella and me and starvation now.

Ahead of me on the beach, Bella squatted down and picked up something I couldn't see from where I stood. She ran back to me, holding it and her lamb against her chest with both hands. The lamb fell to the sand and when she bent over to pick it up, the object she was carrying fell, too, and I had to laugh.

"Need some help?" I asked as I walked toward her.

"I can do it!" she said as she picked up her lamb. By that time, I'd reached her and saw that the object was a huge pale gray whelk, the biggest I'd seen on our beach, and I'd seen some big ones over the years.

"Wow, Bella, you hit the jackpot."

"It's a whelk," she said. She gave up trying to hold both the shell and the lamb and sat down on the beach instead.

I sat down, too, and examined the shell. *Busycon Carica*. It was nearly one and a half times the length of my hand and totally flawless, the interior the pale peachy color of a sunrise. I was so glad she'd found it. We'd been collecting shells on the beach since she was a toddler, but most of them had been ruined in the fire and now we were starting over.

"Do you remember what lived inside?" I asked.

"A snail!" she said. She sat cross-legged, gently touching the knobby shoulders of the shell with her fingertips.

"Right. An animal like a snail," I said.

"That's right." Like me, she loved hearing anything about marine life. I felt my own father's spirit inside me when I was on the beach with Bella, teaching her something. I'd hear his voice coming out of my mouth. I wish they'd had a chance to know each other, my dad and Bella. They would have gotten along so well.

"It liked to eat clams!" Bella said.

"Very good. What else did it like to eat?"

She scrunched up her face, thinking. Her nose was a little pink. I'd forgotten sunscreen. "Scabbits?" she tried, and I managed not to laugh.

"Scallops." She could never get that word right. Someday, she'd be able to and I'd miss the way she said it now.

She petted the shell like it was a puppy. "Is this the one, Daddy, where the boys turn into girls?" she asked.

I let out a little sigh. Franny was right; I gave this kid way too much information. She really didn't need to know about hermaphroditic gastropods at age three. Almost four. I'd probably been seven or eight when my father gave me that bit of mind-boggling information.

"That's right," I said simply. "Should I put it in the bag and we can look for more?" Over my shoulder, I carried the canvas tote bag we always used for the shells we found.

"Okay!" She hopped to her feet and took off ahead of me down the beach. I followed a few steps behind, moving closer to the water to let it swish over my feet. There was one big difference between my dad and me, I thought. He'd been a plumber with his own successful business and he kept me fed and clothed. I might not have grown up rich, but I never went without. He didn't fail me the way I felt I was now failing Bella. I wanted more than anything to be the kind of man who would make my father proud. I wasn't doing such a great job of it right now.

Honestly, if Robin's father had still been alive, I might have asked him for help. He had plenty of money. The contract he'd made me sign said I would never contact Robin herself—and I was still so pissed at her that she was the last person I'd turn to for help anyway—but I didn't think her father would be cruel enough to turn his back on his own granddaughter if she was starving. Didn't matter. He was dead. Mom had been an obituary reader, always checking to make sure her friends were still above ground. I'd felt kind of numb, hearing that he was dead. That man and I had never liked each other. The first time I held Bella in my arms, though, I sort of got where he was coming from. I felt this awesome need to protect her. I'd do anything to keep her safe. That's all Robin's father had been trying to do. Protect his daughter. I got it then, even if I still hated the dude.

Bella and I watched the dolphins and pelicans for a while, then started walking home. I'd been feeling so content on the beach, so far away from my problems, that I started heading in the direction of our burned-down house before I remembered and turned toward Franny's. The tote bag on my shoulder was a little heavier than when we'd started out. Walking away from the beach and back toward my real life, *everything* felt a little heavier.

6

Robin

2004

DR. MCINTYRE HELPED ME DOWN FROM THE examining table. "Have a seat in the lounge while I chat with your father," he said. I'd been seeing him for years and he always ended my examinations with a private talk with my father, but something felt different this time. Daddy held the door open for me and as I walked past him, his face looked a hundred years old. He hadn't quite closed the door behind me when I heard Dr. McIntyre say, "I believe her condition's significantly worse than your wife's was at this age." The door closed before I could hear my father's response, but it would have been lost on me anyway. I was shocked. I walked down the hall to the lounge, my legs feeling like they were moving through mud. I'd known, hadn't I? Deep down inside, wasn't I worried that my mother's fate—death at twenty-five—would be my own? I knew I was worse off than I'd been even six months ago. I'd never been able to run as fast as my friends or ride my bike for miles like they could. But now, any teensy little bit of exertion left me winded and dizzy. Just the day before, my friends and I were dancing around my bedroom and after two seconds, I had to sit down. From my seat on the bed, I watched them laugh together as they perfected their moves and it was like I could actually *feel* them drifting away from me.

Now I sank into one of the leather chairs in the lounge and waited. Even if I hadn't heard what Dr. McIntyre said, I would have figured it out because by the time my father walked into the lounge, his eyes were red. He motioned for me to walk with him and he held my hand tightly as we headed through the double doors and out to the parking lot. Neither one of us said a word until we reached our car. I don't think either of us could speak.

"I love you so much, Robin," he said finally, as he opened the car door for me. "I want everything good for you."

"I heard what Dr. McIntyre said," I admitted, "about my heart being worse than Mom's. Does that mean I won't live as long as she did?" I'd just turned fifteen. That gave me ten years, max.

"You'll live longer," my father said quickly. "Probably even a normal lifespan, because the doctors know more about your condition now than they did ten years ago, and more people are signing those donor cards, so when you need a heart, you'll get a heart."

I wasn't stupid. I knew it wasn't that easy. I slid into the passenger seat and my father shut the door and walked around the rear of the car while I stared at the dashboard.

"I want you out of PE altogether," he said once he was back in the car and turning the key in the ignition.

I was already sitting on the sidelines for just about every activity we did in Phys Ed anyhow, but I hated one more thing that was going to set me apart from my friends.

"It's not like I'm exactly straining myself in there," I said.
"And I'm going to drive you to school from now on."

"Dad," I said. "You have to get to the university early."

"I'll rearrange my schedule."

"What's the difference if you drive me or I ride the bus?"
I felt him chipping away at my freedom. He'd always been
super overprotective. I had the feeling it was going to get a
lot worse.

"You have to walk to the bus stop and there's just too
much...*excitement* on the bus."

"No, there's not! What are you talking about?"

"Just...humor me, okay? I want your life to be as easy and
peaceful as possible."

What he wanted was to be with me every minute. Protecting me. Suffocating me. Soon, he'd have me chained to
his side.

For the first time that night, I understood real fear. In
bed, I felt my heart pounding against my ribs and heard the
blood whooshing through my head, and I was afraid to go
to sleep. My mother had died in her sleep, her heart stopping
without warning. So I stayed awake for hours listening to
every echoey *thump,* like I could somehow keep my heart
going if I just paid attention to it.

My father drove me to school the next morning. I caught
up with my friends as they got off the bus and they were
all talking about a boy my best friend, Sherry, liked and a
party they all wanted to go to and how Sherry hoped the
boy would kiss her there and how maybe there'd be beer and
weed. I couldn't find a way into their conversation and they
forgot to slow down for me as we walked into the school.
Sherry and I broke away from the rest of them as we headed
for our science class, and we didn't seem to have much to

say to each other. I could hardly keep my eyes open, worn out from a nearly sleepless night. While my friends had been dreaming about boys and parties and getting drunk, I'd been doing my best to stay alive.

There was a new boy in our science class. We sat at two-person tables, and since the boy who usually sat next to me was absent, Miss Merrill stuck Travis Brown in his place. He looked more like he belonged in the sixth grade than the eighth. Short and skinny. When I handed him the stack of papers Miss Merrill wanted us to pass around, he didn't look me in the eye. He had these really long eyelashes and thick hair that hung over his forehead. He looked like a girl and he seemed really sad. He was the kind of boy who'd be a target for some of the idiot bullies at my school.

"Robin," Miss Merrill said from the front of the class-room, "after class, please share the assignments from the last few weeks with Travis so he can get caught up to the rest of us."

"Okay," I said, because I couldn't really say I didn't want to. From a few rows in front of me, Sherry turned to give me an *I'm glad she asked you and not me* kind of grin.

The last thing I wanted to do after class was hang out with this weird new kid, so I told him I'd email him the assign-ments that night. As I was walking out of class, though, Miss Merrill called me to her desk.

"I picked you to help Travis for a reason," she said to me. "His father died recently. I thought you might be able to understand what he's going through."

"My mother died a long time ago," I said. "It's not really the same."

"Isn't it?" She raised her eyebrows.

"Not really," I said again, but as I walked to my next class, Travis's email address and phone number in my pocket, I knew she had a point. We were both half-orphans. You never got over that.

I emailed him the assignments that night, but when he didn't understand something I'd typed, I impulsively decided to call him.

"Miss Merrill told me your father died," I said, after explaining the assignment to him. "My mother died when I was four. So I think that's why she picked me to help you."

"Not really the same," he said.

"That's what I told her."

"You've had your whole life to get used to it."

"It's still terrible," I said. "I don't remember her very well, but I still miss her. Miss having a mother."

He was quiet. "My father was so cool," he said after a minute.

"Do you have brothers and sisters?"

"No. You?"

"No." I felt the loneliness suddenly. Mine. His. "It's hard."

"Yeah, it sucks. And then we had to move on top of it. We couldn't afford our house in Hampstead anymore and my mother has friends at the church here, but I hate it. We're renting this old dump. I hate your stupid school, too. The beach is the only good thing about living here. My father always took me to Topsail and we'd hang out on the beach." It was like I'd plugged him in and suddenly all these words were spilling out of him.

"Where do you live?" I asked.

"Carolina Beach."

"Oh." I never hung out with the Carolina Beach kids at school. My father had always seemed to look down on them, an attitude I guessed I'd picked up without meaning to.

"What about you?" he asked. "Where do you live?"

"In a condo in Wilmington near UNC, where my father

teaches." We talked about our neighborhoods and I knew we were living totally different lives. Mine was clean and orderly and middle class and his sounded sort of thrown together in an emergency.

"At least you have friends here," he said, "I'm starting all over."

"I *used* to have friends," I said. "Not so much anymore." Wow, was that true? I felt like I was finally admitting it to myself. When was the last time Sherry called me instead of me calling her? When was the last time she texted me? My friends were moving on. Leaving me behind.

"What do you mean?" he asked.

"They're… I don't know. They're changing in a way I'm not. They don't talk about anything important anymore." I made it sound like *I* was leaving *them*. Not the other way around.

"Most girls are like that," he said. "Airheads."

"Major generalization."

"Maybe."

He told me about his old friends in Hampstead and how cool they were. I told him who was okay at my school and who he should watch out for and then we started talking about music we liked and before I knew it, it was ten o'clock and Daddy was knocking on my door telling me to go to bed.

"Is that your father?" Travis asked.

"Yeah. He wants me to get off and go to bed."

"It's only ten."

"I know." I looked over at my bed, remembering how I'd stayed awake most of the night before, trying to keep my heart going. "I'm afraid to go to bed." I bit my lip, wishing I could take back the words. I couldn't believe I'd said that to someone I hardly knew.

"Why?"

"It's just… It's stupid," I said. I didn't talk much about my heart. I didn't like people to think I was weak. The scrawny, girly image of him suddenly popped into my mind. Why was I talking to him at all? But the words wanted to come out in the worst way. "I have this…I have the same heart problem my mother had," I said. "And yesterday I found out it's even worse than my mother's was, so last night I kept feeling it beating when I was in bed and it freaked me out and now I don't want to go to bed."

"Wow." He was quiet for a few seconds. "You could call me," he said finally.

"What do you mean?"

"Call me from your bed and we'll talk about other stuff. It'll keep your mind off your heart. And keep my mind off my father," he added.

"That's crazy."

"You could," he said.

"No, thanks," I said. "And I have to get off. I still have to read a chapter for history and you have all those assignments to check out."

"Like I'm really going to do that," he said with a laugh. "See you tomorrow."

I hung up the phone and got ready for bed, thinking about what a total dork I was for spending an hour on the phone with him. But once I was lying in bed, my heart started hammering against my rib cage and I felt like I couldn't pull a full breath into my lungs and before I knew what I was doing, I reached for the phone and hit Redial.

He answered so fast, I knew he'd been waiting.

He became the person I looked forward to seeing at school. Not Sherry or my other long-time friends. As I was losing them, I was gaining Travis. He didn't fit in well with the other boys. It wasn't only his looks, although honestly, I was starting to think he was cute. He had really nice gray eyes beneath those insanely long eyelashes and although he didn't smile often, when he did, he kind of tipped his head to the side in a way that made me smile back. He was too down over his father's death to make much of an effort to fit in. He talked to me a lot about him, and I felt jealous that he'd gotten to know his father so well when I'd been cheated out of knowing my mother. His father sounded amazing. I loved my own father and I would have said we were close, but Travis's father was almost like a best friend to him. A really, really good father.

We talked on the phone more than we emailed and it took me a while to realize the old computer he shared with his mother was always breaking down and they didn't have the money to get it fixed. I didn't know what it was like not to have enough money for something as necessary as a computer. We had three in our condo for just Daddy and me. Travis had to use the one at the library sometimes to get his work done—and he *did* get it done even though he always acted like he didn't care about school. My father drove me to his house every once in a while so we could study together and afterward Travis and I would slowly walk the two blocks to the beach and he'd talk on and on about the tides and the surf and the marine life—all the things he'd learned from his father. My own father seemed to like Travis and called him "that nice little boy at the beach." He was happy I was no longer hanging around my old friends, who were getting wilder by the minute. The nice little boy at the beach struck him as much safer.

By the time summer rolled around, I was hardly speaking to Sherry and everybody, and that was okay. We had nothing in common anymore and they always wanted to put distance between themselves and Travis, who seemed like such a loser to them. That summer, Travis and his mother spent the entire two months with his aunt in Maryland, and when he came back he looked completely different. It was such a shock. When I saw him the first day of school, I honestly didn't recognize him. He'd had a growth spurt so huge it must have hurt. He was taller than me and he had muscles where he used to be all skin and knobby bones. He actually needed to shave! No one would ever think of him as girlish again. *Especially* not the girls, Sherry and my former friends included. They practically threw themselves at him, but he hadn't forgotten how they treated him. And he hadn't forgotten the one girl who treated him like he mattered: me.

I'd changed, too, over the summer. I suddenly understood my old friends' fascination with guys and I saw Travis in a whole new way. We settled back into our friendship pretty easily, but there was something new and exciting cooking beneath the surface and we both knew it. We still spoke on the phone nearly every night, but our conversations were different, full of unexpected twists and turns.

"I met a girl in Maryland," he told me one night, soon after school started.

I tried to act cool, though I felt ridiculously jealous. "What was she like?" I asked.

"Nice. Pretty. Sexy."

I didn't think I'd ever heard him use the word *sexy* before and it set all my nerve endings on fire. I was dying at the thought of him kissing her. Touching her body.

"Did you do it?"

He laughed, sounding a little embarrassed. "Almost, but no."

I felt relieved. "Are you still… I mean, do you want…"

He laughed again, and this time I knew he was laughing at me. "Spit it out," he said.

I shut my eyes. My heart was beating so hard I could feel it pounding through my back into my mattress. "Are you going to see her again?" I asked. "It's not like Maryland's on the other side of the country."

"No, I'm not. It wouldn't be fair to her."

"Why not?"

"Because the whole time I was hanging with her I wanted to be with you."

Yes. I couldn't believe how much I'd wanted to hear him say that! "I love you," I said. I blinked my eyes open and stared at my dark ceiling, biting my lip. Waiting.

"Since when?" he asked. Not exactly the response I'd wanted. But I thought back.

"Since that first night we talked on the phone. Remember? How you said talking would keep me from thinking about my heart and you from thinking about—"

"I love you, too," he interrupted, and suddenly everything was different.

I missed tons of school that fall because I was weak and kept getting sick. My father was afraid every time I left the house for "the germ factory," which is what he'd started calling my school. Travis was driving by then, this little old Honda of his mother's, and he'd pick up assignments and books for me and bring them to our condo after school. My father didn't like it. At first, I thought it was because the books and papers were coming from the germ factory, but then I realized he didn't like Travis and me being alone together. Daddy'd had no problem with Travis when he looked like a harmless, skinny little kid. Now, though, he looked like a man, and suddenly Daddy wasn't crazy about him. When Travis finally asked me to a movie, my father said I couldn't go. Daddy and I were sitting in our den. I was doing my math homework on the sofa while he answered email and he didn't even bother to look at me when he told me no.

"Dad," I said, looking up from my work, "we're just friends. It's no big deal."

He took off his reading glasses and set them on the desk. Whenever the glasses came off, I knew we were in for a long conversation about what I could and couldn't do. It had been that way for years. "Honey," he said, "one of these days you're going to have a new heart and you'll be able to live a full and active life, but until then, staying healthy and taking it easy are your top priorities, and—"

"Sitting in a movie with my best friend isn't going to tax my heart," I argued. I rarely fought back. I'd been taught not to argue by both my father and my doctor. They'd taught me to avoid conflict and stress for the sake of my failing heart. I was supposed to breathe slowly and repeat the words *peace and calm* in my head over and over again until the urge to fight passed. But some things were worth fighting about and this was one of them.

"You may consider him your best friend," Daddy said, "but I know how boys think and that's not the way he's thinking about you."

"Yes, it is." The lie felt so natural to me. I wasn't going to let my father screw this up.

"Boys and girls can't stay friends when they become men and women," my father said. "Hormones come into play and it's impossible. Travis is the wrong boy for you to get involved with, anyway."

"First of all, we're not 'involved,'" I said, although when my father said that word, all I could think about was holding Travis's hand in the movie and kissing him afterward. "Second, there's nobody who cares about me more than he does. Besides you," I added quickly.

"I was a boy and even the nicest boy has one thing on his mind." My father swiveled his chair to face me. "But even if…all that wasn't a concern, I still wouldn't want you with Travis. It's time to cool down that friendship, honey. He could drag you down."

"Are you talking about money? It's not like we're rich and he's poor."

"We're not rich, but we're very comfortable," he said. "Travis…isn't. I doubt he ever will be. It's not his fault. I know he hasn't had the advantages you've had, but that doesn't change the fact that he's not the sort of person I want my daughter to end up with. So there's no point in giving him any encouragement. And that's that."

"That's so unfair!" My cheeks burned. I felt the heat in them as I slammed my math book onto the coffee table. My father was instantly on his feet, holding his hands out in a calming motion.

"Settle down," he said. "Settle down. You know better than to argue—"

"You're always telling me to treat people equally and all that and then you say that just because he has less money than we do, I can't go out with him. He's smart, Daddy. He wants to be a biologist someday."

"Listen, honey." He sat down next to me on the sofa and put an arm around my shoulders. "I don't want you going out with *anyone* right now, okay? You don't understand how serious your condition is."

"You're upsetting my heart more than Travis ever would," I said.

"Then stop arguing with me." His voice was so annoyingly calm. "You have to trust that I know what's best for you right now. If you want, I can have Dr. McIntyre talk to you about this. He'll agree with me. Until you can get a new heart, you need to—"

"To stay locked up in my room without friends or ever doing anything fun."

"You need to be careful. That's all I was going to say."

I knew it was time to back down. I could feel my heart hurting, though it was more like a heart*ache* than anything to do with my condition. I would find a way to see Travis. I would just have to hide what I was doing from my father. I'd never done anything behind his back before, but he wasn't leaving me much of a choice.

So, I *did* go to the movies with Travis. I told him we needed to keep it from my father because he was worried about my health and didn't want me to date. I didn't tell him Daddy didn't want me going out with *him*. I'd never hurt him that way. Travis was sweet and sensitive, which was why I'd loved him back when he was a scrawny little boy and why I was falling into something deeper with him now. He wasn't like the other guys I knew who were all about drinking and hooking up with girls. The guys my old girlfriends hung out with and drooled over and talked about day and night.

It was amazing to sit next to Travis in the theater, holding his hand, feeling electricity between us where there used to be just the warmth of friendship. In his car, he kissed me and made me feel a little crazy with the way he ran his hands down my body over my clothes, and I thought: *I could die tomorrow, so there's no way I'm going to deprive myself of this today.* I decided right then that I was going to squeeze every drop of living into my life that I could.

Every single drop.

7
Erin

I'D BEEN LIVING IN MY BRIER CREEK APARTMENT for nearly a week when I discovered a coffee shop tucked into the far corner of the shopping center's vast parking lot. The tan stucco building looked very old, as though it had been there for decades and the shopping center had grown up around it, but I knew that couldn't be the case. It was simply designed to look old to give it some personality. The shop's name was painted on a board that hung above the wood-and-glass front doors and I couldn't read it until I was nearly on top of it. *JumpStart.* I walked inside and was transported from the bustling parking lot with its zillions of cars and the illusion of squeaky-clean newness into a warm space that felt almost like a living room. The furniture was organized into intimate little groupings set apart from one another by bookcases and a fireplace—not burning, since it was still very warm outside. Then there was the long counter with a menu made up of pastries and salads and coffees and teas. Music played softly in the background. It was something jazzy, which I didn't usually like, but I didn't really care about music one way or another anymore. Music, books, politics, art, sex—what did any of it matter? It was all so insignificant to me now.

Half the chairs and tables and leather sofas were occupied, mostly by people my age typing on their computers or doing paperwork. Three young women shared a table and they were laughing at something on a computer screen. A man was talking about real estate with an older couple. I heard the words *town house* and *too many stairs.* Another couple was in the midst of an intense conversation, an open bible on the table between them. I knew the moment I walked inside that I'd be spending a lot of time there. I felt anonymous and I liked the feeling.

I spotted a leather chair that I wanted to claim for my own. Although it was part of a grouping—three chairs and one sofa—no one was sitting in that little circle. I liked knowing I would have that space to myself, at least for a while.

I ordered a decaf latte and a bagel I knew I would only nibble. I'd lost twenty pounds in the five months since Carolyn's death and I had to force myself to eat. I couldn't taste anything and food seemed to stick in my throat. The barista, a dark-haired guy whose nametag read *Nando,* smiled at me, showing off a deep dimple in a handsome face. I did my best to smile back without much success. I noticed a tattoo of a unicorn on his forearm as he handed me my bagel.

I settled into the brown leather chair, pulled out my iPad and did a quick check of my email. Michael wrote that he missed me and asked how I was doing.

Okay, I typed. *In a coffee shop right now. It's nice. Hope you're okay, too.* We'd had a similar exchange every morning since I left and I guessed that would be the nature of our communication for a while. Polite and bland. Empty words. The sort you might write to an acquaintance you checked in with once a year instead of a man you'd shared your life with for so long. A man you'd made love to and laughed with and cried with.

We used to email each other all the time during the day. The days I worked in the pharmacy, I'd check in to talk about dinner or household things or simply to tell him I loved him. The days I was home, I'd describe what Carolyn and I were up to and he'd write back saying he was sad that he wasn't with us. He meant it, too. My friends had envied that, how close he and Carolyn were. How capable Michael was of taking care of her. If my friends had to leave their kids with their husbands for some reason, they worried the guys wouldn't be able to manage. I never worried about that with Michael. He'd take Carolyn to the park or just make up a game to play with her on the spot. I'd admired that about him. He was so creative and fun and Carolyn always looked forward to "Daddy Time."

How did he stand it, losing her? He'd loved her so much. How could he just go back to normal, talking about having another baby like nothing had happened? I didn't understand my husband.

I deleted a bunch of spam, along with a confirmation email from Judith about our next appointment, and that was the sum total of my mail. A few weeks ago, I realized someone had taken me off my neighborhood Mom's Group email list. I'd been part of that list for four years. It was a way of staying connected and sharing experiences and advice. We made plans for birthday parties or announced a spontaneous get-together at the park. After Carolyn died, they took me off the list for a week or so while they figured out how to help Michael and me. They divvied up food responsibilities, bringing us casseroles and meatloaf and chicken potpie every night. Michael and I didn't need to think about cooking for a month. The only thing was, we couldn't eat. Or at least I couldn't. Some of that food was still in our freezer.

Then they put me back on the list, but that was torture of the first order. How could I read about what they were doing with their kids? Debates about vaccinations, recommendations of pediatric dentists and ideas for birthday gifts. Temper tantrums and preschool problems and, the worst, the get-togethers I would no longer be part of? The moms emailed me separately to find out how I was doing, but gradually that stopped. I wondered who made the decision to take me off the list? Who said, "She never participates anymore. We should just remove her" or "Maybe it's hurtful to her to be on the list? Should we take her off?" Yes, it was hurtful to be on the list and just as hurtful to be off it. But what hurt the most was how everyone had disappeared, as though I didn't matter anymore because I didn't have a child. I honestly didn't blame them. We were in different worlds now. My world was scary to them and theirs was painful to me.

So now I had Harley's Dad and Friends, and I navigated to that group to see what everyone was up to. I read through the most recent messages. There were some new people and I welcomed them and offered sympathy. They shared their stories in long, wordy, tearful paragraphs and I nodded as I read them. My heart expanded to take them into my world. I'd asked Judith, "Is it nuts that the people I love the most right now are these strangers in the Harley's Dad group?" and she'd just smiled and said, "What do you think?" turning it back on me as she usually did.

There was an angry comment written by Mom-of-Five whose sister told her "Life is for the living and you need to get over your grief for the sake of your other children." I felt indignant on her behalf and I typed an empathetic response, my fingers flying over the iPad screen. In my mind, I lumped her sister together with Michael and with anyone else who dared to tell someone she was grieving the wrong way.

Early on, Michael and I had been in the same place when it came to our sorrow. We were both in that denial stage where we walked around crying and shaking our heads and saying "I just don't believe it" and "This can't be happening." We held each other and cried for hours and I loved him with all my heart. He was my connection to Carolyn, the person who shared the deepest love of her anyone could imagine. But then he returned to work, just a week after she died. He wanted to go, and I didn't understand how he could possibly concentrate on work. Right then, I couldn't imagine *ever* going back to my job. But Michael simply threw himself into some new project. I used to admire his work. He'd convinced me that his style of video game design went way beyond sport to something with far greater significance. "It's about social connection," he'd say. "It's about people working together to solve problems." He'd won a few awards for his games and I'd been proud of him. Now, though, I thought his work was superficial and silly. Games! What on earth did they matter? Still, you'd think he was saving the planet with the hours he put in. He'd work till six, then come home, eat dinner, and work some more in our home office. On the weekends, he started doing all the handyman jobs he'd put off for years. Repairing the deck. Painting the family room. Keeping busy so he didn't have to listen to me rant and rave. As far as I could tell, he was finished grieving.

We saw Judith together a few times, but Michael was done talking about Carolyn by then, while I felt as though I was just getting started. I *needed* to talk about her. The way that one lock of hair on her forehead would never lay flat. The way she'd sing to herself in bed at night or come into our room to cuddle with us on Saturday morning. Chatty. She was always chatty. When I started talking about that terrible night on the pier, sifting through every detail of it, I wasn't surprised when Michael got up and left the room. "This is pointless," he said over his shoulder to Judith. "She can't let go of it."

After he left the room, I looked at Judith. "See?" I said. "He's done with her and I'll never be done with her."

"Men and women grieve differently," Judith said. She was fiftyish with straight, chin-length gray hair and vivid blue eyes. My doctor had recommended I see her shortly after Carolyn died, when no matter what drug I took, I couldn't sleep. When I did doze off, I'd be back on that pier, reliving the whole thing all over again.

"I can *accept* that men and women grieve differently," I said, "but I can't *live* with it any longer." That was the day I decided to move out.

After an hour in the coffee shop, I felt a little guilty sitting there with my empty cup and half-eaten bagel, even though no one was fighting for my seat. I went up to the counter and asked Nando for a refill.

"You're new here," he said as he filled my cup.

"I just moved to the area last week."

"You working nearby?"

"No, I'm taking a little time off."

"Room?" he asked.

"I... What?"

"Room for cream? I don't remember how you took that first cup."

"Oh. No. Black, please."

"I'll remember for next time," he said with that dimply

smile as he handed me the cup. "So, where did you move from?"

"Just...not far. A different part of Raleigh." I wanted to get back to my seat. "Thanks for the refill," I said.

"Anytime."

I sat down in the leather chair again and opened my iPad. There was a new father in the Harley's Dad and Friends group and he was in major pain. I wanted to respond to him. To let him know he wasn't alone. I couldn't imagine Michael ever baring his soul so openly, online or off. I typed a few lines to him. *Donald, I'm so sorry you have to be here, but I'm glad you found us. It sounds like your daughter was a truly special little girl.*

Nando started singing something in Spanish as he waited on another customer. I glanced over at him. He'd said he'd remember how I liked my coffee. So much for anonymity. I'd sounded rude, the abrupt way I'd answered his questions. Questions were becoming a challenge. It was nobody's business why I'd moved from one part of Raleigh to another. It was nobody's business that I was taking time off from work. I felt a sudden ache of loss in my chest, not for Carolyn this time as much as for my old life. The ache expanded and I had to clench my teeth together to keep from crying. I'd loved my job and I'd loved my life. Cooking, fixing up the house, taking care of Carolyn, making love to my husband. I pressed my fingers to my breastbone as if I could rub away the pain. Then I looked down at my iPad again, returning my attention to Donald and Mom-of-Five and the other people who understood how, on a warm April evening on a long moonlit pier, the life I'd loved and treasured had ended.

8

Travis

THE TRAILER WASN'T A PRETTY SIGHT. THE exterior was white—or at least it had been white at one time—with patches of rust and plenty of dings. It was maybe twice as long as my van and it sat on concrete blocks above the sandy soil. It was in a line of other trailers in all shapes and sizes, most of them empty now that summer was over. There was a car parked in front of the gold trailer next to ours, though—a sparkling new green VW Beetle convertible that looked out of place in a sea of grungy old trailers. I'd borrowed the money for my first week's rent from a buddy. I hoped it wouldn't be too long before I could pay it back, but I wasn't optimistic.

I slid open the side door of my van and helped Bella out of her car seat.

"This is our new home, Bell," I said. "At least for a while. Let's go inside and explore." *Explore* was the wrong word for what we'd be able to do inside a one-room trailer, but it didn't matter. Bella stood staring up at the thing with her wide gray eyes. She'd turned four the day before and we'd had a little party for her at Franny's with balloons and ice-cream cake and not much in the way of presents. I think Franny was actually celebrating our departure, but whatever.

"It's not a home," Bella said, staring at the trailer. Her lamb and pink purse were in her arms and she didn't move from the side of the van. My mother had given her that purse for her third birthday and I was so glad Bella hadn't lost it or the lamb in the fire. They let her hold on to something familiar. Inside the purse, she had a picture of the three of us—my mother, Bella and me—sitting on the beach around a sandcastle we'd built. She had a tiny little doll that one of the women I'd gone out with had given her. She loved that doll because it had really long, blond hair she liked to comb. And the third and final thing in her purse was a picture of Robin. Just a little headshot I'd had since we were in high school. I was glad I'd never given in to the temptation to toss it. Bella knew Robin was her mother, but that was it. Someday I planned to tell Bella all about her, though how I was going to explain why Robin didn't want her, I had no idea.

"Well, we're going to make it into our home," I said now. "It's not a *house* like we're used to. It's called a trailer and lots of people live in trailers. It'll be an adventure for a while. Let's go see what's inside, okay?"

She took my hand and we climbed the steps to the door. I unlocked it and we stepped into a space so dark I couldn't see my hand in front of my face. I could *smell* the place, though. It had that musty, closed-up, "beach place" odor and something else I hoped had nothing to do with cats.

"I can't see anything, Daddy." There was a sound in her voice that told me she was going to lose it any second. Sort of a mini-whine that only I could pick up. Even my mother never heard it, but sometimes Bella would say something and I'd whisper to Mom, "Meltdown coming," and sure enough, five seconds later, the crying and wailing would begin. It didn't happen much anymore, but I had the feeling it was going to happen now. My kid had been through too damn much in the past couple of weeks.

"We need to open all the shades and let in the light," I said, prying my hand from hers to reach for one of the window shades, which I could make out only because of the line of sunlight around it. It sprang open so fast I blinked at the light pouring through the filmy glass. "That's better!" I said. "How many windows do we have, Bella?"

She looked around the dim interior. "Three," she said.

"I think there's one more. Do you see it?"

She turned in a circle. "I spy!" she said when her gaze landed on the long narrow window above the kitchen sink.

"Good job!" I finished opening the shades.

Bella ran to the only inside door in the place and pulled it open. "That's the bathroom," I said.

"Where's my room?" she asked.

"That's the cool thing about this trailer," I said. "It's all one big room instead of separate rooms. So it's our living room—" I pointed to the futon, then to the small table and two chairs beneath one of the windows "—and our dining room, and our kitchen, and your bedroom." I pointed to the double bed crammed into the other end of the trailer. "You'll sleep there and I'll sleep on this futon."

"What's a futon?"

"Couch. It's another name for a couch," I said. "I think the first thing we should do, even before we bring in the bags with our clothes, is find a place to display your new shells."

The people at my mother's church had collected clothes and sheets and towels for us. They'd been so good to us that for a few days I thought I might start going back to church like when I was a kid, but the mood passed. Now I was into survival mode and I had my priorities: shelter, food, job, child care. My soul was going to have to wait.

"I want my *old* shells back." The whine was there, not so little this time. A stranger would be able to pick it up now. She was tired. No nap today, and this was a kid who definitely still needed naps.

"Yeah, I wish you could have them back, but you'll always have the memory of them."

"I don't want the remembery. I want *them* back. And Nana back, too."

I'd told her she'd always have the memory of Nana, but I knew she wouldn't. As she got older, she'd forget her. You didn't remember people from when you were four. Maybe vaguely. I kept thinking about that—how my mother, who had done so much for her and who loved her more than anything, would just disappear from her memory. Whoosh! It seemed like one more unfair thing in a whole bushel of stuff that sucked.

"I'm going to get your new shells," I said, hoping to avoid the meltdown.

"I don't want them," she whimpered.

I went out to the van and got the canvas bag with its lame collection of shells and carried it and the garbage bag filled with sheets and towels back into the trailer. The floor made a hollow sound when I stepped on it. This was going to take some getting used to.

Bella was curled into a ball on the futon, her lamb clutched in her arms, her lower lip jutting out in a pout that was so damn cute I had a hard time not smiling. I used to laugh when she'd pout like that until my mother said I was encouraging it. Mom said she'd turn out to be one of those girls who'd get her way with guys by acting like a pouty baby and I can tell you, that thought wiped the smile off my face. I wanted my daughter to be strong.

"Now, where's a good place for these?" I asked, looking around the room. At home, we'd had them on the mantel above the non-working fireplace.

She was still pouting, but she sat up a little straighter and started looking around the room. I could see the only ledge in the whole place—under that long narrow kitchen window—but I waited for her to find it on her own. And she did. She hopped off the futon and ran to the sink, pointing to the window. "Up there," she said.

"Perfect!" I handed her the bag. "You give them to me one at a time and I'll put them up there."

She handed me the first one, the giant gray whelk, which was clearly going to be the foundation of her new collection. It was her favorite. I put it right in the middle of the window ledge. She handed me an orange scallop shell and frowned. "The mantel was better," she said. "There's no room up there."

I was kind of impressed she could figure that out. It seemed pretty smart for a four-year-old to realize there wouldn't be enough space on that ledge as her collection grew. Mom said I had an inflated idea of her brilliance, but what did I know? She seemed smart to me. "Well, you're right, and when we run out I think we'll have to put some of them in a bowl, okay?"

"They'll break."

"Not if you're care—"

"Knock knock!"

I turned to see a girl standing in our open doorway. The way she was silhouetted in the sunlight, I couldn't make out her face, but her voice was unfamiliar and I was sure I didn't know her.

"Come in," I said, and she stepped inside. I'd definitely never seen her before. She was the sort of girl you wouldn't forget. Twenty, maybe, and hot. *Smokin'* hot. Maybe a little too skinny, but she had blond hair in a long ponytail that hung over her right breast and she was wearing just about nothing—shorts and sandals and a halter top. I felt myself go hard and had the feeling she knew it. She had one of those *Let's get it on* smiles, or maybe I was just fantasizing. It had been months for me and I needed to go back and adjust that list of priorities I'd come up with.

"Hey," she said. "I'm Savannah. Your next-door neighbor."

"Cool." I moved forward to shake her hand. "I'm Travis and this is Bella." I squeezed Bella's shoulder and she wrapped one arm around my leg, the other holding the bag of shells.

"Hey, Bella." Savannah squatted down, giving me a really nice view of her breasts. "Welcome to the neighborhood, honey," she said. "What do you have in the bag?"

I expected Bella to pull away from her. It usually took her a while to warm up to strangers. But instead, she opened the tote bag and let Savannah peek inside. I wondered if Savannah reminded her of the long-haired doll she carried around in her pink purse.

"Shells!" Savannah's eyes lit up and she actually sat down on the ratty thin carpet, cross-legged, and patted the spot next to her. "Will you show me? I love shells."

Okay, I thought. *This is finally a stroke of luck.* I could have gotten a trailer next door to a crazy old dude who walked around in his undershirt and had a thing for little girls. Instead I was living next to a hot girl who had a way with kids.

"The Beetle is yours?" I asked as Bella took out the rest of her shells and showed them to Savannah, one by one.

"Uh-huh." Savannah didn't look at me. Her attention was on Bella and she said nice things about each shell. "I've been living here three months and I'm glad to finally have a neighbor. I mean a *real* neighbor. There were plenty of people over the summer." She rolled her eyes. "*Too* many. But now that the season's over, it's lonely here."

"Do you... I mean, why are you living here?"

"I waitressed during the summer and I'm taking a couple of night classes now. Cosmetology. And I need a cheap place to live and this is about as cheap as it gets."

I laughed. "Tell me about it."

Okay, so she wasn't a rocket scientist, but neither was I. Although at one time, I'd had higher expectations of myself. Those days were gone.

"I wanted to invite you and Bella over for dinner." She got to her feet and dusted off her hands. "Just mac and cheese, if that's okay."

Bella drew in a quick breath. She was still sitting on the floor and she looked up at me with a little smile. Damn, she was cute. I grinned at her. "Mac and cheese work for you, Bella?" I asked. It was her favorite, and she nodded.

"What time?" I asked Savannah.

"Six?"

"Excellent. We'll settle in. Maybe one of us will take a little nap."

We exchanged phone numbers and I didn't tell her I probably wouldn't have my phone much longer. I hadn't been able to pay the last bill. I thought about the magnetic signs I had on the sides of my van: Brown Construction, with my phone number below it. I wasn't taking those signs down, no matter what. I had a thing about them. They were more than just magnetized plastic to me. My dad had had Brown Plumbing signs on the sides of his truck, and when I put my own up, I thought about how he must have felt about those signs. Proud to have his own business. Proud to have a way to support us, the way I'd supported Bella and my mom before the economy totally tanked. What use would those signs be if I had no phone, though?

Savannah's trailer was a step up from mine, which wasn't saying much, but you could feel a girly touch when you walked inside. First, it smelled a lot better, between the macaroni and cheese cooking and some other scent. A candle, maybe. Second, she'd put some nicer rugs on top of the old carpeting. Maybe I could do that, too, when I got some money. Third, she'd thrown this gold-striped fabric over the couch along with a bunch of pillows, and there were lamps all over the place. It just felt homey. I could see into the second room, where her bed had a bunch of pillows on it, too, and a yellow quilt. There was one thing that bugged me, though, and that was a bong sitting out on her kitchen counter. I didn't do drugs. I was even careful with booze. Maybe I messed with it a little after things went south with Robin, but once I had a kid to raise, I cooled it. I didn't care if Savannah smoked weed. It was no big deal, but the bong right out in the open like that with Bella there…well, I didn't like it. But I was liking *her* well enough. She'd changed into a skimpy dress. No bra. She was so thin she didn't need one, but the fabric of her dress hugged her nipples and I was having trouble keeping my eyes on her face. She'd taken her hair out of the ponytail and it was very long and gold. Smooth and silky. The kind of hair you'd see on a shampoo commercial. I wanted to touch it. Just grab a big fistful of it in my hand.

I needed to slow the hell down.

"Thanks for asking us over," I said. "I didn't have a chance to go to the store yet."

"I know what moving day's like," she said. She reached into the fridge, pulled out a beer, uncapped it and handed it to me. "What about for Bella?" she asked. "Juice? Milk?"

"Juice," Bella said. Usually I'd give her the milk, but tonight was a special occasion.

"Please," I reminded Bella.

"Please," she said.

Savannah poured some orange juice into a tall plastic cup with a cap and a straw. Perfect.

"You act like you understand kids," I said as I settled Bella at the table with a puzzle I'd brought with me so she wouldn't get bored. She loved puzzles and this one had Cinderella on it. She loved her princesses.

"Oh, I've got a slew of nieces and I volunteered in a day care for a year or so. This age—" she motioned toward Bella "—so adorable. The best. Still innocent, you know?"

I nodded, but I was thinking about what she said. She'd worked in a day care? Was there a chance I'd stumbled across not only the hottest neighbor a man could hope for but child care, as well?

Savannah pulled a bunch of salad stuff out of the refrigerator and set it on the counter, then seemed to notice the bong and quietly moved it inside one of the lower cabinets. I didn't say a thing except, "Can I help?"

We worked together in the kitchen, talking about where we were from—me, from right there in Carolina Beach; her, from Kinston—and did a little "Do you know so and so?" but we definitely moved in different circles. I told her about the fire and she stopped chopping celery to look at me. She rested her hand on my shoulder. "I'm so sorry, Travis," she said. She glanced at Bella, who was quietly working on her puzzle. "This must completely suck for both of you."

I nodded. "Yeah, it does."

She still had her hand on my shoulder and she lowered it, running it down the length of my arm, slipping her fingers into my palm. She was coming on to me. I hadn't had any kind of long-term relationship since Bella came into my life. I didn't want one now, either. It would just confuse things. But I could use someone to sleep with. That I couldn't deny, and the way she'd touched me let me know she knew what she was doing. She would be as good in bed as she looked.

I focused on the lettuce to keep my wits about me. "The thing is," I said, "I really need to get work. My final paycheck literally went up in smoke with the house. And if I find work, I need somebody to watch Bella for me. Do you know anyone who does child care?"

She shrugged with a smile. "I know *me,*" she said. "I've had experience. I told you I worked in a day care. My classes are at night and all I do all day right now is hang out. I'd love to watch her."

"I'd pay you, of course. I mean, as soon as I get work."

She nodded. "Not easy to find right now, huh?"

I shook my head. "Twenty guys for every job, at least," I said.

"Well, if you find a job, you've got a sitter. Except..." She hesitated, taking a few more chops at the celery. "I have to go out of town sometimes. I have friends I visit in Raleigh when I don't have class. But I could probably find someone to cover for me then."

"Okay," I said, thinking that I wouldn't want to leave Bella with someone I didn't know. But then, what did I know about Savannah herself? I should probably ask to speak to the day care where she'd worked, but I was afraid that would sound like an insult. What I knew about Savannah was that she grew up in Kinston and was taking night classes to learn how to do hair or nails or whatever and that she drank beer and smoked enough weed to have a bong on her kitchen counter. I wondered if she did anything heavier than marijuana. I'd keep an eye on how much she drank tonight. What if she had friends who hung out with her at the trailer? I didn't want a bunch of losers hanging around Bella. I wondered if *I* was one of the losers now. Maybe that's what Savannah was thinking.

"Where's Bella's mom?" she asked quietly as she dropped the celery into the salad bowl.

"Beaufort," I said.

"Is she... What's her name?"

"Robin."

"Was she unfit or what? How come Bella's with you?"

"It's a long story," I said. Robin wasn't my favorite topic, especially not with someone I didn't know well.

"Does Bella ever see her?"

"Sure," I lied. It was none of her business, and the lie seemed the easiest way out of the conversation. "Want me to shred some carrots for the salad?"

"Sure." Savannah smiled. Touched my arm. "I think Bella's a lucky little girl to end up with you," she said.

Over dinner, we did most of our talking to and through Bella, but beneath the table Savannah ran her bare foot up my leg. The first time, she looked at me with a question in her eyes, like "Is this okay? Are we on the same page?" and I gave her a little smile back to let her know it was as okay as it could be, even though I knew hooking up with her might be really stupid. I needed her to take care of Bella more than I needed a lover. But right then, with her foot inching closer to the inside of my thigh, I wasn't thinking all that much about child care.

We watched a little TV with Bella after dinner, then I settled her down on Savannah's couch. I didn't think she'd go right to sleep. It usually took her a while, especially in a strange place, and she was used to me reading to her in bed before lights out. She'd had a ton of books that burned in the fire, but Franny'd given us *The Cat in the Hat* when we first moved in with her, and Bella didn't seem to mind hearing it over and over again. Even when we were finished reading, she'd rarely just drift off. She'd ask for water or get up to tell me or my mom something that couldn't possibly wait until morning and generally wear herself out. But the lack of a nap was working to her advantage tonight. *My* advantage. I covered her over and watched while she sank into a deep sleep, and as I tucked the light blanket tighter over her shoulders, Savannah leaned over and nuzzled my neck.

I stood up and put my arms around her. "Listen," I said. "I'm not ready for anything ser—"

"Shh." She kissed me. "I don't care about serious," she said. "I'm all about living in the present moment." She took my hand and we walked into her bedroom and, for a couple of hours, I forgot about the fire and my lack of a job and just about everything except my body and hers.

9
Robin

ONCE MY BED-AND-BREAKFAST GUESTS WERE well fed and ready to explore Beaufort for the day, I left my assistant, Bridget, to clean up and headed next door to Hendricks House. The fact that, at thirty-three, Dale still lived with his parents had seemed weird to me until I saw his apartment. He had the entire second story to himself with a separate entrance. Once we were married, we'd have a place of our own, of course. Just two weeks ago, a few days before Hannah was born, we'd signed a contract on a small house a block from the water. Or at least Dale had signed the contract. The Beaufort-style bungalow would be in his name until we were married. We'd close in a month and I couldn't wait to fix it up. I'd still manage the B and B, although Bridget would take over my roomy first-floor apartment and I'd do less of the day-to-day grunt work. If Dale had his way, I wouldn't be doing any of it. I could be a lady of leisure, he said, just doing volunteer work like his mother. He didn't like it when I talked about going to school. I wasn't sure if I wanted to be a nurse or some kind of medical technician, but I was absolutely certain I'd need more in my life than the garden club and playing golf and tennis, two games I hated to begin with. Dale thought I should just take it easy. He was always worrying about my health. I took a couple of handfuls of pills a day and had to be careful around germs, but I refused to live my life in a bubble the way he wanted me to.

I walked across the driveway that ran between the B and B and Hendricks House and spotted Mollie working in the garden by the front steps. They had a gardener, of course—a bunch of them, actually—who took care of both properties, but the garden that ran the width of the house belonged to Mollie.

"Hi, Mom," I said as I neared her. She sat back on her heels and adjusted her straw hat to look at me.

"Hi, sweetheart." Her smile looked a little tired and I guessed that having a baby in the house was taking a toll on everyone's sleep. I'd started calling Mollie and James Mom and Dad at their insistence right after Dale and I announced our engagement a year ago. Calling Mollie "Mom" came easily to me. I loved how kind she was to me. I didn't remember my own mother and I'd spent most of my life wishing I had someone I could call Mom. Calling James "Dad" had been tougher, though. My own father had still been alive then, so I already had a dad. Plus James always held his distance. Oh, he was really nice to me and I knew he loved me in his own way, but he was such a politician. I was never certain if what was written on his face was what he was really feeling. I'd seen him smile warmly at too many people he'd later put down in private to trust him completely. I sometimes saw the same trait in Dale and it shook me up.

"Alissa's going to be so happy to see you." Mollie brushed a speck of dirt from her khaki shorts. "That baby was up all night."

"Did she keep you awake?" I asked.

She shook her head. "Ear plugs. I've worn them ever since I married James. I'm going to give you a pair as a wedding gift."

I laughed. I started to say that Dale didn't snore, but thought better of it. I honestly didn't know if they realized how often Dale stayed over at my apartment. Anyhow, it would be "indelicate" of me to say. I was learning a lot about what was tolerated in a family that needed to keep a polished public image. The word *indelicate* came up a lot. That's why they dealt so openly and quickly with Alissa's pregnancy, making lemonade out of lemons.

I'd adored Alissa from the moment I met her. She'd been barely fifteen with silky-straight, long, dark hair and a wide, white smile. For the longest time, I'd thought what an amazing teenager she was. She seemed so together. Straight-A student. Popular, with a sweet, shy, lovable boyfriend named Jess. She was a whiz with anything to do with the computer. She set up the website for the bed-and-breakfast herself at fourteen. If anyone should have been able to see through a facade, though, it should have been me, and even I missed it. Only when she was five months pregnant did she tell her parents and Dale. Then, for the first time, I saw all hell break loose in the Hendricks family. When James and Mollie and Dale started talking about contacting Jess's parents, Alissa owned up to the truth: Jess had been nothing but a cover. He was Alissa's best friend, as gay as the day was long, and he'd been helping her sneak around to see Will Stevenson, a boy she'd been forbidden to go out with. Jess would pick her up for a "date," then drive her to wherever she and Will were hooking up. I'd never met Will, so I couldn't pass judgment on him, but the rest of the family seemed to hate him for reasons that still seemed small and wrong to me. I guessed there were enough small reasons that when you added them together, it was enough to equal one giant one. For starters, he was a high-school dropout doing custodial work for some businesses. His mother was a housekeeper—in fact, she'd been the Hendricks' housekeeper when Alissa and Will were toddlers. His father was in prison for something to do with drugs. Plus Will was nineteen, two and a half years older than Alissa. The Hendricks all acted like that was a big deal. Since Dale was eleven years older than me, the age difference seemed like a pretty weak argument, but it was one of those family issues I knew I'd better stay out of. Anyhow, Alissa hadn't been allowed to see him and when she announced he was her baby's father, the shit hit the fan. We were all sitting in the living room when she told us the truth. James and Dale went ballistic. Seriously, I was afraid they were going to get the rifles from the gun rack in the den and hunt Will down.

The family kept Will's name out of the whole mess, simply painting him as an older guy who took advantage of their vulnerable daughter. "Please let us deal with this family matter in private and protect a young girl who made a mistake and is taking responsibility for her actions," James had said in a statement to the press.

I felt sorry for Alissa. She was sixteen years younger than Dale, a change-of-life baby, Mollie told me, and it was like she had three parents instead of two. They started monitoring her cell phone and computer to make sure she and Will had no contact, and I honestly thought she'd lost interest in him until she mentioned him in the labor room. I'd asked her about that once since Hannah was born but she said she was just "crazy" that day and that she really didn't care about him anymore.

It was strange that I never connected what Alissa was

going through with what I'd gone through with Travis. Maybe because Alissa was so healthy and together and I'd been anything but. Maybe because she had two parents and a brother and I'd just had my father. Maybe because I'd never met Will, so it felt almost as though he didn't exist. The one thing I knew, though, was that my sympathy was with Alissa more than with her parents or Dale. I was careful about ever saying that, but I hoped Alissa knew I was in her corner. I could hear Hannah crying as I neared Alissa's room. The door was open, and when I walked in, Alissa was sitting in the rocker by the window while Hannah wailed in her bassinet.

"Is she hungry?" I asked, walking to the bassinet to peer down at Hannah. I couldn't stand it when she cried. I just wanted to fix whatever was upsetting her. "When's the last time you fed her?"

Alissa held up a bottle. "I was just going to," she said, although it looked to me like she'd been pretty relaxed for a while in that rocker. "You want to do it?"

"Is the bottle still warm?" I asked.

"Yeah. I made it too hot and was waiting for it to cool down."

I bent over to lift Hannah into my arms. I could finally hold her without crying. That first day in the delivery room when I held her in my arms had opened up a whole part of myself I'd buried. Now I couldn't get enough of her. I helped Alissa every chance I got, though Mollie had hired a nanny, an older woman named Gretchen, who came in several hours a day—hours I wasn't needed and left me wishing I was. Everyone thought I was hormonal or something, the way I'd get so emotional around Hannah, and maybe that was it. I'd seen plenty of babies since my own was born four years ago, and I'd never had this reaction before. It was like I was *ready* now. Ready to let myself admit it had all happened, though I refused to dwell on it.

Through the bay window, the sun fell on Alissa's long, reddish-brown hair, and for the first time since Hannah was born, she looked strong and well and pretty. I took the bottle from her and settled down in the wing chair opposite the rocker. I could see Alissa's desk from where I sat. The book I'd given her on baby care was tossed on a messy pile of other books and magazines. I doubted she'd even glanced at it, although I'd read it from cover to cover myself before I gave it to her.

"Mom said she was awake a lot last night," I said. I touched the nipple to Hannah's lips and she trembled as she took it in her mouth as though she couldn't get to the formula fast enough. It made me smile.

Alissa rocked a little. "I couldn't get her to settle down," she said. "Gretchen said I should make little swishing sounds in her ear, but it didn't work."

"Frustrating," I said. Gretchen had told Mollie and me that Alissa wasn't bonding well with Hannah. We were supposed to keep an eye on her. Make sure she wasn't sinking into some major postpartum depression. I just thought she needed sleep, but maybe it was more than that. She was such a social girl and I knew she'd felt cut off from her friends, first by the pregnancy and now by the baby. She'd go back to school in another month and maybe that would help her mood.

Hannah opened her eyes and stared right at me. I wondered if she did that with Alissa. I hoped so. How could you feel those dark eyes on you and not be hooked for life? "Hi, sweetie," I said to the baby. "Is that good?"

From her seat by the window, Alissa watched Hannah drink the way she might look at a puppy she hadn't quite decided whether to take home or not. I smiled at her. "She has such a good appetite," I said.

"She's so much better for you than she is for me."

"You'll get the knack of it in no time."

"But you never had a baby and it's natural with you. It's totally *not* natural to me. Gretchen said I need to relax when I hold her, but I get all tense."

"Be patient with yourself," I said.

She looked out the window toward Taylor's Creek. "Maybe you and Dale should raise her," she said, without glancing back at me.

"We'll be right there to help you with her, Ali. Don't worry."

She let out a long sigh. "I am so trapped," she said.

"But soon you'll be back with your friends."

"With a baby."

"It'll be fine," I said, but I knew she had an uphill battle in front of her. Things would never be the same between her and her old friends.

I stayed with her another hour, until it was time for me to get back to the B and B to check on the housekeepers and answer messages. I'd burped Hannah, changed her and settled her back in her bassinet when Alissa grabbed my hand.

"I'm so glad you came along," she said. "I'm so glad Dale ended up with you instead of Debra."

Dale had told me about Debra, his former fiancée, early on, when we were just getting to know each other. He'd been crazy about her and she'd told him she'd never been serious about anyone before. Some reporter, though, wrote an article about the Hendricks family in the local paper and he'd dug up the fact that Debra'd been married before. Not a crime. The crime was that she'd never told Dale about it and he was hurt and humiliated by her deception. I saw it in his eyes when he told me. The pain had still been raw then, and I'd felt sorry for him.

I bent over to give Alissa a hug. "I'm glad, too," I said. "Call me if you get lonely."

I left her room and was nearly to the front door when I spotted James and two well-dressed men in the living room. "Here's our Robin!" James boomed, and I slowed my pace to a more ladylike walk.

"Hello." I smiled.

"Come in, come in!" James held out an arm to motion me into the room. I walked in, and he introduced me to the men, whose names I quickly forgot. Dale told me I was going to have to do better with names. I just couldn't keep everyone straight the way he did.

"Robin's going to be the newest member of the Hendricks family," James said. He sounded proud of me and I tried to look worthy, but in my shorts and T-shirt with a little bit of baby spit-up on my shoulder, I doubted I was pulling it off. I hoped he wasn't upset that I was such a mess.

One of the men held my hand in both of his. "All my wife can talk about is your wedding," he said. "She said it's been too long since she's been to one. You'll have to meet her beforehand so when she starts crying, she'll at least know the person inspiring her tears."

"I look forward to meeting her," I said. I was getting so nervous about the wedding. It seemed like everyone in town was being invited. I'd had almost nothing to do with the plans. Mollie took over, picking out the invitations and the flowers and the cake. Well, I did say I wanted chocolate, but she picked the style. She also picked out my dress, but since it had been hers, I couldn't criticize her for that, and it was beautiful. Just amazing. I was trying to think of the event as a dream wedding, but I kept waking up around two in the morning, feeling as though it was more of a nightmare. My life these days seemed a little out of my control.

"I have to run," I said to James. "Need to see how things are going next door."

"Of course, of course," he said, and I heard him say to the men as I headed out the front door, "Isn't she lovely?" The words made my eyes burn. The people in this family were sometimes two-faced, sometimes back-stabbing, sometimes calculating. But one thing I felt sure of: they loved me. And as I walked across the yard to the B and B, I had to ask myself if a lie of omission was just as bad as the outright lie Debra had told Dale.

In the B and B's kitchen, I started putting together the casserole for tomorrow's breakfast, thinking of James's sweet words and what a miracle my life was turning out to be. My girlfriend Joy, whom I'd known from the cardiac rehab center where we'd both been patients, had been the one to tell me about the job opening at the B and B. She'd been working as a waitress at a Beaufort restaurant and she encouraged me to leave Chapel Hill and move in with her in Beaufort. I'd been at loose ends. Dad was pushing me to go to college. But while college was definitely in my plans, I wanted a taste of freedom. I felt as though I'd been locked in a closet of a life for years, first by my illness, then by my recovery. After my year of rehab, I didn't feel like studying. I just wanted to enjoy being alive for once.

After the family hired me, Dale gave me a crash course about Beaufort so I'd at least know more than my guests about the area. He walked me along the waterfront, introducing me to every shop owner, pointing out the boats, telling me about their owners. In the distance, we could see a few of the ponies standing in the surf on Carrot Island.

Dale and I fell in love on those walks. I was moved by how much he adored Beaufort and how much he wanted to do for its people. Even then, he was planning to be mayor one day, though I didn't realize he'd be running so soon. I was so attracted to him. I'd forgotten that part of myself while I was sick. The sexual part. It's so weird when your entire life is consumed by illness. Sometimes I'd felt like a heart instead of a person. With Dale, I felt the rest of me coming back to life. When he took my hand, I felt every cell in my fingers as though I'd just noticed them for the first time ever. And his beautiful gray eyes! I hadn't yet seen those eyes turn stormy back then. Oh, wow, could you see thunderclouds in his eyes sometimes! Dale had a gentleness to him, a real honest warmth, but there was steel behind it. He didn't bend easily, and I was learning that if I wanted to do something he didn't want—to change the way we handled something at the B and B, maybe, or even to watch a movie he wasn't crazy about watching—I had to approach the subject carefully and slowly if I stood a chance of breaking through that stubbornness. But there were compromises in any relationship. I'd learned that growing up with my father. This was nothing new.

My father was thrilled when I told him I was seeing Dale Hendricks. Since he taught political science, my father had always been tuned in to state politics and he knew exactly who Dale was: heir apparent of the Hendricks empire. Daddy had wanted me to be taken care of. He knew if I became a Hendricks, he'd never have to worry about me again.

I was tired of talking about my heart by the time Dale gave me my Beaufort tour, but he asked tons of questions about it and I answered them all. He said I was amazing, and I said the people who were really amazing were the donor's family. And then I cried, which is what I always did when I thought about the people I would never know who gave me the greatest gift I'd ever receive. We'd been sitting in the public gazebo looking out over Taylor's Creek, dusk falling around us and the colors of the sunset in the air and the water. Every single moment of my life was beautiful, but that one was like a painting in my mind, permanently hanging on the inside of my forehead. Dale put his arm around me. He brushed away one of my tears with the back of his fingers. Then he turned my face toward him and kissed me. It had been so long since I'd been kissed, I'd forgotten how the simple touch of lips could send sparks to every other part of my body. How it could make me lose all reason. How it could lead me to do things that were a little crazy, like sleeping with a man I barely knew. Yes, we walked back to Hendricks House, quietly climbed the outside stairs that led to his private apartment, and I was pulling his shirt out of his pants before we'd even reached his bedroom.

I smiled at the memory of that night as I covered the casserole with foil and slid it into the refrigerator. Then I picked up my cell phone and dialed Dale's number.

"Can you come over earlier tonight?" I asked, leaning back against the counter. "I miss you."

I could hear my baby crying from somewhere in the B and B, but I couldn't get to her. I knew I was dreaming, but that didn't make me feel any better. I ran through the house, which in the dream was made up of rooms that led into other rooms that led into yet more rooms, some of them so small I had to crawl through them on my hands and knees, others as big as a ballroom. The crying was heart-wrenching—she needed me! The sound seemed to come from one direction, then another, and I couldn't find her.

When I looked down at the T-shirt I was wearing in the dream, I had two round wet patches over my nipples.

"Robin!" The voice sounded far away. "Wake up, Robbie. You're dreaming."

I opened my eyes. In the darkness, the only thing I could see was the blue LED light from the small TV on my dresser. I was winded from running in my dream and confused about where I was. The hospital? My childhood bedroom? I touched my left breast through my tank top. Dry.

"Sit up, honey." It was Dale's voice. I was in the B and B, and Dale's body was nearly wrapped around mine as he lifted my shoulders from the bed.

"Are you all right?" he asked. "You're breathing so hard. Is your heart—"

"It was just a dream," I said, to myself as much as to him. I knew my heart was fine. It was probably stronger than his. It had come from a fifteen-year-old girl killed in a car accident. When I had nightmares, they were usually about her. I dreamed about her last moments, lying injured and alone in a car that had flipped over into a ravine. I dreamed about the life pouring out of her body and into mine. Sometimes I dreamed we both lived and I'd wake up feeling this impossible joy until I remembered.

"Whew." I leaned forward and Dale massaged the back of my neck. I was embarrassed. "I hope I didn't scream or anything." I tried to laugh. "Freak out the guests." When Dale and I became lovers, we experimented to see how much noise could be heard from my room in the guestroom right above. Dale went upstairs and I stayed in my room and made erotic-sounding noises and rocked the bed to make it squeak. He promised me he couldn't hear a thing, but the whole thing cracked both of us up. "Was I actually screaming?" I asked now.

"No," he said. "You were just whimpering and breathing hard." He locked his arms around me and rocked me a little. He could be so sweet. "Tell me about the dream," he said.

I hesitated a moment but could think of no reason not to tell him. "I had a baby in the dream," I said. "She was crying and I couldn't get to her. I couldn't find my way through the house to her. It was very… I just wanted to get to her." My tears were a sudden surprise and I was so glad it was dark in the room. This wasn't the first time I'd had a dream about my baby in the two weeks since Hannah was born. During the daytime, I was fine. No problem. But when I was asleep and had no control over my thoughts, there she was, crying for me from a distance and I could never, ever reach her. In one of the dreams, I was upset that I didn't know the baby's name, just as I didn't know the name of my own child. What had Travis named her? Was she happy and healthy? I knew she didn't have my heart problem. My father told me they checked her out right after she was born and she was fine, which was a miracle because of the medications I'd been on when I got pregnant with her. Most of the time, I could push that baby out of my mind. Now, suddenly, she was trying to get in.

Dale laughed a little. "You're spending way too much time with Alissa and Hannah," he said. "Seriously, though," he added quickly, "you've been such a help to her. She's really… She's not adjusting that well to motherhood, is she."

"I think her hormones are still screwed up," I said. "Once she's back in school with her friends, she'll probably be fine." I didn't really believe it. Alissa was right to be nervous about her future. None of her friends would have to run home after school to take care of a baby.

"You're going to be such a great mother," he said and I was glad it was so dark because I didn't want him to see how I cringed. I'd told him I might never be able to have children. I'd been honest about it. The antirejection meds made it extremely risky. My doctor had said having children was "unlikely but not impossible" for me, and Dale seemed to have completely wiped the "unlikely" part of that sentence from his mind. "We'll find a way," he'd said, and I'd let it go, like I always let go of anything that might lead to conflict. I wanted children, but I would have been happy adopting. I knew from the way Dale and his parents reacted when Alissa said she wanted to place her baby up for adoption that it wasn't an idea they'd take to easily.

I thought I heard the baby again, way in the distance, even though I was now wide-awake. I leaned away from Dale to turn on the light on my night table. The darkness was getting to me.

The light caught Dale's gray eyes. They were a metallic silvery-gray, the color of the ocean on an overcast day, and they were suddenly familiar to me in a whole new way. I nearly gasped. I knew all at once why I'd fallen for him. I knew why, the moment I first saw him at my interview, I'd wanted to put my arms around him. I'd thought then that it had been love at first sight, but my subconscious had been messing with me. Suddenly I knew it had been Travis I'd seen in him. "What?" he asked, and I realized I was staring at him like I'd never seen him before.

"Nothing." I shook my head. "Just a little spaced out." I shivered. Something was happening to me and I didn't like it. Alissa's baby was shaking me up in some strange new way and with all I had going on right now, I didn't need shaking up. The very last thing I needed was memories of Travis and the baby tormenting me. What was *that* about?

Your baby's safe, I told myself. *She has a father and mother who love her and she's healthy.*

I hardly ever thought about her. I'd had a heart transplant and that was what defined me, not having a baby, who was nothing more than a footnote in my life. When I did think about her, it was with zero emotion. Tonight, I thought I understood why and it scared me. My brain had been protecting me from something that could rip me apart. Now with Hannah in my life, the seams were beginning to fray.

"You ready to go back to sleep?" Dale rubbed my shoulder.

I nodded, though I wasn't sure I'd be able to sleep for the rest of the night. The dream seemed long ago now, yet it had left so many disturbing feelings behind that I was almost afraid to turn out the light. I did it, though, and snuggled close to Dale, trying to breathe in his scent, to remember who he was. Trying to think about how great my life would be when I was married to him. Instead, I heard my father's voice in my ears.

The baby never happened, he'd said. *Put it all behind you, Robin. That part of your life never happened.*

I thought of the dream and my desperate need to reach my baby, and I knew in that instant you could love someone you didn't know and never would know. You could love her with all your heart.

10

Erin

EVER SINCE THE ACCIDENT, I HATED GOING TO bed. As soon as my head hit the pillow I'd see the pier stretching out in front of me, so I'd never even walk into my bedroom until I could barely keep my eyes open. Then if I was very lucky, sleep would find me before the pier did. That was why, about two weeks after I moved into the apartment, I was still awake at 2:00 a.m. and caught the late-night airing of *The Sound of Music* on TV.

I'd always been a night owl, but my job had forced me to go to bed no later than midnight. Now, though, with no job and no husband, I could stay up as long as I wanted. I'd sit on the too-hard sofa in the living room and watch something mindless on TV, like the home and garden channel or a classic movie, and I'd play solitaire on my iPad or check in with the Harley's Dad group. Michael didn't think much of solitaire and it gave me a perverse pleasure to play it. "It doesn't connect people with other people," he'd gripe. He liked games that tied people together, whether in competition or cooperation. Farmville and World of Warcraft, that sort of thing.

I liked living alone as much as I was capable of liking anything these days. I didn't have to worry about cooking a meal on time or what clothes I put on in the morning. A few nights, I actually slept in my clothes and just wore the same thing the next day. Michael would have been on the phone to Judith to report that I was spiraling down and needed more help than she was giving me. That was the best thing about living apart from Michael. I could do whatever I wanted and not worry about his reaction.

The Sound of Music was Michael's favorite movie. I always teased him about that because I thought it was sappy. I wasn't sure I'd ever actually watched the whole thing, always busying myself with Carolyn or some home project when it came on. But Michael would watch it all the way through every time. Now I found myself caught up in a scene or two, finally setting my iPad aside to give myself over to the movie. For the first time, I thought I understood the pull it had on Michael. It was all the kids. Seven kids. He was one of seven, right smack in the middle, and when we were dating, he'd told me he wanted seven of his own. I'd thought he was joking, but he wasn't. He finally told me he'd settle for as many as I'd be willing to have. I thought three would be just right, and he countered that four would be better so no child would have to suffer the fate of being the middle child alone. I'd loved that about him, the fact that he wanted a bunch of kids. That he was a family man. We'd been trying to conceive when Carolyn died, and although I'd been frustrated at our lack of success, I was so glad now that I hadn't been pregnant. The timing would have been so very wrong. Michael didn't agree. One night, only a couple of weeks after Carolyn's death, we were holding each other in bed, both still caught up in raw sorrow. Back when we seemed to be suffering in unison.

"If only you were pregnant," he said then. "It would make all this pain a little more bearable."

I sat up, unable to believe what I was hearing. "She's not replaceable!" I shouted.

"I know, I know," he said, pulling me back into his arms. "That's not what I meant."

I twisted free and glared at him. "That's *exactly* what you meant," I said.

Maybe that was the moment I first felt hatred toward him. It was definitely the moment the enormous wedge began forming between us.

Now I looked at the TV. At those seven children, all lined up in their dirndls and lederhosen, happily singing *Do-Re-Mi* together. This was why he loved this movie, I thought. It represented what he longed for: a family, united.

I used the remote to check the TV guide and saw that the movie was airing every night that week. I picked up my iPad and wrote an email to Michael letting him know in case he wanted to record it. Then I raised my feet to the sofa and wrapped my arms around my legs.

I'd lost a child, I thought. Michael had lost a dream.

11

Travis

SAVANNAH PUT THE EMPTY CONTAINER OF potato salad back in the cooler next to her on the blanket. We'd eaten dinner on the beach—Bella, Savannah and me— and now we watched the tide rolling in.

"What are those people doing on our beach?" Savannah had a snarky smile in her voice as she nodded toward an old couple strolling barefoot across the sand, the water rippling over their feet.

"Trespassers." I speared a strawberry from the bowl on the blanket between us.

"What's trespers?" Bella asked. She was curled up on my legs and I had my free arm wrapped around her. She felt skinny to me. We were definitely missing my mother's cooking.

"It's only a joke, Bell," I said. "Trespassers are people who walk where they don't belong, but this is a public beach. A beach for everybody. So those people belong here as much as we do."

"Then why'd you say that word? Trespers?"

"Trespassers. Because this time of year when there's not

many people on the beach, it feels almost like the whole beach belongs to us."

"You explain too much to her," Savannah said. "She doesn't understand."

"Yes, I do." Bella understood enough to be insulted.

Why did everybody want me to talk down to my daughter? Yeah, some of what I told her went over her head, but she took in a lot of it. I never knew which part would stick, so I said it all. Every once in a while, Savannah would do what she just did—criticize how I dealt with Bella. She did it often enough that I was going to have to say something to her about it if she kept it up. She was watching Bella for only fifteen bucks a day, so I figured I had to put up with some flak. I'd had a job building an interior staircase last week because the contractor's regular guy was recovering from surgery, but now he was back and there was no more work for me. The wages had sucked, anyway, but at least I hadn't had to worry about food. The phone and rent, though—I didn't want to think about them. The phone company cut off my phone the day before yesterday. I decided not to take the signs off the sides of my van, even though the number wouldn't do me much good. But maybe someone would see the sign while I was parked someplace and ask for an estimate. *Dream on,* I thought. It was a matter of pride, really. If I took those signs down, I was just another loser driving around in a dinged-up white van.

I was late with the rent money. I had about half of what I needed and the old guy who owned the trailer was no bleeding heart. "All or nothing," he said. "You have till the end of the week." Savannah had money. Not a lot, but she had some decent things in her trailer and her nice little car and she never seemed to have trouble buying food and beer. I didn't want to borrow, though. She wasn't offering, anyway.

I was grateful to Savannah, which was another reason I put up with any noise she gave me about Bella. She and Bella were doing well together. The two of them really seemed to hit it off, but when I got home from work at the end of each day, Bella just wanted me. Ever since the fire and losing her nana, she didn't like to let me out of her sight. She seemed so relieved when she saw me, as though she was afraid that, even though I told her I wasn't leaving, I might decide to go to heaven myself.

I lay back on the blanket and straightened my arms to lift Bella into the air. She giggled, putting her arms out at her sides, pretending she was a plane. I'd done this with her since she was tiny and she was getting way too big for it. The other night, after I'd worked on that staircase, my arms hurt like a bitch when I lifted her in the air this way. It had felt so good. The kind of ache that let you know you'd put in an honest day's work. Now I felt nothing. Just the light weight of my skinny little girl sailing through the air.

"So, you didn't say how the job hunt went today." Savannah popped the cap on a bottle of beer and took a sip. She was right. I'd talked about anything I could think of other than the sorry state of my job hunt. Now, I sat up and lowered Bella to the blanket and watched as she got to her feet and ran toward the line of shells.

"Zip," I said. "There's nothing. I bought a Wilmington paper and maybe I could use your phone tomorrow to make a couple of calls, but I'm not holding my breath."

"Maybe you need to get training to do something else, like I'm doing," she said. "You might have to do a different kind of work."

"And how do I support Bella while I'm training? And training for *what?*" I knew I sounded angry. Feeling frustrated always put me in a shitty mood. I'd wanted to go to college. My grades had been okay, but not good enough for a scholarship and my mom and I didn't have money to spare. Then Bella came along and that was that.

"Well, like, what are you interested in?" Savannah asked.

"I always wanted to be marine biologist," I said. I didn't tell many people that, and was sorry I'd told Savannah when she laughed.

"You'd have to be really smart to do that," she said.

"Give me a break, Savannah." I wanted to tell her my SAT scores, which hadn't been half bad, but I doubted she'd even know what SAT stood for.

"Sensitive, aren't we." She tipped the bottle back to take a long swallow. "Look," she said, "I have an idea. I know where you can get work."

"What are you talking about?"

"I didn't want to tell you about it because I didn't want you to leave."

"Leave…?" I wasn't sure what she meant.

"Leave here. Carolina Beach. But I know where there's work that pays really well."

"I'm not leaving the beach," I said.

"What if it's a choice between the beach or food on the table?" She nodded toward Bella, who was bending over to pick up something from the row of shells.

I speared another strawberry, but didn't put it in my mouth. "You know of a for-sure construction job someplace else?" I asked. "Like where?"

"Raleigh."

"I don't know anyone in Raleigh." I popped the strawberry in my mouth. I wasn't going to Raleigh.

"Well, you *will* know someone if you take this job. I have a good friend there. Roy. Don't be jealous," she added quickly. "He's not like a boyfriend or anything."

I wasn't jealous. I didn't care if she had a boyfriend. As a matter of fact, it might be a good thing. The heat I'd felt for her the first few times we got together was just about gone. Yeah, she was a knockout, but she was also an airhead, and her snarkiness could get under my skin. You couldn't talk to Savannah about what was really going on inside you—it didn't feel safe. I just hoped the occasional snarky attitude wouldn't rub off on Bella. I needed Savannah's help. She'd said she was falling for me—her exact words—so I was walking a fine line, trying to keep her happy without giving her the idea we could ever be more to each other than we were right now.

"Why can't he find somebody in Raleigh?" I asked. "People are desperate for work everywhere."

She shrugged. "I don't know all of that. All I know is I told him about you when I talked to him the other day and he said 'Send him to me and I'll fix him up.' His exact words."

Whoa. I had to admit, that sounded tempting.

"Is he a general contractor or what? Is it residential work? I was starting to do some fine carpentry before the fire. I'm not a master carpenter or anything like that, but I can do more than just general construction." Was I actually considering this?

"I'll tell him that," she said.

"Where would we live, though? And what would I do with Bella? I don't know anyone—"

"You could leave her with me, I guess, though—"

"Uh-uh, no way," I said. Raleigh was only a few hours away, but it might as well be the moon if I left Bella behind. I might've considered leaving her with my mother for a couple of weeks just to get the bucks, but I wasn't leaving her with Savannah. If Savannah's feelings were hurt, she didn't let on.

"Well, like I told you," she said, "I want to be able to get away sometimes, too, so it probably wouldn't work leaving her with me anyway. Even though I love her to pieces."

"So forget the whole Roy and Raleigh idea," I said.

"He has to fill the job by next week," she said, "so you have a few days to think about it."

"No. I appreciate it, Savannah. Really. But I can't leave here. This is home. It's Bella's home. I can't shake up her life again so soon after—" I watched my daughter playing tag with the waves "—after everything."

"I get it," she said.

"I'll find something here. It'll just take a little more time."

"I hope you do," she said. "I wasn't even going to tell you so you wouldn't leave. 'Cause I really love you guys."

I kept my eyes on Bella because I knew Savannah had just dumped something on me that she hadn't meant to say and there was no way I was getting into any talk about love with her.

"Yeah," I said, reaching for another strawberry. "She loves you, too."

12

Robin

WHAT MY FATHER DIDN'T KNOW COULDN'T hurt him.

That's what I decided when Travis and I began sneaking around to see each other. It wasn't easy. Daddy had pulled me out of school and set me up with a teacher who came to the house. I usually had no more than two hours between the time my teacher left and my father got home from work, but Travis would come over during that time. At first, we just listened to music or watched part of a movie and kissed a little—well, we kissed a lot, I guess, so much that one day my father asked me about the rash on my face when he got home.

I texted Travis that night. We have 2 stop kissing so much. Daddy saw rash on my face.

Don't want 2 stop, Travis wrote back.

Have 2 do things that won't leave rash where he can see it. I smiled as I pressed the keys, then stared at the display on my phone, waiting for his reply. It took a little while to come.

But your heart?

He was worried about me. That was sweet.

It'll be ok, I wrote. I wasn't one hundred percent sure about that. My heart was pounding in my throat from the texting alone. Tomorrow? I typed.

Cool!!!!!!

Condoms!!

Not an idiot. I'll bring 10. Enuf?

I giggled. Can't wait.

We ended up going to his house instead of meeting at mine. I was too nervous about my father coming home, so I lied and told Daddy that Sherry had gotten back in touch and we were going to a movie. The worst part about lying was seeing his face light up when I told him. He was so happy I'd heard from one of my old girlfriends. He loved me so much and wanted me to be happy. Just not with Travis.

Travis picked me up and we drove to his little house in Carolina Beach. His mom was at her waitressing job and would be gone for hours. His house smelled like smoke and fish, but you never saw a speck of dust anywhere. I loved it. He always called it a dump and the outside *was* falling apart, but inside it was full of knickknacks and afghans and feminine things that made my condo seem sterile. Like a hospital.

Travis started kissing me as soon as we were in the door. "Are you sure about this?" he asked.

"Totally sure," I said, though I didn't think he'd be able to stop even if I said I was having second thoughts. I'd never seen him like that, so intense and hot. He grabbed my hand and nearly pulled me through the living room and hallway to his bedroom, but when he lowered me to the bed, he did it gently, like I was made of glass.

"You don't have to do anything," he said. "You can just take it easy and I can—"

"I *want* to do things." My hand was on his belt buckle. The bulge in his jeans was right in front of me, close to my cheek. My mouth. I was breathing hard and I felt the muscles tighten around my heart, but I didn't care. All I wanted was to have him inside me.

I knew it was supposed to hurt, but it didn't. Not even a little bit. It was over so quickly I was disappointed. I'd wanted it to go on and on and he promised me the next time it would. Then he touched me with his fingers, slipping one inside me, pressing the others against me in some magical way that made me breathe so hard and fast I thought I might actually die, but still I didn't care. I let out a shout and he caught it with his lips and then it was over. From start to finish, no more than seven or eight minutes. The best seven or eight minutes of my life.

"Pretend I'm your father," he said afterward, when he'd settled down next to me on the bed, his arm around my shoulders.

"What?"

"So how was the movie, Robin?" he asked in a voice that was nearly as deep and stern as Daddy's.

I laughed. "Amazing," I said.

"The sort of movie you'd go to see a second time?"

"And a third and a fourth."

Travis rolled against me, hugging me hard to his naked body, his face buried in my hair. He whispered something that sounded like *forever* and I whispered the same word in return, and then I cried because I was so, so happy.

"I have some big news," my father said at dinner the next night. It was my turn to cook, so we were eating stir-fried chicken and vegetables, which was just about the only thing I knew how to make.

I looked up from my plate and he was wearing that smile of his that meant he wasn't sure how I was going to react to something. "What?" I asked.

"I've accepted a position at UNC-Chapel Hill."

I set down my fork. My heart did a little sputter in my chest. "What do you mean?"

"I know the timing's not great now that you've reconnected with Sherry and I'm sorry about that, but you'll make new friends in Chapel Hill and the most important thing is that we'll be close to the very best medical care for you."

"The medical care is fine here," I said. "I don't want to move." I was already doing the calculations in my head. Chapel Hill was three hours away. When would I ever get to see Travis? I felt panicky.

"I'll breathe a sigh of relief when we're closer to excellent care," he said. "I know I'm springing this on you kind of suddenly, but I didn't want to tell you until I knew for sure. Everything fell together today. Both the job and finding someone to rent the condo here. Plus I know of a condo there we can rent until I'm ready to buy it. That practically dropped into my lap." He smiled again. "So we need to start packing right away. I'm having cartons delivered tomorrow and you can just begin putting your clothes and books and things into—"

"When?" I said. "When are we moving?"

"I have to call the movers, but I hope I can find someone to do it a week from Friday. I have to start work the following Monday."

"Dad!" I said again. "You should have told me. You should have given me some warning!"

"Peace and calm, honey," he said, and I felt like throwing

my fork at him but of course I didn't. "I suppose I should have let you know what was going on, but I didn't want to get you upset and then have it fall through. Until this morning, I thought it might not work out."

"I'm not hungry." I set down my fork and stood up. I had to call Travis. I had to tell him what was happening.

"Sit down," my father said. He spoke in that calm voice he used to try to settle me down. I didn't dare walk away, but I didn't sit down, either. "I know you've been seeing Travis," he said.

"I have not." My cheeks burned. How could he know? How *much* did he know?

"Don't lie to me. One of our neighbors—who shall remain nameless—told me he's been here several times while I've been at the university."

"It was only a couple of times," I said. "He brought some...books over." I stared down at the plate of stir-fry, afraid to look him in the eye.

"Were you really with Sherry last night?"

"Yes," I said.

He sighed like he didn't believe me but wasn't going to push it. He didn't need to. He was going to make sure I never saw Travis again. "Go ahead to your room," he said. "Start thinking about what you want to take with you and what you can donate to charity." He grabbed my hand as I walked past his chair. "It's puppy love, honey," he said. "You'll find a more suitable young man one of these days. I promise."

The move happened so quickly that I had no time to get away from my father to say goodbye to Travis in person. It was a horrible couple of weeks. I'm sure my father knew about the move long before he told me about it. Yes, I believed we were moving partly for his job and partly to get me the best medical care, but I knew he was looking for a way to put some distance between Travis and me. He had no idea how close we were, though. How distance wasn't going to put an end to the fact that we loved each other.

Our new condo was smaller than the one in Wilmington, but it was in a very upscale building on a street near the university and students walked together outside our windows, chattering to each other, making me lonelier than ever. Travis and I stayed in constant contact by phone and text and email and I would have died of loneliness without him. I had a new home teacher but zero friends. How did you make friends in a new town when you were cooped up in a condo all day? My father finally figured out what was going on between Travis and me from the phone bills. He was more scared than angry and told me I needed to make new friends in Chapel Hill.

"How am I supposed to do that?" I asked him. I told him how lonely I was and he got me involved in a support group with other sick kids, which was more depressing than anything else. After that, Travis and I stuck to email for our contact, and we began to make a plan. We picked a Tuesday early in January, when I knew my father would be at the university for the entire day. Travis would ditch school, come pick me up, and we'd go to Jordan Lake to spend the day together. It would be chilly, but we wouldn't care. For the first time since the move, I walked around with a smile on my face.

"I knew you'd like it here once you settled in," my father said as we watched TV together that night.

"Right," I said. What he didn't know wouldn't hurt him. I hadn't stopped to think it might hurt *me*.

13

Travis

SOMETIMES, LIFE DIDN'T GIVE YOU MUCH choice.

My landlord gave me three days to get out of the trailer. It wasn't like people were dying to rent the thing now that it was fall. He was just being hard-assed and although I told him I would pay the back rent once I started working again, he didn't want to hear it. I guess he knew what I knew deep in my gut: "working again" wasn't going to happen anytime soon. So I told Savannah I'd take that job with her friend in Raleigh. "Roy'll know someone who can watch Bella for you," she said. "He knows everyone. He's totally connected."

I was building Roy up to be my savior. Construction workers were a dime a dozen, but this guy was holding a job for a stranger. He was taking a chance on me just because I was a friend of Savannah's. And to make things even better, he had connections to child care? It felt like I didn't have anything to lose.

I had an old mattress in the back of the van that had been there from when I'd carted around sheets of glass for a job, and I was glad now that I'd never taken it out. Bella and I were going to have to live in the van until I got a paycheck and could find an apartment or room or something. For the first time ever, I thought I could be in danger of losing Bella. If someone knew how screwed up my circumstances had become, could they do that? Report to social services that I didn't have the money to take care of her? I didn't. It was the truth. But I was going to get by somehow. I'd never let Bella be taken away.

"Do you ever think that maybe you should give her to her mother?" Savannah asked me the night before we left. We were drinking beer on the steps of her trailer while Bella slept inside on the couch. Savannah had set up an interview for me with Roy for the day after tomorrow and given me his phone number to find out where to meet him. I was going to have to buy a prepaid cell phone so I'd have a number to give him.

"I can't believe you'd even ask me that," I said.

"I know you love her and you're a great father and all that." She brushed a strand of her amazing hair over her shoulder. "But let's face it. You can't really take care of her now and maybe her mother, Robin, maybe she could—"

"Let's talk about something else," I cut her off.

"You're being selfish," she said. "Couldn't Robin at least take her till you get on your feet again? Or if that didn't work out, maybe she'd be better off in foster care for a while. She could have so much more than you can give her right now."

I was royally pissed off. "You really know how to kick a guy when he's down," I said.

"I just wondered," she said.

The truth was, once or twice since the fire, I *had* wondered if I'd screwed up Bella's life. I never used to feel like I'd made a mistake when I derailed Robin's plans for Bella to be adopted. *Let her go to a couple who can give her everything,* people argued with me when I told them I was going to fight for her. Maybe someone else *could* have given her every material thing she could ever want, but they couldn't give her *me.* Her father. Growing up, I cared about *having* my father, not about what he could give me. I cared about those walks with him on the beach and all the things he taught me. My mother had agreed with me about taking Bella and supported me all the way. But since the fire and my lack of money, I'd lie in bed at night and feel a boatload of guilt pour down on me. Now I was going to uproot her again just when she was getting used to the trailer and Savannah, and I was going to take her—and me—inland. When I traveled thirty minutes from the coast, I always felt like I was fighting for air. Three hours from the beach, I'd suffocate. But lots of people had to rearrange their lives for work, so it was time to get a grip on myself and go. Savannah loaned me fifty bucks for gas, and I had another fifty in my pocket for food and the cell phone. Maybe this Roy guy could give me an advance. I'd work my butt off for him if he could help me out.

"Stay over tonight," Savannah said as I got to my feet.

I shook my head. "I have some things to get ready before we take off tomorrow." Mostly, I didn't want some drawn-out, sloppy goodbye with Savannah. Ever since that day she'd said she loved us, I'd been nervous that she'd press me to say something back to her. That she'd want promises I was never going to keep.

"Okay," she said, and I was surprised she didn't put up a fight.

We went inside and I picked up my sleeping daughter and carried her back to our trailer. I tucked her into the double bed. A week ago, I'd been upset that we were moving into this pathetic tin can. Now I was moving us into my van. I only hoped the next step wasn't the street.

"We're going on a trip today, Bella," I said the next morning as I poured the last of the Cheerios into her bowl. "An adventure."

"Where?" she asked, reaching for her spoon.

I sat across the small table from her. "A city called Raleigh," I said, "where I can find a job. For a few nights, we're going to live in the van. Won't that be cool? Kind of like camping out."

"Like when we slept in the tent?" She didn't look happy and I realized *camping* had been a stupid word to use. During the summer, I thought it would be cool to take her camping, so I set up my father's old pup tent in our backyard. Bella had hated every minute of it and begged to go inside until I finally gave in.

"No, not like camping," I said. "Totally different, actually. Just like having Moby Dick be our little house on wheels for a few days until we find a real house. Or apartment." Or whatever.

"Are we going where Nana is? Is she in the Raleigh place?"

I let out a breath. "No, baby. I told you. Nana's in heaven. We can't see her anymore."

She poked her spoon at her Cheerios. "Until I'm an old lady and go there, too?"

"Right," I said with a sigh, and I stood up to begin packing her collection of shells.

I'd hoped we could have one last walk on the beach, but it started to rain. It was a chilly rain that fit how I was feeling. I would have walked on the beach anyway if I'd only had myself to think about, but the last thing I needed was Bella getting sick.

I packed up the rest of our stuff. There wasn't much of it. I helped Bella buckle herself into her car seat, then dodged the raindrops to knock on Savannah's door to say goodbye. She came out and hopped in the van, scrambling across the backseat to give Bella a hug. She ran a hand over Bella's fine hair and said, "I'll miss you, cutie pie," and she looked so sad I thought she might cry. She really did love Bella, I thought as I stood in the drizzle next to the van. I gave Savannah a hug and thanked her for everything. I owed her.

"Maybe I'll see you in Raleigh sometime," she said.

"Maybe," I said, but I knew that the moment the economy picked up, I was coming back to Carolina Beach. There was no doubt about that in my mind. I wouldn't tell her that, though. She needed to be able to convince this Roy dude that I was trustworthy and motivated. Someone he could count on.

Bella and I waved to Savannah as we drove away, and once we pulled onto 70, I started singing "You Are My Sunshine" and she joined right in the way she always did, and I tried to convince myself that we were heading for a future that would be a whole lot better than what we had now.

14
Robin

"SO I THINK WE'LL PUT THE DELANEYS AT TABLE seven and the Beckers at eight."

Mollie had spread her chart out on the dining room table and it covered nearly a third of the surface. Dale and I sat on one side of the table staring down at the dozens of circles that represented seating for the guests at the wedding reception and the long rectangle reserved for the small wedding party. Alissa would be my maid of honor, of course, and my friend Joy, who'd recently moved to Charlotte, would be my bridesmaid. Dale's best friend, a guy he went to college with and who now lived up north someplace, would be his best man, and one of his fellow lawyers would be a groomsman. I didn't have a lot of close friends. After I got sick, I never really had the chance to make them. I'd loved Joy like a sister, but even she and I had drifted apart since her move to Charlotte. Or maybe it wasn't so much her move as my total adoption by the Hendricks family.

Dale stretched back from the table with a yawn. "Are we done with this?" he asked his mother, who didn't seem to hear him.

"At any party," she said to me, "you want to put the talkers and the quiet people together. The talkers will keep things moving and the quiet people won't have a chance to feel awkward."

I nodded. The truth was, ninety percent of the guest list was made up of people I'd never met, so I was completely dependent on her to know who was a talker and who was quiet and what to do with the people who didn't fall neatly into one category or the other.

One thing about the wedding that made me sad was that my father wouldn't be there. He would have loved to walk me down the aisle and see me marry Dale. I tried not to think about it, but every book on weddings that Mollie shoved into my hands talked about roles for the bride's parents. I was used to not having a mother, so I didn't feel the same heart pang that I did when I read about the bride's father. One of the books said that the father/daughter dance was one of the "most cherished moments in any woman's lifetime." I read that sentence over and over again. I wanted my father back. We hadn't always gotten along, but he was the one person I knew loved me more than he loved himself. I'd lost him to pneumonia only ten months ago. It had been unexpected and devastating and the only thing that had gotten me through that time was Dale and his family.

James offered to give me away, but that felt too weird to me. I didn't say that, exactly. I didn't know *what* to say when he suggested it, but Dale seemed to pick up on my discomfort and suggested we walk down the aisle together. That appalled Mollie at first, but she got over it. "You're both adults," she said. "I guess you can do it whatever way you want." I was grateful to Dale for that. Every once in a while, he did something that told me he understood me better than I thought.

Mollie could have gone on all night with that chart on the table, but I heard a whimper from down the hall and saw my chance to make a break.

"I'm going to see if Alissa needs any help before I go back to the B and B," I said, pushing back my chair.

Dale gave me an envious smile for coming up with a way to escape. He stood up himself, bent over and kissed his mother's cheek. "Thanks for doing this, Mom," he said.

"Well, it must be done," she said, as if she wasn't enjoying every single second of the planning.

Dale gave me a quick kiss on the lips. "Call me when you get home," he said, and I knew he planned to sleep over at my place.

"Okay." I headed for the hallway. "Later."

Hannah was crying full throttle when I knocked on Alissa's closed bedroom door. "It's me, Ali," I said. "Want some help?"

"In a sec!" She sounded breathless. I thought I heard a man's voice behind the baby's cries. Did she have her TV on? I heard something small fall to the floor. "Damn it!" she said.

I opened the door a crack. "You okay?" I asked. "Can I come in?"

She was bending over her keyboard, the screaming baby precariously balanced in one arm, the mouse in her other hand. A young blond guy stared out from her computer monitor and I knew I'd caught her talking to someone on Skype.

"What's going on?" the guy asked. "Do you need to—"

His image disappeared from the screen as Alissa clicked her mouse. I moved forward to take Hannah from her and Alissa turned toward me, her face flushed. She bit her lip. "Don't tell," she said.

"Was that Will?" I asked, lifting Hannah to my shoulder. "Shh, baby, shh," I whispered against her warm little ear.

"Promise," Alissa begged. "Please, Robin."

I could feel Hannah's heavy diaper through her onesie. "She's wet," I said, moving to the changing table. "I'll change her."

"Oh, shit." Alissa sat down on the edge of her bed. "Please, Robin. If you tell Dale, he'll—"

"They'll know you were talking to him without me telling them, won't they?" I asked as I undid the snaps on Hannah's onesie. The baby was crying so hard her little body shook. "They monitor everything you do online."

"This was the only time," she said. "He had a right to see his daughter."

"Her diaper's soaked." I felt angry with Alissa, not so much for talking to Will as for ignoring Hannah's needs.

"I was just going to change it," she said.

"It's been wet so long, it's cold, poor baby."

"I love him," Alissa said.

I looked up from the changing table. "Oh, Alissa," I said, more to myself than to her. I doubted she could hear me over the crying. I put a fresh diaper on the baby and lifted her to my shoulder again. Almost instantly, she settled down. "She hates being wet," I said. "You'd hate it, too." I sat down in the rocker and patted Hannah's back. Did all babies smell this sweet? I rested my cheek on her downy blond hair.

Alissa was chewing her lower lip. "Please, please don't tell," she pleaded.

"I won't," I said. My anger was losing its steam. I wanted Alissa to be able to talk to me and turning her in wasn't going to help.

"I hate my family," she said. "I mean, not you. But they're all so old. I have a brother who's practically old enough to be my father. He doesn't understand me at all. And my parents! You know what they're like, Robin. All they care about is money and power."

"That's not true," I said. "They love you and Hannah very much and they care about your happiness and your future. They don't want to see you throw it away on someone who doesn't deserve you." I couldn't believe what I was saying. The Hendricks party line was spilling out of my mouth, and I realized it had been my father's line about Travis, as well. How could I possibly be sounding like my father? I shuddered, pressing Hannah closer to me.

"The only reason they—and *you*—think he doesn't deserve me is because he doesn't have money and power, right?" Alissa asked. "Isn't that right?"

"You know all the reasons, Ali. And maybe they're not fair. Maybe they have too much to do with protecting your father's image, but Will didn't exactly do anything to win them over. He snuck around with you. He got you pregnant. He gave them plenty of reasons not to approve of him."

"Robin, don't tell! I'm begging you, please don't. It was only this once and I wanted him to see—"

"I told you I won't, and I won't, but that doesn't mean I can't talk to you about it. I *love* you, Ali. I know it's been hard to be cut off from your friends and you've been brave. I think you just miss Will because you're isolated. It'll be better when you're back in school."

"No, it won't." She shook her head, her eyes filling with tears. "I have no friends left. They've all moved on without me. And that's so not true about why I miss Will. I *love* him. He's Hannah's father and he can't even see her."

I got to my feet and laid Hannah back in her bassinet, then sat next to Alissa on the bed. I hugged her and she hung on to me. "Don't be mad at me," she said. "I couldn't stand it if you were mad at me."

"I'm not," I said. "I understand how you feel. You can talk to me about it, all right? Let me help you think it through."

I thought of the man, only a boy, really, whose face I'd seen on the monitor, but it was Travis's face I saw. They looked nothing alike, but that didn't seem to matter to my imagination. Ever since I'd recognized Travis in Dale's eyes, he'd been hammering against my memory to let him in. I didn't think I could push him out any longer. I wasn't even sure I wanted to.

I walked back to the B and B, thinking about all that had happened between Travis and me. It still felt wrong, the way my father had kept us apart. Now, there seemed a way I could right that wrong through Alissa. I thought of the image of Will on the screen again. There'd been sincerity in his face, hadn't there? Caring? I'd talk to Dale about it. I would right a wrong.

The next morning, Dale gave me a ride to my cardiologist's office for a routine appointment. The office wasn't far from the B and B and usually I'd walk, but having Dale drive me would give me a chance to talk to him about Alissa and Will. As he started the car and backed it out of the driveway, though, I thought I might chicken out. What was I afraid of? His anger? His disapproval?

I'd been so nervous when we first got engaged and the press was suddenly all over me. I was interviewed for every newspaper and magazine in the eastern part of North Carolina, it seemed, and I even made a couple of local TV appearances. I'd been so worried I might somehow hold Dale back politically, since I didn't come from his world of super wealth and privilege. James had actually told me to please wipe words like *awesome* and *cool* from my vocabulary. When I shared my doubts with Dale before the first interview, though, he gave me a little pep talk.

"You're an *asset* to me, Robin," he insisted. "Your story is a sympathetic one—this innocent young girl who spent her teen years cut off from her peers by illness, fighting for her life, no chance to live a normal adolescence with her friends. No chance to have a boyfriend. Nearly dying. Getting a heart in the nick of time because of the generosity of strangers."

He'd been right about being an asset to him. Everyone in Beaufort seemed to love me and they loved my story. I'd been photographed so many times that people on the street recognized me even more quickly than they did Dale.

As we pulled out of the driveway, though, I remembered his words from that pep talk: *So sweet. No boyfriends. Innocent young girl.* A couple of weeks ago, those descriptions would have felt just fine to me, but a couple of weeks ago, I wasn't haunted by Travis and my baby.

"You're sure you don't want me to go in with you to your appointment?" he asked as we turned onto Craven Street.

"It's just a quickie," I said. "No big deal." It was sweet that he wanted to go with me and I'd let him come to a couple of my appointments, but having him there made me feel like I was a kid again, my father glued to my side.

We were both quiet for a minute, and I tried to get my courage up to talk about Alissa. I finally took a deep breath and dove in.

"I think Alissa's still in love with Will," I said.

He gave a little laugh. "Oh, I don't think so," he said. "She's done with all that."

"I think that's why she's so down." I didn't dare mention

that I'd caught her talking to Will. "She misses him," I added.

"She has the baby blues," he said. "Besides, I don't think she ever *was* in love with him. She's just rebellious." He glanced at me. "I love my little sister, but she's a screwup, in case you haven't noticed." He chuckled. "She intentionally picked a guy she knew would piss my parents off. A guy with a felon for a dad and trash for a mother."

"That's pretty harsh," I said. "Will's not responsible for who his parents are."

He glanced at me with a frown. "Robin, this is a done deal," he said. "Finished. Why even bring it up now? I'm running for office, in case you don't remember. The last thing I need is to have my sister's lowlife ex-boyfriend come out of the woodwork."

"Is everything about politics with you?" I asked, although I felt the thin ice under my feet. Dale and I never argued. I never argued with *anyone*. That "peace and calm" mantra still floated somewhere in my subconscious. But I knew I was edging toward a good fight with him now.

"Oh, come on," he said. "How can you even ask that?"

"You're always talking about my 'sympathetic story.' Like marrying me is going to win you votes." I was going too far. I felt like saying mean things to him. What was wrong with me? I didn't even believe what I was implying. I could see the color rise in Dale's cheeks and his hands clench the steering wheel.

"Hey," he said sharply. "I fell in love with *you*. Not your so-called story or what it could do for me."

I thought of the things I'd left out of my story during the interviews. Travis and the baby. The parts of my existence I'd erased. Exposing those truths about myself would be the end of my future with Dale, my work at the B and B, and the perfect life I was building in Beaufort. I was certain that if Dale had known about the baby from the start, he never would have asked me out, much less asked me to marry him. I would have been just as low in his eyes as Alissa. *A screwup.* Even worse, I'd deceived him by keeping it from him, the way Debra had kept her first marriage from him. He'd be so hurt. Burying that part of myself hadn't seemed wrong before. Now, though, thoughts of a baby I didn't know and a guy I once did were rolling around in my head both day and night. I was living a lie. Suddenly I felt as though I had a noose around my neck.

"What *if* she still loves him?"

"She's seventeen. She'll get over it." He turned the corner. "Don't make problems where none exist, Robbie," he said. "There are things you don't know and have no need to know, so just trust me and forget it."

That stunned me into silence for a minute. What was he keeping from me? And how dare he? Of course, I wasn't exactly letting him in on everything about *my* life, either. "Don't treat me like a child," I said. "What do you mean, I have 'no need to know'?"

"It's not a big deal, all right?" he said. "And what's with you today? Alissa's over him, so don't go planting any ideas in her head. I think the wedding must be giving you…I don't know, romantic notions or something. Will is out of the picture. Alissa has my parents and you and me to help her raise Hannah. She'll eventually find some nice guy to marry who'll love her and the baby and it will be settled. All right?"

I didn't answer. Instead, I looked out the window again. We passed through a residential neighborhood filled with Beaufort's small, inviting coastal cottages. Broad porches and white rockers. The house we were buying was very much like these.

"Do you honestly think she still has feelings for him?" Dale's voice had softened. "Has she told you that?"

"No...I'm just guessing from the way she's acting."

"If you seriously think she still cares about him, help her see the light, okay? You're closer to her than any of us. You have more influence on her, so help her get over him, all right?"

"All right," I said, but I was thinking, *No, it's not all right.* I wondered if Will knew his name was not on Hannah's birth certificate. If that bothered him. "He could try to get parental rights," I said. I was having trouble just letting this go.

Dale looked at me like I was out of my mind. "We've gotten that all settled," he said. "He's out of the picture and fine with it. Now Alissa can move forward."

I stared out the window at the street in front of us. I felt as though I'd failed Alissa with the way I'd handled this and I suddenly thought I might cry. I touched my throat where the noose was tightening. I'd never felt as trapped as I did at that moment. Not even a failing heart had made me feel this way.

My appointment went perfectly. My cardiologist gave me a hug before I walked out her door and I had the feeling she'd picked up on my stress even though I'd told her I was doing great. "Enjoy this time," she said, holding my shoulders and looking me straight in the eye. "You only get married once." She gave my shoulders a squeeze. "Hopefully," she added.

I left her office and began walking toward the waterfront. Tourists dotted the street, strolling, eating ice-cream cones, snapping pictures. I saw a couple of the B and B's guests across Front Street from me and waved. Then, in the space of a single block, I saw two men who looked like Travis. At least, I *imagined* they looked like Travis. I twisted their features in my imagination to make them his. I just wanted one of them to be him. I wanted it so badly that it hurt. *I'm cracking up,* I thought, and I knew I was as trapped by my own head as I was by everything else.

15
Erin

I WAS SIPPING COFFEE IN MY BROWN LEATHER chair at JumpStart, typing a post to my Harley's Dad group when my iPad beeped to alert me to an email. It was from my supervisor, Gene, at the pharmacy. *We're looking forward to having you back a week from Monday,* the email read. I guessed that was his way of not-so-subtly reminding me I was expected back. I was dreading my return to work, but now it was a matter of money as well as what Judith called a "need to reengage with the real world." My Harley's Dad friends *were* my real world, I told her. Nobody realer than the people who understood exactly how I felt.

I was still a little afraid that I'd screw up at work the way I did when I tried to go back the first time. My head was clearer now and I wasn't totally numb like I'd been in the beginning, but I was still overwhelmed by sadness, and the thought of "reengaging with the real world" tired me out.

Right, I answered Gene. *See you then.*

I was reading a post written by Harley's dad himself when, from the corner of my eye, I noticed a man and little girl come out of the men's room and head for the counter. I sat up straight. Carolyn? *Of course not.* She didn't even look like Carolyn, but in the irrational and sometimes scary part of my mind, I could manage to see my daughter in any little girl. Carolyn had been blonde, though, while this child had brown hair. She held the man's hand as they walked toward the counter. He was in his early twenties, I thought, barely. He was dressed in old jeans and a gray T-shirt with a dirty, once-white canvas bag slung over one shoulder. It seemed strange to see a man and child together in the coffee shop, especially on a weekday morning, and especially coming out of the men's room together, although Michael had taken Carolyn into the men's room any number of times. Still, could this guy have kidnapped her? Was he abusing her? Maybe she needed me to rescue her?

Stop it, I told myself. The girl seemed perfectly at ease with him, holding his hand, leaning against his leg as he ordered something I couldn't hear. Her hair was a little straggly and her bangs hung low over her eyes. She wore pale blue shorts, red sneakers and a blue-and-white-striped shirt. I could see a couple of stains on the front of it even from where I sat. A small pink purse hung from her arm, the same arm that clutched a stuffed animal to her chest. She was so darling. I didn't want to look at her. The way I felt scared me. Seeing a little girl whole and alive filled me with such longing it was almost unbearable, and this one, with her straggly hair and dirty shirt, looked like she needed a little more TLC than she was getting. She looked like she needed a mommy.

I forced my gaze back to my iPad and started a new post on the support group.

I'm in a coffee shop, I typed, *and a little girl just walked in with a man (her father?) and even though she doesn't look like C., I thought it might be her. Guess I'm in crazy-grieving-mom mode right now!* I hit Send. I knew I'd get responses within a few minutes, and I could even predict what they would be. Other parents would relate similar experiences. Similar feelings. And I would feel less crazy. Less alone.

I looked up. The man and little girl were walking toward my small circle of furniture. The man sat down on the sofa and the girl climbed up next to him. He smiled at me and she tipped her head back a little to look at me from beneath her long bangs. Her eyes were huge and gray. The same gray as his, only his were fringed with thick black lashes. He was handsome, though tired-looking, and the little girl was equally pretty beneath her messy hair. Father and daughter, most definitely.

"How're you doin'?" He slid the canvas bag from his shoulder and rested it on the sofa next to him. "Is it always this quiet in here?"

I could barely breathe. I felt the way I had when I first saw a horse as a child. I'd been both fascinated and afraid, longing to move closer but afraid it might hurt me. If I looked at this little girl too long, I was afraid of how I'd feel, so I only brushed my gaze over her as I responded.

"It's busy earlier in the morning," I said, "and it'll pick up again around lunchtime."

I looked down at my iPad. No response yet to my post to the Harley's Dad group.

"We're new in town," the man said. "I'm Travis and this is Bella."

"I'm Erin." I should have just said I was working. Tuned him out the way I tuned out the other people in the shop. Even Nando rarely tried to talk to me now beyond a "good morning," and I guessed he thought I was pretty cold. But the little girl—Bella—felt like a magnet to me, and try as I might not to look at her, my gaze kept drifting in her direction. She had me mesmerized by those big gray eyes. "She's your daughter?" I asked.

"Yes, ma'am." He broke the muffin he'd bought into two parts, rested each half on a napkin, and handed one of them to Bella. She was almost dainty as she lifted the muffin to her mouth and took a bite from the corner.

I waited until she swallowed, then leaned forward in my chair. "How old are you, Bella?" I smiled at her and the smile felt anemic and shaky.

She didn't answer. Shyly, she leaned closer to her father's arm. The skin beneath her nose was a little red, the way Carolyn's would get during allergy season.

"Answer Miss Erin," the man said to her. "Tell her how old you are."

Bella held up four fingers, a fat crumb from the muffin stuck to one of them. "Four," she said. She noticed the crumb and nibbled it from her hand. Carolyn would have been four now, if she'd lived. Bella was a little small for four. Thin and waiflike.

"She just turned four a couple of weeks ago," Travis said. Except for dark circles around his eyes, he was a very good-looking guy. If I'd been ten years younger, single and not completely miserable, I would have been captivated by him. Instead I was captivated by his daughter. "We didn't have much of a party," Travis added. "Things were a little rocky. So we're going to celebrate when she turns four and a half, aren't we, Bella?"

Bella looked up at him and gave a nod. I wished she would smile. She didn't look like a very happy child.

"She's sleepy," Travis said. "We had a long drive yesterday and didn't sleep too well last night."

"Where did you move from?" I asked.

"Carolina Beach," he said. "No work there, so we had no

choice but to come to Raleigh." He screwed up his face and I knew he wasn't happy about the move. "I have a job lined up here, though. I interview with the guy tomorrow."

"I hope you get it," I said.

"Oh, it's sewn up. The interview's just a formality. A mutual friend hooked me up with him." He handed Bella the cup of water he'd set on the coffee table. "Do you have kids?" he asked me.

I shook my head. I felt Carolyn in the air around me, hurt and betrayed.

"Then you probably don't know where I can find child care for when I start working, huh?"

I shook my head again. It was the truth. I didn't know the child care options in the Brier Creek area. "Your wife's not with you?" I asked.

"No wife," he said. He pulled a tissue from his pants pocket and blotted Bella's nose in a way that told me he'd done it hundreds of times before. "It's just me and Bella," he said.

Had there been a wife? I wondered. Were they divorced? Did she die?

"So, is it nice around here?" he asked. "Bella and I are used to the beach, aren't we, Bell? We're not used to all the trees and the big buildings."

"It's nice," I said. I was thinking of the fun places we used to take Carolyn. Monkey Joe's and the kids' museum and Pullen Park, but I couldn't talk about them. I couldn't let the image of Carolyn riding the train at Pullen Park into my head right then. "I hope the job's a good one."

"Me too," he said. "We need a break."

Yes, that's how he looked. How both of them looked—like they'd been to hell and back and needed a break.

"Excuse me, Miss Erin," Travis said, "but it's story time."

He pulled a picture book from the canvas bag. *The Cat in the Hat.* Michael and I had read every Dr. Seuss book to Carolyn too many times to count. I had the feeling Travis had read it to Bella many times, too, because the book jacket was ragged-looking and slipping off. I watched Bella climb onto his lap as he opened the book. I remembered how it felt to hold a little girl in my arms that way. How it felt to have her lean back against me while I read. I felt the injustice of it all over again. I wanted my baby back.

I lowered my eyes to my iPad, glad Travis's attention was on the book and not me, because whatever was in my face wasn't meant for anyone to see. The screen of my iPad blurred in front of me and I had to blink a few times before I could read the first response to my post.

Carolyn's always with you, Harley's dad had written. *She's in that little girl and in the little girl's father and in the air that you breathe. Remember that.*

Yes, I thought. I looked over at Bella and Travis where they sat together, absorbed in the book, and I felt Carolyn slip over all three of us like a veil of warm air.

16
Travis

Raleigh

IT WAS CHILLY WHEN I WOKE UP IN THE VAN
the next morning, but Bella slept on, looking warm in the
sleeping bag I'd snuggled her into. It was nearly October and
we weren't going to be able to live in the van for long. We
were parked in the Target parking lot where I was supposed
to meet Roy at one, and I couldn't wait to get this show on
the road. The lot actually made a good spot for our tempo-
rary home. It was part of a massive shopping center and we
didn't stand out. I felt good and anonymous.

I checked the prepaid cell phone I'd picked up in the Target the evening before. I'd only used it once so far—to call
Roy and arrange the time to meet. Roy had been in a rush,
so I didn't get to ask him anything about the job, but he said
Savannah had told him I was a jack-of-all-trades and that was
cool. I said, "Yeah, I guess I am," but I was getting nervous.
What trades were we talking about? I wasn't licensed to do
electrical work, though I could handle plumbing okay. I'd

have to fake the other stuff. I hoped Savannah hadn't built me up to be something I wasn't.

I'd wanted to ask Roy if he knew someone who could watch Bella, but I could tell by how rushed he'd sounded that I'd have to hold off on that. It wasn't the time for a long conversation.

"Hey, sleepyhead." I gave Bella a nudge and her eyes popped open. She'd always been a pretty good sleeper, though she had nightmares after the fire and had wet the bed a few times at Franny's, which hadn't gone over all that great. But usually she slept well and woke up perky. Not like me. I needed my coffee.

I looked across the parking lot at that little coffee shop. It was really too expensive, but it had that comfortable furniture that we'd never find at a doughnut shop or whatever, plus it was right there next to us so we didn't have to use up gas. We'd brushed our teeth and washed our faces in the men's room last night and filled our bottles with drinking water. We could do the same this morning, as long as we bought something. Bella and I could split another muffin. Last night we ate at the McDonald's at the other end of the parking lot, which I could swear was as long as all of Carolina Beach.

I peeled a banana for Bella and she scrambled out of the sleeping bag and took it from my hand. She was still wearing the clothes she'd had on the day before. I checked her pants to make sure she hadn't wet herself during the night, but she was dry. Her nose was runny and I made her blow into a tissue. Her hair looked a little dirty and I ran my comb through it. I didn't see how I'd be able to take a shower or give her a bath till we found a place to live, and I hoped that would be soon. Maybe Roy could hook me up with one of his other workers and we could crash there till we found our own place. Then there was the whole child-care issue. God, my life was a mess. The word *homeless* was pushing its way into my brain and I was trying to keep it out. I refused to raise a homeless kid.

I neatened Bella and myself up as well as I could, and then we walked to the coffee shop. There were more people inside than there'd been the day before, and we had to wait a couple of minutes before we could get into the men's room. Waiting in the hallway, Bella was doing the little bouncy moves that meant she really had to go and I just hoped whoever was in the bathroom wasn't going to take as long as we would. A guy came out dressed in a suit and tie. He looked like he was trying to hold his breath as he passed us. I hoped we didn't smell. I hoped I was just imagining things. Damn.

I washed Bella's face and then helped her brush her teeth before brushing my own. I always sang the same song to her while she brushed her teeth. *Five little monkeys, jumping on the bed...* and even though she'd heard it every day of her life since she started getting teeth, she still giggled. I brushed her teeth more carefully than I did my own and washed behind her ears with the rough paper towels. She was so damned dependent on me and I wasn't doing right by her, and we were in a strange place where we didn't know a soul. *Roy.* We knew Roy. Sort of. *We're going to be fine,* I told myself. Bella was giggling and she hadn't wet herself or had nightmares. We were okay.

And we knew that lady. Erin. A little bit, anyway. A very little bit. I spotted her when we walked back into the main room of the coffee shop. She was sitting in the same chair she'd been in the day before, bent over the iPad on her lap, cardboard cup next to her on the table. Man, I would have loved to have an iPad, but that was only going to happen in my dreams. I was glad to see no one was on the couch near her.

"There's Miss Erin," I said to Bella. "Let's get something to munch and go say hi."

Bella took my hand and we waited in the short line in front of the counter. "Do you want a blueberry or banana nut muffin, Bell?" I asked.

She chewed her lower lip. "Blueberry," she said finally. I bought the muffin and a large coffee, even though it was fifty cents more than the small. I needed it and anyway, in a few hours I'd have a job.

"Good morning, Erin," I said as I sat down on the couch.

She looked surprised to see us. Maybe not all that happy about it, either, and I wondered if we were interrupting her work. She gave me one quick glance before her eyes landed on Bella and stayed there. "Hi, Bella," she said, in the kind, high voice women always used with kids.

"Are we interrupting you?" I asked.

She shook her head. "No," she said. "It's fine." She looked at Bella again, who was starting in on her half of the muffin. "Is that blueberry?" she asked.

Bella pressed herself against my arm. "Answer Miss Erin," I said, and Bella nodded.

"I had one of them myself this morning," Erin said. "It was so good." She looked at me. "Today's your job interview, huh?" she asked.

I liked that she remembered. "Yeah." I thought about the phone in my pocket. I pulled the charger out of my canvas tote bag. "Better charge this thing," I said. I stood up to plug the charger into the wall socket next to the couch.

"So where do you and Bella live?" Erin asked as I sat down again.

"Here and there for a few days till I get this job squared

away," I said. I thought of telling her we were in a hotel or something, but I couldn't lie like that in front of Bella. Bella was being really quiet and I hoped she wouldn't suddenly decide to say something about sleeping in the van.

Erin set down her iPad and leaned in Bella's direction. "I'm totally in love with that purse," she said, pointing to Bella's pink purse.

Bella lifted the purse in the air to give Erin a better look at it and I was glad Erin didn't reach for it or ask her what was inside. I didn't feel like explaining the photographs to her. "It's such a pretty color for you, Bella," Erin said. "Pink goes beautifully with your eyes."

"I have Daddy's eyes," Bella said. That was something my mother always said. *Bella got her daddy's eyes.* I didn't think I'd ever heard Bella say it before, though, and it was sort of like hearing my mother's spirit coming through her.

Erin looked pleased she'd finally gotten some response out of my daughter. "You definitely do," she said. "What color are they?" She peered more closely at Bella as if she couldn't figure out her eye color on her own.

Bella looked up at me as if she wasn't sure what color our eyes were, either. "You know," I said.

"Purple," she said, then giggled for the second time that morning. I wanted to hug her. I was putting her through so much right now and she was being such a good sport.

"Purple!" said Erin. "And I thought they were orange."

"Green!" Bella said, and they went back and forth that way for a minute while I drained my coffee and tried to wake up.

"When does your job start?" Erin asked me when she and Bella had worn out their game.

"Soon, I hope. I hope I can start right away."

"Did you figure out child care?"

"My friend thinks he—this guy—will know someone. Probably some of his other workers have kids and I can get Bella hooked up with them."

"That'd be good," Erin said.

"You live around here?" I asked. I wanted to get the conversation off me and onto anything else.

"Really close," she said. She pointed north of us.

For the first time, I noticed her wedding ring. With girls my own age, I always checked for rings, but I hadn't even noticed with Erin. I wondered what her story was. Why did she hang out here in the mornings? I nodded toward the iPad. "Are you working on that thing or do you use it for games or reading whatever?" I asked.

She glanced at the iPad. "I'm just using this to keep up with email and some…some groups I belong to," she said. "I'm actually a pharmacist, but I've been taking some time off. I go back in a week or so."

"A pharmacist!" I said. Whoa. She was no dummy. It was funny how you could suddenly see a person differently when you learned something new about them. It was like when someone knew me as a construction worker and then found out I'd been a decent student who could have gone to college if things had turned out differently. "Bella," I said, "Miss Erin is like one of those people who work in a drugstore. Remember when you had that cold and the doctor told us to get you medicine at the drugstore?"

"Strawberry," Bella said.

"That's right. Well, the lady who asked you what flavor you wanted in your medicine was a pharmacist, like Erin. Miss Erin."

Bella looked at Erin and I wondered what was going through her little head. Was she following me at all?

"Is strawberry your favorite flavor, Bella?" Erin asked.

Bella shook her head. "Manilla," she said.

"*Va*-nilla," I said. "That's the ice cream you like, right?" I looked at Erin. "She's had the sniffles since we left Carolina Beach and that's how that cold started, so I'm hoping she doesn't end up sick again."

"Do you have any saline spray?" Erin asked.

I shook my head.

"Try that. She's probably just reacting to the change in the weather."

"See that, Bella?" I said, blotting her nose with my napkin. "We've got free advice from a real pharmacist." I wondered how much saline spray cost. "Does your husband work in medicine, too?" I asked.

She shook her head. "No, he works with computers." She looked down at her rings. "We're separated right now. For a while. Sometimes you need a little break."

"Tell me about it," I said, as if I knew what it was like to be married.

I wondered if I could ask her to watch Bella while I met with Roy that afternoon. It was one thing to talk to him about who might be able to watch Bella for me when I was working for him, but another to actually show up with her for the so-called interview. Erin was starting to work on her iPad again, though, and I couldn't bring myself to ask.

"Want a story?" I asked Bella, and I pulled out *The Cat in the Hat* and began to read.

I drove back to the McDonald's for lunch at noon, then returned to our parking place in the Target lot at the other end of the shopping center. You could live your entire life in this shopping center. Anything you needed, there was a store for it. You never had to go anywhere else if you didn't want to. As big as the whole place was, though, it felt suffocating to me because there was no ocean. No open sky, no sparkly blue sea, no white sand. I'd had a trapped feeling in my gut ever since we got to Raleigh. It'd pass, I hoped. Once I got a job and a real place to live, I'd feel a lot better.

On the phone, I'd told Roy where I was parked and that my van had the Brown Construction sign on the side. When he hadn't shown up by ten after one, I was getting nervous. I stood next to the van, waiting. I had all the doors open to air the thing out, and I'd piled a bunch of stuff on the mattress so it didn't look like it was our bedroom. Bella sat inside the van on her wadded-up sleeping bag, using a wooden box as a table as she colored in a coloring book. I was lucky she was a girl. A boy would be bouncing off the van walls on this trip. Bella was usually pretty quiet and able to play by herself.

I spotted this shiny red Mustang driving slowly through the lot. It made a sudden turn toward us, pulling into a space a little ways from the van. I knew it was Roy. There was no reason for anyone else to park way out here in this sea of asphalt. He got out of the car and started walking toward me, and he wasn't exactly what I'd expected for a construction type. He wore a sports coat, his blue shirt open at the neck, his hair neatly trimmed, and I caught the shine of a gold watch on his wrist. He looked like he was doing pretty well for himself in his construction business, and it gave me some real hope. I walked toward him, smiling, hand outstretched.

"Roy?"

"Hey, man." He shook my hand. "How's it going?"

"Good," I said. "I'm looking forward to getting to work, though."

"Excellent. Excellent." He looked past me toward the road and slipped his hands into his jean pockets.

"Daddy?" Bella appeared at the open van door. "Who's that?"

"Ah," I said, like seeing Bella there was a surprise. I waved Roy to follow me the few steps back to the van. "Bella, this is Mr. Roy," I said. "Roy, this is my daughter, Bella. I think Savannah told you about her."

Roy raised his eyebrows. "You have someone to watch her?" he asked.

"Savannah said maybe you'd know someone," I said.

He gave a short laugh, the kind of laugh that wasn't really a laugh at all, and I tensed. "That bitch," he muttered, not quite under his breath, and I knew there was a rough dude beneath his spiffed-up appearance. *Shit.* This was not going to go as well as I'd hoped.

"She thought maybe one of your other workers had kids and would know someone who could watch Bella," I said.

"I'm not a child-care clearinghouse," Roy said. His upper lip curled a little on one side when he talked.

"All right." I felt nervous all of a sudden, like I was moving back to square one. "I'll figure something out." *Damn Savannah.* She'd made it sound like this would be so easy. A done deal. "Tell me about the job," I said. "Savannah didn't know if it was residential or what."

Roy folded his arms across his chest. "Look, I know Savannah told you it was a construction job, right?"

I hesitated. "Riiight…" I drew out the word, waiting for whatever the hell was coming next. I had the feeling it wasn't going to make me happy.

"Well, the good news is, you'll make a nice sum for just a little work," he said.

"What are you talking about?"

"We need a driver with a van." He nodded toward my van. "I lost my other driver, but this will be perfect. Your kid could even come along for the ride if you can't find anyone to watch her."

"Perfect for what?"

He squinted his eyes at me and I felt him sizing me up. "Savannah promised me you weren't an asshole," he said.

"Big of her." I was getting annoyed. "Tell me what the job is, all right? Stop messing with me."

"It'll be the middle of the night," he said. "You'll drive me and a buddy to a truck stop north of here a ways. We'll take some cases of baby formula from one of the trucks, load them into your van, then take them to a drop-off point and collect a shitload of money."

I tried to laugh. "Is this a joke?"

"You'll get five hundred bucks for a few hours' work," he said. "Two hundred at the truck stop, three more when we make the drop-off. The easiest money you've ever made, and if it all goes smooth, we can do it again next week. That'll be five hundred under the table every week."

He was serious and I was stupefied. I stared at him, unable to speak. "Baby formula?" I said finally. "You're talking about stealing baby formula?"

He nodded toward Bella. "You have a kid," he said. "Was she ever on formula?"

I didn't answer. I didn't want this sleazeball talking about Bella.

"They lock it up, some places," he said. "Other stores, you can only buy a certain amount. That's because it's so expensive and people steal it. So what we do is we get a few cases, then the guys I work with resell it online for less than people can get it in the store. So it's like a public service. We're like Robin Hood. We take so few cases, nobody'll miss them, and then we sell them to people who can't afford to buy it in the stores, with the markup and everything."

I remembered, back when Bella was on formula, seeing it locked up in a couple of stores. I'd never really understood why. The stuff *was* expensive, though. That much was the truth. But going to jail wasn't part of my plan and I felt this big empty hole opening up in the center of my chest. I was so pissed at Savannah. And I was so screwed. I'd never felt farther away from home.

"No way I'm doing this, man," I said. "Savannah totally lied about what you had to offer. You're saying there's no construction work?" Could this baby formula just be a sideline? Maybe he was yanking my chain.

"That's right. There's no construction work. I *used* to be in construction, but the economy screwed that up." He grinned. "This is so much better, though. I wish I'd been doing this the whole time. It's easy. Safe. And much more lucrative." He motioned toward his Mustang to convince me.

"Forget it," I said. "I'm not the guy you want." I turned to head back to the van.

"Hey!" he called after me. "You got my number if you change your mind."

I climbed into the van and shut all the doors. I pulled Bella into my arms. She wriggled to get out of my clutches and back to her coloring, but I held her tight. *Okay*, I told myself, burying my face in her hair. *Stay calm*. I had to think this through. There was nothing for me in Carolina Beach. I was in Raleigh now. Big city. More opportunities. I'd find something.

"Daddy." Bella squirmed her way out of my arms. I leaned back against the wall of the van and wondered how I'd feed my daughter and myself until that something came along.

17
Robin

2007

IT HAD BEEN THREE MONTHS SINCE I'D SEEN Travis, and when he showed up at the condo in Chapel Hill for our well-planned getaway to Jordan Lake, I grabbed him and started kissing him. I'd fantasized our reunion a million times and my imagination pictured a long, emotional hug, but when I saw him standing there with his beautiful eyelashes and all that love in his smile...well, I wanted him. That was all there was to it. *You could die tomorrow,* the familiar voice in the back of my head told me, *so you'd better grab today.*

We probably set a record for how fast you could take off another person's clothes, and there, on the living room floor of the condo where my father had locked me away to keep exactly this from happening, we had crazy, wild sex. *Unexpected* sex, since when we'd planned this day, it had been about our drive to the country, the picnic lunch I had waiting for us in a tote bag in the kitchen, and the drive back, which would get us to the condo early enough to let us make love before my father came home. We hadn't planned on breathless, sweaty, hungry *fucking*. Oh, my God. It was so delicious to be with him again! I wrapped my legs around his waist to pull him deeper inside me. The carpet burned my shoulders as we rocked back and forth, and I thought, *I don't care, I don't care, I don't care!* All I cared about was having Travis back in my arms.

When we'd finished making love and were lying naked and cuddled up together, Travis suddenly laughed. "Let's skip Jordan Lake and just stay here," he said. I realized they were the first words he'd said since walking into the condo.

"Oh, yeah," I agreed.

"We can have our picnic right here on the floor. Naked."

"Yeah," I said again, but I wasn't the least bit hungry. As a matter of fact, the thought of the turkey-and-cheese sandwiches I'd made a couple of hours ago was nauseating. I couldn't seem to catch my breath, either. I lay there quietly, waiting for the nausea to pass. I didn't want to let Travis know how bad I felt. I didn't want to spoil what had just happened.

"Oh, shit." He smacked his forehead with his palm.

"What?"

"The condoms. I left them in the car. I didn't expect you to attack me like that." He laughed again. "You think it'll be all right?"

I wanted to say it would, but I didn't seem to have enough breath to push the words out of my mouth. A deep, dull ache was working its way into my chest, sending long fingers of pain into my back. Plus the terrible nausea! I was going to throw up any second.

"Bathroom," I managed to say as I tried to sit up. I felt

Travis's arm around me as I got to my feet, and that was the last thing I remembered before everything went black.

I woke up in the back of an ambulance. It felt familiar to me; it wasn't my first ambulance trip to the hospital. The siren screamed and somebody pressed an oxygen mask to my face. I thought I saw Travis sitting nearby, his face blurry and white. I lifted my hand toward him, but someone was squeezing all the life out of my chest and lungs and the world disappeared again before I could touch him.

Days later, my father sat next to my hospital bed. My eyes were closed, but I knew he was there. He stroked my hair back from my face and I could feel the love pouring from his fingertips. When I opened my eyes, he leaned forward, holding my head between his big hands as he kissed my forehead.

"Hello, sweetheart," he said. "How are you feeling?"

I shrugged. I wasn't sure how I felt. I was hooked up to so many wires and tubes and I had a feeling whatever they had running into my veins was keeping me from feeling much of anything.

"I hope you understand now why I forbade you to see Travis," he said. "It wasn't to be mean, Robin. He doesn't realize how fragile you are. He took advantage of you. Do you understand now?"

I nodded, because it was the easiest thing to do. I didn't have the strength for a fight. He spoke so quietly. So calmly. If he was angry with me, he didn't show it. I thought he'd already spent all his anger on Travis. One of the nurses had told me everything—how he'd threatened to kill Travis outside the emergency room. He'd actually called Travis a rapist and said he'd press charges if he didn't stay away from me. I was so mortified that Daddy knew we'd had sex. I knew all his threats were empty ones from a gentle man afraid for his daughter. Still, lying there weak and winded, I wasn't sure how Travis and I could ever make things work out between us again. My father would have his eye on our every move.

Once I was out of the hospital, I emailed Travis. I told him I was better. Not to blame himself. I told him how much I loved him. I hit Send and then I waited. Hours passed without a response from him. The hours turned into a day. One day turned into two. Two into a week. When a week turned into a month, I knew I'd lost him. I tried calling him, but he'd changed his phone number and the new one was unlisted. Had he decided I was more trouble than I was worth? Was he terrified of my father? I couldn't blame him either way. All I knew was that he was gone, and my life had a giant cavern in it that could never be filled by anyone else.

18
Erin

I COULDN'T CONCENTRATE ON THE HARLEY'S
Dad and Friends group posts as I sipped my coffee at Jump-
Start because my gaze kept drifting to the door. Bella and
Travis had come into the coffee shop every day for the past
week, and it had gotten to the point that I thought about
them all day long and into the evening. Except for Carolyn,
there had never been a more adorable child born into the
world. Those eyes! The past couple of days, Bella had been
more talkative with me, although I didn't think she was
much of a talker to begin with. I could get her to smile now
and occasionally to giggle a little. Every day, Travis read to
her from the same worn-out-looking book that she clearly
knew by heart. I'd only seen her wear two outfits—the
blue shorts and stained blue-and-white-striped shirt, and
short khaki cargo pants and a pink jersey. I wondered if
she had any other clothes. Travis wore jeans and T-shirts
every day and he carried a black warm-up jacket in his canvas bag. Whenever they came into the coffee shop, they
headed straight for the men's room and they were in there a
long time. Travis would come out freshly shaved and Bella's

cheeks would be pink, as though he'd scrubbed her face. Then Travis would plug his phone charger into the wall. I was afraid that all this added up to them being homeless and I was worried about them. Especially about Bella. I knew the job that had brought Travis to Raleigh had fallen through and every day he picked up one of the newspapers other people had left strewn around JumpStart and searched the classifieds. I was sure the pickings were slim for a construction worker these days.

I glanced at the time on my iPad. Nearly nine-thirty and I'd finished my coffee. Where were they? I peered out the windows to the parking lot. I should hope they *didn't* show up. That would mean he'd found a job and someone to watch Bella. I should hope for that, and yet the thought of not seeing Bella today was almost painful.

From where I sat, I couldn't see a single Raleigh newspaper on any of the tables. I bought one so he'd have it to look through, and while I was paying for it at the mobbed counter, I ordered a decaf coffee from the new, clearly overwhelmed, teenage barista Nando was supervising. I'd had enough caffeine for the day, but needed something more while I waited. I wasn't going to leave without seeing Bella.

Travis and Bella walked into the shop while the frantic new girl was making my drink, along with a half-dozen others. Travis waved at me on their way to the men's room, and I added a bottle of orange juice for Bella to my order. I smiled to myself as I moved to the end of the counter to wait with the other customers for my drink.

Nando grinned at all of us as he set a few cups on the counter. "She'll be a whiz at this in a week," he said, nodding toward the new barista as she poured steamed milk into someone's coffee. "Probably be managing the place in a month."

I gave him my usual anemic smile, then carried my coffee and newspaper back to my seat and set them on the end table next to my chair. I paged through the paper to take a peek at the classified section. Not much. This wasn't the right day of the week to find a lot of jobs listed. I thought suddenly of Craigslist. Maybe Travis could find something there? Did he have a computer he could use to check? I doubted it. I remembered his envy of my iPad. I could let him use it to check the ads.

I felt almost happy as I waited for Travis and Bella to come out of the men's room. But when I took a sip of my coffee, I nearly spit it out. It tasted like...I wasn't sure what. Dish soap? Salt? Something that nearly made me gag as I forced myself to swallow the mouthful. I lifted the lid of the cup and saw the milky concoction inside. Definitely not my black decaf. I got to my feet and went back to the counter. Another customer, an older woman dressed in a pink suit was there ahead of me, complaining to the new barista that she'd been given the wrong drink.

"I think we picked up each other's cup," I said.

"I might have got the order wrong." The young barista screwed up her face.

"No problem!" Nando patted the girl on her shoulder. "These two nice ladies will wait while we get it right." He took our cups from us and started over again.

"What *was* that?" I asked the woman in pink, pointing to the cup Nando had taken from me.

"My favorite," she said. "Roasted peanut chocolate Bavarian."

"It's...different," I said, and she laughed. Soon we had our drinks sorted out and by the time I'd taken my seat again, Travis and Bella were coming out of the men's room.

"Hey, Erin," Travis said when they'd reached my chair.

"Hi, Travis. Hi Bella," I said. "I thought you might not make it this morning."

"We're here." Travis didn't sit down, but Bella climbed onto the couch, her pink purse dangling from her arm. She hugged her lamb to her chest and Travis rested a hand on her head. "You sit here while I get our breakfast, Bella," he said.

"I bought some OJ for Bella," I said.

He raised his eyebrows. "What do you say, Bell?" he asked.

"Thank you," Bella said.

"You're welcome. And be careful up there," I said to Travis. "New girl behind the counter. I picked up the wrong cup and thought I was drinking poison."

He laughed, folding his arms across his chest. "I'm always careful with coffee cups. One time I went on a fishing trip with my buddies to Kill Devil Hills," he said. "I picked up a coffee at a McDonald's on my way there and I put it down on the kitchen counter in the cottage we were renting. One of my buddies had the same cup, only his had worms in it."

"Oh, no." I cringed.

"Oh, yeah," he said with a shudder. "I took a nice sip of worm juice."

I laughed. It felt like the first time I'd laughed in months.

"My mother told me that's what I got for eating at McDonald's."

"Nana?" Bella asked him.

He hesitated. "Right, baby," he said. He rubbed her shoulders with a tenderness that put a lump in my throat. "Nana."

I wondered where Nana lived. Couldn't he leave Bella with her grandmother while he tried to find a job?

Travis headed for the counter and I looked at Bella. It was the first time I'd been alone with her—not that we were really alone. Four women sat at a nearby table, the pink-suited woman chatted on her phone, and a few business-men sat here and there in the coffee shop, working on their computers or reading the *Wall Street Journal*. But I only had eyes for the little girl on the sofa.

"You love that purse, don't you, Bella?" I said.

She lifted the purse in the air to give me a better look. "Pink is good with my eyes," she said, repeating what I'd told her a few days earlier.

"It really is," I said. "What do you carry in it? Can you show me?"

She nodded and began trying to pry open the clasp.

"Would you like some help?" I asked. Carolyn had hated it when I'd try to help her with small tasks like that, and I wasn't surprised when Bella shook her head.

"I can do it." She frowned as she struggled, her lips tight in concentration. *Oh, my God.* She was beyond precious. She finally looked up at me in defeat. "I can't do it," she admitted.

"But you almost did," I said. "It's really hard, huh?"

She stood up and took a step toward me, handing me the purse. She rested one hand on my knee. I felt the warmth of her small, fleshy palm through my pants. Or at least, I imagined I could feel it, and I hoped she'd keep her hand there forever. My own hands shook a little as I took the purse from her. "Wow," I said, prying the two sides of the clasp apart. "This is even tough for me to do. No wonder you had a hard time."

"That's so nothing falls out," she said.

I could smell her. Soap. Toothpaste. Musty hair. I took in a deep, deep breath, then handed the open purse back to her. "Do you want to show me what's inside?" I asked.

She nodded and slipped her hand into the pink satin lining. With a flourish, she pulled out a miniature Barbie-type doll with very long, blond hair and a red-and-white-striped bathing suit painted on her body.

"Look at that amazing hair!" I said.

Bella leaned on the arm of my chair and peered at the doll. "Yellow hair is called blond," she informed me.

"Like mine," I said.

She studied my hair, then shook her head. "Yours isn't yellow," she said with the candor no adult would dare to express.

I smiled. I supposed that, between my dark roots and fading highlights, my hair *wasn't* very yellow anymore. "Does she have a name?" I asked.

"Uh-uh." She shook her head, then suddenly gave a little jump. "Oh, yes! Yes, she does. I forgot. It's Princess!"

I laughed at her sudden enthusiasm. "Well, she's beautiful," I said.

Travis sat down on the sofa, resting his coffee on the table. "Here, Bella," he said. "Here's your half of the muffin."

I realized that they'd split a muffin every day I'd seen them. At first, I'd guessed they'd eaten breakfast at home and the muffin was just a snack. Now that I was convinced they had no home, though, I figured this probably *was* breakfast. Half a muffin.

Bella pointed at the doll. "I'm showing her what—"

"Miss Erin," he corrected her.

"I'm showing Miss Erin what I have in my purse," she said.

"Well, put it away for now and eat your muffin," he said. "Then we can have a story."

"Just two more things," Bella said. From inside the purse, she pulled a rectangular photograph and handed it to me.

Nearly leaning on my lap, she pointed to the three people in the picture. "That's me and Daddy and Nana," she said.

They were sitting on a beach wearing bathing suits and broad smiles, the ocean behind them.

"What a beautiful sand castle!" I said, pointing to the castle in the picture. It was big and elaborate, nearly covered with shells. I knew Travis was trying to get Bella to climb back onto the couch and that I was undercutting his parenting, but I didn't want her to move away from me.

"We builded it," she said.

"Where does your Nana live?" I asked.

"She lived with me but she moved to heaven."

Oh, no. I glanced at Travis. Mouthed, "I'm sorry." He gave me a sad nod.

"I bet you miss her," I said to Bella.

"She can't come back," she said, but she was already reaching into her purse again. This time she pulled out a small photograph of a pretty teenage girl. It looked like the uninspired sort of picture kids had taken at school.

"And who's this?" I asked. My best guess was Travis's sister.

"My mommy," she said.

I didn't dare ask where her mommy lived and Travis seemed to pick up on my trepidation. "She lives in Beaufort," he said. He was holding his cup to his lips but not drinking.

"Ah," I said, thinking I'd better not ask any more questions. "Let's put these things back in your purse and then you can have your muffin," I said. I watched as Bella carefully placed the items, one by one, into the purse. As she slipped the picture of her mother inside, I saw the name *Robin* written on the back.

"See? It's got two 'partments," Bella said, showing me how the inside of the purse was divided in two. "The pictures go on this side and the dolly on the other, so the pictures don't get scrunched."

"Good job," I said, when she managed to press the two sides of the clasp together. I watched her climb onto the sofa next to Travis.

"This is my paper," I said to Travis, gesturing to the *News and Observer* on the coffee table. "You're welcome to check the ads."

"Thanks." He looked really tired today, even more than usual. I'd been so focused on Bella that I hadn't noticed, but he seemed beaten down. The shadows around his eyes were darker and his whole face seemed drawn and gaunt. Maybe seeing the pictures in Bella's purse had made him sad. Or maybe he was just fed up with the job hunt.

"Do you know about Craigslist?" I asked. "I hired some yard guys through it once. They have free job listings."

He nodded. "Yeah, actually, we went to the library day before yesterday and I used the computer there to check. There was one job that was a good fit, but by the time I called, the guy said it'd been filled. Twenty or thirty applicants, he said. Something like that." He brushed a crumb from his jeans. "We'll go the library to check again today."

"Use my iPad," I suggested, lifting the iPad from the table. "I'll find Craigslist for you and you can check right now. You can probably find someone to do child care, too, but be sure to check references."

He gave me what I hoped was a mock insulted look. "I've been her dad for four years," he said. "I know what to look for."

"Of course," I said. I found Craigslist on the internet and handed the iPad to him, holding back from giving him instructions on how to use it. I didn't want to insult him again, and he didn't seem to have any problem at all surfing through the ads. He pulled a pen and pad from the canvas bag and jotted a couple of things down. "I'm going to call on this one," he said, reaching for his phone.

Bella held the book in front of him with an expression on her face that asked, *Did you forget about the story?*

"I'll read to you after I make this call, Bell," he said, getting to his feet.

"Would you like me to read to you while your dad talks on the phone, Bella?" I asked.

She jumped off the couch, handed me the book and climbed into my lap, and for the first time in six months, I was holding a child. She leaned against me as if she'd known me all her life. As if she were my own daughter. I breathed in the musty smell of her hair again. I couldn't pull the scent of her deeply enough into my lungs. Beneath my hands, I felt her ribs and the little knobs of her spine. She was tiny for four. Tiny and way too thin. Carolyn at three had been bigger than Bella at four. I rested my chin on the top of her head and opened the only book she seemed to own, and while I read to her, I thought of all the books and toys in Carolyn's room. I could go to the house and get some of them for her. *If* I could make myself go into Carolyn's room. The thought was so unsettling that I lost my place in the book.

"*No*," Bella said. "The *fish* says that part!"

"You're absolutely right," I said. "My mistake."

I read on, thinking about my house. *Michael's* house, for now anyway. Was there any work Travis could do there? Since Carolyn's death, Michael had taken care of nearly every handyman task we'd had, so I doubted there was much left to do. Besides, without my income, we couldn't afford to hire anyone.

I glanced at Travis, who stood in the corner of the coffee shop talking on the phone, and I could tell from his expression it wasn't going well. Reaching into my own purse, I pulled a twenty from my wallet, never missing a beat as I read to Bella. Carefully, I slipped the bill into the pocket of her pants. I knew Travis wouldn't take it if I offered it to him outright. I only hoped he wouldn't be offended when he found it.

19
Travis

BELLA AND I ATE AT MICKEY D'S AGAIN THAT afternoon. My mother would have thrown a fit if she'd known how Bella and I practically lived there. Mom had been a true Southern cook—lots of butter and gravies and pork—but she looked down her nose at fast food, and before this trip from hell, I'd only taken Bella to a McDonald's maybe twice. Now it felt like home. Those cheap Happy Meals. Protein, right? Plus apple slices. Plus the little toys. Bella loved them. She loved everything about Mickey D's, from the sweet, harried teenagers who worked there to the play area. Especially the play area. I loved it, too, frankly. I could sit at a table calling on jobs while Bella climbed through the tubes and hopped around in the germy plastic balls and chattered with other kids and acted like she didn't have a care in the world. That's what I wanted for her. That freedom. And if the price was some artery-clogging food, well, it was worth it.

We'd hung out at the coffee shop as long as we could that morning. Until Erin left, actually. Erin was returning to her job in a few days and I was going to miss her. She was the only person I knew in Raleigh—not that I actually *knew* her—but she was a smile in the morning and she gave us her time and I liked that. She was good with Bella and I liked that even more. Bella needed some women around her.

I'd written down some of the Craigslist ads from Erin's iPad that morning. Building a fence, hauling stuff, handyman jobs. I'd written down anything I thought I might be able to do, and while Bella played, I started calling around. I was going to need to buy more minutes for my phone today. I also needed to buy some fruit and vegetables. A bag of carrots. Something cheap. Something to keep Bella from getting scurvy. Did kids still get scurvy? I'd picked up a bottle of that saline stuff Erin told me about and it seemed to be helping.

The Craigslist ads were a pain in the butt, though. People wanted you to start work *now*. Like ten minutes ago. And I couldn't work until I had somebody to watch Bella, but I couldn't find someone to watch Bella until I had a job that would let me pay them. I thought of Erin. I should've asked her for her number. Maybe she'd be willing to watch Bella for a few hours so I could work and get the money to pay someone for the next day—if the job lasted that long. My brain hurt from trying to figure it all out.

That was the other thing about the Craigslist jobs. Most of them were short, one-day sort of things. Move some old couple into an apartment. Fix a toilet or paint a room. I finally called one of the numbers for a woman who said she could babysit. Turned out she was sixteen and she sounded totally stoned on the phone. While I was talking to her, I watched Bella slide into the sea of plastic balls, her arms high in the air. She looked happy and I smiled and hung up on the girl. Forget turning Bella over to someone I didn't know. Wasn't going to happen.

I was so angry at Savannah. I used some of my precious phone minutes trying to call her. I wanted to chew her out, but I got her voice mail as I had each time I'd tried to call her since I'd talked to Roy. I pictured her checking her caller ID, seeing it was me, laughing at her big joke and not bothering to answer. I didn't know why she'd jerked me around like this, but if she ever answered her phone, I was going to let her have it. It was one thing to mess with *me,* another thing to mess with the welfare of my daughter.

I finally ran out of numbers to call. Then I tried my old boss in Carolina Beach just in case something had opened up, but when he answered he was in Washington, D.C. He'd moved back in with his brother and was looking for work up there. That scared me more than anything. He had skills up the wazoo. If he hadn't been able to find anything at the beach, I didn't stand a chance. Sticking it out in Raleigh was the best choice. At least, it was the best of a bunch of really shitty choices.

"Daddy!" Bella ran from the play area over to me as I was hanging up the phone. "I finded money!" She held a wadded-up bill in her little fist and I held out my hand for it. She dropped it onto my palm, and I unfolded it. Twenty bucks.

I looked toward the play area, thinking *finders keepers,* but what kid would be carrying around a twenty-dollar bill? "Where did you find this, Bella?" I asked. I looked toward the balls. Anything could be buried in there.

"It comed out of my pocket," she said.

"Your pocket? Which pocket?"

She pointed to the left front pocket of her pants.

"Are you sure about that, Bella? Are you sure you didn't just find it in the play area?" But even as I spoke, I knew what had happened. *Erin.* I remembered Erin reading to

her, Bella cuddled against her as she listened, and my cheeks
burned. *Damn.* I wished she hadn't done that. I needed my
pride more than I needed her money—or worse, her pity. I
wished she'd let me have that pride. We couldn't go back to
the coffee shop now. She'd ruined it.

Yet I looked at that twenty-dollar bill and it looked like a
bag of carrots and a couple of apples and maybe some of the
grapes that Bella loved, as well as a couple of gallons of gas
for the van. I let out a sigh.

"Can I keep that in my wallet?" I said.

"In my purse," she said. Her purse and her lamb rested on
the table next to my phone.

"Okay," I said. "We'll go over to the Wal-Mart in a little
bit and use it to get some food, and then we'll keep the
change in your purse. How's that?"

"What kind of food?"

"Grapes?"

Her eyes widened. "Yes!" she said, her face so filled with a
simple joy that I had to laugh. I cupped her head in my hands
and leaned forward to kiss her forehead. I caught a whiff of
little-girl sweat and wondered how ripe I was smelling myself. We needed a motel room. A real shower. A laundromat.

"Can I go back and play some more?" Bella asked as I put
the twenty-dollar bill in her purse.

"Sure," I said.

I sat back in the chair and watched her climb around the
play area with another little girl about the same age. I was
trapped in McDonald's. Trapped in this gigantic parking
lot with stores I'd never be able to shop in except for some
careful trips to the Target. The beach was a million miles
away and just the thought of walking barefoot on the sand,
watching the waves that now held my mother's ashes, and
picking up shells that were free and more beautiful than

anything I could find in one of the nearby stores got to me, and I had to blink my eyes to clear the image away.

Five hundred dollars. Five hundred dollars for a few hours' work. Roy did it all the time. Five hundred dollars sounded like a million to me right then. A motel room for few nights. A tub and a shower and a phone and TV. A few healthy meals for Bella, and a chance to catch my breath.

I just had to drive the van. It was no big deal, Roy had said. I wouldn't be the one doing the actual stealing. Plus, I'd be helping poor parents, right? Poor parents like me. What if Bella was still young enough to need formula instead of cheap Happy Meals? I'd be helping those parents feed their kids. I didn't let myself go too deep with that thought. Not deep enough to see the wrong in it.

What if Roy had found someone else to do it by now? A panicky feeling suddenly hit me. This was my only chance. Five hundred bucks. Why was I being such a tightass? I'd be an idiot to pass it up.

I'd do it. What would I do with Bella while I was driving the van, though? I thought of what it would be like to do this job with her buckled into her car seat behind me. No way. The thought of Roy and his buddy—two total assholes, I was sure—being around Bella made me feel sick.

And then I remembered Erin.

20

Robin

2007

I HAD A SHORT, SPOTTY PERIOD A COUPLE OF months after Travis and I made love that last time, but my periods had always been irregular because of my heart medication, and with the heart attack, hospitalization and missing Travis, my cycle was the last thing on my mind. So by the time my doctor shocked me with the news that I was pregnant, I was already sixteen weeks along. Both he and my father said I had to have an abortion. The medication I was on could cause birth defects and there was no way I could handle a full-term pregnancy. *You could die tomorrow,* I reminded myself, and the baby was my only link to Travis. I'd recovered okay from the heart attack and felt nearly as well as I had before it, so I refused to have an abortion. My father tried to get a court to declare me a danger to myself and give him guardianship rights so he could force me to abort the baby, but the judge was a pro-lifer who was on my side all the way.

I wanted to tell Travis. I didn't know how he felt about me now, since he'd never answered my email. Had he moved on? Was he with someone else? I told my father we needed to tell him, that it was only right. Even if Travis wanted nothing to do with me, I argued, he should know he was going to be a father. I knew I was secretly hoping maybe the baby could bring us together again. But Daddy said there was no way he'd let Travis back in my life. I'd fought my father in court and won, though, and that gave me courage, so I emailed Travis and asked him to get in touch. That I had something really important I needed to talk to him about. Months had passed since the whole mess with my father in the E.R., and I guess I believed Travis loved me enough that he'd write back, but he didn't. The pain of that—of not hearing back from him when I really, really needed him— was so bad. I remembered what my father had said about puppy love so long ago. Maybe he'd been right. Maybe that's all it was for Travis.

In order to continue the pregnancy, I had to stop taking a couple of my medications and that's when I discovered how sick I really was. Those drugs had been keeping me stable. Making me feel well when I was anything but. Without them, I grew sicker and weaker. So weak that my father traded in my home teacher for a home nurse and I spent most of my time in bed, barely conscious. I'd had a couple of sonograms and everyone seemed amazed that my baby girl looked perfectly normal, which made me so glad I was giving her a chance at life. Lying there in bed, day in and day out, I felt her move and kick and punch my belly and I hoped she would keep going like that. I hoped she was full of fight, because I was losing all of mine. It was all I could do to drag myself to the bathroom without passing out.

Finally, thirteen weeks before my due date, they moved

me to the hospital, where I would have to stay until the
baby was born. I was so, so sick. Dozens of doctors passed
through my room, all of them messing with a concoction of
medications and IVs, all of them trying to keep the foolish
girl alive. I knew what I'd never wanted to admit: my father
had been right. I should have had an abortion.

After two more weeks had passed, I didn't need my father
or my doctor or the hospital social worker to tell me that
if I survived the pregnancy—which was now an honest-
to-goodness concern—I would be far too sick to take care
of a baby. I didn't even want the baby by then. I'd been so
stupid. My father hired a lawyer who could help me arrange
an adoption. The lawyer came to my hospital room, cranked
up my bed and logged me into a website that described a
bunch of couples, all of them longing for a baby of their own.
I was too tired and weak to care by then and their images
and profiles ran together in front of my eyes.

"I don't care," I said to the lawyer. "You pick."

He looked hesitant. "Well," he said, "I'll tell you about
three of the couples, all right? And you can decide between
them. I want you to have a choice in this. If... *When* you
recover, I don't want you to feel as though you were coerced
in any way."

He described three couples but I couldn't keep them
straight. Which was the guy who worked for IBM? Which
was the woman who'd lost three babies? Which was the
airline pilot who planned to retire to be a stay-at-home dad?

"The middle one," I said, after the lawyer had described
all three. I thought he said the middle couple was rich. I
wanted my baby to have everything if she couldn't have me.

"The Richardsons." He looked pleased as he closed the
computer screen. "They'll be so thrilled, Robin. You can
be as involved in your baby's life as you want. You can—"

"I just want her out of me," I said. "She's killing me."

He took a step away from me and I thought I'd shocked him. I was too tired to explain that I didn't mean it quite the way it sounded. Or maybe I did. I was sorry I'd fought so hard to have this baby. She *was* killing me. I would do everything I could to make sure she got her chance at life, but I was angry she seemed to be stealing mine while she was at it.

Every day, one doctor or another would explain his or her treatment plan to me and I began to lose the ability to make any sense of what they were saying. I knew they were telling me they'd take the baby early. I knew I would have a Cesarean section. I knew that I wouldn't be leaving the hospital until they found a new heart for me. I knew I'd done it all to myself when I chose the baby's life over my own. The doctors' words grew mushier in my head day by day, until I slipped into a world where I couldn't hear them at all.

One day, while I was stuck in that foggy world between life and death, I became vaguely aware of a woman leaning over the side of my bed. She was holding something in her hands. A notepad or chart or something. She lifted the side of the oxygen mask from my face.

"Are you awake, Robin?" she asked. "I need the name of the baby's father for the birth certificate."

"Not supposed to..." I murmured, trying to remember what my father had said about the birth certificate.

"Are you awake, dear? Who's the baby's father?"

"Travis Brown," I whispered, and it felt so good to feel those two words on my lips. She was out the door before I remembered they were the words my father had told me never to say.

21

Erin

I PULLED INTO THE DRIVEWAY OF THE HOUSE I'd shared with Michael for the past ten years and was disappointed to see his car through the windows of the garage door. It was five o'clock and I'd hoped I'd beat him home so that I could get in and out of the house without having to talk to him. I knew he'd be working on a game in his first-floor home office and I wondered if I could just sneak by him.

Travis and I had talked for a long time at JumpStart that morning. It had been obvious by the way he'd handled my iPad that he was no stranger to computers and the internet, and when I pointed that out, he told me he used to use a friend's Mac to design cabinetry. We started talking about the internet and before I knew it, I was telling him about Michael being a video-game designer. Travis was fascinated.

"I never knew someone could have a full-time job inventing games," he said. "Cool."

"They're not your usual games," I said. "They're collaborative, so thousands of people play at one time, and they're designed to try to solve real-world problems. Like the energy crisis or forest fire prevention. He won an award for a game that had the goal of curing a certain kind of cancer." I felt some of my old pride in Michael rise to the surface as I talked.

"Very cool," he said again, and I wondered how someone who couldn't find a job, had a child to feed and was probably homeless could possibly see the redeeming qualities in game invention.

"He thinks games are a cure for everything," I said, moving into my putting-Michael-down mode, where I was more comfortable these days. "Pollyanna thinking."

"I bet he's a nice guy," Travis said.

I nodded. "Yes," I said because I couldn't argue with that. Suddenly, I missed him. I missed our "before everything went wrong" life. "He *is* a nice guy."

Our 1930s craftsman-style house was small and cute and it sat on a corner in Five Points, one of my favorite neighborhoods in Raleigh. I loved our house, even though space was always at a premium. We knew we'd have to move to a larger home once we had a second child and we'd been carefully saving for that day. Now it all seemed pointless. Our savings were being eaten up by my rent.

I turned off my car and took the short path around the side of the house to the back door. How many hundreds of times had I walked this path? How many times had I fiddled with my key chain, searching for the back door key? How many times had I climbed these old porch steps, which I now noticed Michael had painted? He'd rebuilt them before I left as one of his many recent home maintenance tasks, designed to keep him from thinking about the unthinkable. The things I'd pleaded with him to do for years were suddenly all getting done.

I was about to slip my key into the lock when he opened

the door. His smile was wide and I hoped he didn't think my showing up there meant anything.

"Hey," he said. "It's good to see you."

"You too," I said, politely. Even though I hadn't wanted him to be there, it *did* feel good to see him and that surprised me. We hugged awkwardly. I kissed his cheek without thinking and felt something visceral and traitorous in my body as the familiar scent of his aftershave caught me off guard. I let go and took a step away from him.

"I'm sorry to just barge in, but I need to pick up a few things," I said, moving past him into the room and setting my purse on the kitchen table.

"Sure." He motioned toward the box of penne on the counter. "I was just about to make dinner. Why don't you get what you need and then join me?"

"I can't," I said. I hoped he wasn't eating pasta every night. That made me feel guilty. I was the cook in the family, he was the cleaner-upper. "I'm starting back to work next week and need to get some clothes." It was a lie. I'd packed plenty of clothes when I moved out. You didn't need much in the way of a wardrobe when you wore a white jacket all day. What I'd come to the house for was in Carolyn's room— books I could give Bella. Maybe a toy or two. Something small she could carry in her purse.

"That's great, Erin," he said. "It's going to be so good for you to start working again."

"Right," I said.

"Do you need some help?" he asked as I headed for the stairs.

"No, thanks."

"Give a shout if you change your mind."

I climbed the stairs, hoping he'd stay in the kitchen because I didn't want to explain what I was doing in Carolyn's room, a room I'd only peered inside once since her death. That one glimpse had been too much. I'd psyched myself up for this visit on my way to the house today, though, picturing myself walking into the room and straight to the bookcase. I even knew which books I would pull out: The *Winnie the Pooh* books Carolyn had been a bit too young and hyper to sit still for, but which I thought Bella might love. And there was also a book about a blue-eyed lamb somewhere on those shelves. Bella would like that one, too, since she never let go of that stuffed lamb of hers. I imagined Bella sitting on my lap as I read the books to her. New-to-her books, unlike *The Cat in the Hat.* Unimaginable to have only one book. Carolyn had been so lucky. We had *all* been so lucky, once.

As I reached the top of the stairs, I pictured myself walking to Carolyn's bookcase, picking out the books, then looking up at the shelf where we'd kept most of her stuffed animals and pulling one of them down. Maybe the giraffe. That hadn't been one of Carolyn's favorites so it wouldn't be worn or soiled. It wouldn't hold any scent of her. Carolyn's favorites had always been lined up on her pillow and I assumed they still were—except for the fuzzy brown dog she'd had with her on that trip to Atlantic Beach.

The hallway was long and the old floorboards creaked exactly where they'd always creaked, surprising me with homesickness. At one end of the hall, the door was open to our bedroom. Michael's and mine. There were four other doors—one to my combination home office and guestroom, one to the bathroom, one to the attic and one to Carolyn's room. That was the only door that was closed and hanging from the knob was a sign she'd made in preschool the week before she died. Below a felt flower, her name was spelled out in wooden beads, the *Y* and *N* crammed in the cor-

ner below the *Carol* because she'd run out of room. I stood
still in the hallway, staring at the sign, remembering how
much she'd loved it. How proud she'd been of it, because her
teacher told her she'd picked colors that harmonized beautifully, and *harmonize* became her new word of the week. "Do
these colors harmonize, Mommy?" she'd ask, looking at the
pages of one of her picture books. "Do these colors harmonize?" she'd ask, picking out a shirt to go with her shorts.
Standing in the kitchen, Michael and I had sung "Way Down
Upon the Swanee River" in passable harmony to try to teach
her a second meaning of the word. She'd pressed her hands
to the sides of her head. "That hurts my ears," she'd said,
and Michael and I had laughed. Even now, remembering, I
smiled before I caught myself. Judith had told me, "Someday
memories of Carolyn will make you smile as well as cry." I
hadn't believed her. Smiling had seemed like a betrayal, and
standing outside Carolyn's room, I thought *I won't tell Judith
about this.* Why not? Would it mean progress? Did progress
mean I was leaving Carolyn behind?

"I will never leave you behind, sweetheart," I whispered
to my daughter as I turned the doorknob to her room.

I opened the door and stood there for a moment, taking
in the room. It smelled a little stale and the scent of her was
truly gone. It was lost forever, and I wondered if Michael
had opened the windows to get rid of it or if somehow the
air moving in and out of the room over the past few months
had simply carried it away. Her big-girl bed was neatly made
as it had been that Friday morning we'd left for the beach.
Five stuffed animals were lined up in front of the pillow on
the blue-and-green bedspread she'd picked out herself. *Do
these colors harmonize, Mommy?* In the corner stood her play
kitchen, and across the room was a low table flanked by two

small chairs. Sticker books, coloring books, crayons and small containers of clay were piled neatly on one side of it.

"I love you," I whispered to the air. "I will always, always love you."

Across the room from where I stood was her bookcase. It was long and low enough to fit beneath the windows. I could see the spines of the books and from where I stood, I could make out a couple of the titles I wanted. The others, I would have to dig for a little. It would take me five steps to cross the room. One minute to squat down and pick out the books. But I felt frozen in the doorway. The floor of her room might as well have been the Grand Canyon.

"Erin?"

I turned to see Michael in the hallway behind me. I hadn't heard him on the stairs.

"I haven't touched her room," he said.

"I know. Thank you."

He stood next to me. "Do you want to…I don't know… Would it help you to go through her things? Start cleaning it out?"

"I'm nowhere near ready to do that," I said. "I don't want to touch it." Maybe that was why I couldn't cross the room to take the books. It was like taking Carolyn out of the room, piecemeal. A book here, a toy there, until she was gone.

"All right. I just thought…" His voice trailed off. "Seriously, I made way too much pasta. How did you always manage to make just the right amount?"

"Remember how she'd ask if colors harmonized?" I asked. "Remember when we sang 'Swanee River' in the kitchen?"

"Yes, I remember." He was talking to me in that slow, measured way he'd used ever since things started falling apart, as though he was afraid he'd pick the wrong word or the wrong inflection and send me into a crazy-woman tirade again. I really couldn't blame him for that.

"Do you ever come in here?" I asked.

"No," he said. "I don't like to. It's too hard." Gingerly, he rested his hand on my back. "I think all her toys and clothes should be donated, Erin. I think we should—"

"*Stop,*" I said. "I know what you think. That we should take all her stuff out and bring in a treadmill, but that's not going to—"

"I wasn't going to say that." He sighed, dropping his hand from my back. "Look, I'm going downstairs. I just wanted to say, this house is still your house. Your home. You can come anytime. You don't need to apologize for showing up without calling. I miss you."

"You miss the old me," I said. Just like I missed our old life. "You can't honestly miss the me I am now."

He looked down at the floor, hands in his pockets. "How's it going with Judith?" he asked. He was waiting for the magic cure.

"It's fine." I stepped back into the hallway and pulled Carolyn's door shut. "I'll get the things I need and leave," I said, knowing I'd be bringing nothing of Carolyn's to the coffee shop for Bella. I'd go to my closet, take some clothes I didn't need and then I'd drive away, wishing I'd never tried to come home at all.

22

Robin

I SAT ON A CHAIR IN THE BRIDAL SHOP HOLDING Hannah on my lap and staring into her amazing little face. She was a month old now and I couldn't see Alissa or any of the Hendricks family in her features. Her hair was blond and flyaway and she still had the dark, blue-gray eyes of an infant. Eyes that followed every move I made, I could swear, though Mollie said that just wasn't possible yet.

Mollie circled the platform where Alissa stood sulking in her sleek black bridesmaid's dress as the seamstress pinned the hem.

"I told you I'd never fit into this thing!" Alissa said. The dress *was* a little snug. It had been hard to order the right size for her when she was pregnant, since we had no idea how much baby weight she'd lose by the wedding.

"It looks great on you, Ali," I said. "You'll probably drop another pound by the wedding and it will be perfect."

"What if I don't? And my boobs are *still* enormous."

"Enjoy it while you have it," Mollie said. I liked that about Mollie. Appearances were important to her and she was probably slightly freaked out about the poor fit of Alissa's dress, but she acted like it was no big deal and that was really kind of her. I could tell how self-conscious Alissa felt on that platform and that self-consciousness on top of her depression was just too much for her. I knew better than anyone how upset she was these days. She was confiding in me a lot now, and I felt the weight of her secret longing for Will. That relationship had been far deeper and gone on far longer than anyone knew. Not only had her friend Jess taken her on those pretend dates where she'd meet up with Will, she'd also sneak out in the middle of the night and meet him in the Old Burying Ground. She told me the caring things he'd say to her and all the plans they'd had for the future. Every time I pictured those clandestine meetings, Will's face would morph into Travis's in my imagination.

I'd already had my turn on the platform. The seamstress had altered Mollie's wedding gown to fit me a couple of weeks ago and had only had the hem to do today. I'd stared at myself in the mirror as she worked. The dress was amazing. The only real change the seamstress had made to it was to add a bit of lace to the neckline to hide my scar. Yet I hadn't liked my reflection. Maybe it was because my hair was down and sloppy and I wasn't wearing any makeup, but in spite of the dress, I didn't look like a bride. I looked like a girl playing dress-up, wearing a dress that didn't really belong on her. Mollie and the seamstress oohed and aahed over it, but I wondered if they, too, could see how false I looked. I'd felt the same way the day before at the jeweler's, where Mollie took me to have Dale's grandmother's wedding ring resized for me. I was already wearing her engagement ring, the diamond so big I felt silly in it. The wedding ring would add another band of diamonds to my finger. The jeweler actually touched the nail of my index finger. "I can give you the name of a good manicurist," she said, and I curled my untended fingertips beneath my palm. Mollie just laughed, but I wondered if she was thinking the same thing.

Now I gently stroked Hannah's fluffy hair with those hands, my eyes on the baby's face. My thighs were locked together and Hannah rested in the valley they formed, her head near my knees. I loved holding her this way so I could take in every inch of her. Had someone held my own baby like this, staring into her face, filling up with love? The emotion was so deep and pure. It was unlike anything I'd ever felt before.

Early that morning, I'd strolled through the Old Burying Ground with an elderly couple from Tennessee. Over breakfast in the B and B's dining room, they'd asked me questions about the cemetery and I'd volunteered to bring them over. I'd been feeling sort of emotionally low the past few days. If my period hadn't just ended, I could have blamed it on PMS, but that wasn't the case. I thought playing tour guide might lift my spirits and I loved the cemetery. I loved the deep shade of the trees and the peaceful greenness of the place. Still, it hadn't done much to cheer me up. It actually had the opposite effect. Well, it was a *cemetery*. What had I expected?

I showed the couple the grave of the army surgeon who died on his wedding day in 1848, a thought which gave me a chill, since my own wedding day was such a short time away. I showed them the crooked old headstones of sailors and soldiers and the women who died in childbirth. They asked questions and I was pleased to know every single answer. Days like this, I felt like a native Beauforter. I *wanted* to be a native. "You'll be a native by marriage," Mollie'd reassured me. "People will accept you more."

I was already perfectly well accepted, and it took me a while to realize that Mollie meant "accepted" on a deeper level. On a "Who are your people, darlin'?" sort of level. It reminded me of my father telling me Travis wasn't "like us." But then again, everything was reminding me of Travis these days.

We came to the grave of the girl buried in a barrel of rum.

"Oh, my word!" The woman pointed to the only bit of tackiness in the ancient cemetery. The small raised grave was covered with stuffed toys and trinkets. A flag bearing the image of Blackbeard, another of Beaufort's famous—or, in his case, infamous—visitors, jutted from the side of the grave, and a purple baseball cap hung from one corner of the of the impossible-to-read headstone.

I told them the story about the little girl whose seafaring father had preserved her body in a keg of rum, and although I'd told the story a dozen—maybe *five* dozen—times before, it suddenly choked me up when I imagined the father losing his child so far from home. We continued walking through the cemetery while they chatted about the girl in the rum keg, and for the first time I noticed all the babies. Okay, maybe there weren't all that many, but their little headstones jumped out at me and I pictured every one of them alive in the arms of a loving father. A loving mother. A parent who would never recover completely from that baby's loss.

You could block things from your mind for years at a time. You could make them go away because you know that if you let them in, the pain could nearly kill you. That's how it was with Travis and the baby for me. I blocked them out, and I'd been successful at it until I held Hannah in my arms and wondered about that other baby. The one I couldn't wait to get out of my body. The child I had made a decision never to know.

"Robin?" Mollie asked. "Did you hear me?"

I looked up suddenly, realizing only then that Mollie had

been talking to me and I'd been so absorbed in Hannah and my memory of that morning stroll that I hadn't heard her.

The seamstress laughed. "She only has eyes for that baby," she said.

"We've got to get this girl married as soon as possible," Mollie said. "She has the worst case of baby hunger I've ever seen." Mollie touched my shoulder with affection. "Let Dale get settled in office before you go having a baby, now, okay?" She smiled.

I smiled back, but it felt false. How could I tell her it wasn't Dale's baby I was hungry for? It was my own. The baby who felt like a phantom. Like a dream.

Alissa had changed out of the dress and we were ready to go. I got to my feet, slipping the baby into the sling I was wearing, and we headed for the door, my mind a hundred miles away.

Did my baby and Travis still live in Carolina Beach, I wondered? Would Travis and his wife ever tell her about me? I hoped the woman he'd married was a great mother to my baby girl. Did she ever wonder about me, that woman? Was she starting to feel the tug on her daughter as I pulled her toward my heart?

Back at the B and B, I stared out the bay window of my apartment and felt nearly overwhelmed by the same sadness I'd felt in the Old Burying Ground. I didn't know exactly what was wrong with me lately. Why I couldn't shake the blues. It wasn't like the depression I'd suffered as I recovered from the transplant. It was more like a pall hanging over me. I needed to focus on gratitude, I told myself. I was alive and healthy. When had I started taking good health for granted? I had to be grateful for all the things that were going spectacularly well in my life, and there were plenty.

I stood up, walked into the little room I used as my office and sat down at my computer. I logged on to the Facebook page for Taylor's Creek Bed and Breakfast and added a status update: *Took visitors to the Old Burying Ground today. They were fascinated by the girl in the rum barrel.* I pulled a picture from my computer of the girl's grave and inserted it into the post.

And then I did what I knew I'd wanted to do all day—I typed the name *Travis Brown* into the search box. I held my breath for the one second it took Facebook to pop up with the names. There were two Travis Browns and a bunch of near misses—Travis Browning, Travis Byron, that sort of thing. The first Travis Brown was a black man, so I could skip him, but the other Travis had a boat instead of his picture as his profile image. My heart gave a little extra thump when I saw it. Travis could have a boat by now, living in Carolina Beach. He'd always wanted a boat. I hoped he put a life preserver on his daughter when he took her out in it. There were no other photos on this guy's profile, but his information told me he lived in Florida and was married with two children. And born in 1966. Not my Travis. *My Travis.* I actually thought that. Not good.

My imagination was definitely getting away from me. I looked on Google for Travis Brown and culled through the results without any luck. If someone searched for me— Robin Saville—they'd find tons of information. They'd find the bed-and-breakfast, of course. Loads of articles about me being engaged to Dale. They'd see that professionally shot photograph of me in pearls and the little black dress Mollie had bought me, my hair done up like I was a born-and-bred Southern belle. So not me. Born and bred, yes, but no belle. But I would do whatever I had to do for the sake of Dale's campaign.

So whatever Travis was doing these days—assuming he

was alive, which he absolutely had to be or I just couldn't bear it—he wasn't doing something that caught the radar of a search engine. I pictured him living a quiet life with his wife and daughter, working his butt off to support them.

I was making myself crazy imagining all the possible turns his life and my baby's life might have taken. I was thinking about him way, way too much.

Last night, Dale had sat with me here in my office as we compared our calendars for the next few weeks and he suddenly got really quiet.

"I feel like you're pulling away from me lately," he said

"What do you mean?" I felt busted. "Why?"

"You're much quieter than usual. You don't seem excited about the wedding. You haven't wanted me to stay over. You used to beg me to stay over." He gave me a smile.

"Oh," I said, looking away from him. "I'm sorry. I think I'm just nervous about the wedding. You know, being the center of attention." I felt guilty and dishonest, like I was living a lie. How could I be in the same room with Dale, beautiful Dale, and be thinking about Travis? I was becoming one of those sick women who tried to track down former boyfriends and totally mess up their own lives while they did it. When we were married, these feelings would go away like magic. I was counting on that.

"Most women love being the center of attention at their wedding," he said.

"I know," I said. "And I'm sure I will. It's just the…the anticipation that's getting to me." I wondered, as I did every once in a while, if someone from the media could dig up the fact that I'd had a baby, the way they'd dug up the truth about Debra and her first marriage. I should have told Dale long ago and dealt with the fallout. But why would I have told him about something I'd pretended never happened, even to myself?

I was logging off the computer when my phone rang and I saw Alissa's cell number on my caller ID. I could hear Hannah crying in the background when I answered.

"Can you come over for a while?" she asked. "Gretchen's not coming till four and Hannah's driving me crazy. She won't stop."

"Sure," I said.

I stood up with a sense of relief and headed for the door. I was glad to get away from the computer and my thoughts about Travis. It felt like a sickness to me and I refused to trade one sickness in for another. I was done being sick.

I found Alissa in the parlor pacing back and forth, jiggling Hannah against her shoulder as she tried to quiet her.

"Want me to take her for a while?" I asked.

"Hell, yes," she said, and I knew neither her parents or Dale must be home for her to talk that way. I took the baby from her arms and rocked her from side to side just to try something different. The way she was crying was enough to break my heart.

"Why don't we take her for a walk?" I said. "You've been cooped up in the house with her and it's beautiful out. We can try out her new stroller."

Alissa smoothed her long brown hair back from her face and fastened it into a ponytail. "She's just going to scream her head off while we're walking and everyone will think we're child abusers or something," she said.

"Maybe it will calm her down," I said.

She let out a long, world-weary sigh. "All right," she said.

We got the stroller from the mudroom at the back of the house and settled Hannah, still screaming her little head off, into it. It took both of us to carry the stroller down the back stairs, but as soon as Alissa started pushing it along the sidewalk, Hannah stopped crying.

"It's a miracle," Alissa said as we walked.

"Now we know the secret."

"I only wish I could do this when she's screaming in the middle of the night."

I pointed toward the water. "Let's walk along the water-front," I said.

"No, I want to go this way," Alissa said, turning onto Orange Street and away from Taylor's Creek.

"Really?" I said. "It's so pretty by the water today."

"Too many people," she said. "I don't want to go past all the shops where everyone will want to talk to us and see Hannah and everything."

I thought I understood. It was true we would attract attention from the locals. I couldn't go anywhere anymore without people recognizing me. Alissa wouldn't be quite as recognizable, since the Hendricks had done all they could to keep her out of the paper. The only picture that floated around the media of her was a school picture from a couple of years earlier, and she'd really changed since then. But seeing her with me, people would put two and two together and realize who she was and that she was walking the illegitimate baby the Hendricks family had welcomed so tolerantly.

"That's fine," I said, and we walked one block away from the water and then another and another. Hannah was a perfect angel. Neither Alissa nor I seemed to be in the mood for talking, and I was secretly glad. When she talked to me these days, it was usually about how much she missed Will and then I was stuck feeling like I was carrying around her secrets as well as my own.

"Want to turn around now?" I asked, when we'd walked

about half a mile. We were in a poorer neighborhood, the houses small, some of them in obvious need of repair. "I bet she'll sleep for a while now and you can get a nap."

"Let's go one more block," Alissa said, and I was surprised by how much she seemed to be into the walk now. When we reached the middle of the next block, she suddenly slowed down. "See that house two doors up on the right?" she asked.

I looked at the house. It was small, just one story, and it stood out from the others because it looked freshly painted. The siding was a creamy white, the shutters a pale aqua. The plants in the garden looked like they could use watering, but they still gave off some color.

"Uh-huh," I said. "What about it?"

"That's where Will lives."

So. This was the real reason she didn't want to walk along the waterfront. I put my hand on her arm.

"We should turn around," I said. "You're only torturing yourself."

"I just wanted you to see," she said. "I wanted you to see that it's a nice house. It's not like he lives in a slum or something. My parents and Dale totally suck."

"Let's turn around, Ali." I felt uncomfortable. I didn't want Will to suddenly pop out of his house. I already felt like I was deceiving Dale by talking with Alissa about Will. Bumping into him would be something else altogether. "Come on," I said. "Let's go back."

She obeyed but her eyes were red-rimmed. "Thanks for never telling Dale about that time I talked to Will on Skype," she said.

"You haven't done it again, have you?

She was quiet a moment, glancing back over her shoulder

at his house. "I tried once, but he said they could catch me and we shouldn't."

"He's right." I thought it was a good sign that Will was putting her needs first. "Right now, you need their support in every way, so it's best to just go along with them."

"Dale would be angry if he knew you talked with me about him," she said.

Yes, he really would be. "This is between you and me," I said. "Not Dale and me." That felt wrong enough to make me squeamish. I was letting Alissa know that I kept things from Dale. Letting her in on the biggest problem between Dale and me: secrets. "What I mean is, this is girl stuff. I love Dale and I'd never do anything to hurt him, but as long as you're not acting on your feelings for Will in a way that could hurt you or Hannah, you should be free to talk about them. Does that make sense?"

"I love him so much, Robin." She stopped walking long enough to stomp her foot on the sidewalk like an angry kid. "And I *hate* them for keeping me from him."

"I know," I said. I was relating way too strongly. Will wasn't Travis. Travis wasn't Will. The Hendricks family wasn't my father. I'd been sick. It was all so different. And yet I could feel her hurt and longing clear down to my toes. I put a hand on her shoulder.

"After the election and the wedding, when everything's settled down, I'll talk to Dale again about Will, all right? About you still being in love with him and—"

"No," she said. "Talking doesn't do any good. They're so stubborn and stupid. Once I'm out of school, I can do whatever I want. Hannah and me can move in with him and his mother. He said he'd wait for me."

Would he? Will was a young, good-looking guy. Would

he hang in there for another year of no contact with Alissa? I was so afraid of her getting hurt.

"I don't want to see you throw away your family," I said. "Maybe there's a way they can be convinced. They came around when they found out you were pregnant. They supported you and—"

"Oh, come on, Robin," she snapped. "They figured out a way to *use* me to get votes. That's what they do with everything, don't you get it? Somebody in the family has a pimple, they figure out how to use it to their advantage. Maybe appeal to the acne crowd or something. Just the way they're using you and the wedding."

I stopped walking, truly hurt. "They're not using me," I said, although I'd just accused Dale of that very thing, hadn't I? Hearing Alissa say it fed my insecurity.

She laughed. "No? You had this, like, major illness, but Dale loves you anyway. That makes him look good, right? It makes all the voters think he's this awesome guy and everything."

"That's ridiculous," I argued, but I knew in my gut there was truth in what she was saying.

"You're pretty naive," Alissa said. "My brother is not the saint you think he is."

"What do you mean?"

"I just know him better than you, that's all. He's not all that perfect."

"I know he's not perfect. No one is."

"Okay," she said. "We'll leave it at that."

Okay, I thought. *We will.* She was just angry with him because of Will.

We walked on, but Alissa's words about the wedding, about Dale, about *me* were rolling around inside my head. I remembered Dale telling me there were things I didn't know or need to know, and as we walked, I wondered if I was less a part of the Hendricks family than I'd thought I was. There was, for the first time, a little bit of relief in the idea. I wasn't one hundred percent sure right now that I wanted to belong.

23

Erin

I SAT ACROSS FROM JUDITH IN HER OFFICE, anxiously checking my watch. I'd almost canceled my appointment with her this morning because I was afraid that by the time I got to JumpStart, Travis and Bella would be gone. If I hadn't already known I'd become way too attached to Bella, I knew it then. I'd stopped in a store the evening before and bought her a couple of *Winnie the Pooh* books, since I'd been unable to walk across the floor of my daughter's room to take them from her bookshelf.

"You keep looking at your watch," Judith said to me. She was dressed in one of her usual outfits—a brightly colored, flowy top and long skirt. She always looked like a rainbow.

"I do?" I said, as though I didn't know I was repeatedly checking the time. "I have a dentist appointment."

I liked Judith. Actually, I thought I loved her. I knew that was called transference. She'd become my mother and my sister and my best friend, all rolled into one. Judith let me talk and talk and talk. When Michael and my friends were sick of hearing me describe what happened that night, sick of hearing me say *Why? Why? Why?*, Judith listened. She would listen forever if she needed to, and that's what I loved about her. She loved adages and always ended our session with one. *Sometimes the best way to hold on to something is to let it go,* she'd say. I hated that one, because I didn't agree with it. I would never, never let Carolyn go. *To know the road ahead, ask those who are coming back,* she'd say. That one, I liked. It made me think of the Harley's Dad group, how the parents who'd been grieving years longer than me were helping me survive the journey.

Judith had suggested I bring in pictures of Carolyn, something I still wasn't ready to do, and she thought it was fine that I didn't want to change Carolyn's room. She made me feel not crazy, while Michael and my friends made me feel as though I was grieving the wrong way. *Ruminating,* as Michael would say.

But there was one thing I didn't feel ready to talk to Judith about in any depth and that was how I was feeling about Bella and Travis. I wasn't sure why. I'd known Bella and Travis for ten days now and I was so afraid she'd say it was unhealthy that I was growing attached to a child who was essentially a stranger to me. I just didn't feel like examining my feelings about Bella with Judith. Not yet. Which is why I lied about my reason for checking my watch. Judith believed me about the dentist appointment; I could tell she did. But I'd never been a comfortable liar and the guilt finally did me in.

"I just lied to you," I said.

"What about?"

"I don't have a dentist appointment. I'm just...I'm afraid to tell you why I'm in a rush today."

"What are you afraid of?"

"It's that... You know how I hang out in that coffee shop every morning?"

She nodded.

"I told you about that man and his daughter who came in about a week or so ago?"

She nodded. I'd mentioned Bella and Travis to her, but that was before my feelings for them had mushroomed into something that seemed out of my control. "Well, they come in every morning now. The little girl—her name is Bella—is four."

"The age Carolyn would be now."

"Right. And I..." I straightened my wedding rings on my finger. They'd gotten so loose. "I like seeing her. Talking to her." *Holding her.* "I'll be getting there late this morning and I don't want to miss getting to see her."

"You've avoided your friends' children," Judith said. "You've said it's too hard to be around them. Why is this different?"

I thought about it. "I'm not sure," I said. "With my friends, we were always doing things together. My friends and their kids and Carolyn and me, so now when I'm with them it's uncomfortable for me and I can tell it is for them, too. Our kids were what we had in common. I don't think they want me there. But with Travis...he has no idea about Carolyn. He doesn't know I have...*had* a child. So it's just easier. And the little girl is nothing like Carolyn, really. She doesn't look like her. She's not as outgoing and chatty and happy-go-lucky as Carolyn was. She's adorable, though." I smiled. "She carries this stuffed lamb around with her and a little pink purse. I think they may actually be homeless, though I'm not positive. I'm worried about..." I stopped. Took in a deep breath. "I'm rambling," I said.

"You can ramble in here anytime you like," Judith said.

"The past few days, when I get up in the morning, I'm

actually looking forward to something," I said. "But that's sick, isn't it? They're strangers to me."

"Connecting with other people isn't sick," Judith said. "And they're no longer strangers, either. Are you interested in this man? Travis?"

Her question took me by surprise and I laughed. "No, not at all! He's half my age. Well, I mean, he's in his early twenties. Hot, though. Very hot. If I were twenty and single, yes, I'd be interested. At least physically, but as I said, he seems hard up. He's trying to find a job and everything keeps falling through for him. I feel sorry for him and worried about Bella." I looked at my watch again.

"Are you worried this is becoming an obsession?" Judith asked.

I shook my head, but thought, *Yes,* it's becoming an obsession, and no, I wasn't worried about it. I welcomed it.

Judith leaned forward, a small smile on her lips. "Do you remember when I said you'd know you're beginning to heal when you start looking forward to something with happy anticipation?"

"Well, this is not exactly happy anticipation," I said. "It's just…" I shrugged, my voice trailing off. It was the word *happy* that got me. I couldn't let myself be happy about anything. It felt wrong somehow.

"Do you want to end early?" Judith asked.

I nodded.

She smiled again. "All right," she said, "but here's your adage for the week."

I reached for my purse and stood up. "What?"

"Honor the past, but live in the present."

"Right, okay," I said, the words barely registering as I rushed out the door.

★ ★ ★

Minutes later, I sat in the leather chair at JumpStart, trying to read the morning's posts from the Harley's Dad group, but I couldn't concentrate. I kept glancing through the windows of the coffee shop to the parking lot, watching for them. It was after ten. Where were they? They'd been here by this time every morning, and with each passing minute, my heart sank deeper in my chest. I looked down at my iPad. Sad-Mamma had posted that her in-laws were coming to town tomorrow and she was dreading it. Mom-of-Five wondered if she might be pregnant and didn't know whether to hope that she was or wasn't.

I spotted them outside. Travis was walking quickly toward the Jumpstart entrance, holding Bella's hand as she trotted next to him, her skinny little legs trying to keep up with him. I felt a smile spread across my face as he pushed open the door and both he and Bella immediately looked in my direction. I waved, so relieved to see them. *Happy anticipation.* Yes, there was no other way to describe what I'd been feeling.

"Hey," Travis said when he and Bella reached the circle of worn leather furniture where I always sat. He was holding a small bunch of flowers at his side. I noticed the two young women sitting at a table near the window eying him up and down, then whispering to each other. "How's it going?" he asked.

"Good." I smiled at Bella. "Good morning, honey." I reached out to touch her arm. "How are you today?"

Bella leaned against Travis's leg, her ragged stuffed lamb clutched to her chest and the pink purse dangling from her wrist. "We had Tic Tacs for breakfast," she said.

"Well, we'll get something a little better here," Travis said. He smoothed his hand over her messy brown hair and

I wondered, as I had every morning, if that hair was ever combed. I wanted to smooth her too-long bangs off her forehead.

"Did you?" I asked. "Were they yummy?"

She nodded. Her nose was a little runny as usual, the skin beneath it raw, and I had to stop myself from reaching out with my napkin to clean her up.

"We need to use the bathroom, don't we, Bell?" Travis asked. "You'll be here a minute?"

"Oh, I'm not going anywhere."

"These are for you." Travis reached toward me with the fistful of wildflowers. "Bella picked them for you this morning."

"How pretty!" I looked into Travis's clear gray eyes as I took the loose bouquet from him. I knew why he was giving the flowers to me—it was the only way he could say thank you for the twenty-dollar bill I'd slipped into Bella's pocket. I put the flowers on the coffee table. "Thank you, Bella," I said.

"Looks like Miss Erin has a new book to read you." Travis nodded toward *Winnie the Pooh,* where it rested on the table next to my chair.

"I got to go potty, Daddy," Bella said.

"Right." Travis reached for her hand again. "We'll be back in a sec," he said to me.

I watched them walk toward the men's room, where I knew they'd be a long time, as they were each morning. It was their routine, just like mine was sitting in this brown leather chair with my coffee and iPad and the Harley's Dad group. Next week, I'd be going back to work and I'd miss seeing Travis and Bella more than I could say. I didn't even want to think about it.

When they returned, I moved the book from my lap to

the arm of the chair. "I think you're going to love this one, Bella," I said, holding my arms toward her. She stepped into them so easily now and I lifted her up and set her on my lap. This was the third day in a row I'd read to her, the third day I'd been able to hold her like this and feel her rib cage beneath my hands and smell the little girl musk of her hair. The third day I'd fought the burn of tears in my eyes.

"I'm going to grab my coffee and our muffin," Travis said. "Can I get you anything, Erin?"

"I'm fine," I said. He asked me this every day even though I always said no. "I picked up an OJ for Bella," I added, pointing at the carton on the end table. Buying her orange juice was getting to be a habit. Travis glanced at the carton and I thought he was going to protest, but then he gave a little nod.

"Okay," he said. "Thanks."

I began reading to Bella. She rested her head against my chest in a way that took my breath away.

"That's bumblebees!" She interrupted my reading to point to an illustration of bees.

"Right," I said. "Do you know what they make?"

"Bzzzzz," she said.

"That's the sound they make." I smiled. "But they make a kind of food, too—"

"Honey!"

"Right. And Winnie the Pooh loves honey," I said, and then went back to reading the story.

Travis returned with a small cardboard cup of coffee for himself, a plastic cup of water for Bella and a blueberry muffin I knew he'd split with Bella, as he did every day.

The young women by the window glanced in his direction again. The blonde fanned her face as though she was burning up, and her friend laughed.

"Come over here to eat your muffin so you don't get it all over Miss Erin," Travis said to Bella when I'd finished reading the first chapter.

"Oh, she's fine here," I said. "Just set the water on the table."

I was surprised when Travis handed Bella the entire muffin on a napkin. It was the first time I hadn't seen him split it. She'd probably spill crumbs all over my yoga pants, but I didn't care. I wanted to hold her as long as she'd let me. *My happy anticipation.* I rubbed her back lightly and she leaned into my touch.

"So, just a couple more days till you go back to work?" Travis sipped his coffee, looking at me over the top of the cup.

"Don't remind me," I said.

"Do you ever feel, you know, *tempted* being around all those drugs all the time?" Travis asked.

My glance was sharp and for the first time I wondered if he might be an addict. It would explain his slender frame. His lack of money. But I didn't think so. It didn't fit with what I'd learned about him in the past week and a half, and I just plain liked him too much to believe it. Yet how well did I really know him?

"Not even a little bit," I said, although that was a teeny tiny lie. That one day I'd gone back to work, the narcotics had had an appeal to me they'd never had before. I could take a handful of them and the pain would go away. "And please don't tell me you *would* be tempted," I said to him. I held Bella a little tighter.

"No way," he said. "It's not my thing." His grin was familiar, but I realized there was something different about him today. He seemed a little wired, bouncing his knee up and down and tapping his fingers on the arm of the leather couch. I wanted to ask him if he had any job leads, but he had to be tired of me asking that question. As if reading my mind, though, he took another swallow of his coffee, then said, "I've got another interview today."

"Great!" I said. "You found something on Craigslist?"

"No, my friend came through," he said, tapping his fingers faster. "I hope this one works out."

"Oh, me too, Travis." Maybe I *could* help him find child care. Maybe one of my old friends knew someone in the area. "I guess it's in construction? Is it for a business? Or residential? Or—"

"I've got the info in my van," he said, standing up suddenly. "Can you watch Bella a sec and I'll go get it? I can tell you the address and maybe you can tell me how to get there."

"Sure," I said.

He hesitated a moment, then leaned over, cupping Bella's head with his hands and pressing his lips to her temple. His face was close to mine, but he turned his head away quickly and walked to the door. The young women by the window stared after him as he walked down the sidewalk and around the corner of the building toward the parking lot.

"Read some more?" Bella asked, her palm on the cover of the book. "Please?"

I opened the book and read for about ten minutes, wondering what was taking Travis so long. I read another chapter, my mind only half on the story, my worry mounting. I kept glancing through the windows at the sidewalk. This was a little weird.

"Where's Daddy?" Bella asked finally, looking toward the door. I checked my watch. It had been twenty-five minutes, at least. The two women stood up and left.

"Maybe he got sidetracked," I said, closing the book. "Let's go see if we can find him."

Bella held my hand—oh, that feeling!—and we walked out to the sidewalk and around the corner of the building where I'd seen Travis disappear. There were rows upon rows of cars in the massive parking lot and I realized I had no idea what his looked like. A van, he'd said. I walked with Bella down the first row of vehicles, then the next. "What color is your Daddy's van?" I asked Bella.

"White," she said. "Its name is Moby Dick."

"Like the white whale?"

"Uh-huh."

There were no white vans. One white pickup, but I didn't think that was it. "I guess he had to run an errand," I said.

"What's an errand?"

"Go to the store."

Bella looked toward the endless sea of stores that lined the parking lot. He could be anywhere. I had no idea what to do. I looked at my watch again. He'd been gone close to an hour now. *This is unreal,* I thought. I felt as if I were in a dream, one with the potential to turn into a nightmare. The whole world felt out of kilter. The sky was an unnatural blue. The sun bounced off the sidewalk in sharp bursts of light. And the shapes of the cars in the parking lot ran together in a multicolored sea of metal.

The only thing that felt real to me was the trusting little hand in mine.

24
Robin

2007

WHEN I WOKE UP—*FULLY* WOKE UP—A FEW days after my heart transplant, I had two memories. One was of a view from the ceiling of the operating room, looking down at the doctors frantically working over my open, bloody chest. I remembered feeling calm and curious as I watched them. I wanted to tell them how peaceful I felt, because they seemed so scared down there. The second memory was less clear. My father's voice came to me through a haze of beeping machines and the hiss of the ventilator. Against my ear, I felt the rough material of the mask he had to wear in my room. *The baby never happened,* he whispered to me, like a hypnotist. *Put it all behind you, Robin. That part of your life never happened.*

As the nurses helped me sit up, both memories slipped out of my head at the same moment, leaving me with a searing pain in my breastbone, a foggy brain and the realization that my life had changed forever.

Over the next couple of weeks, I learned that by the time a heart had been found for me, I'd only had days to live and that I actually *had* died in the operating room, but they were able to get me back. My surgeon's face went white when I told him I'd watched the whole thing from the ceiling, but by then I wasn't sure if I'd made it up or not.

I started rehab, which was grueling and painful and amazing, because my heartbeat was so steady and my breathing improved each day. My father came to the live-in rehab center nearly every day to encourage me. I felt as though whatever anger I'd had toward him had left with my old heart. This new one seemed pure and open, ready for me to fill it with new experiences. New emotions.

One day, a couple of months into my rehab, Daddy walked me back to my room. That wasn't unusual, but his quietness and the way he tightly cupped my elbow was, and I had the feeling something was up. Sure enough, when we were nearly to my room, he put his arm around me.

"I need to tell you something, Robin," he said, his hand gently massaging my shoulder. "I wasn't going to tell you at all, but the social worker thinks you need to know. She said if I didn't tell you, she would, so we'll discuss it just this once and then never again, all right?"

I stopped walking, suddenly worried. Was something wrong with my new heart? "What are you talking about?" I asked.

He nudged me toward my room and I walked ahead of him inside, then turned to face him. He looked past me, toward the window. He didn't seem to want to look me in the eye. I thought it was good my roommate wasn't there because something was definitely wrong. "What's going on?" I asked.

"It's about the baby," he said.

From the time I was twenty-eight weeks pregnant to the time I woke up from my heart transplant, I'd had almost zero awareness of anything going on around me. I had no memory of that baby being taken from my body. I'd never seen her. Never cared about seeing her. "Is she all right?" I asked.

He closed the door and stood in front of it. "As far as I know, she's fine," he said. "But...you had them write Travis's name on the birth certificate, honey." He reached out to touch my arm, as though he was forgiving me for doing that. "So he had to be notified about the adoption. The potential adoption. And he fought it." He shook his head as though he couldn't believe Travis was that stupid. "I tried to prevent him from taking custody," he said. "Such a monumental, asinine mistake. But he won." He shrugged. "The couple you wanted to adopt her didn't get her."

"Oh, no," I said, lowering myself to the edge of my bed. One reason I could so easily push that baby from my mind was because I knew I had done the right thing for her. She'd have two parents who had the money to give her everything. And yet, she belonged with Travis, didn't she?

"I tried to fight Travis in court," my father said, "but he's the baby's father and that won the day for him."

I'd been wrong about my new heart being completely empty of my old emotions. At the mention of Travis—just hearing the two syllables of his name—my heart nearly turned itself inside out from missing him. *She'll have love,* I thought. Maybe she'd never have her own TV or the most expensive computer or go to private schools, but when it came to love, she couldn't do any better than Travis.

I hadn't said a word and my father was staring hard at me. "Are you all right?" he asked. "The social worker thought—"

"I need to talk to him," I said.

"No." He gave a violent shake of his head. "Don't even think about doing that, Robin."

"I don't want a say in raising her or anything," I said quickly. That was the truth. I felt no attachment to her at all. "I just want to tell him I know he has her and it's okay with me." I was *glad*, in fact. The more I thought about it, the more right it seemed.

"You don't owe him that," Daddy said. "You don't owe him anything."

"Okay," I said, deciding not to fight with him. I'd email Travis on my own. My father never needed to know.

"Seriously, Robin, just put this out of your mind."

"I said okay."

He said nothing for a moment, and I knew he didn't believe I was going to let it go this easily.

"You never could understand what he did to you," he said. "How callously he treated you. You sounded like a naive little girl in the email you wrote, telling him not to blame himself. Well, *I* blame him. I—"

"*What?*" I frowned at him. "How could you know what I wrote to him?"

He ran his hands through his hair. "It doesn't matter," he said.

"How could you possibly know that?"

"You were so sick, hon—"

"Did you go on my computer?"

He sighed and leaned tiredly against the door. "For your own good," he said.

I couldn't believe what I was hearing. "You were *spying* on me?"

"When you're a parent you'll understand. You were at a vulnerable point in your life, Robin." He began to pace around the room. "I had to protect you. You kept putting your health in jeopardy. I was doing everything I could think of to keep you healthy and you sabotaged me at every turn. That boy...that *idiot*...you think he loved you? He doesn't know what love is. All he was thinking about was himself and what he wanted, not what you needed. I'm not the least bit surprised he didn't put the best interest of his child first. I wasn't going to let him destroy you, so yes, I blocked him on your computer and I stopped your email from going out to him."

I stood up, furious. "That was so unfair!" I shouted. "That was cruel!"

"Shh. Peace and calm."

"How could you *do* that to me?"

"Let it go," he said. "You're over him, thank God. Now you have a new heart and you'll—"

I tried to hit him, but he caught my arms and pulled me into a hug I couldn't escape from. I'd never felt so much anger before and I didn't know what to do with it.

"This is why I didn't want to tell you," he said. "I knew it would only upset you. You were doing so well, but the social worker—"

I struggled free of his arms. "Guess what, Daddy?" I said. "I can use the computer *here* any time I want and you can't do a thing about who I email."

"He's married, Robin."

"What?" I felt the fight suddenly go out of me, my arms dropping limply to my sides.

"He's married. He met someone right after you two broke up and if you care about that baby at all, you need to just leave them alone to become a family. I only hope whoever he married has more sense than he does."

He was married? While I was so sick and out of it, he'd met another girl. Fallen in love with another girl. I turned away from my father. I didn't want him to see how hurt I was that Travis could so easily forget about me. Now that I knew he'd never gotten my emails, how could I blame him? Did that girl have a father who saw past Travis's social status and supported their relationship instead of tearing it down?

"You need to move on with your life and let Travis move on with his," Daddy said.

I had to be an adult about this. It was good the baby had two parents, I told myself. It was good she was with her biological father and hopefully he'd found someone who'd treat the baby like her own. I let those thoughts run through my mind. Maybe in time I would really believe them.

"I'm tired," I said, pulling back the covers on my bed. "I'm going to take a nap."

"Good idea, honey." He moved toward me and rested his hand on the side of my head. "I know this was all hard to hear, but you're a strong girl and I know you'll be fine."

"Right," I said again, and I climbed into the bed and lay down with my back to him.

"I'll see you tomorrow, then," he said.

Go, I thought. *Just go.* All I wanted was to be alone with the hurt I was feeling. And the loneliness. And the part of my life that never happened.

25
Erin

AFTER BELLA AND I HAD SEARCHED THE parking lot for Travis's van for nearly an hour, we walked back into the coffee shop.

"We'll wait here for him," I said, sitting down on the sofa next to Bella. "I'm sure he'll be back in a few minutes."

"Maybe he went to fill her up," Bella said, her gaze on the door.

"Fill her up? You mean get gas?"

Bella nodded. "Moby Dick needs a lot of gas."

"That's probably it," I said, but I was both disappointed in Travis and angry. Worried, too. Could something have happened to him on his walk to the van? But then, wouldn't the van be there? This didn't make any sense.

"You didn't drink your juice yet," I said as I sat down again. I pulled the straw from the side of the carton, unwrapped it and stuck it into the juice.

"Read me more of the book again, please," she said.

"I like your manners."

"What's manners?"

"When you say *please* and *thank you*. That's good manners."

She leaned forward to pick up the book from the coffee table. I opened it and began reading, but I was no longer putting my heart and soul into it. I was watching the door with a mounting sense of dread.

The chapter took all of ten minutes to get through and by the time I'd finished, Bella was done with her juice and getting squirmy. She climbed off my lap and ran to the door, pressing her small hands and forehead against the glass as she peered outside.

"Bella," I called, "stay with me, honey."

She came back to the couch and sat down. "Where did Daddy go to fill her up?" she asked.

"I don't know." I didn't want to say those empty words *He'll be back soon* to her again, because I now had the sinking feeling they would be a lie. "I think he must have gotten sidetracked."

"What's sidetracked?"

I let out a sigh. "He must have gone into a store or something." I glanced at my watch. Something was very, very wrong.

"I got to go potty." Bella stood up again.

"Okay." I took her hand and headed with her toward the ladies' room. "Do you want privacy?" I asked as we walked into the room. I expected her to say "What's privacy?" but instead she said, "I don't like to be alone."

"Okay," I said. "I'm right here."

She lowered her pants and I spotted the corner of a piece of paper sticking out of her pocket. "What's in your pocket?" I asked.

With her pants around her thighs, she pulled the piece of paper from her pocket. "Did you put it in?" she asked, handing it to me.

I took it from her and she climbed onto the toilet. The paper was nothing more than a gas station receipt dated the day before, so I could rule out the "went to fill her up" theory. I was about to toss it in the trash can when I saw handwriting on the other side.

Just for tonight. Please keep her safe. Thank you.

"Oh, my God," I said, staring at the paper. "Why didn't he just *ask* me?"

"Ask what?" Bella said from her perch on the toilet.

"A favor," I said. "Your daddy wanted a favor." He probably couldn't show up at the interview with a little girl in tow. Was he afraid I'd say no—which I probably would have, because I was not equipped, physically or emotionally, for a four-year-old in my apartment. That was the real reason for the flowers. A thank-you in advance.

Bella reached for the toilet paper, wiped herself and stood up, bending over to pull her pants up.

I knew what any one of my friends would do in this situation: they'd call the police. I didn't know what Travis's problems were, but I did know he loved his daughter. This was really wrong of him. Really stupid. But I wasn't going to turn him in for it and have Bella end up in foster care overnight. Travis was trusting me with her. When I turned her over to him in the morning, I'd have a major talk with him. I'd ask him point-blank about his living situation. We'd get everything out on the table. I'd figure out what kind of help he needed. If it was child care, I'd get serious about helping him find it. I'd help him, but I'd chew him out, too. He left his daughter with me, but what did he really know about me? Barely anything. How did he know he could trust me with her? My brain was going a mile a minute.

"Well, guess what, Bella?" I said, as I lifted her up to the sink so she could wash her hands.

"What?"

"This note is from your Daddy and he asked if I could babysit you tonight." I looked at our reflection in the mirror and felt the slightest jolt at the image of me holding a child other than Carolyn.

"Where?" she said, back on the floor and drying her hands. "In the burned-down house?"

"What burned-down house?"

"Where Nana babysitted me?"

Burned-down house? Nana in heaven? Oh, God. I hoped there was no connection there.

"No," I said. "At my house." My apartment was as un-child friendly as a home could be. Plus I had no car seat in my car. How was I going to get her to the apartment and back to JumpStart again in the morning without a car seat? This was ridiculous. *Ridiculous!* I could buy one in Target, I thought, but I knew where there was a car seat. Same place there were books and toys and anything else I could possibly need to occupy a child for an afternoon and evening.

I suddenly had the strangest, almost unrecognizable feeling—*happiness*. I was *happy* Travis had dumped this on me. He'd given me something to do. Something useful. And I would have nearly twenty-four hours alone with Bella.

"Let's go," I said. I took her hand and we walked out of the shop and into the parking lot again, this time to my car. "Now, I don't have a car seat in the car," I said, "so I'm going to buckle you in like a big girl in the backseat and drive very carefully, but then we're going to get a car seat at my old—" I stopped talking. This was going to be way too much explanation. "We have two stops to make," I began again. "I used to live in a house where there's a car seat we can use and lots of toys and books and things we can take to the house where I live now. Then we can play and read all evening and in the morning we'll go back to the coffee shop and your daddy will be there. Okay?"

Her lower lip started to quiver and I held her hand tighter. Standing next to my car, she was so tiny, her big gray eyes filling with tears of confusion. I bent over and lifted her up, held her close, her cheek to mine. "It's going to be all right," I said. "We'll have fun. I promise."

I buckled her into the backseat, wishing I had something I could use to boost her up a little. Bella cried, but quietly, as though she didn't expect me to fix things for her. As though she was used to her life not going according to plan.

"It's all right, sweetie," I ran my hand over her dirty hair. She'd get a bubble bath tonight. A shampoo. "You'll see," I added with a smile. "Everything's going to be just fine."

Michael was at work, thank God, so Bella and I had the house to ourselves. I talked her into leaving her purse along with mine on the kitchen table, but she insisted on carrying her lamb with her upstairs. She'd stopped crying, though she had grown very quiet, and she didn't say a word as we reached the upstairs hallway. I chattered nonstop to try to keep my nerves under control. "A little girl used to live here," I said, "and she would love it if we packed up some of her toys to play with and her books to read."

I licked my dry lips and opened the door to Carolyn's room. I stood in the doorway, but Bella didn't notice the invisible wall that kept me out. She walked straight through it and over to the play kitchen. She stood there for a moment, studying the knobs on the plastic stove, the pots and pans and the bowls of wooden fruit and vegetables. Then she smiled and started playing make-believe.

"Will you cook me something?" I asked.

She looked up at me. "You sit here," she said, pointing to one of the tiny chairs at the small table in the corner.

"That chair's too little for me, I think," I said. "How about I sit on the bed?"

"Okay." She was putting wooden tomatoes in a plastic saucepan, so she didn't see me as I stepped through the invisible wall. I walked the five steps to Carolyn's bed and fell onto it more than sat down on it, my knees giving out. My heart was beating at a ridiculous rate. I rested my palm flat on the bedspread with its harmonizing blues and greens. "What are you making?" I asked. There was a tiny crack in my voice.

"Momlet," she said, opening the brown plastic eggshells to let the rubbery fried eggs drop into the pot with the tomatoes.

"It looks delicious," I said. "Do you like omelets? Maybe we can have one for dinner?"

She looked at me like I was as loony as I was feeling. "This is just *pretend* momlets," she said.

"Oh, I know. I was thinking we could have real ones later. What do you like in yours?"

She didn't answer. Her face was full of concentration as she stirred the noisy concoction together in the pan.

"I need to go in the attic to get a car seat," I said. "Are you okay here by yourself? I'll be just two minutes."

"I'm okay," she said.

I left the room and headed for the hallway door that led to the attic stairs. I was halfway up them when I heard Bella scrambling behind me. I turned. "You decided to come with me?" I asked.

"I'm not okay by myself," she said, reaching for my hand.

"Okay, that's fine."

I had no idea where in the attic Michael had stored the car seat. The attic was unfinished and dimly lit even after I pulled the chain on the bare light bulb at the top of the stairs.

"What *is* this place?" Bella asked.

"It's an attic," I said. "Have you ever been in an attic before?"

"Are there ghosts here?" She stayed close by my side.

"Oh, no," I said with a laugh. "There's no such thing as ghosts." But there *were* ghosts up here. At least one. I could feel her leading me to the corner of the attic as surely as if she'd taken my hand, and there it was—the car seat wrapped in a clear plastic bag. "I found the car seat!" I said. "Now we can buckle you safely into my car."

"Right now? I wanted to play in the little girl's room more."

"You can," I said. "As a matter of fact, I'll get a tote bag and we can take some of the toys and books you like over to my house. My new house."

"Okay." She held the railing and walked down the stairs one at a time, just the way Carolyn used to, and I felt one tiny panicky moment of confusion about what child I was with. Oh, I knew it was Bella. I knew exactly what was going on, but I seemed to *want* the confusion. I wanted to believe that Bella could turn around and it would be Carolyn's brown eyes I'd be looking into. I wanted the impossible to be possible.

Back in Carolyn's room, I squatted in front of the bookshelf. For some reason, this seemed like the hardest thing to me. The books were so loved. Carolyn knew all the words to nearly every story. She'd correct me or Michael if we screwed up and got a sentence wrong. She didn't care if she'd heard a story a thousand times before, she wanted to hear it again. Bella was that way, too, with *The Cat in the Hat*. When Carolyn was little, she'd point to each picture, telling me what it was or asking me if she didn't know or couldn't remember. When she was a little older, she'd grow impatient if I read too slowly, turning the page herself before I'd finished reading it. It had always been hard for Carolyn to sit still for long even though she still loved the books.

I pulled one of them from the shelf. "Do you want to help me pick out some books, Bella?" I asked. She'd deserted the play kitchen for one of Carolyn's dollhouses. Carolyn had two of them. There was the elaborate Victorian that Michael's father had built for her, decorated with gingerbread on the outside and wallpaper on the inside. It was beautiful, but she usually ignored it in favor of the second—a small, plastic princess dollhouse that she adored. Bella, too, went right to that dollhouse. "I'll just pick out a few books," I said, and I grabbed a handful without looking at them. Easier that way. No memories in a handful.

I was wrong about the book selection being the hardest thing to do, though. Bella needed clothes. I opened two of Carolyn's dresser drawers and pulled out pants and shirts, pajamas and underwear, without really thinking about it. I dropped them on the bed next to the books.

I walked into the master bedroom to look for a tote bag in the closet. I was astounded to see the bed was made. I didn't think Michael had made the bed once during all the years we were married. I found the tote bag and carried it back into Carolyn's room. "Pick out four toys to take with us," I said to Bella, putting the books in the bag.

"This one." She pointed to the princess dollhouse.

"That won't fit in here, but we can carry it. It folds up. So that's one. What else?"

Bella glanced at the play kitchen and I was about to veto that choice when she looked past it to Chutes and Ladders on a shelf above the plastic stove. Carolyn had never shown any interest in that game. It had no memories attached to it and that was just fine. I added the game to the books in the bag. Bella reached for the stuffed polar bear on the bed and I almost said "No!" but stopped myself. *Carolyn's not here. She won't miss it. And she'd share it, anyway.* No, actually, she wouldn't have. Carolyn hadn't been big on sharing. I'd worried that was because we'd put off having a second child too long, and that she'd have trouble adjusting to a new baby when we finally had one. Stupid, the things I'd worried about. I'd worried about all the wrong things.

"Good," I said as Bella dropped the polar bear into the bag. "One more toy. Would you like a DVD?"

"No, thank you." She wandered around the room thoughtfully, a finger to her lips. She pointed to a plastic box containing Carolyn's little tea set. "What's this?" she asked.

"It's a tea set," I said. "We can play with it later, if you like. We can have a tea party."

She handed me the box and I put it in the bag.

"Okay," I said. "We're all set."

We went out to the car and I fastened the car seat in the backseat, my hands working from muscle memory. There was a small stain on the edge of the cushion from the day Carolyn spilled her cranberry juice. I'd never been able to get it out. I had to look away.

What would Judith have to say about all this? I'd gone into Carolyn's room. I'd touched her things and hadn't fallen apart. Would she think I was crazy to take care of a child I didn't really know? A child whose father had dumped her on me without leaving me a phone number or, I realized, even his last name? I *was* crazy. Still, I was doing it, and suddenly I was living in the here and now. *Honor the past, but live in the present.* I shivered with a smile. Judith was always one step ahead of me.

Bella climbed into the car seat, pushing my hands away as I tried to buckle her in. "I can do it," she said, and she did.

I chatted with her about lunch as I drove back to Brier Creek. I was going over what I had in the house in my mind, hoping I didn't need to stop at the grocery store.

"How about a cheese sandwich for lunch?" I asked.

"Do you have any mac and cheese?" she asked.

"Actually, I do." It was a Weight Watchers frozen macaroni and cheese dinner—with my meager appetite these days and my lack of interest in cooking, I'd gotten big into those little frozen dinners. "I'll make you some."

We ate lunch in my kitchen and then I let Bella explore the small apartment with me at her side. I wanted her to know her surroundings and feel safe here. I'd never noticed before how sunny and bright the apartment was. Beams of sunlight danced over the glass-topped coffee table and lit up the beige carpeting. On the floor, we played with the princess dollhouse and her doll until she started getting cranky and asking for Travis.

"Would you like a nap?" I asked.

She shook her head, then nodded. "My sleeping bag's in Moby Dick," she said.

I was right, then. They were homeless and living in Travis's van. "Is that where you sleep, honey? In the van?"

She nodded. "I used to sleep in the burned house before it got burned. Then in the trailer. Then in Moby Dick. It's cold."

Yes. The nights were definitely getting chilly. I could

imagine how cold it would be waking up in a van in the morning. I could give her a much better life than that.

What are you thinking? I scolded myself.

"Well, I have a big bed we can share," I said. The one extravagance the landlord had added to the simply furnished apartment was a king-size bed. "You'll be warm tonight. Come on. Let's go check it out."

We walked together into the bedroom.

"This is the biggest bed I ever seen!" Bella said. It was high, too, and I had to help her up onto it. I brought one of the dining room chairs into the room and pushed the back of it up against the bed, just in case she was a roller. I smiled as I settled her under the covers, her little lamb tucked under her arm. She was so cute. She looked a little lost, both in the vast sea of the bed and in this long, strange day. I bent forward and kissed her forehead.

"Sleep tight," I said, for the first time ever to a child that wasn't mine.

"You'll stay here?" she asked.

"Absolutely," I said. "I'm going to take a nap, too." I walked around to my side of the bed, slipped out of my yoga pants and shoes and climbed in.

"Sleep tight," she said back to me. "Don't let the bedbugs bite."

In less than a minute, she was asleep. I lay on my side and studied her face as her eyelids fluttered with her dreams. I knew I wouldn't sleep. I wanted just to watch her. I wanted to savor every moment of this day that felt so bittersweet.

26

Robin

I WAS ASLEEP WHEN MY PHONE RANG. MY FIRST thought was that my father had taken a turn for the worse—that's how out of it I was. *It can't be Daddy,* I reminded myself as I reached for the phone on the night table. *He's already gone.*

"Hello?" I said. My voice was barely a whisper.

"She's dead!" Alissa screamed. "Hurry! She's dead!"

"Who?" I sat up quickly.

"Hannah!" she wailed. "Hurry!"

"Call 911!" I flung the phone onto my bed and raced out of my room, somehow remembering to grab the key to Hendricks House from the key rack near my front door. I ran barefoot across the lawn between the houses.

James and Dale were at a conference in Raleigh, but I reminded myself that Mollie was home. Alissa was not alone. It was amazing how quickly different scenarios could fly through your brain. Alissa had killed her, stabbing her in a post-partum depression fury for ruining her life. No, she wouldn't do that. *SIDS.* Hannah had rolled onto her tummy and suffocated. Or a fall. Alissa might have drifted off to sleep while feeding her and dropped her. By the time my trembling hands unlocked the front door of Hendricks House, I'd imagined all these things and more.

I heard Alissa's sobs coming from her room as soon as I opened the door. Mollie was in the hallway, pulling on her robe. "What's going on?" she asked as she headed for Alissa's room.

"She just called me to say the baby..." I couldn't say it. I let my voice trail off, and Mollie pushed open the door to Alissa's room.

Alissa sat on the bed clutching Hannah to her chest, rocking back and forth and crying. She looked more like twelve than seventeen, and Mollie and I were at her side in an instant.

"She's alive," Alissa said, "but she was *blue* when I found her. I don't know what made me wake up. I just did. It was like she was too quiet or something. It was time for her to eat and somehow I knew it and woke up and I knew something was wrong and I turned on the light and she was blue!"

"Let me see her," Mollie said, reaching for Hannah.

Alissa slowly unfolded her arms from around the baby, who screwed up her face and began to whimper. I let out my breath in relief. Mollie took the baby from Alissa carefully, laying her in the bassinet as she began to check her over.

"That book you gave me," Alissa said to me. "It explained how to do mouth to mouth in it...you know, breathing into her nose, too? And I did it." Her lower lip trembled. "I did it and she let out this little gasp and started breathing and then her face got pink again." She started crying again. "Oh, my God!" she said. "I was sure she was dead."

I sat down next to her and put my arms around her. "You

did a great job," I said. I was floored, first that she'd actually read the book I'd given her and, second, that she'd been clearheaded enough to put what she'd learned into action. I wasn't sure I could have done what she did. I whispered in her ear. "You really do love her," I said, and she nodded slowly.

"I love her," she whispered back.

"She seems okay," Mollie said, "but I think we should take her to the hospital to be checked out. Was she on her back when you found her?"

"Yes," Alissa said. She reached into the bassinet and pulled Hannah into her arms again, holding her close against her damp cheek as if she never wanted to let her go.

We spent the rest of the night at the hospital. It was hard on all three of us as we watched Hannah being stuck with needles and hooked up to monitors, looking so tiny in the little plastic bassinet. But it was hardest on Alissa, who'd discovered all in one night how much she loved her daughter. It had taken me four years to learn what she'd learned in the past few hours.

The doctor on call told us that Hannah had suffered no permanent damage, but he suggested we get an apnea monitor to alert Alissa if Hannah ever stopped breathing again. He congratulated Alissa on her courage and skill and Alissa cried all over again.

We were exhausted by the time we got back to Hendricks House. Mollie offered to stay up to watch Hannah, but I could see how tired she was and besides, I wanted to do it. I knew I'd drag through the next day, but I told Mollie I'd stay until six, when I'd need to get back to the B and B to get things ready for breakfast. I'd wake her up then and she could take over until Gretchen arrived.

Alissa didn't seem to want to sleep, though. She fed Hannah with a tenderness I hadn't seen in her before, and it took all my power of persuasion to encourage her to put the baby back in the bassinet. She sat on the edge of her bed, one hand on the bassinet as though she needed to stay connected to Hannah. She looked over at me where I stood near the window.

"I want to tell Will," she said. "Don't you think he has a right to know? Don't you think *I* have a right to my baby's father's support right now? I don't mean money. I mean *emotional* support. Don't you think I have the right to that?"

Yes, actually, I did.

I sat down next to her. "Why hasn't he fought to be a part of her life, Ali?" I asked gently.

"They wouldn't let me put his name on the birth certificate."

"But he could go to court. Ask for a paternity test."

She shook her head. "I don't know. He probably doesn't realize that. I need to see him. Tell him."

"Maybe after the election," I said. "Maybe Dale would agree—"

"*Fuck* the election," Alissa said, but she kept her voice low for Hannah's sake. "Do you hear yourself, Robin? You're becoming just like them. This is all so wrong."

It was. She was old enough to take care of a baby. To save that baby's life. She was old enough to make other decisions about her own life. I'd caved to my father when it came to Travis. I wouldn't stand by while Alissa caved to the Hendricks. I pictured her reunion with Will, their embrace filled with emotion after they'd been kept apart all this time.

"I'll help you," I said.

"What?" she asked softly, disbelieving.

"I don't know how yet, Ali, but I'll help you and Will get together. I promise."

27
Travis

I WAITED FOR ROY IN A WAL-MART PARKING lot. I'd moved to that lot on the other side of Route 70 in Brier Creek on the off chance that Erin called the cops. All that miserable day, I'd hung out in the van. If I'd known where Erin lived, I would have gone there to take Bella back. I just hoped she'd discovered the note. Really idiotic scheme I'd come up with, but I kept telling myself how stable Erin seemed. She was separated from her husband, but she still seemed to have a sane and normal life. She'd handle it okay. Bella was safe and in the morning she'd be back with me again. I made it through this shitty day without her. Now I had to get through this insane night with Roy and the whole baby formula fiasco, and then I'd have money in my pocket. A lot of money.

I'd called Roy to tell him I'd moved the car, and he'd said he'd come to the Wal-Mart lot around eleven. Now it was eleven forty-five and no sign of him. I thought we'd gotten our signals crossed and was about to call him, when I saw a car turn into the parking lot. It passed under a light and I saw the candy-apple-red color and knew we were about to get the show on the road. Finally.

He pulled up next to me and got out of his car, alone. There was supposed to be two of them. He'd sworn I didn't have to do any of the actual stealing. Just drive. He opened the passenger-side door of my van and got in, carrying two heavy-duty flashlights.

"Where's your buddy?" I asked.

"Coming separately." He looked at his watch. "Should be here any sec." He reached into his jacket pocket and handed me a cell phone. "This is in case something gets screwed up," he said. "We'll each have one, and after the job, you toss it, understand?"

"What can get screwed up?" I asked. "You said this is a piece of cake."

"Quit whining." He looked toward the parking lot entrance and I followed his gaze to the headlights coming toward us. It wasn't until the car pulled up next to Roy's that I recognized the green Beetle.

"Is that *Savannah?*" I asked.

"You got it," he said.

I flew out of the van and met up with her as she was getting out of her car. "What the hell!" I shouted. "What the *hell?*"

"Not so loud." She pressed a hand to my chest as if she could shut me up that way. "And is that any way to greet an old friend?"

Roy was next to us now and he nodded in my direction. "This guy's a loose cannon," he said to Savannah.

"He'll be fine," she said.

"You set me up!" I shouted.

"Would you shut it?" Roy gave me a shove, but I barely felt it. I was seething.

"I got you a job," Savannah said. "And a better paying job than any you'd ever find in Carolina Beach, so just settle down."

"Okay, boys and girls, the reunion's over," Roy said. "Let's get on the road."

"I'm not doing this," I said. It was the principle of the thing now. Being taken for a fool wasn't sitting well with me, five hundred bucks or not.

"Yes, you are," Savannah said. "Look, Travis, I've made this run lots of times. The money's amazing and you need it, right? Where's Bella?"

"None of your business."

"How're you feeding her, huh? Are you living in the van? Winter's coming."

"Just shut up." I spun around to face her. "Stop patronizing me. You're—" I shook my head, still in disbelief that she'd made me into such a fool. "You are one piece of work," I said.

She laughed. "Just a small change from being your piece of ass, huh? Which is all I was to you, right?"

"Okay, okay," Roy said. "You two can settle your lovers' quarrel later. Right now we have a run to do, so let's get it over with."

The two of them headed for my van while I stood there trying to figure out what to do. I was furious—at Savannah and at myself for getting suckered into this. But she was right, wasn't she? I needed the money and she knew it. I climbed into the van, my face burning.

Savannah was in the passenger seat, Roy behind us. None of us spoke as I drove out of the parking lot. "Which way?" I asked when I got to the main road.

"Right," Roy said. "Just stay on this road for a while."

"How long have you been doing this?" I asked Savannah. I was still steamed.

"A few years. You asked me how I could have nice stuff in the trailer and a good car. Well, this is how. And I'm moving out of the trailer soon. I'll probably move here to Raleigh and—"

"Shut up, Savannah," Roy said.

"What?" She turned to look at him.

"You mouth off too much. Nobody needs to know your business."

"I'm not 'nobody,'" I said. "I'm the guy you found to be your patsy. Why me? There have to be a hundred other guys you could corral into this."

"You're not a patsy." Savannah rested her hand on my forearm and I gritted my teeth so hard my jaw hurt. "You're part of the team now, so don't get all wimpy on us. We used to work with another guy but he screwed up on a job and ended up—"

"Stuff it," Roy said to her.

"Oh, go to hell."

I remembered Savannah telling me how she couldn't agree to watch Bella every day because she sometimes went out of town. So these were her out-of-town trips. She needed more money, she made a baby formula run.

"What happened to the other guy?" I asked.

"He screwed up," Roy said. "You're not going to screw up, right? So you have nothing to worry about."

"Did he get caught or what?"

"He got the 'or what.'" Savannah laughed.

"Shut the fuck *up*, Savannah!" Roy shouted.

What the hell was I doing? Nothing was worth the risk of going to jail or ending up dead or whatever. "I'm not doing this," I said again, searching the side of the road for a turnoff. "I'm taking you back to the parking lot. Next place I can turn around—"

"Oh, shut up." Roy sounded sick of me. "Christ," he said to Savannah, "you didn't tell me what a pain in the ass this guy was going to be."

"He seems to forget how desperate he is," Savannah said as if I wasn't there.

"I'm turning around," I said.

"No, you're not," Roy said, and I felt something cold against my cheek just in front of my ear. In my rearview mirror, I could make out his face a few inches behind mine and it took me a second to realize that he was holding the barrel of a gun against my head.

"Get that thing away from me," I said.

He lowered it. "You cool now?" he asked. "Just keep going straight."

The whole game had changed with the appearance of the gun, and I did as I was told. I thought of how a guy in a movie would act in my place. He'd come up with some brilliant scheme. Some way out of this mess. But I felt anything but brilliant. I was an idiot and all I wanted was for this night to be over and to get my baby girl back. I felt tears burn my eyes and was glad of the darkness.

We were mostly quiet for the rest of the drive. It took about an hour. Savannah asked me a few questions about Bella. How she was doing. How much she missed her.

"I don't want to talk about Bella," I said. I felt like it made Bella dirty or something, talking about her with them. Bringing her into the van. I hoped she was sleeping in some really comfortable bed tonight, safe in a warm house with Erin. I kept her in my mind as I drove. *I will never do this to you again, Bella,* I thought to myself. I'd find some other way for us to get by. I'd never let her out of my sight again. We passed a sign welcoming us to Virginia. So now we were crossing state lines. Didn't that change the nature of a crime? Involve the FBI or something? I had no idea and I kept my questions to myself.

"Truck stop's off this exit," Roy said.

"Get in the right lane," Savannah told me.

I took the exit ramp and after a short distance, we pulled into a huge parking lot where a couple dozen semis were parked.

"Turn off your lights and drive slow through here," Roy said.

I turned off my lights and cruised slowly between the rows of trucks that dwarfed my van. Tall lampposts threw scattered light here and there in the lot, but for the most part, we were in darkness. At the far end of the lot was a gas station and a low building that must have been a restaurant, because the blinking pink neon sign out front simply read EAT. Savannah leaned forward, eying the trucks. They all looked alike to me. I figured most drivers of these big eighteen-wheelers slept in their rigs and I wondered if we were being watched. I thought of the license plate on the back of my van. It would be hard, maybe impossible, to read it with my lights off. Same with the magnetic Brown Construction signs on the sides. Still, if anything happened, it was me and my van they'd be after, not Roy or Savannah. I figured that was part of the plan.

The lot was quiet. There was the occasional sound of passing cars from the nearby highway, but there wasn't much traffic this time of night. Everything in the lot seemed eerily still, the only motion that blinking EAT sign in the distance.

"That one, by the fence," Roy said.

I'd barely noticed the truck he was talking about. It was

parked away from the others. Away from any of the overhead lights.

"Pull up next to the rear of it," Savannah said.

I pulled up so that the rear door of my van was about even with the rear of the truck.

"How will you get in?" I asked.

"It'll be unlocked," Savannah said, and I realized the driver must be in on the whole thing, too.

Savannah twisted in her seat to look at Roy. "How did they mark the cases this time?" she asked.

"Just the usual *X*'s," Roy said.

"How many?"

"Fifteen."

"Wow." She sounded pleased.

"What are you talking about?" I asked. "Why would they mark—"

"You don't need to know," Roy said. "The less you know, the better."

He was probably right. If anything went wrong, the less I knew the better off I'd be, but I felt so pissed off and taken advantage of and just plain stupid that I needed to know. And suddenly, I got it. "You're not really stealing baby formula, are you," I said.

Savannah laughed. "Oh, we absolutely are. You'll see. Cases of it."

"Baby formula no babies' lips will ever touch," Roy said as he slid open my van door and got out.

"What does he mean?" I turned to Savannah.

"You are such a rube." Savannah started to open her door, but I grabbed her arm.

"Spill it!" I said. "Is it drugs?"

"What do you think?" she said, trying to twist her arm free. "It's coke. Cut with formula. We take a few cases, deliver them to our middlemen. Then we collect a ton of money and we're on our merry way."

"Shit!" I let go of her and pounded the steering wheel. "Get the hell out of my van. I'm leaving."

It was her turn to grab *my* arm, her nails digging into my skin. "You do that, and social services is going to get a nice anonymous tip about a homeless little girl living in a van with a pathetic asshole of a father."

Roy knocked on my window with the barrel of his gun and I jumped. Savannah leaned closer until her face was inches from mine. "We understand each other?" she asked.

I swallowed. I had to pick my poison—do this drug deal or lose Bella. No contest. I gave Savannah an angry shove. "Just make it fast," I said.

Roy knocked on my window again and I rolled it down. "You're lookout," he said. "You see anyone in the lot, let us know."

I didn't say anything. Didn't react in any way. It was like I was disassociating from the whole thing. I wanted it to be over with.

One of them opened the rear doors of my van and all I could see behind me was the black night. I couldn't see the back of the truck from where I sat, but in my side-view mirror, I could just make out Roy's and Savannah's legs in the darkness. I heard the rear doors of the semi creak open, the sound loud and echoey as it bounced off every other truck in the lot. I watched as Roy's legs disappeared from my view, and I guessed he'd climbed inside the truck. In a minute, Savannah appeared in my rearview mirror as she loaded a case of formula into the back of my van. I didn't turn around.

"Just think about the money," she said to me. I didn't answer. I wondered just how much the drugs were worth to pay everyone involved in the heist. My cut was no doubt the smallest amount anyone was making.

I could hardly see anything from where I was parked, so I didn't feel like much of a lookout. Rows of trucks blocked my view of the gas station and the EAT sign, and the part of the lot I could see was filled with pools of light and stretches of jet-black shadow. I felt more tense as the minutes passed, turning my head from side to side, trying to peer between the trucks for a sign that someone was onto us, but everything was quiet. The only sounds besides the occasional car on the highway were some muffled words between Savannah and Roy, an occasional grunt, and the sliding of another case into the back of my van.

I'd almost relaxed when something caught the corner of my eye. I leaned forward, squinting. I was sure I'd seen something or someone move, way in the distance at the end of one of the rows of trucks. I stared in that direction until my eyes watered, and just as I began to think it had been my imagination, I heard the faraway sound of footsteps, coming fast. There was more than one person. I couldn't see a thing and the sound echoed around me so that I wasn't sure exactly where it was coming from.

Suddenly, two men ran into one of the pools of light no more than thirty yards in front of my van.

"Hey!" one of them shouted, their arms waving in the air. They yelled something else, but I had no idea what they were saying. It was like my brain was misfiring, only one thought running through it: *get the hell out of here!*

I turned the key in the ignition and squealed away from the truck. Roy shouted at me and I heard the unmistakable crack of gunfire as he fired a shot toward the men. I felt the weight of my open rear doors swinging behind the van as I swerved past the men, pressing the gas pedal to the floor, thinking, *Don't let them read my sign. Don't let them see my plate.* I heard more bullets sing out, so close the sound made me duck. I didn't take the time to look in my rearview mirror to see if either of the guys had been hit as I sped through the lot. My eyes were focused on the exit and soon I was careening down the long ramp toward the highway.

I went about half a mile before I pulled over, my heart hammering against my rib cage. I climbed out of the van and shut the rear doors, but not before I saw the cases of formula tumbled all over the place on the mattress that had become Bella's and my home on wheels.

Back in the van, I took off again, my foot like a pile of lead on the gas until I realized I'd better stick to the limit. I slowed to sixty-five, and the van grew quiet enough that I could hear my breathing, hard and fast.

What the hell should I do? I'd stranded Roy and Savannah with those two guys. I didn't want to picture the scene in the parking lot. Roy and his damn gun. Should I try to go back? *No way.* I was done with this. So finished. I got off at the next exit and turned around to head back to North Carolina. They'd tricked me into this mess. Now they could find their own way out of it.

But I was the one with thousands of dollars worth of cocaine in my van, no money in my pocket, and my little girl probably wondering if her daddy had gone to heaven and was never coming back.

28

Erin

I HAD THE FEELING I WAS NEVER GOING TO fall asleep. I was still awake at one in the morning, maybe because Bella had asked me to leave a light on and I'd never been a good sleeper unless my bedroom was totally dark. I didn't have a night light in the apartment, so I'd left the closet light burning and the door open a couple of inches. That seemed to satisfy her, but the light lay in a swath across her face as she slept and I had to stare at her because every time I looked away, I forgot she wasn't Carolyn. I needed to keep reminding myself this was some other little girl in my bed and in my heart. I'd felt crazy plenty of times since Carolyn died, imagining that I saw her on the street or heard her voice from across the room. But tonight I felt perfectly sane. Almost content. Yes, this was a screwy situation, but for this one night, I was thinking about someone other than myself. My God, I'd been wrapped up in me! I hadn't even realized it until tonight. All of my energy had been funneled into *my* grief, *my* dread of returning to work, *my* sad day-to-day existence. Tonight, I'd barely thought of myself. I'd thought of making Bella feel comfortable and secure.

Travis had given me a gift, and I wondered if on some level he knew it.

We'd had a good evening, Bella and me. Before dinner, we took a walk around the little lake near my apartment complex. There was one spot where a short bridge crossed over a creek, and I had to run across it holding my breath. I tried to make it into a game with Bella to hide my anxiety, but ever since the night on the pier, I hated being on any structure above water. I used to love to dive, but even the diving board at our neighborhood pool gave me the jitters now. It had gotten ridiculous.

On the other side of the bridge was a small playground, and Bella played on the swings and slid down the sliding board, but most of the time, she stayed close to my side, not running ahead as Carolyn would have. *Oh, Carolyn.* If only Carolyn *had* been a little more clingy. A little more afraid. If only I hadn't listened to Michael that night. *You're so over-protective sometimes, Erin. You're going to make her afraid.* Maybe if Bella had been with Travis, she would have struck out on her own with a little more courage, but she only wanted to hold my hand as we walked, and I didn't mind a bit.

She helped me make dinner, tearing the lettuce for our salads. We had soup, salad and bread. That was just about all I had in the apartment unless we dipped into the frozen dinners again. She didn't eat her salad and she made me cut the crust off her bread and then surprised me by eating only the crust, but she did eat half a bowl of chicken-and-rice soup. Then we had a little tea party with cookies for dessert, and finally I did what I'd been dying to do ever since finding that note in her pocket; I gave her a bubble bath and washed her hair.

"What's a bubble bath?" she'd asked when I told her my plan.

"You've never had a bubble bath?" I asked in disbelief.

She shook her head. "I had baths in the tub in our burned-down house," she said.

I wanted to ask her about that house. How had it burned down? But I thought better of asking her anything that might make her sad when she was already feeling pretty vulnerable.

I ran the bath for her and loaded it with bubbles. There must have been ten inches of bubbles on top of the water and from her wide-eyed reaction as the foam expanded in the tub, I believed she'd been telling me the truth about never having a bubble bath before—or at least not one so wildly extravagant. She undressed herself, skinny little thing, and she weighed just about nothing as I lifted her over the side of the tub and settled her in the water. I used the shower head to wash her hair, careful not to get my shampoo in her eyes. I had a new unpackaged toothbrush that was way too big for her mouth and she whimpered while I brushed her teeth, but she toughed it out. She was squeaky clean, her cheeks pink and shiny, when I tucked her into bed, and she leaned against me the way Carolyn used to as I read to her from *Winnie the Pooh,* and her body grew heavy with sleepiness. I went to bed then myself, not wanting her to wake up alone and afraid, but I hadn't been able to sleep at all.

Now I picked up my iPad from the night table and logged into Harley's Dad and Friends. There were a couple of messages asking *Where's Erin?* and I realized that for the first time in many months I hadn't checked the group since early that morning.

I read through the posts from the day. It was the usual stuff. There were a couple of new people with fresh, raw grief. A few more in the same stage as me. Some of them blamed family members or doctors or God. Some had a ton of guilt over things unsaid or undone. For a moment, I felt distant from it all, like I had left these online friends, so precious to me, behind in the past day.

Hi all, I typed. *Sorry to go AWOL. It's been a crazy day. I'm actually babysitting a little girl C's age.* I was one of the parents who didn't share our children's names. I would have been okay with it, but I'd promised Michael I wouldn't share identifying details about her or our family. *So it's been a strange day,* I finished.

Within a few minutes, I'd received a string of responses.

Wow, I don't know if I could do that!

I bet it's been good for you. You have such a good heart, Erin.

I quickly felt at home with my online friends again, wrapped up in the understanding of these strangers. We wrote back and forth for a while, then I tried to read but my eyes kept drifting to Bella. She was sucking her thumb, her lamb clutched tightly against her cheek. Carolyn's polar bear had been discarded on my sofa.

At two, I closed the cover on my iPad but still couldn't sleep. I had sleeping pills I could take, but I wanted to be alert in case Bella needed me. So by two-thirty, I was every bit as awake as I'd been at eleven, and I finally got out of bed and walked into the kitchen to make a cup of tea. I'd just sat down on the sofa to sip it when I heard Bella crying. She ran into the dim room looking frightened and confused.

"Bella," I said, "I'm right here."

She ran to me and I lifted her onto my lap. I almost couldn't bear how scared she looked. "Did you wake up and forget where you were?" I asked.

She nodded, hiccupping through her tears. She was crying hard, the way a much younger child might cry. So hard she could barely catch her breath. "I want *Daddy,*" she said.

"Oh, I know," I said, rocking her, her sweet, clean hair

beneath my lips. "We'll see him in the morning at the coffee shop. He's going to be so happy to see you." I was going to have trouble letting her go tomorrow. Send her back to living in a van? How could I?

I started to sing. I'd never been much of a singer, but Carolyn loved it when I sang to her, so I went through "Jack and Jill" and "Twinkle, Twinkle, Little Star" and gradually Bella's crying turned to little intermittent shivers. I felt so good that I could calm her and that she felt safe in my arms. But then she said, "Stop singing now," in a tone that told me my voice had grown more grating than relaxing and I had to laugh.

She suddenly climbed down from my lap and ran to the sofa for the polar bear and her purse. She climbed back onto my lap with the lamb, bear and purse surrounding her. She tried to open the purse.

"You want your dolly?" I asked, helping her with the clasp. We'd put the doll back in her purse after playing with it in the dollhouse. I didn't want to forget it in the morning.

"Yes," she said.

I opened the purse and she dug her hand in and pulled out the little doll with the long blond hair. Then she slipped her hand inside again and pulled out her toothbrush. It had never occurred to me that Travis might have "packed" anything for her. "Oh, honey," I said, "here's your toothbrush! We can use this one instead of that big one in the morning, okay?"

"I got money in here, too," she said, turning the purse upside down. A bunch of coins fell out along with a five and a one and the two photographs.

"You *do*," I said. I was curious about those pictures. I turned on the light next to the sofa and lifted the photograph of the teenage girl.

"That's my mommy," Bella told me again.

I hadn't gotten a good look at the picture when I saw it the other day in the coffee shop. Now I could see that the girl, who couldn't have been more than fifteen or sixteen, was wan-looking. She had a really pretty smile, but her skin looked as though you could see clear through it. So pale. The picture was old, or maybe the edges were simply felt-like and damaged from spending so much time in Bella's purse.

"She loves me very much," Bella said, "but she lives too far away for me to see her." I could hear Travis telling her this. Hear her repeating his words. I wondered if she could be dead, but then I remembered Travis saying that she lived in Beaufort—certainly not too far away for Bella to see her. I wished I knew their custody situation. Why did Travis have her? I looked at the pale, pretty teenager again and wondered if she missed her little girl. Maybe Travis *had* kidnapped her. That thought would never have crossed my mind a day ago, but now it was clear that Travis wasn't making the best decisions for his daughter. My heart did a little flip-flop at the thought of the girl in the photo—Robin—aching for her daughter. Her *missing* daughter. I imagined how she longed for her. *You're projecting.* I could practically hear Judith's voice inside my head. Of course I was projecting. I couldn't imagine my daughter being alive somewhere without feeling a desperate need to have her with me. I was going to have a long heart-to-heart with Travis when I saw him. He'd dragged me into this situation and now I had a right to know exactly what was going on.

29

Travis

COULD YOU HAVE A HEART ATTACK AT TWENTY-three? I lay on the mattress in the van, curled between crates of cocaine-laced baby formula, staring at the dark ceiling for hours, and my heart wouldn't slow down. It pounded against the mattress and all I kept thinking was that I couldn't die. I couldn't die and leave Bella without a dad. For what her dad was worth right now, which didn't feel like much.

I was back in the lot by the Target, wondering how bad I'd screwed things up. Pretty bad, I guessed. I just hoped nobody was dead. Not the two guys Roy shot at. Not Savannah or Roy, even though I felt like killing them myself. I didn't want this whole stupid scheme to have gone that wrong. And I didn't want to land in prison either, but carrying a van-load of stolen goods was going to take me there, wasn't it? I had to dump this stuff. Where, though? And I wanted Bella back. *Bella.* I couldn't go there in my head. If I thought about Bella, I wasn't going to be able to clearly figure out what I needed to do.

Around four in the morning, the phone Roy had given me rang and I grabbed it and flipped it open.

"What happened?" I asked.

"You fucking asshole," Roy growled. "You are so fucked."

"What do you mean?"

"'What do you mean?'" he mimicked me in a singsong voice. "I'll give you the address for the drop-off and you take the goods there tonight. Ten—"

"Uh-uh," I said. "No way. I'm done. You and Savannah can just—"

"Shut the hell up!" he shouted. "You have no choice, got it?"

"I said I'm not doing it. I'm done."

"Ten sharp. Not a minute before or a minute after. You'll get your money then, minus a hundred for the fuck-up in—"

"What don't you understand about 'I'm done'?" I shouted back at him.

"What I understand is that you've got the stuff, man, and you're not keeping it."

"I don't want it!"

"Well, I'm telling you what to do with it and if you don't do it, you're dead. Simple as that."

I shut my eyes. I'd take the address now and figure out what to do later. I wrote it down along with the directions. The drop-off was about a half hour from where I was. "Let me take it to them right now," I said. "I want it out of my van." There was no way I could have Bella in the van with cases of coke. I didn't want her involved in any of this mess.

"You can't take it right now," he said. "This is a structured operation, bro. They're getting other deliveries right now. Tonight at ten. That's it."

"You come get it from me now and take it to them yourself." I cringed the moment the words left my mouth. If I met up with him now, he'd kill me. What would stop him?

He'd take the stuff, put the cold barrel of his gun to my head, and that would be that.

"Christ, you're dense," he said. "If I wanted to cart around fifty pounds of half-baked cocaine, I wouldn't have needed you in the first place."

"I'm getting off."

"You do this or so help me God, I'll hunt you down. Your little girl, too. Bella? Is that her name? I'll blow her brains out first so you can wa—"

I flipped the phone shut, my hands shaking. I got out of the van and made it to the grass before I threw up. I had to lean over to catch my breath, hands on my knees, my body torn between fear and fury. Just the sound of Bella's name on his lips was enough to rip me apart.

It wasn't cold, but I was shaking all over by the time I got back in the van. I sat in the driver's seat, resting my head against the steering wheel and when I shut my eyes I saw Robin's father, his face ugly with hatred. "You can't raise yourself, much less a child," he'd shouted at me. "You need to think about what's best for that baby!"

I groaned, lifting my head from the steering wheel to rub my temples. Just what I needed right now was the ghost of Robin's father telling me what a piece-of-crap father I'd be. I never before thought he was right.

I remembered the day Robin and I had sex when she landed in the hospital. That was the beginning of the end for us. Man, I nearly killed her. I was so stupid. I came on way too strong that day. I hadn't been with her in so long and I'd missed her. I didn't stop to think how fragile she was.

As soon as her father showed up in the E.R., they threw me out on my butt, but he wasn't done with me. I sat on the wall outside, praying Robin didn't die, and after a while he came through the doors and headed straight for me, head down like a bull. He would've killed me if the security guard hadn't held him back.

"You raped her!" he shouted.

"No, man, I didn't!" I was backing away, hoping the guard had a good grip on him 'cause he was ready to pound me.

"She was a sick little girl, you son of a bitch!" he shouted. "You're going to hang."

"Is she all right? Is she—"

"Let's go back inside, sir," the guard said to him. He was starting to cry and go limp against the guard's chest and I didn't know what to do.

"Just tell me she's all right!" I shouted as the guard led him toward the emergency room entrance.

He turned back to me. "You just better say your prayers she doesn't die," he said. "Say your prayers."

I kept calling the hospital, but they wouldn't put me through to her room, so I was never sure just how bad things were with Robin. I wanted to talk to her, but I was locked out. A couple of days after everything happened, her father called to tell me if I ever tried to get in touch with her again, I'd go to prison for rape. He could make the charge stick, he said. Sick girl, brutal guy. I was still seventeen, but seventeen was an adult in North Carolina. Juvenile hall was one thing. Prison was another. My mother knew everything that happened and she tried to reason with him on the phone, but he wasn't having any of it. I never knew what strings he pulled to get our phone number changed and unlisted so Robin couldn't call me, and I knew he changed hers, too, because I tried to call and couldn't get through. I started wondering if she'd actually told him I raped her. If she said that to get herself out of trouble. I couldn't picture her doing that, but how would I ever know?

So for a long time, I just thought about her and worried

about her and wondered if she'd blamed everything on me, and the next thing I knew, this agency calls to tell me Robin had my baby and wanted to put her up for adoption. *Baby?* I was blindsided. If she'd been well enough to make it through a pregnancy, she'd been well enough to find a way to tell me about it. I felt like the girl I'd loved had disappeared. She was going to give our baby away. She had the parents picked out and everything. I told the lady from the agency I wanted custody, and next thing I knew, Robin's father was calling me, telling me not to be a fool. Not to be so selfish. "You need to think what's best for that baby!"

"She should have told me!" I shouted into the phone. "Why didn't she find some way to tell me?"

"Because she hates you, why do you think?" he said. "She's critically ill. She had a heart transplant. She needs her life to be peaceful and calm, and here you come making waves. Again! She's furious you won't respect her wishes. She risked her life because of you and she has every right to decide what happens with her baby."

"I want my kid!" I yelled. "She's mine! It's only right."

He laughed. "Just try and get her," he said. "I'll fight you, and you can bet I have a lot more resources for a fight like that than you do. You'll never win. You can't raise yourself, much less a child."

Yeah, he had resources and he fought hard but I had blood on my side. He pulled out the rape card, but the judge didn't buy it since he'd never pressed charges against me for it. Robin was in no shape to put her two cents in; he was telling the truth about her being really sick. Maybe dying. My feelings about her were so mixed up at that point. I was really angry with her, but I sure didn't want her to die.

The one thing her father won, if you could call it that, was my signature on a contract saying I'd never try to contact

Robin. I'd leave her alone for the rest of our lives, it said. I signed it. I had my little girl. That was all I'd wanted right then, and it was all I wanted now.

I didn't sleep for the rest of the night, sitting on high alert in the van. Instead, I watched for Roy's car. Or Savannah's. Or the police. I didn't know *what* I was watching for. All I knew was that I couldn't let down my guard. Around six in the morning, I remembered the magnetic signs on my van and got out to peel them off. Those two guys at the truck stop—what had they seen? And were they still alive to tell anyone?

The Target parking lot was dead quiet. There were a few other vehicles parked here and there and I wondered if they had people sleeping in them, too. Living in them. Did the cops ever come around and check on them? Suddenly I felt extremely paranoid. As I was getting back into the van after removing the magnetic signs, I saw headlights turn into the far end of the lot. Cops? I tossed the signs in the back of the van and climbed into the driver's seat and slumped down. The car was still in the distance, but as it passed under one of the lights, I thought I caught a flash of red. Roy's Mustang? *Shit.* I grabbed the keys out of my pocket and rammed them into the ignition. I pictured my body being discovered in the van in the morning, the mattress soaked with my blood, and Bella with no daddy. I hit the gas and squealed out of the parking lot even faster than I'd squealed out of the truck stop.

I didn't know where I was going. I turned onto the main road in the direction of downtown Raleigh and just drove for a while, checking my rearview mirror every two seconds. No one behind me. No one. *That wasn't Roy,* I told myself. *Everything's cool.* Besides, he'd said he didn't want the stuff in his car, right? So why would he be after me? Though maybe

he'd kill me and then drive my van to the drop-off and…
My imagination was out of control. All I'd wanted was a
legitimate construction job! Lumber and hammers and saws
and nail guns. Damn it!

I pulled onto a side street and, once I was sure I hadn't
been followed, I climbed into the back of the van and lay
down on the mattress, trying to figure out what to do. I
should go to the police myself. That made the most sense.
I'd tell them the whole story and take whatever lumps they
dished out. Then I started counting up the charges they'd
have against me. The heist itself, for starters. And what if
Roy had killed one or both of those guys at the truck stop?
Murder in connection with a robbery? What would I get
for that? I could plead ignorance all I wanted, but I doubted
it would do me any good. The thing that kept me frozen to
the mattress, though, the thing that kept me from picking
up the phone, was that they'd take Bella away from me.

I wished I had a way to get a message to Erin. I'd ask her
to keep Bella one more night—that was, if she hadn't already
gone to the police. I played it out in my mind. I could go to
the coffee shop this morning and ask Erin if she could watch
her for another day…Bella would see me, though. I couldn't
walk away from her one more time. I was rolling this around
in my mind when the phone Roy had given me rang again.
I checked the display. It wasn't his number and I stared at it
a second before flipping it open without saying a word.

"Travis?" It was Savannah.

"Thanks a lot, Savannah." I leaned up on my elbow.
"Thanks for screwing up my life."

"I know, I know. Travis, I'm so sorry. I'm sorry I dragged
you into this mess."

That wasn't the reaction I'd expected. Was she crying?

"A little late for the apologies," I said. "Now I have a van full of drugs and I was supposed to pick up Bella today. If you'd told me what you were really up to, I'd never—"

"I know. It just got so...so screwed up. I'm sorry. You have no idea how sorry. I split with Roy. He's crazy. I didn't realize how crazy."

I hesitated. "Did he kill those guys?" I wasn't sure I wanted to hear the answer.

"No, but he shot one of them in the leg. We had to climb a fence and hang out in some woods and then Roy stole a car to get us back here. But I don't blame you," she added quickly. "I was mad at the time, but...now I'm just exhausted and I wish last night could go away. I never should have gotten you involved."

"Damn straight." I pictured her climbing the fence. Stranded in the woods more than an hour from Raleigh. I remembered her calling me a rube. *You are such a rube,* she'd said. I didn't buy this sudden transformation.

"Where do you have to pick Bella up?" she asked.

"Nowhere, now," I said. "I can't pick her up while I have a van full of drugs."

"You have to make that drop tonight," she said. "Roy will never leave you alone unless you do. And once you do, you'll have money."

"What about you?" I asked, curious to hear her answer. "If you've split from Roy, how do you get your share?"

"I will. I'll make sure of it."

"And what if I don't make the drop?" I asked.

"You don't want to know." Her voice was nearly a whisper. "Oh, Travis. If you only knew how whacked he is. Our last driver... That was so messed up. You have to make the drop. When I left him he was talking about finding Bella if you don't."

"Let's leave Bella out of this."

"He thinks you found someone to babysit at that coffee shop where you hang out."

I squeezed the phone tight in my fist. How did he know where I hung out? We'd been watched, Bella and me. More paranoid than ever, I moved to the driver's seat so I could see the road, still clutching the phone to my ear. "Sure, that's what I did," I said. "I just walked up to someone and asked, 'Could you take my kid for the night?'"

"I figured you took her to her mother's in Beaufort. I hope that's what you did, anyway. That she's, you know, totally safe."

"Right," I said. "That's where she is."

"That's a major relief," she said. "Because you don't want to know what Roy likes to do with little girls."

My blood felt like ice water in my hands. *"Savannah,"* I said. "How could you have hooked up with this guy?"

"Money can make you crazy."

"So can lack of money," I muttered.

"So you'll make that drop tonight?"

"I thought of taking it to the cops."

For a moment she didn't speak. "Are you *insane?*" she finally asked.

Yeah, I thought. *I am.*

"Look," she said, "you're in more trouble than you know. Do you honestly think taking the signs off your van makes you invisible?"

I dug in my pocket for the car keys. "I'm getting off," I said, and I shut the phone before she had a chance to say another word. I rammed the key into the ignition and turned it. How did they know I removed the signs? I remembered the car I'd seen in the parking lot in the middle of the night. Were they following me right now? I thought I'd lost him. I could have sworn I'd lost him.

The one thing I knew for sure: I didn't dare go to the coffee shop this morning. The only way to keep Bella safe today was for me not to be around her.

And for me to drop off the drugs tonight.

The only way.

30
Robin

I WAS SO EXHAUSTED THE MORNING AFTER
Hannah nearly died that my vision was blurry as I carried the
breakfast casserole into the dining room. I had two couples
this morning, and the women made swooning noises when
they saw the casserole. I hoped my smile didn't look as tired
as I felt. I answered questions about the ponies and the mu-
seums and the ferries and when I was sure everything was
under control, I left Bridget to finish up and went into my
apartment to get my purse. I planned to drive to Morehead
City to pick up the baby monitor this morning. I was still
shaken by Alissa's middle-of-the-night phone call. *She's dead!*
I had no trouble tracking down the monitor the doctor in
the E.R. had recommended. I took it to Hendricks House,
where I found Alissa sound asleep and Gretchen changing
Hannah. Mollie was at a luncheon, politicking for her son.
Gretchen and I quietly set up the monitor and talked a little
about what had happened the night before. We whispered
to keep from waking Alissa.

"She didn't sleep a wink till I got here," Gretchen said.

"It's a terrible thing, what happened, but I think it finally woke up her mommy instincts."

I nodded. I watched as Gretchen snapped Hannah back into her onesie and lifted her from the table. I would have liked to hold the baby for a while, but it was clear I wasn't needed and I was so, so tired. I looked at Alissa, sound asleep beneath the light quilt on her double bed, and decided I could use a nap myself.

I was just getting into my bed at the B and B when Dale called.

"Hey, you," he said when I answered the phone. "Got some good news. The *News-Times* endorsed me."

I heard the joy in his voice. We'd been waiting and hoping for this, though it struck me as weird that he didn't even mention the fact that his niece had almost died the night before. "Oh, Dale," I said, "that's fantastic!"

"So we're going out for dinner tonight," he said. "Blue Moon?"

"Awesome," I said, then caught myself. "I mean, *wonderful*."

He laughed. "How's the baby doing today?" he asked. "Sounds like it was pretty terrible last night."

It suddenly hit me that he always called Hannah "the baby." I didn't think I'd ever once heard him call her by name. But at least he'd mentioned what happened.

"She seems fine," I said. "I bought the monitor in Morehead City, so we're all set."

We talked a few minutes longer, and then I curled up under the covers and closed my eyes, but I knew I wasn't going to sleep. I thought about how I could bring up the subject of Alissa and Will with Dale again. It hadn't gone well the first time on that drive to my doctor's appointment, and now I felt nervous just thinking about it. He could intimidate me,

I realized. He was so much older than me. Smarter. Wiser. More worldly. He wasn't afraid of conflict. Of saying no. Was I going to feel this way the rest of my life? Afraid to bring up topics that might set him off? I had to learn to do it. I just needed to be firm.

But not tonight. It would ruin the evening. Ruin his good news and his good mood. I knew what he'd say, anyway: *no way.* I'd be screwing up his careful campaign if I invited Will into our lives.

But why did I need his permission? I sat up and looked out the window, arms folded across my chest. I was part of the Hendricks family now. I had some of their power. I was closer to Alissa than any of them and I had a mind of my own. I'd talk to Will myself. I'd find out how he felt about the whole situation and then I'd take it from there.

That couldn't hurt anything, could it?

31
Erin

"WHEN'S DADDY COMING?" BELLA LOOKED UP from her coloring book. We'd been sitting in JumpStart for nearly an hour and I was beginning to get anxious. It was ten o'clock, well past the time Travis and Bella usually showed up in the coffee shop. What was he waiting for?

"I'm not sure, honey," I said. "Probably pretty soon. Should we play I Spy again?"

She let out a very long sigh. "Okay," she said finally, but her gaze was on the door. So was mine. *Come on, Travis.* I had my lecture ready to deliver to him, but it was changing by the minute. *It's one thing to leave her with me the way you did, another to not show up on time to pick her up.* Although he really hadn't given me a time, had he?

"Erin?" I turned to see a woman standing a few yards away from me. She was silhouetted against the window and I couldn't make out her features. "I thought that was you," she said.

I shaded my eyes and recognized her as the mother of one of the kids from Carolyn's first year of preschool. I couldn't remember her name.

"How are you?" She took a few steps closer and sat down on the arm of the couch.

"Good," I said, my brain scrambling for her name. "How about you?"

"We're all fine." She smiled with a shake of her head. "I have to say, I'm so glad to see your little girl here." She nodded toward Bella. "I'd heard a rumor——" she blushed "——I heard she'd...that there was an accident, but it must have been someone else they were talking about, and I'm just so relieved."

I wasn't sure what to say. I didn't want to get into it with her. This was why I'd moved away. Why I hadn't wanted to go back to work. All the acquaintances and customers asking questions and making comments and offering relentless sympathy. And now this misunderstanding that left me speechless.

"I don't remember her name," the woman said. "What's your name, honey?" she asked Bella, who glanced at her and then at me before returning her attention to her coloring book. It looked like neither of us wanted to talk with the woman.

"Bella," I said. I felt like I was betraying Carolyn with the lie.

"*Bella.* I don't remember that. She's a little one, isn't she? Jade is ridiculously tall now. Is Bella still going to preschool?"

I wanted to escape. I looked at my watch. It was the only thing I could think of to do. "Oh, wow, I was supposed to make a call fifteen minutes ago." I dug in my purse for my phone. "I'm so sorry," I said, pulling it out. "It's great to see you."

"Oh, you too, Erin," she said, standing up. "Bye-bye, Bella."

"Bye," Bella said without looking up from her coloring book.

I faked my phone call until the woman had left the coffee shop, but no sooner was she out the door than Nando stopped by my chair with a tray covered with samples of cake.

"It's our new red velvet cupcake," he said. "Would you and Bella like to try a piece?"

"I don't think so, thank—"

Bella was on her feet in a flash, her hand on my knee and her gaze on the tray. "Can I?" she asked me.

I smiled and put my hand on her back. "Sure," I said, and I took one of the little chunks of cupcake and handed it to her.

"Where's her dad today?" Nando asked.

"I'm babysitting her," I said. "He's working."

"My daddy's coming soon." Bella spoke around the cake in her mouth.

"Oh, that's great he found work," Nando said.

"Yeah, it is." I nodded. "Thanks for the cupcake."

"Thank you," Bella said, swallowing.

Nando laughed. "She is one cute kid," he said, and then he carried his tray toward the tables by the windows.

Another hour passed. Bella and I played games, did puzzles, walked around outside the store, split a muffin and ate a packet of dried fruit. It was clear he wasn't coming. How could he do this? How could he just dump his child on someone and disappear?

Finally Bella flopped down on the sofa. "I want my *daddy*," she whined. She'd been so good all morning, but I could see her disintegrating by the minute. Soon she'd need a nap, and then what? What if I took her back to my apartment and then Travis showed up at JumpStart? Although, frankly, I'd given up on that happening. Something was just plain wrong about this whole situation. I knew what I needed to do—exactly what I *didn't* want to do; I needed to call Protective Services. I hated those people with a vengeance. I understood they had a job to do. I knew they saved some kids' lives. But after Carolyn died, they'd badgered Michael and me relentlessly, asking so many questions as they looked for someone to blame. Of course, there were never any charges. It had been an accident, pure and simple. But I was on their radar. If I showed up now with a child who didn't belong to me, I could just imagine the questions. They would never end.

One o'clock, I thought. If he didn't show up by one, I'd have to make the call.

One o'clock came and Bella had reached the end of her rope by then and so had I. I tried to figure out what to do. I didn't want questions; I only wanted Bella to be safe. Somehow, I'd have to turn her over to Protective Services without giving my name. I wrote a note on a napkin. *Her name is Bella Brown. Her father's name is Travis. They're from Carolina Beach…or at least that's what he told me. He abandoned her.* I opened her purse and slipped the napkin inside when she wasn't looking.

If I called the police from my cell phone, they'd have my number and the questions would begin. I looked around at the few women and men sitting in the coffee shop. I could ask to use someone else's phone, say that mine had died, but I was too familiar a face in JumpStart. It would be too easy to track me down.

I knew I wasn't thinking straight. All I knew was that I needed to get help for Bella and to keep myself out of it. I watched her as she paged through one of the books, her cheeks red from crying.

"Come on, Bella," I said, getting to my feet and gathering up our books and stuffed animals. "Let's get some lunch."

"Mickey D's?" she asked.

"Yes." Actually, McDonald's would be perfect.

We went out to the car and buckled ourselves in. Then I drove down the long row of stores in the parking lot, trying to figure out my next step. If the shopping center had any pay phones, they were well hidden. Maybe in the Target. I parked the car in the massive lot and unbuckled my seat belt. "We need to run in here for just a minute," I said, "and then we'll go to Mickey D's, okay?"

I thought she was going to start crying again, but she seemed too worn out to make a peep. She clung to my hand as we approached the store. On the sidewalk out front, a teenage boy was organizing the shopping carts.

"Is there a pay phone in the store?" I asked.

He looked at me blankly as though he'd never heard of a pay phone. He was so young that maybe he hadn't.

"No, ma'am," he said finally. "I don't think there's one anywhere around."

"Okay, thanks." I held Bella's hand as we walked into the store and over to the service desk. We had to wait in line with a bunch of adults, and I looked down at her, knowing all she could see was a sea of grown-up legs. She leaned against me the way I'd seen her lean against Travis and I remembered how loving Travis was with her. How much he clearly cared about her and how jittery he'd seemed the morning he left her with me. I wished I knew what was going on. I wished I could find him and talk to him and see what kind of help he needed before I put into motion this unstoppable train.

We'd reached the front of the line.

"Yes, ma'am?" the woman behind the service desk said to me.

"I was wondering if you have a phone I could use," I said. "My cell died and I need to make a call."

She gave a little roll of her eyes, but nodded me over to the end of the counter and set a chunky black phone in front of me. "Thank you," I said, and I dialed 911 with a trembling finger, then turned away from the service area so I wouldn't be overheard.

"What's your emergency?" the dispatcher asked.

"There's a little girl sitting alone in the McDonald's in the Brier Creek Shopping Center," I said. "She's been there for a while. She's about four years old."

"What's your name?"

I hung up.

"Come on, Bella," I said. "Let's get some lunch."

I wondered if the police would get there before I did, and I rushed Bella into her car seat and drove the length of the shopping center as fast as I dared. I pulled into a spot in front of McDonald's. It was late enough that there was only one other person, an elderly man, in line in front of us. Bella knew exactly what she wanted—a Happy Meal—and I ordered nothing for myself. We sat down near the window. My plan was this: as soon as I saw the police car, I would tell Bella I needed to run to the restroom and then I would leave. Leave McDonald's. Leave her. Drive away. Maybe I would park a short distance away and watch to be sure they found her and took her with them.

And then she would have been deserted twice, I thought.

I couldn't do it. Couldn't leave her that way. I needed to tell them about Travis. I needed to explain.

Bella picked at her burger and handed me the toy to unwrap. A little fairy. Or maybe it was Tinker Bell? I didn't look too closely as I handed it back to her.

So, they would ask me questions, I thought as I watched Bella make the fairy hop across the table. They'd stick my name in their system and say, "Oh, she was the mother of that little girl who fell off the Stardust Pier in Atlantic Beach back in the spring. And now she shows up with this kid and a far-fetched story?" But I couldn't desert her. I'd have to work with the authorities. Be a grown-up. Do whatever I needed to do to help Bella. Maybe they'd let her stay with me as they tracked down Travis or her mother? Not once they realized who I was, they wouldn't. They'd see it as a little sick that I'd taken this child in so easily, wouldn't they? A woman clearly not recovered from the death of her own daughter? *Was* it a little sick?

It took another twenty minutes before the police car showed up in the parking lot along with a car that read *DSS* on the side. Department of Social Services. A male police officer got out of the cruiser, and a woman got out of the DSS car. From where I sat, they both looked stern-faced and annoyed. They said a few words to each other, then headed toward the entrance. The woman was about fifty and she was as big as a mountain. She had to be nearly six feet tall and while she wasn't obese exactly, she was huge. I looked at the tiny little girl sitting across the table from me.

"Go to the moon!" Bella said to the fairy, and she made it jump from the top of her Happy Meal box to the table and then up my arm. She smiled at me, all pearly baby teeth and big trusting eyes.

I wasn't turning her over to these people. No way.

The officer and social worker walked into the restaurant and the few customers looked up at them with curiosity. I tried to pretend I was one of them, just a curious mom bringing my little girl to Mickey D's for a Happy Meal. The officer and social worker eyed everyone in the restaurant, then went up to the counter to speak to the server, but I couldn't hear their conversation although I certainly tried.

"Aren't you hungry, honey?" I asked Bella, who was too busy playing with the fairy to notice her food. "Eat a little more of your burger."

She took a bite, watching me, an impish look now in her eyes. The toy had cheered her up, and she chewed her food playfully, mouth partly open as though taunting me to tell her to chew with it closed. I didn't care how she ate. I was just relieved to see the contentment return to her face. I couldn't imagine, not for a second, turning her over to these two people who looked scary even to me.

The officer was moving from table to table, talking to customers, while the mountainous woman walked into the separate play area and studied the two children who were scrambling through the tubes. In a moment, the officer was standing right next to my chair. I looked up at him, trying to think what an innocent woman would say at that moment.

"Is everything okay, officer?" I tried.

"Did you notice a little girl alone in here, ma'am?" he asked.

I shook my head and looked around as though searching for an abandoned child. "We've been here about twenty or thirty minutes," I said. "I didn't notice a little girl, though I wasn't really looking, either." I felt like a criminal and wondered if he could pick up the shiver in my voice. He was staring at Bella, who seemed fascinated by the shiny badge on his uniform.

"Thank you," he said finally, and he walked over to the social worker, who shook her head. They returned to the counter and I watched them exchange a few words with a man who might have been the manager. The officer handed him a card. I watched them leave. In the parking lot, I saw them chat for a moment. Then the social worker shrugged and the two of them climbed into their separate cars and took off. I let out my breath. I hadn't even realized I'd been holding it in.

A few minutes later, Bella and I were driving across the parking lot again. I parked right in front of JumpStart, ran inside to scan the place quickly for Travis, then ran back to my car.

"Nap time!" I sang out.

"Where's Daddy?" she asked.

"I'm not sure, honey, but I bet we'll see him tomorrow." What could I tell her? We'd go back to JumpStart in the morning. Tonight, Bella and I would once again be on our own.

In the apartment, I tucked her in for a nap and was relieved when she instantly fell asleep. Then I called Gene at the pharmacy.

"Something's come up," I said. "I won't be able to start tomorrow. Probably the next day, but—"

"*Erin,*" he said. "We're counting on you tomorrow."

"I know and I'm sorry. This is out of my control. A family matter." I knew that would silence him. My whole absence had been a family matter—Carolyn's death—and I knew Gene wouldn't probe. That didn't stop him from being angry, though.

"Do you know how hard I had to push to get them to keep this job open for you?" he asked.

"I know, I know. I'll call you Wednesday. Don't count on me till Thursday, though, okay? I have something I need to work out. I promise I'll be in Thursday. Absolutely. Really."

I went back into my bedroom and looked at the little girl in my bed, thinking that I'd just made one more promise I wasn't sure I could keep.

32
Travis

AROUND SEVEN THAT NIGHT, I GOT ON THE beltline that circled Raleigh and took the exit for the neighborhood where I was supposed to make the drop. I was three hours early, but I wanted to see where I was going while it was still light out. People did this all the time, I told myself as I drove. Criminals, anyhow. I'd help the guys in the house unload the cases, get my money, and with any luck, I'd be home free. I pictured it all happening, nice and neat.

The neighborhood surprised me. It wasn't run-down, like I'd expected it to be. It was a nice, middle-class neighborhood with winding streets and yards that looked like someone cared about them. I drove past the address where I was supposed to make the drop, not slowing down enough to attract attention. The house was a white split-level, the yard a little overgrown and an old maroon truck in the driveway. There was a kid's tricycle on the lawn. We weren't talking about a bunch of hardened criminals here. That made me feel better, like if this was a family with kids, they couldn't be all bad or all that dangerous. Suddenly Roy and his gun and the whole mess at the truck stop seemed far away. Now

I was picturing a husband and wife helping me unload the cases from the back of my van. I could ask them about their kids.

I parked the van around the corner. I'd wait here till ten, when I was supposed to make the drop. I'd bought a burrito at Taco Bell and I unwrapped it and began to eat. I was so close to this mess being over.

At five to ten, my hands were sweating. I'd tried to sleep, but couldn't. I kept picturing Erin and Bella together and what Erin must have thought when I didn't show this morning. And then suddenly it hit me: Wasn't tomorrow the day she was going back to work? *Shit.* Was it? She would have had to call the cops today, then, wouldn't she? I pressed my forehead against the steering wheel. I'd be at the coffee shop when it opened in the morning. Maybe she still had Bella and she'd try one last time before she went to work, hoping I'd show. And I'd show. Oh, yeah. *I'll be there, Bella.*

One minute to ten. I turned the key in the ignition and started driving slowly. I made a left onto one of the winding streets. I was about two blocks from the house, but I couldn't see it because of the curving road. When I came around the curve, I saw a car behind the truck in the driveway and two more parked by the curb. I stepped on the brake, trying to see if the cars belonged to Roy or Savannah, and that's when I realized they were cop cars. Three of them. I could hear shouting coming from the backyard. It sounded like a couple of men. Maybe a woman. I saw a cop lead a guy down the front walk, and all I could think was *That could have been me.* A couple of neighbors were out on their front lawns, watching what could only be a bust. I heard a little kid screaming, running out the front door after the man being led away. It was too dark for me to tell if the kid was a boy or a girl, and by then I didn't care. I kept on driving, driving, driving, and I didn't stop until I was back on the beltline.

My phone rang and I grabbed it, flipping it open without even checking the caller ID. "There's a fucking bust at that house!" I shouted.

"Right," Roy said. "So plan B. 2:00 a.m. You go out Route 64 to—"

"I want this stuff out of my van!"

"Chill," he said. "We've got it covered."

"We?" I asked. "Are you and Savannah working together again?"

"Savannah and I'll be working together till we're old and gray," he said.

So Savannah'd been playing me. I wasn't shocked. Just pissed.

"She's getting a truck right now," Roy said. He started rattling off directions and I had to memorize them since I was still driving. It sounded like he was sending me to the end of the earth. I only hoped I had the gas to get me there.

"You'll come to a clearing with a couple of tree stumps straight ahead of you," Roy said. "Don't drive past the stumps or you'll be up to your hubcaps in the marsh. You'll see the truck. 2:00 a.m."

"2:00 a.m.," I said.

"We know where you are, bro," he added. "Don't even think of blowing this again."

The place I was to meet Roy and Savannah was a long way off Route 64, clear on the other side of Raleigh. I drove for miles through the darkness, hoping I had the directions straight in my head. Some of the roads were missing street signs and I would have killed for a GPS.

At one forty-five, I reached the clearing. There was no

truck, but I was sure I was in the right place. The dirt road
ended and my headlights picked up the two tree stumps and
the marshy earth beyond. When I turned off my headlights,
the only lights I could see were the stars in the sky and the
half moon. The place spooked me. It had taken me a long
time of driving through nothing to get here. A gunshot
wouldn't even be heard out here. I turned on my headlights
again and inched the van forward. It looked like the soggy
earth bordered a pond, the water scummy. Tree limbs and
a tire stuck up from its surface, and suddenly I could see
myself in there. I saw my lifeless body floating in the water
after Roy did me in. Why wouldn't he? He'd have the drugs,
he'd have my van, and he could keep the few hundred bucks
and get rid of a potential problem—me. A criminal with a
conscience. I knew I'd become more trouble to him and
Savannah than I was worth.

Ten to two. No way was I going to hang out here, waiting to be killed. I turned the van around and left the way
I'd come in, hoping I didn't pass Roy and Savannah on the
road. I took the first turn I spotted and pulled off the dirt
road, tucking the van into the woods, waiting in the darkness until I saw what must have been their pickup pass by
on the main road and then I took off. Took the hell off.

I was relieved when I reached 64 again but I headed away
from Raleigh instead of toward it. I couldn't go back to the
parking lot near the coffee shop, which was the first place I
figured they'd come looking for me. Instead, I found a huge
Dumpster behind a restaurant. I pulled up next to it, opened
the lid and tossed in case after case of formula. They made
a satisfying *thunk* as they hit the garbage.

I felt cleansed when it was over. I'd reclaimed my van. My
life. Now I needed to reclaim my daughter.

33
Robin

I WALKED THE HALF MILE TO THE HOUSE where Alissa had told me Will lived with his mother. There was an old Suburban in the driveway, dented on one side, the paint scraped away and a little rust showing. But the house itself looked well maintained, as Alissa had pointed out to me. Someone had planted pansies in the front flower bed.

I hoped Will was home and not his mother. I was prepared to talk with him, but I wasn't sure what I would say I was doing there if his mother answered the door. Did she know about Hannah? Did she even know that Will and Alissa had been involved? I had no idea.

I climbed the steps to the front porch. The floor of the porch was a little tilted, enough so that I felt off-balance as I neared the door. I rang the bell and heard a series of low, gruff barks from inside, the kind of barking that had a menacing growl mixed into it, and I was glad there was a screen door between me and the front door.

It took a couple of minutes and another ring of the bell, but then the door was pulled open and Will stood in front of me. Blond, blue-eyed, slender. He looked just as he had on the computer screen in Alissa's room. He held the collar of a snarling dog that had at least half pit bull in him. I wondered if I was making a mistake. I'd never allow that dog around Hannah.

I opened my mouth to introduce myself but didn't need to. "Hey," he said, eyebrows raised. "What are *you* doing here?"

"I wanted to talk to you about Alissa and the baby," I said quietly, in case his mother was home.

"Right now?" he asked. "The timing kinda sucks."

I didn't like his answer. "There's no good time," I said.

"Okay," he said. He pushed the door open and stepped out onto the porch, the dog coming with him. I felt a rush of adrenaline as the dog started toward me, but once on the porch, he was friendly, tail wagging, sniffing my hands. My legs.

"He's cool." Will gestured toward him. "Bark's worse and all that." He sat down on one of the two porch chairs and I sat on the other. The dog rested his big square head on my knee and I scratched behind his left ear. "How's she doing?" Will asked. "Alissa?" He was wearing jeans. A blue T-shirt. No obvious tattoos. No pierced anything that I could see.

"She's doing okay," I said. "But she misses you. She really wants to see you. She doesn't know I'm here. I came to find out how you feel. If you want to see her and your daughter. Your baby's beautiful." I smiled. I should have brought a picture but hadn't thought of it. "Alissa's certain you want to see them and I frankly don't think it's fair you're being kept apart, so—"

"You have no idea what's going on, do you?" he interrupted me. He was leaning forward, arms on his knees, frown lines between his eyebrows that made him look older than nineteen. His smile was small and a little mocking.

I was caught off guard. "What do you mean?" I asked.

He didn't answer right away. He looked away from me, out toward the street. "How much do you know?" he asked.

"I know you're the father of Alissa's baby," I said. "I know you two saw each other for quite a while on the sly. I know she loves you and misses you. What do you mean, I don't know what's going on?"

"Your fiancé's kept you in the dark," he said. He made the word *fiancé* sound like something dirty, and I felt the same rush of adrenaline, the same fear, I'd felt when the dog snarled at me.

"About what?" I asked.

He leaned back and rolled his head right, then left as if stretching his neck muscles. "You know my mother used to work for the Hendricks?" he asked.

Ah. I thought I understood. "Yes, she was their house-keeper years ago, right? And I know the family can be… elitist. I know that the fact she's a housekeeper and your father's in prison is upsetting to—"

"Smokescreen," he said. "That might be what they're telling you is the big issue—" he put air quotes around those two words "—but that's not it. I haven't even seen my father since I was three. He's not in my life. Their big issue with him being locked up is just…" He shook his head. "They're blowin' smoke. My father doesn't have anything to do with why they didn't want me and Alissa to see each other. Neither does my mother's work. Or the fact that I dropped out of school."

"I'm afraid it does, Will," I said gently. "I'm afraid that the Hendricks family, much as I love them, have their noses in the air sometimes and—"

"Old man Hendricks—James. *Mr. Mayor.* Him and my mother had a thing."

"Had a...? You mean a disagreement or—"

"An *affair*," he said. "They were screwing each other. Get it?"

I sat back in the chair. "No, they were not," I said.

"Yes, they were. Back when she was working for them. From the time I was ten or eleven to when I was thirteen. I was probably the only person who knew about it and it took me a long time to catch on 'cause I was young and naive, but I finally figured it out. Then Mollie found out and all hell broke loose. They fired my mother, of course, and James gave her this house." He nodded toward the front door. "Used to be owned by the Hendricks and they rented it out, but James turned it over to my mother so she'd keep her mouth shut. He still pays for the upkeep on it. Check out the new paint job. Nice, huh?"

I shook my head in disbelief. Could he be making this whole ugly thing up? It was too far-fetched *not* to be the truth, though. I had a sudden thought. "This whole relationship between you and Alissa," I said, "this wasn't some sort of...revenge, was it? Do you care about her?"

He let out a long breath and sat back in the chair, his hands behind his head. "When I met Alissa, I didn't realize who she was. I liked her a lot. She was nice to look at. Cool. I knew she was too young for me, but she seemed older, you know what I mean? We just hung around for a few weeks before I knew her last name. Then I thought, *Oh, shit.* I told her how my mother used to work for her family and she remembered her, but not real well. I didn't say anything about what happened with her father, though. I didn't want to hurt her." He patted his thigh and the dog moved from my side to his. "You could say I was falling for her then," he said.

"You love her?"

He leaned over to rub the dog's chest. "I don't know if I love anybody," he said.

Hannah, I thought. He wouldn't be able to look at Hannah without loving her.

"I didn't know how her parents would react when we started going out, but I found out soon enough. They nixed it, but by then, Alissa and I were in too deep to just quit, so she got that gay dude—Jess—to play like he was her boyfriend, which worked okay till she got pregnant. Dale called me then. Said I had to stay away from Alissa and the baby. He said his mother had a cow when she found out Alissa was seeing me, because of my mother. The last thing Mollie wanted…probably James, too…was having my mother back in their lives. My mother's beautiful," he added. "I mean, she's forty-two and all that, but you put her next to Mollie Hendricks and Mollie fades away, you know what I mean?"

I could imagine how upset Mollie had been when she found out Alissa was dating Will, but seriously. They had to put Alissa and Hannah first, didn't they? They had to let go of the pettiness.

"What if I could smooth things out somehow?" *How?* I wondered. "Would you want that? I mean, do you still care about Alissa? Do you want to be part of your daughter's life?"

His smile was weird. Sort of…sly. "Do I care about Alissa?" he asked. "Sure. But I can live without her."

I sat back in the chair, drawing away from him. "That's harsh," I said. "What about your daughter?"

"She'll be just fine with the Hendricks and better off without me. I don't have any strong, like, paternal pull or anything."

He stood up and reached into his jeans pocket, taking out a slightly crumpled piece of paper. "You're not the first person from the Hendricks family to visit me today," he said.

He handed the paper to me and I flattened it on my thigh, shocked to see that it was one of Dale's personal checks, made out to Will Stevenson for $4500.

I looked over at him. "I don't understand," I said.

"Like father, like son." He shrugged. "James bought my mother's silence with this house," he said. "Dale's buying mine now. I'll leave Alissa alone. I'll never go public with what I know about James. I'll never try to be a part of that baby's life. Frankly, I'd rather have the money."

My mouth felt dry as dust. I shook my head. "Did you do some work for Dale, maybe?" I held the check in the air. "Maybe this was to cover the painter?" I nodded toward the house. "He wouldn't give you this much money for nothing."

"Staying out of Alissa's life seems to be worth it to him."

"Well, $4500 might seem like a lot to you now," I said, "but having your child in your life is worth a lot more than that."

He laughed. "Forty-five hundred dollars is a drop in the bucket of what Dale's given me," he said.

I couldn't speak. I had no idea what to say. I felt as though the past two years of my life were falling apart too quickly to ever be put back together.

"He delivers it in dribs and drabs," Will said. "Did you ever study those rat experiments when you were in school?"

"Rat experiments?" I shook my head, numb from head to toe.

"Yeah. If you reward them irregularly—you know, different amounts of rat food doled out at random times—they do more of what you want them to do than if you reward them on a schedule. I think that's Dale's philosophy. I never know when the next check is coming or how much it'll be, but I *do* know it's coming. And *he* knows if it ever stops coming, the deal is off."

I wanted to shout at him. Call him a liar. Suddenly, a woman about my age appeared at the screen door. She pushed it open a few inches and I could see her spiky blond hair, her long bare legs, her tight T-shirt. "Hey, baby," she said to Will. "What's going on?"

"Business," he said to her. "Wait inside."

She looked at me. Assessed me. I could see her deciding if I was a threat, and I could tell the moment she decided I wasn't. She closed the door.

If there was a threat in this whole mess of a situation, it wasn't me. It wasn't the pit bull. It wasn't even Will.

It was the man I was about to marry.

34
Erin

BELLA AND I SPENT ANOTHER QUIET MORNING in the coffee shop, and my brain hurt from trying to figure out what had happened to Travis and what I should do. We were going stir-crazy, both of us, so at eleven I gave up on JumpStart and drove Bella to the lakeside playground by my apartment complex. I liked that small playground because Carolyn had never been there and there was little to remind me of her other than the feeling of pushing a child on a swing.

When we'd tired ourselves out at the playground, I didn't even bother checking out JumpStart again. The coffee shop wasn't the answer. How could I turn Bella over to Travis now, knowing he could just dump her on a stranger?

Back at my apartment, we ate tuna sandwiches and played Chutes and Ladders and then I tucked her in for a nap. I lay next to her on the bed while she slept and opened her pink purse to stare at the picture of Robin. "Do you have any idea what's happening with your daughter?" I whispered to the photograph.

I pulled the shades to darken the room, then climbed under the covers, Robin's picture still in my hand as I drifted off. Suddenly I was back on the playground, only it was Carolyn I pushed on the swing. As she swung away from me, she turned her head to call out. "It was a mistake, Mommy!" she squealed at me as I waited for the swing to bring her back to my hands. When it did, I caught her. Held on to her. Buried my face in her soft blond curls. "You thought I was dead but I'm really alive!" she said.

I jerked awake, my breath in my throat and a huge smile on my face—until reality hit. I looked at Bella, whose fist was curled beneath her cheek. Her lamb peeked out from beneath the covers. I lightly touched her hair. "Where is your mother?" I whispered to her. "Does she dream of holding you in her arms?"

I turned on the night-table lamp and stared at Robin's picture in my hand. I would give anything to have my daughter back. Anything. Is that how she felt?

Beaufort. Not far. Two hours? Three? I had Robin's picture. I knew where she was. And Beaufort wasn't very large. Someone in that town would recognize her.

I got out of bed and began packing. I'd have to stop at the grocery store for snacks for the road. And JumpStart. Really, Bella and I should stop there one last time, just in case.

"Is Daddy here now?" Bella asked as I unbuckled her from the car seat and helped her out of the car the next morning. I'd parked right in front of JumpStart.

"I don't think so, honey," I said, "but I want to check before we go on a little trip."

"To the swings?" she asked, taking my hand.

"No, farther away than the swings." I planned to make a quick stop by my old house. In the attic was the portable DVD player we always used when we took Carolyn on a trip. I'd thought it was a terrible idea in the beginning, plugging my child into a DVD for hours, but Michael had said, "Why not? Don't you wish you could pass the time in the car watching a movie?" The DVDs had kept Carolyn entertained and happy and I was sure they would do the same for Bella.

As I'd expected, Travis wasn't in the coffee shop. I stopped at the counter where Nando was working alone. The new barista hadn't lasted long. "Coffee, OJ and a muffin?" Nando asked.

"Just coffee for me," I said. I'd given Bella cereal at home and I didn't think I could eat a thing.

"So, Travis is still working, huh?" Nando said as he put the lid on my cup.

"Uh-huh." I handed him a five. "We're having fun, aren't we, Bella?"

"We're going on a trip with *Wonder Pets!*" Bella said. I'd told her about some of the DVDs we had and she grew excited when I mentioned *Wonder Pets!,* so I hoped I could get my hands on it.

"You are?" Nando pressed a few buttons on the register. "Where are you off to?"

"Just to Beaufort for a couple of days," I said.

"Cool." Nando handed me my change. "You have family there?"

"No, it's just a little getaway." I looked down at Bella. "Do you want to use the potty before we go?" I asked.

She shook her head. She'd gone just before we left the house, but it was always worth checking.

"Okay, then." I waved goodbye to Nando, and in a few minutes we were back in the car and on our way to my old house.

★ ★ ★

It never occurred to me that Michael would be home. It was the middle of the day and I didn't even bother to peek in the garage windows as Bella and I walked along the path to the rear of the house. I opened the back door and there he was, standing in the middle of the kitchen, a cup of coffee halfway to his lips. I froze and Bella wrapped an arm around my leg. He looked from Bella to me, a puzzled frown on his face.

"Hi, Michael." I tried to sound casual and upbeat. "This is Bella."

He slowly lowered the coffee cup. "Hi, Bella." He glanced at her briefly before returning his gaze to me. "What's going on?" he asked.

"I'm babysitting Bella and I wanted to get the portable DVD player for the car."

"It's in the attic," he said.

"I know. That's where I'm headed." I took Bella's hand and started to walk past him.

"Can I play with the little kitchen again?" Bella asked.

I stopped walking. Well, *that* cat was out of the bag. I looked across the room at Michael. "We came by yesterday to get some books and—"

"You went in Carolyn's room?"

I nodded. "Bella, you can play with the kitchen while I run up to the attic for the DVD player." I started up the stairs, letting out a long breath. I wasn't looking forward to more of Michael's questions.

I heard Michael close behind us on the stairs. Bella peered over her shoulder as she climbed. "I don't want the man to come with us," she said.

"No, he won't," I said. "This will be a trip just for girls."

"I mean now. I don't want him to come to the little girl's room."

Oh. "He won't," I said. At the top of the stairs I turned to Michael. "Could you wait here a minute, please? Let me get her settled and I'll come out and tell you...what's going on. Maybe you could get the portable DVD player for me?"

He was slow to nod. "Okay," he said.

In Carolyn's room, Bella headed straight for the stove and began playing with the wooden food again. I waited until she was thoroughly engrossed, then knelt down next to her. "I'm going to talk to Michael," I said. "I'll be right outside the door here."

"Okay." She opened the oven door and squealed. "There's all more food in here!" she said, reaching inside for the rubber pork chops and whatever else Carolyn had left behind.

"Cook something yummy," I said, standing up.

Michael was already waiting for me in the hallway, the DVD player and a grocery bag of DVDs in his hands.

"I don't understand this," he said quietly, nodding toward Carolyn's room."

"She's the daughter of someone I met in a coffee shop near my apartment," I said. "I'm taking her to Beaufort, where her mother lives. She sort of... She was kind of dumped on me and I didn't have a choice."

"What do you mean, she was dumped on you?"

I sighed. He'd think I was crazy if I told him the truth. "Her father got work and had no one to watch her, so I... agreed to help out."

Michael looked at the floor for a moment, taking this in. "Good for you," he said, when he raised his head again. He sounded so sincere and he touched my arm with his free hand. "She got you into Carolyn's room," he said. "She did something I couldn't do. That's a big step for you."

I gave a reluctant nod. I didn't know why it was so hard for me to accept kindness from him. I felt a brick wall around myself, unable to really let him in. "Why are you home in the middle of the day?" I asked.

"The game I'm working on… It's just easier here. We're testing it on a focus group and I'm on Skype with the artist and it's quieter. Just…long story. It's going well."

What could I say? *I'm so happy your game is going well?* Maybe I was just envious that he found it so easy to put Carolyn's death aside and throw himself into his so-called work.

"That's good," I said, reaching for the DVD player. Empty words. "Bella and I'd better hit the road."

"Are you just dropping her off and coming back? Maybe we could have dinner tonight or tomorrow night? I want to talk to you about something."

"I don't know my plans," I said. "I may stay in Beaufort a couple of days." How long would it take me to find Robin? "I'll call you, okay? Thanks for getting this." I nodded toward the DVD player.

He glanced into Carolyn's room where Bella was chattering to herself. "I wanted to talk to you about this game," he said. "The one I've been working on the past few months." He looked uncomfortable. "I could use your input," he said, "and the input of that online group you're part of, if they'd be willing."

I frowned. "Harley's Dad?" I asked. "I don't understand."

"It's a game about…about grieving, in a way," he said. "Or really about honoring someone you've lost. That's a better way of saying it, though that's part of the problem I'm having where you could help. How to describe—"

"You invented a *game* about grieving?" I was horrified.

He nodded. "Right now, I'm calling it *Losing Carolyn,*" he

said. "It's like my other games in that it's collaborative and the more people who play, the better it should work. It uses Kübler-Ross's stages of grief, and—"

"Michael." I interrupted him with a shake of my head. "I can't believe what I'm hearing." It seemed so wrong.

"That's why I'd like a chance to talk to you about—" He stopped talking as Bella came out of Carolyn's room. She glanced at him, then looked at me. "How long do we have to stay here?" she asked.

"We can go now," I said, reaching for her hand.

"Will you talk to me about this?" Michael asked.

"When I get back," I said. "But I can tell you right now, the last thing I'd ask the people in the Harley's Dad group to do is play a game about their grief."

He actually smiled, but there was sadness in it. "You might change your mind if you'd give me a chance to describe it to you."

He took a step toward me and I knew he wanted to hug me. I leaned forward and gave him a quick kiss on the cheek. "I'll be in touch," I said, and then headed down the stairs with Bella.

35

Travis

THE SUN WOKE ME UP. MY FIRST THOUGHT WAS *I actually slept. Finally!* My second thought—*What time is it?*—jerked me completely awake and I sat up on the mattress. I'd parked on a narrow road off the beaten track and I could tell by the way the sun poured through the woods next to my van that it was late. I'd wanted to be at JumpStart when it opened. I made my way up to the driver's seat and reached into the cup holder where I'd put my watch. Eight-forty. *Damn.*

My phone had rung as I'd drifted off to sleep the night before and I'd turned off the ringer. It had given me a sense of power over Roy and Savannah. I no longer had what they wanted. Yeah, they could hurt me out of revenge, I supposed, but right now they couldn't possibly know where I was and they thought Bella was in Beaufort. And yeah, I didn't know exactly what I was going to do when I got Bella back, but I knew I was going to JumpStart and at least that was a plan.

I stood in the woods at the side of the road to brush my teeth and take a leak. There wasn't another soul around. I wasn't sure exactly where I was; I'd pulled onto this road in the dark the night before, just glad I was far away from Roy and Savannah and closer—I hoped—to Bella. I ran my hands through my hair, then climbed back into the van, turned the key and started driving. I hadn't gone more than two yards before I knew I had a flat.

I sat there feeling paralyzed for a few minutes, remembering the flat I'd had a month or so ago in Carolina Beach when I drove over a nail. I'd used the spare and now I had none. This isolated parking place which had seemed like such a great idea a few minutes ago now seemed like a big mistake. I had no idea where I was and the eighteen bucks I had in my pocket wouldn't buy me much in the way of road service.

I got out of the van and looked at the tire. Flat as a pancake. If I drove on it, I'd wreck the wheel. I put the phone in my pocket and started walking. I didn't think I'd driven that far off the main road the night before, but I'd been so tired I couldn't really have said. I'd walked about ten minutes when I saw a car turn into a small dirt lot a short distance ahead of me. A little white clapboard chapel, not in the best shape, was tucked into the woods. *Jedediah Baptist,* the sign out front read. A man got out of the car and headed for the chapel's side entrance and I started walking toward him. His hand was reaching for the doorknob when he noticed me, and he lowered it to his side.

"Can I help you?" he asked. He was all duded up. Suit and tie. Clean-cut. Big, good-looking black guy, maybe forty-five or fifty. I imagined how I looked to him: skinny young white guy in dire need of a shower. Dirty clothes. Dirty hair. *Homeless* written all over me.

"I'm parked down the road," I said, pointing behind me, "and I've got a flat."

He frowned like he didn't believe me. Like he thought I might be there to smack him over the head and rip off the church's poor box. He looked down the road though he couldn't possibly see my van from where we stood.

"Have a spare?" he asked.

I tried to smile as I shook my head. "I had a flat about a month ago and used it then. I ran over a nail on a construction site where I was working," I added, hoping the fact that I'd had a job would raise his estimation of me a little.

He tilted his head. "What are you doing out here on this road, son?" he asked.

"I needed a place to sleep last night."

"Where are you headed?"

"Anywhere I can find work," I said.

"What sort of work you do?"

"Construction. Handyman. Plumbing." I smiled again. "At this point, anything."

He shook his head and I sensed he was starting to relax about me. "Rough out there right now, is it?"

"Yes, sir," I said. "I was wondering if you could tell me the name of this road and if you know of a service station that has road service." I pulled the phone out of my pocket.

"Yeah, I know a place," he said. "Come into my office." He unlocked the door and I followed him through a short hallway and into a small room. The plaque on the door read *Reverend Winn*. He sat down behind a desk and began looking through an old-fashioned Rolodex. His fingers stopped at a particular card. He tapped it a couple of times, then looked up at me. "They'll probably have to tow you in," he said. "Or at least take the tire back to their shop."

"Right." My hopes for today were rapidly sinking. Where was Bella now? I felt like hitting something and letting go with a string of cuss words. If a man of the cloth hadn't been sitting in front of me, I would have. I wanted my daughter back!

He wrote the phone number on a Post-it note. "You have money to pay for this, son?" he asked, before handing me the slip of paper.

I hesitated. "I have eighteen bucks," I said.

He rubbed his chin and looked out the only window in the room. "You have any tools with you?"

"Yes, sir."

"I tell you what," he said. "The door to our kitchen is warped. You take care of it and I'll cover the work on your vehicle."

It was the best I could hope for. More than I could hope for, to be honest. "That's generous of you," I said. "Thank you."

He got to his feet. "When's the last time you ate?" he asked. "Ladies' luncheon was yesterday and the refrigerator is full." He put a hand on my shoulder and led me into a small kitchen.

I bet this guy was a good minister, I thought. I felt like telling him everything. Pouring the whole mess out. But of course I told him nothing. I would eat the leftovers from the church ladies' luncheon and I'd fix the door while waiting for my tire to be plugged, and all the while I'd imagine Erin washing her hands of me, taking my confused four-year-old daughter someplace where I'd never be allowed to see her again.

It was twelve-thirty by the time I was sitting in my van again, pulling my thoughts together. I had four decent tires, a full stomach, and in my pocket, a twenty-dollar bill the reverend had handed me before I left his chapel. If not for the fact that I was running way too late, I could call the flat a lucky break. But I *was* late. Most likely, Bella was in foster care and Erin was at her job at the pharmacy. Maybe someone in JumpStart would know where she worked. That was the best I could hope for.

Before I started the car, I finally turned on the ringer on my phone and checked the messages. There were five of them, four from Roy and one from Savannah. I didn't bother listening to them, but the phone rang again as I turned the key in the ignition, and when I saw Savannah's number, I let out a sigh. They were going to keep hassling me as long as they thought I had their stash. I turned off the engine and flipped the phone open. "I don't have the stuff," I said.

"Why didn't you show?" she shouted as though she hadn't heard me. "What is wrong with you? You are so dead, Travis. So totally screwed. If you try to unload the shit yourself, Roy'll kill you."

"It's gone," I said tiredly, but she must have been passing the phone over to Roy because the next voice on the line was his.

"You're really pissing me off, man!" he said. "Where are you?"

"Like I'd tell you. Look, I don't have the stuff anymore, so just forget about it. Write this off as a loss, okay? That's what I'm doing."

"What are you talking about? You don't have the balls to do a deal on your own."

"I dumped it."

"What the fuck are you *talking* about?"

"I dumped it!" I shouted. "I don't have it. So leave me alone."

"Do you have a clue what that stash is worth? Get it back or you're dead. Your daughter, too."

"Leave her out of this."

"Same place, same time tonight," he said. "You hear me?"

I sighed, like he'd won. "A more public place," I bargained, although it didn't matter. I wasn't showing up, but I'd keep them in the dark about that so with any luck, they'd leave me alone today and I could focus on getting Bella back. I wished that Bella and I could be a million miles away by tonight.

"Public doesn't cut it," Roy said.

"You want the stuff or not?" I said. "I'm not meeting you out in the middle of nowhere."

I heard Savannah say something in the background and it sounded like they were arguing back and forth for a minute. Finally, Roy was on the line again. "The lower level lot by the Sears at Crabtree Valley Mall," he said. "You know where that is?"

"I'll find it."

"Last chance, fool," he said, and he hung up.

I closed the phone slowly, then turned on the engine and drove down the narrow road, giving a little wave to the chapel that had been my home for the morning. I made a left on the main road. Glenwood. That would lead me right to Brier Creek. I almost smiled. *You're the fool, Roy,* I thought to myself, but I kept checking my rearview mirror for the candy-apple-red Mustang. That was a habit that was going to die hard.

I pulled into the parking lot near the Target and the paranoia was back full force. I was as sure as I could possibly be that I hadn't been followed. Definitely not by Roy's car, anyway, but I parked close to the Target entrance instead of near JumpStart, anyway. Then I walked across the lot toward JumpStart, dodging between the parked cars like I could throw someone off my trail that way. I was winded by the time I got to the coffee shop, not so much from the exertion of the walk as from the tension. I must have been holding my breath half the way. I walked into the coffee shop and scanned it. No Erin. No Bella. I sank into the chair Erin usually sat in, unsure what to do.

"Hey, Travis," Nando called from behind the counter. "I hear you found work, dude. Good news, huh?"

What was he talking about? I stood up and walked toward the counter. "Have you seen Erin?" I asked. "You know. The lady who—"

"Yeah, she was in with Bella this morning."

Bella was still with her! I had to hold on to the edge of the counter to keep from jumping for joy. I had to keep my cool.

"Erin's been watching her for me," I said. "I was hoping to catch them."

"Before they took off on their big road trip, huh?" Nando swiped a spot on the counter with a rag.

"Road trip?" I sounded dense and thought I'd better try to recover. "Oh, you mean…" I didn't know what to say. What *did* he mean?

"Beaufort, right?" he asked. "You want coffee, man? You look like you need it."

Beaufort. Why would she go to Beaufort? I could think of only one reason. I remembered her looking at Robin's picture and me giving my usual explanation. *That's her mom. She lives in Beaufort.*

"What time did she leave?" I asked.

"A couple of hours ago," Nando said. "Why don't you call her?"

"Good idea," I said, pushing away from the counter. "I've got her number in the van." I raced out the door. He probably thought I was one weird dude, but with any luck, I'd never have to see him again.

I wove through the parking lot one more time, dodging the eyes I imagined were following me until I got to the van. Quarter of a tank of gas. I'd give it a few bucks' worth. Just enough to get me where I needed to go.

36
Robin

ALISSA AND I WERE ALONE IN THE HOUSE WITH
Hannah, although the housekeeper was vacuuming down the
hall in the living room. I knew the two housekeepers who
worked for me in the B and B very well and I cared about
them as people, not just as my employees, but I barely knew
anything about the Hendricks' housekeeper other than her
name: Ella. Mollie gave me a gentle lecture early on about
how to treat the B and B staff. I was too friendly with them,
she said, and that would make it hard if I ever needed to ask
more of them. "Keep it professional at all times," she told
me. I'd tried to find the right balance between my friendly
nature and my role as their employer. Behind Mollie's back,
though, I still asked the B and B staff about their boyfriends
and their home life and I'd even loaned one of them a few
dollars on a couple of occasions. But now I understood why
Mollie had kept her distance from her staff. I understood
why their housekeeper was an older woman, industrious,
quiet and plain. I imagined all those qualifications were what
Mollie demanded in a housekeeper after James's fling with
Will's mother.

I fiddled with the baby monitor while Alissa rocked Hannah on her thighs. She was studying Hannah's face the way I had when the baby was first born. She was a little late with her bonding, but it was intense now and it was real. What I knew about Will—if it was the truth—would hurt her so much.

I could only imagine how Mollie had felt when she'd learned the truth about her husband. Then what a shock for her to discover Alissa was seeing the son of "the other woman"—and carrying his baby! How painful for her. I hoped it would be at least a few days before I bumped into James. I felt disgust toward him that would take a while to go away. I would never be able to look at him the same way. *He's only human,* I told myself. Well, so was I, but I would never betray my spouse that way. Would Dale? *Like father like son,* Will had said. I had the sickening feeling that Dale was already betraying me.

I wanted to be wrong about that. I wanted Will to be lying to me. I wanted an explanation! I needed one. *There are things you don't know and have no need to know.*

Screw you, I thought to myself, stepping away from the baby monitor.

"I just remembered I left a scarf in Dale's apartment," I said to Alissa. "I'll be right back."

"Okay," she said without looking up from Hannah.

I climbed the stairs to Dale's apartment and let myself in with the key he'd given me shortly after we'd started dating. That key had meant so much to me back then. It had meant he was serious about me and that he trusted me. That he had nothing to hide from my eyes.

I walked across his living room. The door to the room he used as his office was closed but unlocked, and it let out a squeak when I opened it. I rarely went into that room.

I'd always viewed his office as his private space. It was tiny, almost claustrophobic, the walls lined with law books, the oversize desk as neatly organized as Dale himself. My heart pumped hard as I sat down at that desk. What would I say if he came home and found me in here? It was a risk I had to take. I felt intrusive and sneaky, but also justified. If he found me, I'd tell him the truth and hope against hope that he had an explanation for his payment to Will.

And yet, as I opened the top right drawer and pulled out his checkbook, I knew it didn't matter. There was nothing he could say to explain away that check in Will's pocket. Regardless of what I found, I knew I no longer loved him. I wasn't sure *what* I felt, but it wasn't love. I loved Alissa. Hannah. Mollie. Whatever love I'd felt for Dale had eroded over the past few weeks. Maybe it had been disintegrating for months.

I glanced through the check register. It showed the last one he'd written, number 1432 to "W.S." for forty-five-hundred dollars. I flipped back through the pages and counted seven more checks to W.S. for as little as two thousand and as much as eight thousand. Random rewards to the rat. I closed the checkbook, slipped it back into the drawer and slowly got to my feet. I left the office, not even bothering to close the door behind me. What did it matter? I now knew exactly what I felt for Dale: disgust.

37
Erin

On the Road

BELLA WAS AN EASY TRAVELER, MESMERIZED BY
Wonder Pets! and *Dora the Explorer,* but I wasn't having that
comfortable a time of it. The sound of Carolyn's old DVDs
playing in the backseat was disorienting and I kept having
to check my rearview mirror to remind myself it was Bella
back there, not my daughter. I was still thinking about my
conversation with Michael. A grief game? I tried to muster
up the annoyance I'd felt when he first mentioned it, but I
was having trouble doing it. That was always the way Michael viewed the problems of the world, wasn't it? *How can I
create a game to solve this problem?* he'd ask himself. I felt torn
between my anger at him and my empathy. He'd been grieving all along, just in his own unique way. I shook off the
thought. The empathy I suddenly felt toward him didn't fit
well with the wall I'd built around myself to keep him out.

I felt more and more anxious as we neared the coast and
I thought it was because my plan to find Bella's mother

seemed half-baked. I had an old picture and a name. That was it. What if no one recognized Robin? What if Travis had custody of Bella because Robin was an unfit mother? But as we passed the exit for Atlantic Beach, I understood the real source of my anxiety. The exit sign caught me by surprise and I quickly looked away from it. *Ridiculous.* I needed to get over this. Judith once told me I might need to walk out on the pier again to rid myself of the haunting visions I had from the night Carolyn died. I'd need to face the fear. "You've built the pier into something it isn't," she'd said. That was true. The pier was a soul-eating monster. "If you can walk out on it someday," Judith had said, "it might put an end to those visions." I'd told her to forget it. She might as well have been telling someone with a phobia of high places to leap from the Eiffel Tower. And yet, maybe she was right.

I took the next exit and got back on 70 heading in the opposite direction. I stared directly at the sign for Atlantic Beach and drove onto the exit ramp.

"We're going to take a little side trip," I said to Bella. She didn't respond. She was trying to sing along with a song on the DVD, stumbling over half the words but completely absorbed.

Atlantic Beach was quiet and there was plenty of parking at the pier. I allowed myself no time to think, getting out of the car quickly and opening the back door for Bella, but I felt the tremor in my body just beneath my skin. Bella was still glued to the video screen.

"We're going to go for a little walk," I said, reaching for the buckle of her car seat.

"No!" she said. "I want to watch this." She was going to need a nap soon. There was a large inn in Beaufort. Michael and I had stayed there many years ago. This time of year, there'd almost certainly be vacancies. As soon as we checked in, we'd take a nap. Then we'd walk around town, Robin's photograph in hand, and start asking people if they knew her. I pictured us walking from shop to shop on Front Street, and suddenly the whole idea seemed even more far-fetched and overwhelming, but it was the only thing I could think of to do.

Right now, though, I had a more pressing need.

"Come on, honey," I said. "You can watch again in a few minutes. We're just taking a little walk to see the ocean, okay?" I sounded so brave and calm! I held her hand as we walked toward the pier. Inside the tackle shop with its smell of fish and metal and oil and salt, I paid a dollar and received our tickets. Then we walked through the open door and out onto the pier. The first wide strip of boards was over land, but even so, my heart raced.

The day was brilliant, but only a handful of fishermen were on the pier, and the scene was nothing like it had been the night Carolyn fell into the sea. In daylight and uncrowded, it was almost unrecognizable as the same pier. But there were the horizontal wooden slats along the railings. There were just two of them, but they were wider than in my memory. Safer. I pointed to the fishermen in the distance. "People are fishing out there," I said to Bella. I tried to calm myself by speaking in an even voice, but I must have been hyperventilating because I needed to stop between the words *fishing* and *out there* to take a breath. We walked along the part of the pier that stretched long and high above the beach, but when we reached the strip above the crashing waves, I couldn't take another step. I could see the end of the pier far in the distance, the place my daughter had disappeared forever, and the boards turned to cotton beneath my feet. I grabbed the back of one of the built-in benches to steady myself. I would never be able to do this. I lifted

Bella into my arms, turned around, and nearly ran back to the exit.

"I want to see the fish!" Bella wailed in my ear.

"We need to get back to the car," I said, winded. "You can watch *Wonder Pets!* again. Then pretty soon we'll have some lunch and then a nap."

In the car, I let her buckle herself in, my hands trembling too hard to help even if she'd needed me to. Then I sat behind the wheel and shut my eyes as I leaned back against the headrest. *Premature,* I thought to myself. If I couldn't manage the diving board or the bridge over the creek at my apartment complex, how did I think I could possibly manage this? I drove out of Atlantic Beach and my breathing didn't settle down again until I was back on 70, heading for the safety of Beaufort.

The inn was still there. It was a long, three-story building with a porch that faced the water. It was nearly empty on this October afternoon. I checked us in, and it wasn't until we were riding the elevator to the third story that I realized our room—333—was the same one Michael and I had stayed in. With all the empty rooms, how did I get that unlucky? I thought of taking the elevator back down and asking for a different room, but by that time, Bella was so irritable that I didn't dare.

Once we were in the room, I tucked her into the queen-size bed for a nap. Then I went onto the balcony and looked out over the shops across the street and the waterfront beyond. In the distance, I could see Carrot Island and I thought I could make out a couple of ponies by the water's edge. I was only now beginning to calm down from those few minutes on the pier. I tightened my jacket around my shoulders and sat down on one of the white rockers, leaving the door to the room open so I could hear Bella if she woke up. I remembered this view from when Michael and I shared this room so long ago, when Carolyn had been an idea in the future, one of our three or four imagined kids. Our family. That future that had seemed so full of hope and simple then. We thought we could plan it. Control it. I remembered loving Michael so much. I remembered making love to him over and over again. *There's magic in this room,* we'd decided. We would set out for a walk through town but make it only a block or two because we couldn't wait to get back to our room to make love again. I was working on my pharmacist license back then and I'd talk about drugs and chemicals and he'd ask questions as if I was talking about the most fascinating thing in the world. And he was just discovering the "social power of gaming," he called it. I thought he was the most remarkable man. A passionate idealist. That was long before he ran away from us. From Carolyn and me. Metaphorically. *Literally.*

We'd been drowning and he ran away.

38

Travis

I ROLLED INTO BEAUFORT ON FUMES, THE needle on my gas gauge hovering right above empty. The whole way there, I was thinking how crazy this was. I always told people that Bella's mother lived in Beaufort, but the truth was, she could be anywhere. She'd definitely lived in Beaufort after she got out of her cardiac rehab program because my mother knew someone who knew someone who knew Robin's father. But now? More than two years later? I couldn't imagine her staying in a little place like Beaufort. When I let myself think about her, I pictured her back in school getting the education she'd always wanted. Becoming a nurse or maybe even a doctor—unsaddled by the baby she never wanted me to know about.

The only reason I could think of for Erin to be here, though, was because she thought Bella's mother was here. I pictured her trying to find Robin with only that old photograph to go by. Beaufort was small, but it wasn't so small that everybody knew everybody else.

I didn't have Robin's picture, but I had her last name. Unless she'd gotten married. *Whoa,* that felt like a knife to my heart, but why should it? She'd cut me out. And then I had another thought: she might not even be alive. I hoped she was. I really did. I hated the thought of her dying before she'd had a chance to live. Wherever she was, though, whatever she was up to, I didn't think she'd welcome Bella with open arms if Erin showed up on her doorstep.

My main hope right now was that she was still in Beaufort and Erin and I would both be able to find her. She'd be the point of intersection. The only way I could get to Bella. But I couldn't deny that I wanted to see Robin. I'd be shaking up her life one more time and putting her in a really weird position, but yes. I wanted to see her.

I stood on the boardwalk that ran along the waterfront. On one side of me were the docks and a dozen or so gleaming white boats that screamed *Money!* On the other side was a long string of shops and restaurants. Touristy places, though. If she still lived in Beaufort, what was the chance she ever set foot in them? Although if she still lived in Beaufort, maybe she *worked* in one of them. I headed down the boardwalk and walked into one of the shops—a small place that sold pottery and jewelry and kitschy souvenirs.

"Excuse me," I said to the gray-haired lady dusting one of the display shelves. "I'm looking for someone who lives in Beaufort and I know this is a long shot, but would you happen to know a girl named Robin Saville?"

She turned to face me, looking me up and down, and I thought I saw her nostrils flare for just a second. I hoped I didn't smell as grungy as I felt. "You don't look like a reporter," she said.

It was a weird comment. "No, I'm not a reporter," I said.

"You're not from Beaufort, either, are you?" she asked.

I shook my head again. "Do you know her?"

"Everybody knows her, honey," she said. "She's engaged to the guy who thinks he's going to be our next mayor."

"Let's *hope* he's the next mayor," said an elderly man sitting behind the glass jewelry case. I hadn't even noticed him and his voice gave me a start.

"We're not in agreement there," the woman said, "but we can probably agree on Robin, can't we? I don't know what a sweet girl like that wants with a family of money grubbers."

I felt like I was going to keel over. "Robin *Saville?*" I asked. There couldn't be another woman with that name, but I was having trouble getting it through my head that the first person I asked knew her. That *everyone* knew her.

"Can you tell me where I can find her?" I asked.

Now she looked suspicious. "Why do you want to know?"

I could imagine how I looked to them. She was engaged to a guy running for mayor? Some clean-cut dude who apparently had money? And here I stood—this scruffy, smelly guy. "We're old friends," I said, and I thought how lame that sounded. How made up. Yet my throat choked up when the words came out of my mouth. "I knew her when we were kids, but I haven't seen her in years and I thought since I was passing through Beaufort, I—"

"She runs that Taylor's Creek Bed and Breakfast place right down the street," the man said.

"Hush!" The lady shook her duster in his direction. "Don't tell him that!" she said. "You don't know who this boy is."

"Oh, what're you worryin' about?" the man said.

"It's okay," I said to her, heading for the door. "Really. We're old friends. No problem."

Back on the boardwalk, I started running toward my van, my heart pounding in time with the slap of my sneakers. I was so close to her! I hoped she wouldn't slam the door in my face. I hoped she could remember at least a little of what had choked me up in the shop—that friendship we'd thought would tie us together forever.

39
Erin

MY PLAN TO FIND BELLA'S MOTHER WAS START-ing to seem more ridiculous by the minute. Bella and I walked along the waterfront, stopping in the shops and restaurants, showing her picture to everyone we met. After our fifth unsuccessful stop, we were about to cross the street when a red Mustang pulled up to the curb in front of us. A woman threw open the passenger-side door and nearly burst from the car.

Bella suddenly let out a squeal and did a happy little jump at my side. She let go of my hand and ran toward the woman, whose hair was very long and very blond. No wonder no one I'd shown her picture to had recognized Robin! She'd dramatically changed her looks since that youthful photograph had been taken.

"Bella!" The woman lifted Bella into the air and spun her around and my hand felt empty where Bella had been holding it. But this was what I'd wanted, right? What I was here for? I'd wanted to see this reunion between mother and child. I pressed my hand against the lump in my throat.

The woman hoisted Bella a little higher in her arms, then looked at me. "Hi, Robin," she said. "I'm Savannah."

What?

"I'm not Robin," I said. "I thought *you* were Robin."

She frowned at me. "What do you mean, you're not Robin?"

"I'm not. I'm actually *looking* for Robin."

She started to laugh. "Oh, come on," she said. "If you're not Robin, what are you doing with Bella?"

"I…" I was so confused. "Who are you?" I asked. "How do you know Bella? Are you a friend of—" I was going to ask if she was a friend of Robin's but my brain felt like mush. It was like waking up from a dream and trying to separate the real world from the unreal.

The passenger window of the red car rolled down and the woman leaned over to speak to the driver. "She says she's *looking* for Robin," she said.

The driver—a man I couldn't see well—said something I couldn't make out.

"I don't have a clue," Savannah said to him. She straightened up, lowering Bella back to the sidewalk. Then she opened the car door and folded the front seat forward. "Hop in," she said to me. "We'll help you find Robin."

"Great," I said, sliding into the rear seat. Bella climbed in after me. No car seat, of course, but hopefully we didn't have far to go. The car smelled of cigarettes and fried food.

The driver turned to smile at me. He was fortyish and very good-looking, but he held a cigarette in his hand where it rested on the steering wheel and I wished he'd toss it out the window.

"Hey," he greeted me, and as if he'd been in on my thoughts, he opened the window a crack and flicked the cigarette into the street. "What's your name?" he asked.

"Erin." I laughed. "And I'm totally confused. I came here to find Robin and now I find you guys and—" I noticed the gun. A toy? Something he was trying to hand to Bella to entertain her in the car? He was twisted in the front seat now so that he nearly faced me and he was pointing a gun not quite at me over the top of the seat. His eyebrows were raised and he was quiet as he waited for me to react to it. I reached for a door handle, but remembered the car was a two-door. We were trapped.

"What's going on?" My voice came out in a whisper.

"Is Daddy with you?" Bella asked Savannah.

"No, cutie," Savannah said. The driver handed the gun to her, then shifted the car into gear and started driving. I put my arm around Bella and tried to pull her close to me, but she was too wound up to cuddle.

"Why do you have Bella?" she asked me.

"I've been taking care of her while her father's working."

Savannah looked at the driver. "This makes no sense," she said to him.

"Doesn't matter. We've got the kid."

"Look," I said, "please let us out. I don't know what you—"

"And you just happen to be in Beaufort, where Robin lives?" The driver's voice was cynical and mean. He was watching me in the rearview mirror and the eyes I'd thought were attractive a minute ago now looked slitted and cruel. "You're a friend of hers, right? Just come out with it and tell us where she is if you want to save your own skin. There's no point in gaming us now."

"I don't *know* Robin," I insisted. "Travis left Bella with me in Raleigh and—"

"In Raleigh?" He sounded as though he didn't believe me.

"Yes. He asked me to take care of her for just one night,

but he didn't come back. I knew her mother was in Beaufort, so I came here to try to find her. Please just let us out. This is a big misunderstanding or—"

I was starting to tremble, but Bella seemed oblivious to the tension in the car. She leaned forward to play with Savannah's hair where it hung over the front seat, and one thought ran through my mind like a mantra. *Keep her safe. Keep her safe. Keep her safe.*

The driver pounded the steering wheel so hard that even Savannah jumped. "Fucking wild goose chase!" he shouted.

"We have Bella," Savannah said to him. I could tell she was trying to calm him. Soothe him. I hoped it would work.

"Once we get the shit from Travis," the driver said, "he's dead."

"What…shit?" I asked, but I knew. I didn't live in a bubble. This had to be about drugs. *Damn it, Travis.*

Bella started to whimper. I didn't know if she'd understood the man's comment about Travis being dead or she'd picked up the angry tone of his voice. Either way, she was now crying and I pulled her toward me. This time she let me hold her. Let me rub her back. "It's okay," I whispered. "Everything's going to be okay."

"Would you cool it, Roy?" Savannah said. "You're scaring her."

"Don't you go soft on me," the man—Roy—said to Savannah, and I watched her draw back, leaning into the passenger-side door a bit. Roy glanced at me in the mirror again. "We can dump her and just keep the kid. This one's only in the way."

I should have felt more afraid than I did. They had a gun. They were talking about getting rid of me. The man behind the wheel was crazy and the woman in front of me was not much better. But I felt steel inside my arms. Inside my chest.

I wouldn't let them separate me from Bella. I pictured the pier. Carolyn vanishing. A gun was nothing compared to that image in my mind. *Keep her safe.*

40
Robin

THE HOUSEKEEPERS WERE WORKING UPSTAIRS, my guests were all out, and I was in the kitchen putting together the casserole for tomorrow's breakfast. I was content doing that, or as content as I could be, given what I now knew about Dale. I thought of how he wanted me to turn over the day-to-day business of the B and B to Bridget once we were married. I'd agreed to that, even though I didn't want to, just like I'd agreed to practically every other thing he asked of me. Why did I always go along with his demands? He was so controlling. Every thought of Dale was infuriating to me right now. I chopped onions and peppers with a vengeance, the knife blade slapping against the cutting board in a satisfying rhythm. Why should I give up something that made me happy? Why was it always about what *he* wanted? Dale had no idea what it meant to be able to truly *live* every minute of his life. Those meditative things like cooking and straightening up were work to him, while they were a joy to me. We were so, so different. It was over between us. He was not the man I thought he was and definitely not the man I wanted. Now I had to think of how to end our relationship without hurting the rest of the family—and myself—in the process.

The doorbell rang as I pressed aluminum foil over the top of the casserole. The sound surprised me. I wasn't expecting any guests to check in that afternoon. I walked into the foyer and through the sidelight I could see a white van parked in front of the house. Had I set up an appointment with a worker and forgotten? I thought of the dripping faucet in the front upstairs guestroom and the shingles that had blown off the roof in the last storm. But I was certain those guys were coming next week.

I pulled open the door and there he was. *Travis*. For a moment, neither of us said a word. We stared at each other and I was glad I had a healthy heart; my old heart wouldn't have held up to the extra beats and the wrenching nostalgia that overwhelmed me. Hundreds of memories. A thousand regrets.

"Robin," he said finally, and I heard so much in that word. An ache. An apology? It scared me. Something was wrong. Something with my child. *Our* child.

I pressed my fingers to my mouth. "Is she okay?" I asked.

"I think so." He stretched a hand toward me and I took it, pulling him inside and wrapping my arms around him. I didn't know which of us was holding the other tighter. We were silent. I knew in the deepest part of myself that he felt exactly what I felt—love that had taken root when we were kids. Love that had been forced underground. We'd blocked it from our minds and our hearts, but it had never disappeared. Certainly not for me, and I knew by the way he held me, not for him, either. *I love you; you love me,* I thought. He didn't need to say the words for me to know it.

I finally pulled away from him. "There are people here," I said quietly. "Come with me." I took his hand and walked with him through the foyer and into my apartment. In the living room, I closed the door behind us, then turned to face him, hand over my mouth again in utter disbelief that Travis Brown was actually standing in front of me. He looked gaunt and tired. He hadn't shaved in a few days, either.

"I thought you'd be angry," he said. "I promised I'd never get in touch, but—"

"I'm anything but angry," I said. I grabbed his hands and pulled him over to the sofa. "Tell me everything," I said as we sat down. "Why you're here. Where's my...your daughter. What do you mean, you *think* she's okay?"

"That's why I'm here," he said. "I screwed up, Robin. I think someone might be bringing her to you. As a matter of fact, I was hoping she might already be here." He glanced around the room as though I might be hiding her. "You haven't heard anything?"

I shook my head. "I don't understand," I said.

He stood up and started pacing. He was so much thinner than I remembered, but his eyes. Those lashes. As beautiful as ever. "It's a long story," he said.

"Tell me." I got up myself to check the intercom by my apartment door, making sure it was on so that I'd hear the doorbell if it rang. "Where is she?"

"With a...this friend. This woman." He sat down again on the sofa, his hands resting on his knees. "How are you?" he asked, as if testing me to see if I could handle whatever the long story was he had to tell me.

"I'm fine. I'm good." I sat on the edge of the chair nearest him. "Tell me what's going on."

"You look..." He shook his head, unsmiling. "You look amazing," he said. "I'm glad to see that."

"Tell me," I said once more.

"Bella and I were living with my mother," he began. "But there was—"

"Bella is your wife?" I asked.

"My wife?" He looked confused. "I'm not married. Bella is my daughter. *Your* daughter."

Bella. Beautiful. My daughter had come to life for me in a new way these past few weeks since Hannah's birth, but now I had a vibrant picture of her in my mind.

"The daughter you never told me about," he added, and I heard some anger in his voice.

"I tried to, Travis, but my father monitored my email and by the time I found out, you were already married."

He frowned. "I was never married."

"My father said you were. Maybe you were just… Were you living with someone?"

"He told you I was married? I haven't even had a girlfriend since Bella was born. Nothing serious, anyway."

"My father said…" I let out a sigh, my shoulders sagging. "He lied, Travis. He told me you were married and I should leave you alone. Who knows what else he lied about."

"He told me you were furious I tried to get Bella."

"I *was* upset at first, but then I was glad. He died last year. My father."

"I know. My mother saw the obituary. My mother died, too, Robin." He ran his hands through his hair. "That's what started everything going downhill. We lived with her and she took care of Bella while I worked. I've been doing construction."

"You wanted to be a marine biologist," I said. "You were good at science and math. You were—"

He brushed away my words. "What I'm trying to tell you is that our house in Carolina Beach burned down and my mother was killed."

"Oh, no." I pressed my hands to my cheeks. "Oh, Travis, I'm sorry." I didn't want to picture it. I couldn't imagine the horror. I remembered his mother. "She was always really nice to me," I said. She *had* been, and the way she'd treated me had only made me angrier at my father for his coldness to Travis.

"So then I had no one to watch Bella and I was laid off from my job and...like I said, it's a long story. But..." He shut his eyes. "I'm ashamed, telling you this. You wanted a good home for your baby. I did really well with her till now, Robin. Honest, I did and nobody could love her more than I do and I have to find her!"

I moved to the sofa and sat next to him, my hand on his arm. It seemed so natural to touch him. "I believe you," I said. "But what's going on now? Where's this friend? Why is she coming here?"

"Your father said you didn't want anything to do with the baby," he said. "Was that a lie, too?"

"No, that was true," I admitted. "By the time she was born, I was so sick that...I don't even remember a lot of what happened. I loved you, but honestly...your perspective changes when you're that sick. All I thought about was surviving. Lately, though..." I shook my head. "It's so strange that you're here now, because lately, you and the baby are all I can think about."

"You don't want to think about me," he said. "I'm so messed up, Robin. You've got this great house." He waved his hand through the air to take in my living room. "The person who told me where you lived said you're engaged to a guy who's running for mayor."

"I hate him right now."

"I have nothing," he went on as if he hadn't heard me. "I have *less* than nothing. That's what I'm trying to tell you. A friend...or I thought she was a friend...she told me about a job in Raleigh, but when Bella and I got there, it turned out it was driving a getaway van for a drug deal."

I pressed my back against the chair. "Drugs? You were never into drugs. Never—"

"I didn't know what I was getting into. I know that sounds lame, but it's the truth. They told me it was just baby formula and I swallowed the whole story. I was completely broke. I mean completely. Bella and I were living in my van. I finally said I'd do it once. Just to get some money for food and to keep us going while I kept looking for work."

"What happened?"

"Everything went wrong. But here's the main thing. I met this girl—this really nice woman—in a coffee shop in Raleigh. She's older...I mean, in her thirties...and she was really good with Bella, so I left Bella with her while I did the job, but when everything went wrong, I couldn't get back in time to pick her up. The place I was supposed to drop off the drugs..." He rubbed his forehead, looking at the floor. "Ah, shit," he said. "It doesn't matter. What matters is that I ended up dumping them. Tossed them in a Dumpster to get them out of my van. It was cocaine in cases of baby formula."

"Baby formula?"

"I dumped them, like I said, and this guy—his name is Roy—he was threatening me. I was afraid of leading him to Bella, so I couldn't go to the coffee shop where the woman had her. When I finally got there this morning, someone told me she'd gone to Beaufort. The only reason she'd come here, as far as I can figure, is because I told her Bella's mother—*you*—lived here."

"But does she know my name? How would she find me?"

"She knows your name is Robin and she has a picture of you."

"How could she have a picture of me?"

"That picture you gave me when we were together. From your sophomore year?" For the first time, he smiled.

"Why did she have my picture?"

"Because Bella carried it around with her. She has this little purse and she has that picture of you in it. She knows it's a picture of her mother."

She was so real in my mind now, that little girl. I could see her carrying her purse, taking out the picture of me every once in a while. Looking at it—at the mother she didn't know. My eyes began to sting and I blinked. "Why does she think I'm not with her?" I asked.

"She knows you're sick. Or you *were* sick. That's what I've always told her. That you love her but are too sick to take care of her."

"Oh, Travis, I want to see her! Have you tried calling the woman who has her?"

He rubbed his palms on his thighs and let out a sigh. "I know this is going to sound terrible, but I don't have a number for her and she doesn't have one for me. I don't even know her last name. All I knew about her was that she was... you know, *solid*. She's a pharmacist, but I don't know where. I had no idea it would turn into this big mess. I had no idea I was putting Bella in danger." He stood up, pulled his wallet from his back pocket, and handed me a photograph. I wasn't ready for the picture. *Oh, my God.* It was a studio shot, the sort you'd get from one of those places in a mall. Travis sat on a stool with a little girl, maybe two years old, on his knee. He was clean-shaven. Smiling broadly. Nothing like the worried, haunted look he was wearing now. The little girl smiled, too, and they had the same clear gray eyes, but I saw myself in her face. I saw my own childhood pictures. She had the same little rosy coins of color in her cheeks that

I'd complained about all my life, except for the years I was so ill. Every part of me—my mind, my body, my heart—longed to hold her. I stared wordlessly at the picture. When I looked up at Travis, he was a blur in front of my eyes. His smile was slow. "I've wasted the past four years being angry with you," he said. He bent over, hands on my shoulders, and kissed my cheek. A sweet little kiss filled with a lifetime of affection. I grabbed one of his hands and held it between both of mine.

"What do we do?" I asked. "How do we find her?"

"Maybe I should go into town and look around for them, but I don't even know what kind of car she drives."

"Then stay here," I said. "Practically everyone knows who I am. If she's looking for me, she'll find me." It was strange. If any other man had told me this story, I would have pulled away from him, bit by bit. Instead I felt myself pull closer to him until I had my arms around him, my cheek pressed to his hair, and I knew that no matter what he'd done, no matter whether he was rich or poor, I belonged with him.

41
Erin

WE KEPT DRIVING AROUND WITH BELLA AND me trapped in the backseat of the Mustang, Roy and Savannah talking quietly in the front. Occasionally, Roy raised his voice and Savannah would either snap back at him or shut up. Either way, Roy's anger sent little lightning strikes through my nerves. He let us out of the car only once and that was to use a restroom. When I told him Bella needed to go, I hoped he'd let us off at a fast food place so there'd be people around and I might be able to alert someone that I needed help, but no luck. Instead, he drove us to a rest area and Savannah walked us into the empty ladies' room. I thought of grabbing Bella and running, but run where? The building was surrounded by grass on all sides. There was nowhere to hide and I had no phone. Roy'd taken it away from me not long after they first picked us up.

Every once in a while, Roy would sing this gleeful little tune in a singsong voice: *We've got his kid, we've got his kid*. It sent a chill through me. Bella was afraid of him, but not at all of Savannah and I began to get the picture—Savannah had been a trusted friend to Travis and she'd betrayed him.

They kept asking me where he was and I finally convinced them they knew a lot more than I did about where he'd spent the past couple of days. At one point, Savannah started to explain the whole situation to me—something about Travis not showing up at a drop-off point—but Roy shut her up with one nasty look. She'd said enough to let me know Travis had been afraid of them, or at least of Roy. Whatever he'd gotten himself into had been against his will.

"I'm hungry," Bella complained after we'd been driving aimlessly around Beaufort for a couple of hours.

"Me too," Savannah said to Roy. "Can we stop and get something?"

He blew a long stream of smoke toward the windshield, then took a quick left onto Front Street. "All right," he said. "We'll eat and then we'll call Don and see about the boat."

A boat? I guessed that had been part of their whispered conversations. I'd try to listen more closely. I needed to know what Bella and I were up against if we stood a chance of getting away from them. A boat didn't sound like good news to me. I wouldn't get in one. I hadn't been in a boat since the night Carolyn died.

Roy pulled into a parking place in front of a restaurant. We were just blocks from the inn and I longed to be back on that porch overlooking the waterfront, Bella safely napping in the room behind me.

Roy handed Savannah a couple of bills. "Get whatever," he said. "And make it fast."

"Can we go with her to use the restroom?" I asked, although I didn't have to go.

"You just went," he said.

"I have to go again."

He didn't even bother to answer me. Instead he pulled

out his phone and began scrolling through phone numbers or email. I couldn't see from where I was sitting.

"I'm hungry," Bella said again.

"I know, honey," I said. "Savannah's getting us food."

She pouted and leaned against me and I put my arm around her. But then I noticed a woman walking down the street and realized she'd be no more than a few yards away from the car as she passed us. She was walking briskly, a big straw purse over her shoulder. I glanced at Roy. He was engrossed in his phone. Letting go of Bella, I pressed both my hands flat against the window, my face nearly plastered to the pane, hoping to get her attention as I mouthed the word *Help!*

Suddenly, I felt a hard *thwack* on the back of my head. I yelped and turned to see Roy holding his gun and I knew he'd hit me with it. He shook his head at me, his expression telling me he considered me more of a nuisance than I was worth, and he wordlessly returned his attention to his phone.

Bella started to cry, startled by what had just happened. So was I. I touched the back of my head and my hair was wet where he'd hit me. "I'm okay, honey," I said to Bella. "Shh." I reached into my purse for a tissue and pressed it to the back of my head. It came away smudged with red. The blow had left me dizzy and I could already feel the lump forming beneath my fingers.

We ate fried chicken and French fries. Bella and I only nibbled at ours in spite of Bella's protests of hunger. Then Roy started driving around again. I chatted with Bella, playing I Spy and singing songs, but I was leaning forward as far as I dared to try to listen in on the conversation.

"It'll mean another cut," Roy said to Savannah, and I guessed he was talking about the guy with the boat. "But it's still the best way."

"Yeah, but how can we let Travis know if he's not answering his phone?" Savannah asked.

Roy reached into his pocket and showed her *my* phone. Travis would answer a call from me. I was sure of that, and apparently Roy was, too.

"The one thing he'll give up the stash for is his kid," Roy said.

"But what about..." I saw Savannah give a little nod in my direction.

"Collateral damage," Roy said in a hushed voice, but I didn't miss it. I didn't miss how Savannah turned away from him, either. How her fingers shook as she brushed a strand of that long blond hair behind her ear.

42
Travis

ROBIN WAS BEING SO NICE. THAT SHOULDN'T have surprised me. She'd always been that way, from the first time we'd met as kids. But I didn't deserve her kindness right now. I was embarrassed by the mess I was in. The mess I'd gotten Bella into. I wished I could tell Robin what a good father I'd been before the fire. I wanted her to know it hadn't always been like this. Robin seemed to understand without me saying it, though. She kept touching me—my arm, my shoulder, my hand. They were loving touches and she looked at me with understanding in her eyes. I had to remind myself it was the old Travis she was remembering and reacting to. The boy who'd been full of promise and big dreams. Not the screwup.

She looked so different. She'd always dressed well and she'd always been pretty, but now she looked really healthy: shiny hair, bright brown eyes, perfect skin, small diamond studs in her ears. She looked like the type of girl I'd never been able to relate to.

"You look…I don't know, you look *sophisticated*," I said

as we sat in her living room, waiting for Erin to somehow stumble across us.

She wrinkled her nose. "Not something I ever cared about being." She looked down at her hands. "I'm living in a world where I don't belong, Travis."

"What do you mean?"

"I came to Beaufort looking for a job while I figured out what I wanted to do with my life. My new life with my new heart. But this family—" she motioned in the direction of the house where she'd told me Dale's family lived "—they made me feel so special and it was great, but they've been... *grooming* me. It took me a while to realize it. They've slowly been turning me into someone I'm not. At first I was sort of seduced by it. There was so much money and I could have anything I wanted and I had this handsome guy other women would kill to go out with. I could have this great life. I'd never have to work if I didn't want to. I could play tennis or golf all day if I liked, even though I hate tennis and golf." She nearly laughed. "But it all comes with a price."

"What's the price?" I asked.

"Living a false life. For me, anyway. I mean, it would be a fine life for some people. Maybe even *most* people. But it's not right for me. And then..." She twisted her hands together in her lap.

"And then what?"

"I just found out yesterday that Dale's been buying off the guy his sister's in love with, to get him to stay away from her. It reminded me so much of you and me—the way my father kept us apart. Alissa even has a baby now, and the baby..." She smiled and looked toward the window, but I knew it was that baby she was seeing. "The baby woke up a part of me I didn't even know was there. The part that had a baby. That has a child." She looked at me again. "I started thinking about her…and about you, and I've been… You're all I could think about lately, Travis. It's just so weird that you showed up now. It's like I knew you were on your way back into my life. If you hadn't shown up, I was going to have to find you. I couldn't marry Dale when I was thinking about you all the time."

"But you were thinking about me in the *past,*" I said. "You were thinking about when we were younger, and money and survival and raising a little girl weren't a problem. When all we had to think about was—" I hunted for the right words "—loving each other," I said.

"What else is there to think about?" she asked.

I was about to answer her when my phone rang—the phone Roy had given me. I pulled it from my pocket and set it on the table. "I'm not going to answer it," I said. "This is the guy who wants the drugs I don't have and I'm finished with him." I had nothing to say to Roy, but the name on the caller ID display suddenly jumped out at me. *Erin Patterson.* I grabbed the phone and flipped it open.

"Erin?" I stood up.

"Would you like to see your daughter again?" Roy asked. "Ever?"

He couldn't have her. Couldn't possibly. "What are you talking about? How did Erin's name come up on—"

"Where are you?" he asked. "How quick can you get to Beaufort?"

My mind spun. I didn't know what was going on, but I knew it wasn't good. "I'm *in* Beaufort," I said.

"No shit." He laughed. "Well, that's perfect. Do you want your daughter?"

"What are you talking about!" I shouted.

"I have her."

"No, you don't."

"Oh, yes, I do. Her and Erin."

"Shit." I pressed my hand to my forehead.

Robin moved next to me, her hands on my arm. "What's going on?"

"So here's what you do," Roy said. "Your last and final chance, bro. You bring the stuff midnight tonight to this address."

I motioned to Robin that I needed something to write with. In an instant, she found a pad and pen for me.

"It's at the eastern tip of Beaufort," he said. "Private property, but the owner's cool. Drive around the back and we'll be out on the dock."

"A dock?"

"We've got a boat."

"I want my daughter first," I said. "I want her *now.*"

"Right, like I'm going to give you your kid before I get the stash when you've been so reliable before. I'll see you at midnight."

"Let me talk to Bella!" I said quickly.

"Forget it."

"How do I know you really have her?" Though I *did* know. At the very least, he had Erin's phone.

I heard voices. A woman was speaking in the background. Maybe Savannah? Then suddenly, Erin was on the phone. "Travis?" she said.

"Erin? I'm sorry, Erin! What the hell is going on?"

"You have to do what he says, Travis."

"Is Bella okay?"

"Yes, but this guy is serious. He has a gun. Please just do whatever he says."

I hesitated. "Can they hear me?" I asked softly.

"What? No. I don't think so."

"I don't have the drugs, Erin," I said. "I tossed them. I didn't want them in my van."

She was quiet and I wondered if she was silently cursing me. I was silently cursing myself.

"You need to bring them to the dock, just like he says," she said.

"You don't get it. I don't—"

"At midnight," she said. "You can do it, Travis. Remember Kill Devil Hills? The coffee cups?"

"What are you talking about?" I asked, and I could hear Roy asking her the same question. I heard a scuffle, and the next thing I knew he was back on the phone.

"Midnight," he snarled at me. "And no cops. Cops show up, you'll be exceedingly sorry."

The line went dead and I stared at the phone for a moment, then looked at Robin. "They have Erin and Bella."

"How did they—"

"I don't know, but they do. Roy wants me to bring the drugs to this address at midnight." I held up the piece of paper. "Erin said something weird. When I told her I don't have them, she said 'Remember Kill Devil Hills and the coff—' Oh, whoa." I pressed my hand to the side of my head. "I think I get it, but I… Oh, shit."

"What?"

"I have to buy some cases of baby formula." I reached for the keys to my van where I'd left them on the end table. "A lot of them," I said. "Where can I go?"

43
Erin

IT HAD BEEN A RELIEF TO TALK TO TRAVIS—TO have that connection to someone outside the stuffy Mustang. I'd heard the terror in his voice, especially when he told me he no longer had the drugs. I only hoped he understood what I was talking about with the coffee cups and could pull it off.

Roy drove us back to the rest area after the call to Travis. In the ladies' room, I turned on the faucet so Bella could wash her hands and caught Savannah staring at me in the mirror. I remembered how her hand shook when Roy talked about me being collateral damage.

"I don't know how you got mixed up with him," I said to her in the mirror, "but you can get away. Help me and Bella, please. I'll pay you."

She scowled. "Unless you're a lot richer than you look, you can't pay me what I can make doing this kind of work. Besides—" she looked at her own reflection in the mirror, smoothing her long hair "—it's not that easy to get away from your husband."

"What do you mean?" I asked, handing Bella a paper towel. "You're *married* to Roy?"

"Since I was sixteen." She gave me a small smile. "He can be a charmer when he wants to be."

I washed my own hands, slowly, savoring the time out of the car. I wet a paper towel and pressed it to the aching lump on the back of my head as I tried to think of something I could say to convince her to break free of the man who was holding her hostage as much as he was Bella and me. She spoke first.

"You married?" she asked, as I dropped the red-stained paper towel into the trash.

"Yes," I said.

"Then you know," she said. "Sometimes things are good. Sometimes they suck. There's always this love/hate thing going on."

We walked back to the car, me holding Bella's hand tightly in my own. I thought of my husband, who could turn our grief into a game. He could turn *anything* into a game. Right now, I could have used one of his games. *How to get out of a hostage situation.* One thousand players. One hundred thousand players. *The more players, the more ideas,* he would say. I thought of my Harley's Dad group, how we leaned on each other. Helped each other. *Collaborated.* I suddenly saw the parallel between Michael's way of grieving and my own. The structure might have been different, but the end goal was the same—coping with the devastation of losing a child. Why was my way right and his wrong? I pictured him working on that game, day in and day out. *Losing Carolyn.* It was his way of handling the pain. Of immortalizing her. Right then, I wished I could talk to him. I wanted to tell him I finally understood.

In the car, I asked Roy for my phone to make one quick call to my husband. He turned to look at me.

"Uhh," he said, drawing the word out as though he was actually considering my request, "no."

My eyes stung. What if I *was* the collateral damage Roy'd been talking about? I didn't want to die without telling Michael that I loved him.

Roy dropped Savannah off at a marina where she was supposed to pick up the boat they were borrowing, so it was only the three of us in the Mustang as we pulled into the long driveway of a dark, hulking house. Without Savannah in the car, I felt a thousand times more anxious. Behind the big house, I could see the moon reflected in water. I didn't know if the water was the sound or Taylor's Creek or...I wasn't sure. It was as flat as a mirror, so it wasn't the ocean, but that was all I knew for certain. Roy had taken a circuitous route to get us there and I'd been paying more attention to Bella than where we were going. Bella'd been so good all day. She'd tolerated being stuck in the car for hours, despite the smoke and a lot of hostile conversation, but now the tension was getting to her. I'd tried to fake being calm as the evening dragged on and turned into night, but with Savannah out of the car, Bella was really picking up my anxiety. How could she not? My head ached and my chest felt so tight I could barely pull in a full breath. When I rubbed Bella's back, I felt my fear slipping down my arm, through my fingertips and into her body. She cuddled so close to me, it was like she was trying to get inside me. I wrapped my arms tightly around her and pressed my chin to her head.

I had no idea what was going to happen next. The house looked deserted so I doubted we were meeting up with anyone there. I'd hated the suffocating hours in the car, but at least I'd felt as though Bella and I were somewhat safe. Uncertainty lay ahead of us now as we rode down the long driveway, and I held on to Bella with sweaty palms. When we neared the garage, Roy drove off the driveway and onto the lawn, pulling around the rear of the house toward the water. For a terrifying moment, I was afraid he was going to drive us right into that dark, moonlit water, but what he had in mind was almost worse. He parked on the lawn near a long, long dock, an endless strip of silver in the moonlight. I could barely look at it.

Roy turned off the engine, but made no move to get out of the car. He switched on the overhead light to check his watch.

"What's the plan?" I asked, as if I actually expected him to tell me. My voice came out like a croak, my mouth was so dry.

I thought he wasn't going to answer. He peered hard through the window toward the water, as if he could see something other than the dock and the moon out there in the darkness. "Savannah will be here with the boat any minute." He turned around to face me. "So here's what we're going to do. You and Bella are going to go out to the end of that dock there. That's where Savannah will bring the boat. When Travis shows up, and he damn well better, we'll start loading the cases into the boat. Once they're all in, he can leave with you and the girl. What Savannah and I do at that point is none of your business. Simple."

No. Not simple. "Let Bella and me wait here," I said. "On the lawn. Or even in the car. You can keep us locked in." I'd rather he locked us in the smoky car than make me walk out on that dock.

"I don't think so," Roy said. "As soon as I get the word

from Savannah, we're going out on the dock. Till then, we can all take a little siesta." He lowered the back of his seat until it nearly hit Bella's knees and she curled her legs up on the seat. I pulled her closer, trying to figure out what to do. If he fell asleep, could we... Could we what? We were trapped in the backseat of this car, and yet I had the feeling that once we got out, things were going to be much, much worse.

I shut my eyes, trying to think of some way out of this mess. Some brilliant escape. Yet the moment I closed my eyes, there it was: a long silvery ribbon stretching in front of me in the darkness—The Stardust Pier—and that terrible weekend in Atlantic Beach came back to me in a rush.

That weekend had started out so beautifully, warm and sunny for early April. We'd rented an oceanfront cottage, perfect for the three of us. The water was cold after one of North Carolina's rare hard winters, but we played on the beach and took long walks and did what Michael and I loved to do best—hang out with Carolyn. There was a fireplace in the cottage and we built a fire that Friday night and played games, and Carolyn was blissful, having the total attention of both her parents for a change instead of sharing Michael with his computer and me with some household project. Michael and I made love that Friday night. I'd gone off the Pill several weeks earlier, so we were excited and hopeful and ready to alter our lives again.

That Saturday night, we decided to walk out on the pier. We passed through the tackle shop where we paid for our tickets, and as soon as we stepped out onto the long, broad pier, I felt nervous. A sign warned of all sorts of dangers and I wanted to take the time to read it, but Michael kept walking. The night was black, but the pier was well-lit and crowded

with men and women fishing. I'd been on fishing piers before, of course. I'd even been on the Stardust Pier before, but
never at night. It was a different world. These were serious
fishermen, with specially outfitted carts for their poles and
buckets and bait. They stood shoulder to shoulder against the
railing, their lines in the water, some of them manning half a
dozen poles at a time. Carolyn was enthralled. She wanted to
run ahead of us to peek into every bucket and watch people
reel in fish that glittered in the overhead lights. The hooks
were what worried me. I had visions of one of the fishermen casting his line over his shoulder, the hook catching
my daughter's ear or eye. I wasn't usually that paranoid, but
that image just wouldn't leave my head and I kept calling
Carolyn back to us to make her hold my hand.

"She's okay," Michael said to me. "She's having a blast. Just
let her go." To Carolyn he said, "Don't run too far ahead,
and don't get in anyone's way." He thought that was enough
direction for a three-year-old.

"It's the hooks," I said with a shudder.

"She's okay," he said again. "You're so overprotective
sometimes, Erin."

The pier stretched far out into the sea, high above the
water, and we continued strolling its length. I'd always liked
piers. I liked the way you'd seem to be out in the middle of
the ocean where it was deep and mysterious and yet you'd
still feel the solid planking beneath your feet. This night,
though, I didn't have that sense of wonder or ease.

I remembered seeing her just a few yards ahead of us
where she stood next to a bucket filled with someone's catch.
She was bent over, peering into the bucket, her hands clasped
behind her back.

"Mommy, look!" she cried. "There's seven in this one!"

We joined her around the bucket and marveled at the fish, and then she ran on ahead again.

"Carolyn!" I called. "Stay closer to us."

"She's fine," Michael said. "I like seeing her like this. She's adventurous. Sometimes you hold her back."

"When do I ever hold her back?" I asked, wounded. I was a good mom. I didn't hover.

"Well, like on the beach today when she wanted to poke at that jellyfish."

"It was probably poisonous."

"She was using a stick and it was dead."

Maybe I *had* overreacted. I'd shouted at her to get away from the huge gelatinous blob. I'd shouted so loud that she'd jumped and then looked at the jellyfish like it was a monster that might get her in her sleep. "Well, I don't usually do that," I said.

He put his arm around me. "No, you don't," he admitted, "and that thing was pretty gross." He gave my shoulders a squeeze. "You're a wonderful mother," he said, "and I love you."

I slipped my hand into the back pocket of his jeans. "I love you, too," I said.

I could see the end of the pier ahead of us. Six or eight men and women were lined up along the railing, very little space between them. Carolyn walked toward them quickly, though she wasn't running. Not exactly. Through the slats of the railing a distance ahead of us, I could see the black water that stretched into infinity and I had a flash of apprehension. Just a flash. I pictured Carolyn slipping between two of the broad slats and out into the abyss. I nearly called to her, but I didn't want to hear Michael say one more time, *She's okay,* so I bit my tongue.

Then she was gone. It happened so fast that I didn't even

see it. I couldn't even tell the police exactly what happened. Somehow, she slipped between the floor of the pier and a broken slat in the railing and simply disappeared. If she screamed or made a splash when she hit the water, I didn't hear it, but shouts went up from the men and women lining the pier. The second I realized what had happened, I climbed over the railing in a flash of insanity, leaping into the air, not thinking of anything other than getting to my baby.

I seemed to fall forever before the water hit me like a solid wall of ice. I went down, the breath ripped from my body. My eyes were open and my hands pawed frantically through the black water for the child I knew was there but couldn't see.

The next hour or so was a blur. Someone pulled me screaming and clawing into a tiny boat. I would never forget how it felt to have so many arms holding me down in the rocking and rolling boat, keeping me from diving into the water again to find my daughter. I shoved my fingers into my rescuers' eyes and scratched at their cheeks to let me go, but they imprisoned me in their arms and blankets, shouting words in my ears I couldn't decipher.

And where was Michael during all of this? Still on the pier, running back toward the entrance. Running away from Carolyn and me instead of toward us. How could he not jump in? Maybe it had been stupid, leaping into that cold water. It had certainly been useless. But I couldn't get past it—the fact that he ran away from us instead of toward us. He was running for the beach, he told me later. He thought he could somehow get to us more easily and safely that way. The police told me he wasn't thinking any more clearly than I was and that, since he was not a strong swimmer, he'd done the right thing. Still, maybe if he had jumped in, too.

Maybe if we'd had four arms in that black water, we could have found her in time.

I didn't blame him right away. I didn't even question him until weeks later, because I didn't care about anything other than the fact that Carolyn was gone. I understood then what you always know intuitively about parents who have lost a child: that the fact of that child's death is impossible to believe, that the hole in their lives is bottomless, that the future's been stolen from them, and that they believe in the craziest parts of their beings that there must be *some* way to get their son or daughter back. I always understood all that intellectually. Finally, though, I understood it in my gut, and the experience was completely different and painful beyond endurance.

"I want my daddy," Bella whimpered.

My eyes flew open and I was suddenly back in the darkness of Roy's car, groggy and disoriented. I wrapped both my arms around Bella. "I know, honey," I said.

"I want him *now.*"

"Shut her up," Roy said from the front seat. "She's disturbing my nap."

I should try to distract her, I thought, but I couldn't tear my mind away from the pier. Away from Carolyn. Away from my husband. After the accident, Michael threw himself into a one-man crusade to have more slats added to the railing, and I remembered his fight with an ache in my heart. He'd lost that battle because the railings were found to be safe. One of the slats had been broken just that day by a runaway cart and no one had reported it. By some horrible freakish chance, that was where Carolyn ran to the railing. That was the place that swallowed her whole.

Roy's phone rang and he answered it with a couple of

words I couldn't hear. Then he got out of the car and pushed the seatback forward. "Come on," he said. "Get out."

I grabbed my purse, slipping the strap over my shoulder, and Bella and I got out of the car. My legs were stiff and I felt so dizzy, I needed to lean against the car for a moment. Bella was still hanging on to her purse and lamb. It was quiet, the only sound the water lapping against the bank and the pilings of the dock. Bella tugged on my hand. "Is Daddy here?" she asked.

I bent over. "He might be coming, honey," I said. "I'm not sure." I didn't know whether to hope Travis was coming or not. I had trouble imagining that Roy would simply let Travis, Bella and me walk away with all we knew about him and Savannah. And what if Travis showed up empty-handed? I didn't want to think about it, but even worse, I didn't want to think about walking out on that dock. If not for Bella, I would have taken my chances and run through the darkness back toward the street. With Bella, though, I'd never make it.

"I can't walk out there," I said to Roy, pointing toward the long moonlit dock. "You'll just have to let us stay here."

"Oh, I will, will I?" He gave a sour laugh. "It's not an either/or sort of thing," he said. "You're going out there, so get going."

"Can't Savannah bring the boat up closer to the—"

"Too shallow."

I stood my ground. "It's like a...a phobia, with me," I said. "Please."

"So, this will either cure you or kill you." He was behind me and I felt something hard against my back. His gun? I didn't know and I didn't turn around to find out. I started walking toward the dock, Bella's hand in mine, but when I stepped on the first plank I stopped and lifted her into my arms. It would be too easy to lose her here. Too easy for her hand to slip through my sweaty fingers.

"Keep going," Roy said.

I took a few more steps onto the boards. They were firm and unyielding, but the long dock was incredibly narrow and there were no railings at all. Not even a piling to hold on to. My heartbeat accelerated and I stopped walking. "I can't do it," I said.

"Bitch!" he said, and before I knew what was happening, he tore Bella from my arms. She let out a yelp and her lamb went flying over the side of the dock and into the dark water.

"Lambie, Lambie!" she cried, reaching toward the darkness where it had disappeared. Roy was carrying her like a football under one arm as he walked, and he smacked his hand over her mouth to keep her quiet.

"I'll do it!" I shouted. "Put her down!"

He swung around. "Shut up," he hissed. "Your voice echoes out here." He set Bella on her feet and she ran back to me, grabbing me around the legs.

"You're okay." I lifted her up again. "Hold on tight," I said. "We're going to walk all the way to the end."

I sang "Wheels on the Bus" as we walked, more to calm myself than Bella. It was a breathy, gasping rendition, but I kept singing until we'd reached the very end of the dock. I sat down on the boards, trembling all over, and held Bella on my lap so tightly she said she couldn't breathe. I didn't care. She was safe. For now, at least.

44
Robin

I'D ALWAYS THOUGHT OF TRAVIS AS STRONG, both physically and emotionally, but tonight I'd seen how vulnerable he really was and it was all because of his daughter. Our daughter. He would kill for her. I had no doubt of that. My fear was that he might get *himself* killed for her. I wanted them both to survive this night. I wanted to have a future with them. I didn't know what form that future would take and as he headed out the door at eleven-thirty that night, I didn't care. I just wanted him to live. I knew what I'd be throwing away: money and security, along with hypocrisy and the stress of trying to be someone I wasn't.

We'd had to drive all over two counties to get cases of the right brand of baby formula. We'd hit every Wal-Mart and Costco and Kmart. Some places had limits on the amount we could get. Some places just had the cans loose on the shelves rather than in cases. Travis was dogged, though. We both were. Even so, his van was two shy of the total he needed and I knew he was nervous about that. It would have to do. "Maybe they'll forget how many we had," he said. "They were aiming for fifteen, but I drove off long before we got that many, so maybe they just don't know." By the time we got back to the B and B, he was pale and jittery. I made him bacon and eggs he didn't touch.

"We should call the police," I said, for about the third time. "I know he said not to, but this is too dangerous. Please let them handle this."

"He'll hurt her," Travis said. "He's a psychopath, Robin. He'll hurt her and I'll end up in jail."

But as the evening wore on and we shifted between talking about Bella—I couldn't hear enough about her—and a scared sort of silence, I kept thinking about the police. That was my worldview: you were in trouble, you called the cops to help you out.

I was afraid Dale might stop over, so I called him at eight and told him I was going to turn in early. I was so finished with Dale.

As Travis drove away, I felt terror creep into my bones. I watched his taillights disappear into the darkness. *You're going to lose him again,* I thought to myself. *You're going to lose your daughter again.*

I reached for the phone. Travis would be angry. I'd have to risk that.

Dale's voice was muffled with sleep. "Wake up," I said. "I need you right now. I need you to listen to me. Are you awake?"

"What's wrong? Are you okay?"

"There's a drug deal going on at one of the docks at the end of Lenoxville Road," I said, "and I—"

"Are you having a dream? A drug—"

"I need your help," I said. "You know everyone. People owe you favors. Call one of your friends in the police department and tell them to be very, very careful. There's a little child involved."

"What the *hell* are you talking about?" he asked. I pictured him waking up quickly now. Sitting up in his bed.

"One of the men has a gun," I said. "He's holding a little girl—and a woman—for ransom. You need to get someone over there."

"How do you know this?"

"Later. I'll tell you later. But call someone *now*, Dale. Right now. And Dale?"

"What?"

"The little girl," I said. "She's mine."

45
Travis

I DROVE AROUND THE AREA A FEW TIMES TO get my bearings. The one thing I could tell for sure, even in the dark, was that folks out here had money. There were only about a dozen properties on a spit of land that jutted out into the water. Robin and I had looked up the address on a satellite map. Each property had a long dock that shot way out in the water like the spokes of a wheel. We pinpointed the dock I needed to find, but it had been much easier on a satellite image than from the street in the dark, even with a pretty good moon. The houses were set far back from the road and the yards were full of trees and shrubs, but my headlights finally picked up the house number on one of the mailboxes. I turned into the driveway, thinking about the cases of formula in the rear of my van. I put on the brakes halfway down the driveway. *Damn.* The *X*'s! I should have bought a marker and drawn a small *X* on the side of each case, the way the stolen cases had been marked. Too late now. Anyway, it was dark. Would Roy look at them that closely?

The house came into view, not a light in any of the windows. It was so massive it nearly blocked my view of the water. Roy'd said to drive around back, but the driveway ended at the garage. I drove onto the lawn and around the side of the house, and that's when I saw Roy's car parked near the water's edge and couple of lights bobbing far out at the end of a long dock. Four people out there, one of them tiny, and once I spotted her, she was all I could see.

I didn't like this setup one bit. Deserted area. Darkness. The four of them out on the end of that dock, one of them with a gun. A gunshot would travel across the water out here, but was there anyone around to hear it? I was so wired, I felt like I'd been mainlining caffeine.

I parked my van next to Roy's car, then started running up the dock to get to Bella.

"Stay where you are!" Roy called out. He was walking toward me, fast. Someone—Savannah, I guessed—was holding a flashlight and it was nearly blinding me, but I still saw the gun in Roy's hand. It was pointing straight at me and I stopped running.

"Daddy!" Bella cried, but I couldn't see her well with that light in my eyes. I held an arm over my face to try to block it out.

"Stay right here, Bella," Erin said, then she called to me, "Travis, be careful! Do whatever he says."

"I'm here, Bella!" I called to her. "Everything's going to be all right."

"Y'all shut up!" Roy said.

Savannah moved the flashlight a little and I could see Bella again. She stood in front of Erin, who had her hands locked on her shoulders. I caught a glimpse of the pink purse. I was so close to my daughter, but I'd never felt farther away from her.

"Let me get Bella," I said to Roy. "I can put her in the van while—"

"We load the boat first," Roy said.

I couldn't see any boat but guessed it was hidden from my view by the end of the dock.

"Get one of the cases and bring it out here," Roy said. He wasn't going to let Erin and Bella go until he was sure I had the drugs. I was scared he wasn't going to let them—let *any* of us—go at all.

"Let Erin and Bella come to me and I'll—"

"Shut up," he shouted. "Keep your voice—"

"Just do what he says, Travis," Savannah called.

I wasn't sure I had a choice. I walked to the van and lifted out one of the cases, then started back down the long dock. Roy was near the end of it now, standing with everyone else. It sickened me that he was so close to Bella. That he'd been this close to her all day.

"Daddy!" Bella started crying when I'd gotten near enough for her to see me again. I wanted to drop the case and go to her, but I didn't dare. *No quick moves,* I thought.

"Stay right there, Bell," I called.

"Daddy." She was crying hard.

"Shut her up!" Roy said, and I could just make out Erin leaning over, saying something to Bella. When I was within a few yards of the four of them, I slowly set the case down on the dock and started toward my daughter, but Roy stepped between us, the side of his gun against my chest.

"Stay right where you are," he said.

"Look, let's get this over with," I said. "I don't want this stuff in my van. I don't want to go to the cops. I just want you to let me and Bella and Erin go, all right? So, let's get the cases out of the van and be done with it."

"You should've just done what we told you right from the start, Travis," Savannah said.

Roy stepped away from me to hand something to her. It glittered in the moonlight, and for a moment I was afraid they each had a gun. "Open one of the cans," he ordered her, and as she walked closer to me I saw the knife in her hand.

"You don't need to open a can," I said. "It's all there. I haven't touched it, and the rest of the cases are still in the van." I was starting to panic. "Don't you get it?" I asked. "I don't want it and I never have!" I was afraid I was protesting too much. He'd know I was faking it.

"Open it," Roy said to Savannah. She squatted down next to the case and slit the plastic with the knife. I started shaking, adrenaline pouring through my body. Only a few yards separated me from my daughter and I wanted to scoop her up and run back up the dock, but Roy was holding the gun steady on me. I'd never forget him shooting at those guys in the parking lot, one of the bullets singing through the air next to my van. I didn't dare move. Erin was squatting next to Bella, holding her tight, trying to calm her down. I wanted the chance to apologize to Erin. So weird to have that thought at that moment, when my life and my daughter's were hanging by a thread. I was sorry I'd ever dragged Erin into this mess.

Savannah stood up, a can of formula in her hand. She carried it over to Roy. *Put the gun down,* I thought. *Lose your concentration.*

"Take the lid off," Roy said to Savannah. She squatted down on the dock, setting her flashlight on the planks as she worked at the lid. It took her a couple of tries, but she got it off and peeled back a piece of plastic that I hoped wasn't a giveaway. Did the doctored cans have that plastic seal on top? What did it matter? In two seconds, Roy was going to know the truth and I'd be a dead man.

Savannah picked up the can and her flashlight and got to her feet. She held the can toward Roy, who dipped his finger into the powder, the gun dangling from his hand. I held my breath as he brought his finger to his mouth. In the light from the flashlight, I saw the flare of his nostrils as he tasted the powder. He pointed the gun directly at my chest. "You son of a bitch," he said, and I knew I was going to die.

Savannah was fast, so fast it took me a second to realize what was happening. I saw the puff of white powder as she threw the contents of the can in Roy's face. I froze only half a second before I plowed forward to shove him to the floor of the dock.

"Run!" I shouted to Erin, but she'd already scooped Bella into her arms and was jumping from the dock into the water. I heard the crack of the gun, but if he hit me, I didn't feel it because I was too busy punching him in the face, over and over and over again. Too busy even to register the distant sound of sirens as they grew louder in the dark night air.

46
Erin

THE WATER WAS COLD AND I FELT IT FILL MY nostrils and cover the top of my head, but I bounced to the surface as I heard gunfire, and I expected to feel a bullet tear through my body any second. Above me, I saw stars and the moon and the black slab of the dock. I kicked my feet until I was completely beneath it. Shouting filled the air above me. A scream. The sounds came to me like in a nightmare, and it was a nightmare I knew all too well. The only difference was, this time, I held a frightened, sobbing child in my arms. I treaded water, kissing her cheeks, the top of her head, savoring every whimper that came from her lips, because *this* child was very much alive.

47
Travis

IN THE CURTAINED CUBICLE OF THE EMERGENCY room, I held Bella on my lap. She'd cried herself out and now clung to me, arms around my neck, and I thought *Let her forget this night,* the way I'd prayed that she'd forget the fire or how I'd abandoned her with a near stranger for days. I was asking too much of God, I thought. We were alive. We were alive and whatever happened now was something we'd have to endure. I had no idea how much prison time I'd get for the things I'd done this past week. At least Robin would be in Bella's life, now. That could only be good.

I answered every question they asked me fully and honestly, knowing I should really be keeping my mouth shut until I had a lawyer. I didn't care. I didn't want to play legal games. I wanted to cleanse myself of the past couple of weeks. My body might end up in jail, but I wanted my mind and soul to be free.

I didn't know where Roy was. Maybe the police station? I had no idea. They'd separated all of us. Erin went in one ambulance, though she'd handed Bella over to me before they drove me away. A second ambulance had taken Savannah and

I knew she was in surgery with at least one gunshot wound. I knew, too, that she'd saved our lives. They'd stitched a cut on my head that I had no memory of getting. My neck hurt and I guessed I'd wrenched it when I beat the crap out of Roy. Small thing. Very small thing. The big thing was that Bella was back with me, even if it was only for a little while. She hadn't let go of me once since we got to the hospital, her arms wrapped around my wrenched neck, and I held on to her just as tightly, knowing this might be my last chance to hold her for a very, very long time.

48
Robin

"THEY'RE IN THE E.R.," DALE SAID, FLIPPING HIS cell phone shut. He'd been pacing around my living room on the phone for the past fifteen minutes while I'd been biting my nails on the sofa, waiting to learn Travis's and Bella's fates. "Now tell me what the hell this is all about," he said. He was angry. I didn't care.

"Why the E.R.?" I asked. "Who's hurt?"

"Some woman's in surgery. She was shot. They think she'll make it, though. The kid is okay. One of the men is in police custody. The other—"

"Which man?" I wanted to stand up to be on a more equal footing with him, but I didn't think my legs would hold me.

"I don't know, Robin." Dale sounded disgusted. I knew he felt manipulated by me right now. Too bad.

"What were you going to say about the other man?" I asked.

"He's being treated at the hospital for a head injury. Minor."

"Where's the little girl?"

"With him. And I'm done with the twenty questions." His voice was rising and he stared down at me like I was a political opponent. "Now what the hell is going on?" He was very nearly shouting.

"Shh!" I pointed to the ceiling. "The guests."

"What the hell did you mean about the girl being yours?" he asked. "How do you know these people? How do you have any involvement with them? And what the *fuck* are you trying to do to my career?"

"Don't talk to me that way," I said. "Don't you dare." I was so unbelievably furious with him for everything. Such a rare feeling for me. Rare and empowering. "Shut up for half a second and I'll tell you how I know them. I'll tell you everything. And then I'll tell you what you're going to do for me."

He took a step backward and gave me a look that asked *Do you know who you're talking to?* "Who *are* you?" he asked. "I feel like I don't know you tonight."

"You *don't* know me," I said. "And I sure as hell didn't know you."

"What are you talking about?"

"Here's what you're going to do for me, Dale." I stood up, feeling stronger. If I didn't have him on the defensive yet, I would very soon. "You're going to pull whatever strings you need to, to make this situation go away. You're good at that. I know you know how to do it. The man with the little girl—her father, Travis Brown—you're going to keep him out of jail."

"He was dealing drugs. I can't—"

"No, he wasn't. He was caught up in something he couldn't control. And you know what? It doesn't even matter. I don't owe you any explanation about what he was doing. The only thing that matters is that he doesn't go to jail. You make this go away."

"I can't possibly do that."

"Oh, yes, you can. You have this whole town in your back pocket. Make this go away."

"Who is he?"

"He's the father of my child. That little girl."

Dale's face went white. "What have you been keeping from me? You deceptive... You're going to ruin everything for me."

"No, actually, I'm not. Not if you do what I'm asking."

"Don't you dare try to blackmail me, Robin. Don't even think about it. I've done *everything* for you. You came to Beaufort lost and friendless. A little...*nobody* with absolutely no prospects. Look at you now. You have everything you could ever want. How dare you—"

"I spoke with Will," I said.

He frowned and looked as though he couldn't imagine what I was talking about. "What do you mean?" he asked.

"I mean I know you've been paying him off, the same way your father bought off his mother."

Dale opened his mouth to speak, then seemed to think better of it. He sank down on my sofa.

"You get Travis out of this mess and I won't go public with what I know. I'll pretend we're still happily engaged until after the election and then I'll quietly go away. But if you don't do what I'm asking, I'll expose you for the lying son of a bitch you are."

He shook his head slowly. "You... I can't believe you—"

"People will forgive all sorts of things," I said. "They'll forgive affairs and perversions and prostitutes. They might even forgive you for betraying their trust. But they won't forgive you for betraying mine. You've made them love me,

Dale." I nearly smiled with the power I felt at that moment. "Thank you for that."

"I'll say you lied to me."

"Me *and* Debra, right? Two women duped you? What will that tell the public about you? That you're a fool with pretty bad judgment, not fit to lead, don't you think?"

"I can't do it," he said. "I can't help your...*friend*." He actually sneered. "I have no authority to—"

"You'd better figure out how to do it," I said. "You have twenty-four hours." I walked to the door and put my hand on the knob. "Believe me, I want Travis to be free, but to tell you the truth, it would give me some pleasure right now to tell the world what I know about you."

"The child... Why didn't you tell me?" he asked. "You're an honest person. I know that. Deep down, you are. Why didn't you tell me about her?"

"Because I was pretending she didn't exist. It was the only way I could survive the past few years. But she *does* exist and I want to be her mother, more than I've ever wanted anything in my life."

"You're going to lose everything," he said. "You know that, don't you?"

"I'll have something better to take its place." I thought of the false life I'd been living for the past couple of years. "I'll have something real."

49
Erin

ONE OF THE NURSES LED ME TO THE CURTAINED cubicle in the E.R. and I thanked her and stepped inside. Travis was sitting on a gurney, propped up against the raised mattress. His eyes were shut and Bella was asleep in his arms, her head resting on his chest. He had a bandage on his temple. A cervical collar on his neck. I stood there for a moment in the donated pants and sweatshirt the E.R. social worker had given me. The clothes were too big, but they were dry and warm.

"Travis?" I said.

His eyes opened and he sat up a little straighter, holding tight to Bella. "Erin!" he said. "Are you all right?"

"Totally fine," I said. "What about you, though?" I touched my own forehead where his was bandaged.

He ignored the question. "I'm so sorry for this, Erin." He looked pained. "I'm so, so sorry."

I sat down on a stool in front of the curtain. I could see that Bella was wearing different clothes, too, and her hair was still damp. Her purse was on the rolling tray by the bed, the two photographs lying on a paper towel next to it, their edges curled.

"I know you are," I said, "Are you okay? How's Bella doing?"

He gingerly touched the bandage on his head. "We're alive, and that's the most important thing. I can never, ever thank you enough for keeping Bella safe. Or apologize enough, either."

"I'm all right." I felt so calm. Calmer than I'd felt in a long time.

"I wouldn't blame you if you never forgave me," he said. "I put you through the worst experience of your life."

"No," I said. "This wasn't the worst experience of my life."

"You're kidding." Bella let out a small moan and he rubbed her arm. "You've actually been through something worse than this?"

I nodded. "I have." I took in a long breath. "Do you remember when we first met at JumpStart, you asked me if I had any children and I said no?"

He nodded slowly.

"Well, I did have a child. A daughter a little younger than Bella. She died when she fell from the Stardust Pier in Atlantic Beach." I knotted my hands together in my lap. "That was worse," I said.

He opened his mouth, but I could tell I'd left him momentarily speechless. Resting his head against the pillow, he shut his eyes. "Oh, damn," he said. "I'm sorry, Erin." He looked at me again. "How did you ever survive that? I don't think I could."

"I *wasn't* surviving it," I said. "I was slowly dying. Bit by bit. Day by day. Until you and Bella came along and I suddenly had something to look forward to. And when you left

Bella with me, I had somebody to think about besides my daughter. And myself."

He looked incredulous. "Are you saying I actually *helped* you?" he asked.

I nodded. "You and Bella. Most definitely." I smiled. "Crazy, huh?"

He looked down at his sleeping daughter. Ran his hand over her tangled hair. "Was she good for you?" he asked.

"She was wonderful," I said. "I'm worried about her, though. About both of you. What happens now?"

He sighed. "Well, medically I'm ready to go, so I'm just waiting for the cop to come back to…take me in." He swallowed hard and looked away from me, "And for Robin to come get Bella. She has to talk to social services and get the go-ahead to take her. Bella's never met her, so I'm… It's going to be hard to just turn her over to her."

"Why do you have custody of her, Travis?" I asked.

"Robin was really sick when Bella was born. She needed a heart transplant and there was no way she could take care of a baby. I signed a contract with her father that said I'd leave Robin alone once I had custody." He adjusted the cervical collar with a wince. "There was just a lot of… misunderstanding between us. I hadn't seen Robin until yesterday. When I found out you'd come to Beaufort with Bella, I figured you were looking for her, so I came here and I found her." He smiled. "She's been thinking about us. Thinking about Bella, and what she's missed. If there's anything good coming out of this whole mess, it'll be getting her and Bella together."

"She's never met her?" I asked.

"Never. And she's wonderful. It's sort of like a miracle. I don't know how long I'll be locked up for, but knowing

Bella will be with her mother… It's better than I could hope for."

"Travis." I leaned forward. "If there's any way I can help… I mean, I don't know if having me testify on your behalf would hurt or help, but I know from things I overheard between Roy and Savannah that you didn't really know what you were getting into."

"I knew enough," he said. "I did something really stupid for money."

I couldn't argue with him about that, and yet he never could have known how wrong it would all go.

"How will you get back to Raleigh?" he asked me. "Where's your car?"

"At an inn in Beaufort," I said. "One of the police officers said he'd take me over there when I'm ready, but I didn't want to leave without seeing you and Bella."

He kissed the top of Bella's head. "She's so wiped out," he said. "I just hope she can get over this. She had nightmares after the fire and really…regressed, and now this."

"Did her nana—your mother—did she die in the fire?"

He nodded.

"You've been through a lot," I said.

"You've been through more. Your daughter. Your marriage."

"He's on his way here," I said. "My husband." I'd used the social worker's phone to call Michael. I'd told him as much as I could squeeze into five minutes and he'd insisted on coming, even though I said that didn't make sense. We'd have two cars here then, but the truth was, I couldn't wait for him to get here. We'd stay in the inn, in room 333, and I'd tell him everything that had happened in the past couple of weeks and I'd listen to him tell me about his game. "He and I need to talk," I said to Travis. "I blamed him for what happened with our daughter, but I think I was wrong."

"Why did you blame him?"

"I jumped into the water and he didn't."

He nearly smiled. "Just like you did last night."

"Only the pier I jumped from that night was much higher," I said. "Michael ran back to the beach, thinking he could get to her more easily that way."

"You're a jumper. He's a thinker."

"That really sums us up perfectly," I said with a laugh. "Remember I told you he's a game developer?"

"Uh-huh."

"He told me he's been working on a game about grief for parents who lose their children. It really upset me at first, but now I don't know. I'm ready to listen to him about it."

Travis rested his head against the pillow and looked at the ceiling. "Would the game work if it's a mother who died instead of a kid?" he asked, and he looked absolutely serious, as though he really wanted to know. As though he really *needed* that sort of game.

I got up and walked over to hug him, my arms around both of them, and when I straightened up again, I heard the curtain open and turned to see a beautiful, grown-up version of the girl in the photograph. I stepped away, because I was clearly invisible to her. Her gaze was on the little girl in Travis's arms. She pressed her hand to her mouth.

"Bella," Travis said softly to his daughter. He jostled her a little and she lifted her head an inch or so from his chest. She rubbed her eyes, a cranky, exhausted frown on her face. "Bella," he said again. "Are you awake, baby? I want you to meet someone."

Robin stood about a foot away from the side of the bed.

Travis reached out to take her hand and I could see her pale knuckles as she held on to him, steadying herself.

"Bella?" she said softly.

Bella looked up at her, messy, damp hair falling in her face, and Travis brushed it out of her eyes. She looked from Robin to the picture on the tray and back again.

"This is your mommy, Bell," Travis said.

"The one in the picture?" Bella asked.

"Yes, baby." Travis smiled.

"I'm so glad to finally meet you, Bella." Robin bent close to her, their faces only inches apart, and I heard the hunger in her voice. I knew how much she wanted to touch her. To hold her. I was so, so glad she was getting that chance. I took a step backward to lower myself to the stool again. I didn't think I could stand up one more second.

Bella reached one small hand toward Robin's face. She touched her cheek. Ran her fingers over her brown hair. Robin held still, biting her lip.

"You're pretty," Bella said.

Robin laughed. "Can I hug you?" she asked.

Bella reached out her free arm and wrapped it around her mother, and I watched the three of them close themselves off from the rest of the world, locked in an embrace that had been too long in coming.

Right as they drew away from one another, the police officer poked his head inside the cubicle and looked at me. "You ready to go to the inn, miss?" he asked.

I got to my feet and slung my damp purse over my shoulder. "Yes," I said.

The officer looked at Travis. "Doctor says you're good to go," he said.

"I know," Travis said. "I'm just waiting for you guys to—"

"Like I *said*—" the officer gave him a cryptic look "—you're good to go."

Travis opened his mouth to speak, but Robin pressed a finger to his lips. "Don't argue," she said softly.

Strings had been pulled somewhere, somehow, and I was glad. We said our goodbyes and I walked with the officer out to his patrol car. The night was still dark and I looked at my watch as we passed under a streetlamp. At least another hour before Michael could get here. I pictured the room at the inn, the one we'd thought was so magical when we'd stayed in it back when our marriage was new and our lives filled with hope. I was nervous about seeing him now, worried that something he said would set me off. That I wasn't quite finished with my anger and he wasn't quite finished with his irritation over my need to talk about our daughter. But I had the feeling that this would be our first step toward one another again. We would have to see how much each of us was willing to go the distance.

Maybe, just maybe, there'd be magic in that room again tonight.

Epilogue
Travis

One Year Later

I LIKE LIVING A NORMAL LIFE—YOU KNOW, ONE of those lives where nothing dramatic happens. Where you're part of a little family: dad, mom, child. You have a roof over your head and food on the table and your biggest problem is deciding whether to send your kid to kindergarten when she's just turned five or give her another year of preschool. Robin and I opted for the second choice, since Bella's only had six months of preschool to begin with. Her teacher said she was doing really well, but another year would let her really shine in kindergarten. We decided to wait and let her shine. Which is why she's in the backseat of Moby Dick right now, swinging her legs and kicking my seat. I'll drop her off at preschool. It's my turn.

"You're kicking my seat, Bell," I say, as I turn out of the Brier Creek apartment complex and onto the main road.

"I can't help it!" she says. "I'm too excited!"

"It's just dress rehearsal today," I remind her. I don't think she understands the difference between the dress rehearsal and the actual play her class is putting on tomorrow.

"I know," she says. "And tomorrow you and Mommy come see it."

"You bet." Robin will have to skip one of her classes tomorrow, but she won't mind. She doesn't want to miss a second of Bella's life. She feels like she's already missed too many.

"And you know who else is going to be there?" I ask.

"Who?"

"Miss Erin and Mr. Mike."

She sucks in her breath. "And the baby?" she asks.

"The baby's not ready to be born yet," I say. "A few more months." Actually, by the time Erin and Michael's baby is born, Robin, Bella and I will be living in Wilmington.

It was funny how things turned out. How all of us jumped around like game pieces. After the whole mess in Beaufort, Erin moved back into her house with Michael, but she still had months left on her lease on the apartment and she insisted Bella and I stay there until I got my act together. Robin played out the charade of being engaged to Dale Hendricks—now *Mayor* Dale Hendricks—and then she shocked everyone in Beaufort by "chickening out" of the wedding. She took the heat, making it sound like it was all her doing. "I suddenly realized how young I was," she told the press. "Dale is so wonderful and I was afraid of rushing into something I'd later regret, and that wouldn't be fair to him." She vanished from Beaufort and changed her name to Brown so quickly that no one had been able to track her down. At least not yet. She was going to be another one of those mysterious Beaufort legends, like the girl in the rum keg and Blackbeard the Pirate. The Hendricks family—

except Alissa—was glad to see her go, along with the secrets she knew about them. I know Robin misses Alissa and Hannah, but that clean break had been the only way. I'm doing everything I can to make her new life worth what she had to give up.

We've had some ups and downs this past year, Robin and me. Her father had a point about the whole social class thing, especially since the Hendricks family had her in their clutches for two years. Sometimes I feel beneath her. She never treats me that way—except that she wishes I wouldn't call people "dude." Most of the time, though, we get along great.

"Do you have preschool today, too, Daddy?" Bella asks as I pull into the driveway of her school.

"College, Bell," I remind her with a laugh. I'm beginning to wonder if she makes that mistake on purpose because it cracks me up, it's so cute. "And yes. I have a class later today, so I'll be working hard just like you." I hand her the lunch I packed and demand a kiss, which she's been forgetting lately because she's so psyched about getting to her classroom. "Bye, baby," I say. "Have fun." I watch her fly up the sidewalk to her teacher, who gives me a wave from the doorway. Her teacher last year told us Bella drew a lot of guns, which had me worried, but this year she's back into princesses and animals. She's the most resilient kid.

I pull out of the parking lot and make a right, still smiling at Bella's comment about preschool. Robin and I are both in college and I'm working part-time. Robin has classes in Raleigh, but I'm doing this distance-learning program at Cape Fear Community College, getting some of the required courses out of the way so when we move to Wilmington I can start working toward a degree in marine biology. It's been a while since I was a student, but I think I'm more ready for school at twenty-three than I was at seventeen. I'm doing pretty well.

At first, I hadn't wanted to pay for school with the money Robin inherited from her father. I didn't want anything from that man, but Robin convinced me I was letting my pride get in the way. She said he would have wanted his grand-daughter to have two well-educated parents. Maybe, but I know for a fact he didn't want one of them to be me. I have to admit, once I got over the humiliation of having to rely on his money for school, it gave me a perverse kind of plea-sure. I wouldn't tell Robin, but I sort of liked the thought of him rolling over in his grave.

I park in the lot closest to JumpStart and walk inside, where Nando's arranging the pastries in the glass display.

"Dude!" he says, and he tosses me my blue apron. I pull it over my head and tie the straps as I walk behind the counter. I remember that day I ran out of JumpStart, heading for Beaufort, never expecting to set foot in the place again. Now here I am, making coffees and cappuccinos and roasted pea-nut chocolate Bavarian lattes. I try not to wonder if I could have had this job a year ago. While I was searching my butt off for construction work, could I have been making a little cash ten feet from where I was sitting with Bella? But then, I wouldn't be with Robin and I don't even want to think about that. Who would've guessed the nightmare of my life would turn out to be the best thing that could've happened?

A guy walks into JumpStart with two little girls, maybe four and five. I've seen him in here before and I like how he treats his kids, helping them order, telling them to say please when they ask for their muffins. I always stare into his eyes, trying to figure out what's going on in his life. He probably thinks I'm pretty weird. It's just that I've learned that somebody's appearance doesn't always match what's going on inside him. You can't look at a guy's face and see his demons.

I make his coffee, then take two muffins out of the display case and slide them into separate bags for the kids. It reminds me of how I'd packed Bella's cookies and grapes when I made her lunch that morning.

"You're the best dad," Robin had said as I added a juice box to Bella's lunch sack. How she could say that after what I'd put Bella through, I had no idea, but I've learned not to argue.

I hand the coffee to the guy and the muffins to the little girls and watch them head over to the chair and sofas were Bella and I used to hang out. The man unpeels the paper from one of the muffins for his daughter. I wonder if he'll ever be tested the way I was. If he'd make better choices than I'd made. Most likely, he would. But I'm done beating myself up about it. I have to focus on how good my life is today.

So, I'm a barista and a student and someday, with luck and a lot of work, I'll be a marine biologist. Today, though, all I really care about is being a good father.

★ ★ ★ ★ ★

ACKNOWLEDGMENTS

There are so many people who helped *The Good Father* travel the road to publication. As always, I'm grateful to my fellow authors and dear friends from the Weymouth Seven: Mary Kay Andrews, Margaret Maron, Katy Munger, Sarah Shaber, Alexandra Sokoloff and Brenda Witchger. I don't know what I'd do without your brainstorming skills and friendship.

Thank you to my agent, Susan Ginsburg, who quite simply rocks in every way, and her assistant, Stacy Testa, who shares Susan's positive attitude and always brightens my day with her emails.

My smart and savvy editor, Miranda Indrigo, can look at a manuscript and instantly zero in on what works and what doesn't. Thank you for making my books the best they can be, Miranda. I'm grateful to all the people at Mira Books who help behind the scenes: Michelle Renaud, Melanie Dulos, Emily Ohanjanians, Maureen Stead, Stacy Widdrington, Ana Luxton, Diane Mosher, Alana Burke, Katharine Fournier, Katherine Orr, Craig Swinwood, Loriana

Sacilotto and Margaret Marbury. In the UK Mira office, I'm particularly grateful to Kimberley Young, Jenny Hutton and the rest of the team who have worked so hard to make my books a success with United Kingdom and commonwealth readers.

My assistants at various points in the writing—Denise Gibbs, Eleanor Smith and Lindsey LeBret—tracked down sources for research, kept my office running smoothly and helped me polish my internet presence. Thanks, you three!

Other people who helped by offering suggestions as I struggled with a plot element or by providing bits of necessary research include Jessica Tocco, Jennifer Thompson, Julie Kibler, Sylvia Gum and Deborah Dunn. Kelly English was forced to listen to me talk about the story for three days straight while we were stranded together during a storm on Topsail Island. Thanks for both your tolerance and your ideas, Kelly!

Thank you Facebook friend Colleen Albert for coming up with the name of the coffee shop, JumpStart. Kelli Creelman of Rocking Chair Books shared her experiences growing up in Beaufort, North Carolina, and Dave DuBuisson, owner of the Pecan Tree Inn Bed and Breakfast in Beaufort, taught me a bit about the running of a B and B.

A couple of three- and four-year-olds were immensely helpful in the creation of Bella. Thank you Claire and Garrett, as well as your moms, my stepdaughters Caitlin Campbell and Brittany Walls.

As always, thank you John Pagliuca for being my first reader, brainstormer, in-house photographer and computer guru, as well as for your unflagging support and belief in me.

1. There are three narrators in *The Good Father*: Travis, Erin and Robin. Whose story is it? To which character did you feel most connected?

2. One of the central themes of *The Good Father* is "What makes a good parent?" Discuss how that theme plays out in the story with regard to each of the three central characters.

3. Another theme in the book is that of desperation and how it can drive people to do things they would never otherwise think of doing. Could you feel Travis's mounting desperation? What events ultimately led to the choices he made? What other avenues were open to him?

4. Why do you think the author chose to open the story with a prologue in which Travis left Bella with Erin? Did the knowledge that this scene was coming increase or decrease the tension for you as you read?

5. Which character do you think had the greatest personal growth during the story and why?

6. Many people told Travis that he should allow Bella to be adopted. Do you think he made the right decision? Why or why not?

7. Travis had an excellent relationship with his own father. How do you think that played into his relationship with Bella? How did it impact his feelings about Robin's father?

8. The relationship between Travis, Bella and Erin developed quickly in the coffee shop. Why do you think that happened? What was in that relationship for each of them, both at first as well as later?

9. Why do you think the author introduced the character of the barista, Nando, to the story? What purpose(s) did he serve?

10. What would you have done in Erin's position if Travis left Bella with you? How might Erin have reacted differently if she hadn't recently lost Carolyn? How did the fact that Erin lost a child play into the way she related to Bella?

11. Erin not only lost her daughter, but her friends and her husband as well—a husband she'd clearly loved and with whom she'd had a positive relationship. Are there examples you can think of

from real life in which people grieve so differently that it damages their relationship?

12. Carolyn's room nearly becomes a character in the story. Do you think this was intentional on the author's part and how did it impact your experience as you read?

13. When Erin realizes she's beginning to heal from the loss of her daughter, she worries "Does progress mean I was leaving Carolyn behind?" Can you understand that emotion? How has Erin's fear of leaving Carolyn behind impacted her life?

14. Travis tells Erin that she's a "jumper" while Michael is a "thinker." Do you think that's true, and if so, how do we see those labels being played out during the story? Discuss the differences and similarities between Erin's reliance on her support group and Michael's creation of the game, *Losing Carolyn?*

15. Robin was taught to avoid conflict at all costs or risk her health. How did this shape the person she became? Discuss the ways this element of her upbringing led her straight into the arms of Dale and the Hendricks family. How did her need for "peace and calm" both help and hurt her?

16. Robin allowed herself to buy into her father's suggestion that her baby "never happened." Discuss her feelings toward that baby from the time

she learned she was pregnant until she learned Travis had custody of her.

17. Robin was drawn to Alissa for a number of reasons. Explore the experiences from Robin's past and present that led to her friendship with her future sister-in-law.

18. Do you think Alissa knew that Dale was paying Will off? Could there be more to Alissa and Will's relationship than we've learned through Robin's eyes?

19. Savannah is a complex character. Explore her motives in the different parts of the story.

20. How do you feel about the fact that Travis didn't face charges for his role in the heist? Do you think he should have received some sort of punishment, and if so, what form should that have taken? How would that have impacted his life and the lives of Robin and Bella?

Q. What inspired the story for *The Good Father?*

A. Nearly every morning, I take my work-in-progress to a local coffee shop and spend a few hours working there. One day, a man and little girl walked into the shop. I had many of the same thoughts Erin had when she first spotted Travis and Bella: What are a man and little girl doing in here on a weekday? Is he her father? Could he have kidnapped her or be abusing her? The little girl was absolutely adorable. My novelist's mind got to work right away, wondering what I would do if the man asked me to watch the girl while he went out to his car and never returned.

Q. So are Travis and Bella based on this man and his little girl?

A. Not at all. The man and his daughter were my inspiration, but I intentionally avoided getting to know them (they became regulars at the coffee shop) because I didn't want to create characters that resembled them in any way. I've learned over the years that using real people as models for my characters can be very limiting. Once I had the characters of Travis and Bella firmly fleshed out, though, I allowed myself to interact with the man and his daughter. They probably thought I was pretty unfriendly before!

Q. Why did you pick a suburban parking lot as the setting for much of your story?

A. That is a little strange, isn't it? I first planted the coffee shop, JumpStart, in a small North Carolina town, but as the story grew, I knew I wanted an area where Travis could park his van and feel anonymous. The Brier Creek shopping center, with which I'm very familiar, popped into my mind and I knew it was the right location. It's so enormous that no one would stand out, yet everything a person could need is right there. My imagination quickly cooked up the coffee shop in a distant corner of the massive parking lot. Logically, that would not be a very good location for business, but it suited my story well.

Q. Did your background as a clinical social worker and psychotherapist have a role in the creation of *The Good Father*?

A. My former career always has a role to play in my writing, but particularly so in *The Good Father*. I dealt with the grief of parents who've lost a child both in my hospital and private practice work, and that's an experience that will always be with me and influence my writing. Erin and Michael have different styles of grieving, and this is very common when parents lose a child. Those different styles are often hard to reconcile.

On the other hand, although I worked in the adolescent unit of a children's hospital, I hadn't worked with heart transplant patients, so my account of Robin's experience came from a massive amount of research.

The strongest influence my former work has on my books, though, is in the area of character development. I always suggest young people who want to write consider studying psychology. There's no greater background for understanding their characters.

Q. What factors come into play when you begin creating characters?

A. I think about two things: What motivates this character to do the things she does, and in what ways will this character grow throughout the story? Robin, for example, moves from being a dependent young woman who doesn't stand up for herself to someone willing and able to take on a powerful family. When we first meet Erin, she's paralyzed emotionally by the death of her child, but over the course of the story she's moved to take action and begins to heal through that action.

Q. Would you say your books are more character driven or plot driven?

A. Both, I think. As I mentioned above, I usually start a story with a situation: a man asks a woman to watch his little girl for a few minutes and then disappears. But once I have the situation in mind, I begin to think of who will play the roles of the man and the woman, and I intentionally create characters who will have the most difficult time dealing with the situation to increase conflict and tension. So the woman in the situation turns out to be Erin, who has recently lost a little girl and has intentionally pulled away from other people as she grieves.

Q. Hurricane Irene destroyed parts of the North Carolina coast during the time your story is set. Wouldn't that create a good number of construction jobs for Travis?

A. It was ironic that, shortly after I typed "The End" on the manuscript, Hurricane Irene did indeed create work for someone like Travis. I considered changing the dates of the story, but decided to leave them as is. In my fictional world, Hurricane Irene never happens.

Q. Why did you make Michael a games inventor?

A. I was listening to an NPR interview with alternate reality games inventor, Jane McGonigal, who talked about games being a resource for solving real world problems. I was fascinated by her ideas—they made me view collaborative computer games such as those you find on Facebook—in a whole new way. I contacted her about Michael's grieving game idea to be sure this was a realistic concept and she responded positively. It wasn't until I was deep into the writing that I saw the parallel myself between Michael's collaborative game and Erin's support group. For anyone wanting to explore Jane's take on games, check out her website at www.JaneMcGonigal.com.

Q. Did you have a good father? What would he have done in Travis's position?

A. Intriguing question! I had a great father. He was a school principal, a true academic who inspired me to read, research and learn. I'm having trouble, though, imagining him in Travis's situation. It's absolutely impossible for me to picture him stepping outside the law. Yet like Travis, he was the sort of man who took great pride in supporting his family, so there's no telling what he would have done to keep us fed and clothed. It's hard to predict what someone would do in that sort of situation, which was precisely what inspired me to write the book. I wanted to put a good man in those dire straits and see how he'd react.

Q. What was the hardest part for you in writing this story?

A. Well, writing a novel is always hard for me and even though *The Good Father* is my twenty-first book, it was no easier to write than my first or fifth or fifteenth. If I had to pick one element that I found difficult in writing this story, though, it would be deciding what Erin would do when left with Bella. If a child were left with me in that way, I would call the police and/or protective services. That may be my social work background—I'm not sure. It was hard for me to imagine a sane woman not making that choice. I had to remember though, that Erin is not particularly sane when left with Bella. She's in such emotional distress and has such conflicted feelings about Bella being in her life that I was able to convince myself that she would not contact the authorities. Once she does, she backs out for reasons I feel are believable.

Q. What was the easiest part of writing this story?

A. Bella came to me very easily. I spent some time with children her age (so much fun!) to remind myself what four-year-olds are all about, and she nearly wrote her portions of the book herself.

Q. How can readers get in touch with you?

A. I can be reached through my website at www.dianechamberlain.com (where Bookclubs can sign up for a speakerphone call). I'm also active with my readers on Facebook: www.facebook.com/ Diane.Chamberlain.Readers.Page.

BESTSELLING AUTHOR
DIANE CHAMBERLAIN

Dr. Olivia Simon is on duty at North Carolina's
Outer Banks Hospital when a gunshot victim is brought in.
Midway through the effort to save the woman's life, Olivia
realizes who she is—Annie O'Neill. The woman Olivia's
husband, Paul, is in love with.

When Annie dies on the operating table,
she leaves behind three other victims.
Alec O'Neill, who thought he had the
perfect marriage. Paul, whose fixation
with Annie is unshakable. And Olivia,
who is desperate to understand the
woman who destroyed her marriage.

Now they are left with unanswered
questions about who Annie
really was. And about the secrets
she hid so well.

Keeper of the Light

Available wherever books are sold.

Award-winning author
DIANE CHAMBERLAIN

Joelle D'Angelo's best friend, Mara, is left with brain damage after she suffers an aneurysm giving birth to her son. Alone and grieving, Joelle turns to the only other person who understands her pain: her colleague—and Mara's husband—Liam. What starts out as comfort between friends gradually becomes something more, something undeniable.

Torn by guilt and the impossibility of her feelings for Liam, Joelle goes in search of help for Mara. She is led to a healer in Monterey, California, who is keeping her own shocking secrets. But Joelle soon discovers that while some love is doomed, some love is destined to survive anything.

The Shadow Wife

Available wherever books are sold.